Few literary works (in Arabic or English) have deal Revolution in 2011 as well as *Confessions of a Knight Errant* by Gretchen McCullough who survived the uprising at Tahrir Square. Her novel is appealing and wacky. At one moment she gives us an (alleged) message from Colonel Muammar Qaddafi of Libya. The next moment, she gives us edgy sarcasm about the American lifestyle—bent on overwhelming the globe. Turn the corner and McCullough's plot rips along in the manner of a detective novel. Wait! It's not just that. The reader also gets free lessons in the art of cooking.

> —Sonallah Ibrahim, *Ice* and *That Smell*
> (Leading Egyptian novelist and political activist)

Gretchen McCullough has written a wild ride through Cairo and beyond, a rollicking adventure tale full of grifters, reprobates, scalawags, and scoundrels, with a few femmes fatales thrown in to keep things teetering on chaos. I couldn't put it down!"

> —Tom Lutz, *Portraits*
> (Founder and former Editor-in-Chief of the *LA Review of Books)*

This rollicking, rambunctious, compulsively readable comic novel follows the adventures of Gary, a would-be writer, professor, rebel environmentalist, and accused cyber-terrorist on the run, as he encounters characters galore from Cairo, Egypt, to a girls' summer camp in Texas. Along the way are murder, drugs, stolen antiquities, arson, sexual hi-jinks, and various international conspiracies that add up to a roller-coaster ride for the reader and, perhaps, some resolution for Gary as he takes on various identities, ponders his life, and asks, "Could we ever see ourselves as the Other saw us?"

> —Jennifer Horne, *Bottle Tree*
> (Poet Laureate of Alabama, 2017 - 2021)

Gretchen McCullough's new novel, *Confessions of a Knight Errant: Drifters, Thieves and Ali Baba's Treasure* is a big, garrulous comedy with myriad, memorable characters, and a palpable sense of place. McCullough's vision is darkly comical, but there's plenty at stake: the Egyptian dream the world temporarily shared, goings on between Egypt and Northern Ireland, timely questions about the role of international immigrants, cyber-crime, Egyptian antiquities, at least three writers with books-in-progress, and murder most foul—all played out at a rich folk's summer camp in Texas run by a delightful menagerie of misfits. Deftly intertwined and diverse story lines weave a compelling cautionary tale about international terror and our global connectedness.
    —Allen Wier, *Tehano* and *Late Night, Early Morning*
      (The John Dos Passos Prize for Literature, Truman Capote Prize)

Confessions of a Knight Errant

Drifters, Thieves, and Ali Baba's Treasure

A Novel

Gretchen McCullough

Cune

Confessions of a Knight Errant:
Drifters, Thieves, and Ali Baba's Treasure
by Gretchen McCullough
© 2022 Gretchen McCullough
Cune Press, Seattle 2022

Hardback	ISBN 9781951082758
Paperback	ISBN 9781951082444
EPUB	ISBN 9781614574279
Kindle	ISBN 9781614572640

Library of Congress Cataloging-in-Publication Data

Names: McCullough, Gretchen, author.
Title: Confessions of a knight errant : drifters, thieves, and Ali Baba's
 treasure : a novel / Gretchen McCullough.
Description: [Seattle] : Cune, [2022] | Summary: "Confessions of a Knight Errant is a
comedic, picaresque novel with a flamboyant cast of characters written in the tradition
of Miguel Cervantes with a modern twist." -- Provided by publisher.
Identifiers: LCCN 2022014144 (print) | LCCN 2022014145 (ebook) | ISBN
 9781951082444 (trade paperback) | ISBN 9781614574279 (epub)
Subjects: LCGFT: Novels. | Picaresque fiction.
Classification: LCC PS3613.C3864496 C66 2022 (print) | LCC PS3613.C3864496
 (ebook) | DDC 813/.6--dc23/eng/20220406
LC record available at https://lccn.loc.gov/2022014144
LC ebook record available at https://lccn.loc.gov/2022014145
CPSNo: 08212022

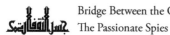 Bridge Between the Cultures (a series from Cune Press)

The Passionate Spies	John Harte
Music Has No Boundaries	Rafiq Gangat
Arab Boy Delivered	Paul Aziz Zarou
Kivu	Frederic Hunter
Empower a Refugee	Patricia Martin Holt
Afghanistan and Beyond	Linda Sartor
Congo Prophet	Frederic Hunter
Stories My Father Told Me	Helen Zughaib, Elia Zughaib
Apartheid Is a Crime	Mats Svensson
Definitely Maybe	Stephen Fife
Girl Fighters	Carolyn Han
White Carnations	Musa Rahum Abbas

 Cune Press: www.cunepress.com | www.cunepress.net

For Mohamed Metwalli

For his *joie de vivre,* love of song,
and quest for the right word ever
since we met thirteen years ago!

Part I

Land of the Pharaohs

Chapter 1

Havoc in Cairo

WE HAD FLED CAIRO TO MALTA FROM THE PEOPLE who must remain unnamed, two years before: Kharalombos and me, his wife, my face covered with a black veil, a complete *niqab*. Of course, if Yasser Arafat could escape the Israelis across the Jordan River in 1967 fully veiled, disguised as a mother carrying a baby, why not me? Hiding out in Malta, I made wax knights at the Knights Templar Museum and enjoyed giving tours with factual tidbits to curious British tourists—a refreshing change from duties on tenure committees. Meanwhile, Kharalombos coached Spanish dancers, who preened and lunged in Who's Got Talent tango contests. I was a rogue professor wanted by Interpol; Kharalombos was wanted by the Egyptians for a problem too sensitive to be named. Even though we had rooms in a pension, with balconies overlooking a shimmery Mediterranean, and feasted on fried squid and red mullet almost every day, I still worried a SWAT team armed with assault weapons could burst through the doors at any time.

But now, we had sneaked back into Cairo to find Kharalombos's son. My novel had been erased by the publishing conglomerate, Zadorf. In a hurry to get out of town, I had dropped my flash drive down an elevator shaft. The very last hard copy of my novel nestled underneath my bed in my old flat in Garden City—I had to find it, or else risk certain obscurity. This time around, I was disguised as a tourist in a loud Hawaiian shirt, wearing Ray-Ban sunglasses and a Howard Cosell-type toupee. Clad in a white suit, with a panama hat perched on his head, Kharalombos resembled a British colonial. I expected the police to appear with handcuffs the moment we got off the plane—straight into the box. My new identity: a vacuum-cleaner salesman from Ames, Iowa, who was going on a once-in-a-lifetime Nile cruise, a bonus for selling beyond quota; Kharalombos was a Greek olive farmer.

We sailed through the airport all the way to customs. Flashing on the arrival sign: Budapest, Cancelled. London, Cancelled. Munich, Cancelled. Moscow, Cancelled.

Only one officer manned the series of booths, immaculate in his black wool winter uniform. He was buttoned up to the collar. When he saw us gaping at the arrival monitor, he gestured to us, "Come in, come in. You are jumping into the fire!"

Kharalombos asked, "Is it really that atrocious?" I could see he was tempted to lapse into Arabic.

Yawning, the officer cleaned his ear with a pen. Why didn't he answer? Then he mimicked the American saying, "Have a nice day!" He stamped the passports, without the usual bureaucratic sense of conviction.

A rail-thin Pakistani, who looked like a student from Al-Azhar, stood next to us at the baggage claim, but avoided eye contact. He clutched a huge Quran, the cover decorated with gold. Did he think we were suspicious?

Our bags came in five minutes—unheard-of in the history of Cairo airport.

Grabbing my tiny suitcase, full of costume props, off the belt, I said, "Kharalombos, are you sure Happy City Tours will pick us up?"

"There have been demonstrations," Kharalombos said, heaving his monstrous suitcase. "Didn't you see the monitor at the Valletta airport?"

True, we had watched the Al-Jazeera video at the Valletta airport. But there were frequent demonstrations in Cairo over the years, all of which had fizzled out, or been squashed. Egyptian citizens raised banners, festooned in Arabic handwriting: "Justice Now!" They chanted: "Bread. Dignity. Freedom. Social Justice!" The image of yet another young man who had been tortured to death in a police station flashed on the screen: his face was disfigured beyond recognition.

We had dragged our bags through the Cairo airport, and exited the hall. The parking lot was completely deserted, except for a few cars. Only one streetlight gleamed; otherwise, it was a forbidding black—four o'clock in the morning. Usually the place was mobbed with relatives, hasslers, and enterprising entrepreneurs. Tour guides who intoned strange-sounding names as they raised their makeshift signs high. But this evening there were no drivers with signs. No Happy City Tours, either. And even the fleet of battered, black-and-white taxis that usually lined up to harass the weary traveler had disappeared. Where were they all?

Kharalombos pulled out his mobile phone. "I'll call my uncle." His uncle was a psychiatrist at the mental hospital, where I had been sent two years before. Kharalombos was my sane, colorful roommate—he was simply hiding in the hospital from the people who must remain unnamed. We had become fast friends and had teamed up to escape the authorities.

"What's wrong?" I asked.

"No line," he said.

"Maybe there's something wrong with your phone?" I asked. "You need another SIM card."

"No," Kharalombos said. "That's not the problem."

He sauntered over to the exit doors, where a policeman stood puffing on a cigarette.

"You'll blow your disguise!" I hissed.

But Kharalombos was unconcerned and ignored me.

He lumbered back to where I was standing. "The government cut the networks. There's a curfew."

I should have stayed in Valletta. Why had I let Kharalombos talk me into returning to Cairo? For the sake of a little adventure, I was going to be arrested for a crime I hadn't committed! I was no Julian Assange. One could understand, though, why Kharalombos would take such a risk to see his new son, Nunu. But was my novel worth ninety-nine years in jail, or even dying? Did I fancy myself the next John Kennedy O'Toole? Or maybe I was more like a dunce. I brushed this disturbing thought out of my mind, like a horsefly, before it had time to bite.

"The policeman said the demonstration against the BIG MAN and HIS MEN has become violent," Kharalombos said. "Anyone who disobeys the curfew will be shot."

The men who must remain unnamed sported the same baggy, black suits and packed big pistols under their belts, their stony eyes hidden by Ray-Bans— they numbered in the thousands on the Big Man's payroll.

In his previous life in Cairo, Kharalombos had been a ballroom-dancing teacher. He had been teaching the Big Man's daughter to waltz, and it had blossomed into a dangerous romance. My own love life blossomed in Malta.

Lonely European women sought out my company in the Roma pension—
I was always having breakfast on my balcony, facing the Mediterranean,
with some charming woman, the latest of whom was Boriana, a slender
Bulgarian, an acrobat in the circus. Before, I had had no luck with Egyptian women, who insisted I marry them after a single coffee for the sake
of their honor. The female American academics I had worked with wore
severe black glasses and issued orders. What had changed? I had embraced
the *joie de vivre* of the Mediterranean and the pleasures of the flesh. But if
I were honest (and who wanted that?), I had saved the gorgeous Boriana
from her burly, abusive husband, Dragomir, the fire eater, by pretending to
be hapless, rather than a gallant knight. Completely thrown off the scent,
Dragomir had left with the circus on an Eastern European tour. Boriana had
stayed behind with me. I now felt a little guilty and responsible, leaving her
alone, unprotected, in Malta, in my quest for my opus. What if Dragomir
returned while I was gone?

I stared at the dark, quiet parking lot of the airport, still in disbelief.
Kharalombos bit his lip.

"It doesn't look good," I said.

"No," Kharalombos said. He had clammed up—and he had lost his sense
of humor. He was chewing his fingernails to stubs.

"In fact, it looks like the desert," I said. "Lots of sand. No camels. No water.
Libya. Or even Saudi Arabia. Reminds me of that famous scene in *Lawrence of
Arabia*...."

"Habibi, please," Kharalombos said, staring at his blank phone. "Let me think."

I turned around. Maybe we could sleep in the airport until...until what?

The exit door whooshed open and a couple emerged. "Good heavens, are
we the only ones here?" the thin man said.

Cocked on the man's head was a panama hat. Had he and Kharalombos
bought their colonial attire in the same shop? The thin man was outfitted in the
same gear, but his tailored white suit was made of linen. A little light for January. His pointy green shoes were crocodile leather, and huge white plastic glasses
enveloped his smallish weasel-like eyes. His wife's hair was styled in a little-girl
pixie cut and dyed a bright orange. While he was tall and slim, she was tall but
very round, her middle ballooning like the Pillsbury Doughboy. Her muumuu,
with huge purple hibiscus flowers against a yellow cotton print, accentuated her

shape rather than diminished it. She toted an enormous green leather purse, the size of a Hefty garbage bag.

"*Ja-aa*," she said, rummaging in her purse. She brandished a lighter she could have used to light a stove, placed a cigarette in a black holder, and lit it with a huge flame. How had she gotten that through the vigilant security at German airports? What moxie!

The thin man beside her clutched two plastic bags from the duty-free shop in each hand. He clinked whenever he moved. "Oi," he said, suddenly noticing me. "Could you assist us, mate? We're newbies."

"Killing crocodiles for a pair of shoes is morally reprehensible!" I said. "How could you?" Wasteful, selfish people were destroying our natural world! I felt the old resentments brewing—why I had urged students to dump over a ton of tilapia at the gates of the university: to protest the complete destruction of the Nile. The university administration had decided I had gone off my rocker, sedated me, put me on leave, and sent me to the mental hospital. I remembered the headline in the *Chronicle*: "Professor Tanks Career Over Contaminated Fish."

Kharalombos put his finger to his lips. Yikes. No tirades.

"*Ja-aa*," the lady with the carrot-red hair said. "They have these wonderful sneakers in America." She showed me her purple Keds. "Cheap."

What did purple Keds have to do with our current predicament, or the price of bananas?

The man chuckled. "She's off her trolley." When he smiled, he had two fangs. "I don't see the sign for the Conrad Hilton. Have they given us the elbow?"

Not so many were off their trolley in the mental hospital—it was, in fact, an expensive rehab for heroin addicts, small-time kleptos, and the manic depressives of the Egyptian upper class. At this moment, I yearned for the lush, peaceful garden, with the purple bougainvillea and palm trees.

Kharalombos exclaimed, "Sir, this is a revolution!"

"You're mad," the man said. "The hotel assured us that the demonstrations would be over in a few days. That'll spoil our Nile cruise."

"Things look bad. Our ride hasn't shown up, either," I said. This fateful day in 2011, had the lid finally burst off the pot?

No Happy City Tours. Had something also happened to Kharalombos's uncle? Was he dead?

"*Ja-aa,*" the large lady said, sighing, "I told you we should go to India, *Liebchen.* You never listen."

"This is most inconvenient," the man said. "Allow me to introduce myself, I am Viscount Triksky." He dropped his heavy bags on the sidewalk. Given the fact that there was not a soul around for miles, he didn't have to worry about someone swiping his loot.

But Kharalombos was gazing, star-struck, at the large lady in the muumuu with the purple sneakers. She was twenty years older, but she was exactly his height and size. Never had he met another giant his size. He had been dancing with upper-class anorexic Egyptian girls for years.

The lady laughed. "We are in a large pickle. Isn't that what you say?"

Viscount Triksky was still extending his hand to Kharalombos. I suddenly blanked and forgot Kharalombos's fake name. How were we going to get into the city? We had no way of getting in touch with Kharalombos's uncle. When Kharalombos had been pursued by the people who must remain unnamed, and I was trying to evade the security officers at the American Embassy, the doctor had hatched the plan for our escape to Malta. His uncle had dreamed up the idea of the *niqab* disguise. A second, more recent *Chronicle* headline echoed in my head: "Professor Creates Computer Virus Called Pure Water. Still Missing." Was some hungry reporter out there, tracking my moves?

Kharalombos couldn't take his eyes off the large lady.

"Gary Smith," I said, extending my hand. "Nice to meet you. All the way from good ol' Iowa. The corn state."

Viscount Triksky winked at me. He had a limp handshake. Was he hitting on me? "You look like a good American egg. Any idea how we can get to our hotel? Looks like you've done this before."

Were we that transparent? Why had I let Kharalombos talk me into it? Was I tired of making wax knights and expounding upon the Knights Templar? Or was I evading further entanglement with Boriana? She would have to divorce Dragomir first . . . and like a chivalrous knight, I had promised to return.

"This is our first visit to Cairo," I said. "We signed up for a Nile cruise."

Viscount Triksky shrugged. "Thought you looked like old hands."

The giantess was smiling at Kharalombos. She introduced herself, "This is Gudrun Grünewald from Schulenburg, Texas. I was from Berlin, but I moved to Texas near a big river. And I have a camp for girls called Clover Flower. Have you been to America? Their sausages are terrible, but I love it."

Kharalombos was entranced. He seemed to have forgotten that we were in serious trouble. "They killed all the pigs here," he said. "I love pork paté."

For crying out loud! "Zorba," I said. "Zorba." I waved my hand in front of his face, but he was hypnotized.

I had to keep reminding myself that Zorba was his phony name. Kharalombos would blow his cover if he started talking about how the pigs were dumped into pits in Cairo and covered with lime during the swine flu panic—something a first-time tourist would not know. The Egyptian government, ignoring the World Health Organization, had killed the pigs anyway—this was not a preventative measure for swine flu, but an expedient for placating Islamic fundamentalists, who weren't exactly fans of pigs.

Suddenly, a sleek, black stretch limo roared out of the dark and screeched to a stop in front of us. The door popped open and a head peered out. The Egyptian man was wearing an Indiana Jones–style hat.

The Egyptian man ordered, "Quickly, enter the car! Before anyone sees Ramses. Everyone will recognize Ramses. They will want my hat! I am not prepared to sign autographs!"

"Do you know him?" I asked Viscount Triksky. I had only seen him in the Egyptian newspapers, in the English newspapers, and on the History Channel. He received more publicity than the Big Man.

"Of course. We studied mummy preservation together at Oxford. Although my doctorate is on ancient pottery. Amulets…" Viscount Triksky said, waving his hand in an effeminate way.

Kharalombos was giving me the thumbs-down sign. Ramses el-Kibir was one of the Big Man's cronies. Was this a trap? Instead of the men in the baggy suits, we would be taken straight to the dreaded Tora prison by an archaeologist.

"I thought you were being picked up by the Conrad Hilton," I asked. Just who was Viscount Triksky? And why had Ramses el-Kibir come to pick him up?

"I'm a consultant for his television show," Viscount Triksky said. "I am sure you must have heard of it. *The Marvelous Adventures of Ramses el-Kibir, the World-Famous Archaeologist.*"

Kharalombos almost guffawed. Instead, he covered his mouth with his huge hand, acting as if he were coughing from Gudrun's cigarette smoke.

"What about your Nile cruise?" I asked.

Viscount Triksky smiled, baring his fangs. "We're combining business with pleasure."

Gudrun said, "*Nein. Nein.* I don't know this man. Where is the Conrad Hilton? You didn't mention any business appointments."

Did she know Viscount Triksky very well? Was he even her husband?

"Get in the car. As soon as people recognize me, they will want my autograph," the Egyptian man in the Indiana Jones hat said. "We don't have time for such things."

"I don't exactly see a teeming crowd," I said, waving to the empty parking lot. In fact, we were the only ones, except for the Pakistani boy we had seen at baggage claim.

"Who are you? You keep acting like you are someone big," Gudrun said. "Big. Big. Bigger than the Pyramids." She waved her thin black cigarette holder in the air at him, as if she were Greta Garbo.

Kharalombos bowed, "Madam, may I have this dance?"

Gudrun giggled. "Can you…?" She gave me the black cigarette holder.

"Put your hand on my shoulder and follow. This is a waltz. One two three. One two three. One two three," Kharalombos said, waltzing in front of the exit door of the airport.

What was he doing?! Yet it seemed so true—this spontaneous attraction. Gudrun had appeared out of the blue and she seemed to match Kharalombos in a way that the willowy, glamorous Yasmine had not.

"Sweet Zorba, we will dance later," she said, sighing. She acted as if she had known him for years. Was this another one of Kharalombos's secrets?

I handed back the black cigarette holder. She winked at me. "You are the butler in Agatha Christie novels, *ja-aa!*"

Not exactly how I saw myself, but why throw a tantrum now? We needed a ride into the city.

"I am Ramses el-Kibir. World-famous Archaeologist," Ramses said, standing close to Gudrun. "One of the Great Explorers of the World."

Gudrun snorted. "Never heard of you. But then, I am in the nature and never turn on the television." She turned to Kharalombos, who had placed his hand protectively around her shoulder. "You could teach dancing at my camp. You know Latin dance? The young people want to learn that. Samba. Cha-cha-cha?"

In the meantime, Viscount Triksky was loading his own suitcases into the back of the limo. "I say, old girl, let's vamoose. Before Ramses changes his mind. We've got to make hay while . . . "

Ramses waved at Gudrun to get into the limo. Unfortunately, she didn't travel lightly and had two enormous steamer trunks, one pink and the other orange. Neither Ramses nor the thin man made a move toward the steamer trunks. They acted as if we were the porters and should load the trunks into the limo.

"Open the boot," Gudrun said, gesturing to the driver. The driver ignored her orders. Or didn't he speak English?

Ramses said, "The back is full."

"*Ja-aa*," she snorted. "Don't tell us. Treasure from the pharaonic tombs. GOLD!"

Ramses sniffed. "Equipment for shooting my show, *The Marvelous Adventures of...*"

I tugged at Gudrun's trunk—what was in it, bricks of gold? "One, two, three," I said. Kharalombos lifted it by a giant loop on the side, but then put it down.

"Set it down for now," Kharalombos said, gesturing. "If there is no place in the boot."

Actually, Kharalombos was so strong he could pick up the trunk with one of his pinkies. But I had always counted on my brains to get me out of scrapes, not brawn. Now that I had left academia, I could see that I was too driven and obsessed with racking up publications. If I went farther back in my history, I also regretted forsaking the high-school thespian club in Oklahoma City. (I wasn't half bad as a woman in *niqab*. I hoped someone would now buy my new identity as a vacuum-cleaner salesman from Iowa.) Dad had wanted me to go out for quarterback since I was fast—he fantasized that I would play for the Sooners at the University of Oklahoma. For a man so practical, my father latched onto the occasional delusion of grandeur.

Viscount Triksky sighed. "Don't be a plank, Gudrun. Get in the bloody car. We're wasting Ramses's time."

Ramses said. "Yes, you're wasting Dr Ramses el-Kibir's time. Tomorrow we have a shoot at the Pyramids."

Did he always talk about himself in the third person?

"*Ja-aa*," Gudrun said. "So you are going to film yourself tomorrow?"

The driver slammed the door and got out of the car. I hadn't noticed before, but he was wearing camouflage fatigues. Why was a soldier driving Ramses el-Kibir around during a military curfew?

"I will have to leave the trunks here," Gudrun said. "There is not enough room for all of us. It's no goot."

"All of us?" Ramses asked. "We are only taking you and the Count."

Gudrun said, "*Ja-aa*, so the ship is sinking and you leave your friends to go down with the ship. What kind of man are you?"

Ramses's face turned red. "My honor as an Eastern man has been insulted! No one talks to Dr Ramses el-Kibir like that!"

The Viscount, not taking any chances, had already settled himself in the car. Peering out the window, he said, "My dear girl, they are mere acquaintances. I say, get in the car. I could use some kip."

A few minutes ago, before Ramses had arrived, the Viscount had been very chummy with us. Kharalombos put his finger to his lips: "SSSshhhh."

Gudrun was sitting on her trunks and refused to budge. She lit another cigarette, as if she had all the time in the world. Kharalombos was mooning over her with pure adoration. He was supposed to be in love with the Big Man's daughter and had risked his life to come see his two-year-old son.

Ramses stood directly in front of Gudrun, his hands on his hips. But she ignored him, exhaling smoke from her nostrils, and stared at Kharalombos, unabashed, as if she were a teeny-bopper. The young soldier in fatigues cleared his throat. He nudged Ramses, pointing to his watch.

"I am told that the car is needed by a general," Ramses said. "And the clock is running out, if you would like to be rescued, madam."

Gudrun exhaled more smoke from her nostrils and tapped out the ashes. "Now, that is the Eastern man, *ja-aa*."

Kharalombos gently pulled her up off the trunk, which had become like a temporary throne.

"We will go," Gudrun said, gesturing for us to get into the limo. We had known this large lady five minutes, but she commanded the authority of Cleopatra, and we were her slaves.

After we had gotten in, she squeezed herself in on the outside. I was sandwiched between Gudrun and Kharalombos. The thin Viscount was sitting to the left of Kharalombos. His duty-free bags took up so much room on the floor that there was no room for our feet. This was a huge vehicle, yet it felt like a Volkswagen bug. The third seat was full of crates, with "For Export" written on the sides in Arabic.

We glided out of the airport easily. The few cars parked in the parking lot were stationary. No one was manning the toll booth at the exit. As soon as we hit Salah Salem, we flew through the streets. Not one pedestrian in sight. No cars. No donkeys. No street sellers. No cleaners. No street urchins. No bicycles. No motor scooters. No pizza delivery. We passed under a bridge. A tank was positioned there. The soldier peered out, alert, at the absolute ready waiting for a surprise attack.

Ramses el-Kibir was saying, "Tomorrow the crew will meet us at the Giza Pyramids to shoot the last show for the season. Did you read the script? Ramses saves Madonna from bats and tomb robbers."

"Smashing," Viscount Triksky said. "It's simply brilliant. First Class A1. Do you think you could also add some camels to the scenario? Maybe a chase across the desert?"

"Do you really think you are going to shoot tomorrow?" I asked. What planet were they on?

Ramses straightened his Indiana Jones hat. "No problem. The Big Man's army will clear the city by tomorrow."

What would happen to Kharalombos if the Big Man's men discovered he was back?

"This is ridiculous. We will not be going on any cruise down the Nile," Gudrun said. "Look at the tanks everywhere. Viscount, we should return to the airport and go to Bombay, instead."

I had attended a conference on Contaminated Water and Cholera in Bombay. I imagined other cities in the world might be a more relaxing alternative.

"*Pssst*, old girl," the Viscount said. "You've been saying you wanted a grand adventure. Here you go. Actually, I was fortunate to be in Ethiopia when Haile Selassie was deposed in 1974. Great fun. Arse-over-tit in the hotel bars."

What was he doing in Ethiopia in 1974? Or was he trying to throw us off the scent?

Crammed in the duty-free bags were Hennessey, Jameson, and single malt whiskey. He had a thousand dollars' worth of booze here. Four bottles were allowed at duty free. Was he connected?

Kharalombos was saying to Gudrun, "I could also teach rhumba at your camp. It's the dance of love."

The driver swerved to avoid burning tires and tree trunks in the middle of the road. I closed my eyes for a minute. I would never even make it to jail because I would be killed in a car accident. Maybe we should have stayed at the airport. Or, in hindsight, stayed in Malta in limbo for the rest of our lives, fugitives.

Kharalombos and Gudrun were holding hands. What had happened to his passion for the Big Man's daughter? How could his resolve have weakened so quickly? Was he this fickle?

Kharalombos pointed to the minibus we had just passed. It looked like a burned pretzel. What had happened to the passengers?

A mob of young men was blocking the bridge. The driver slowed to a crawl. The locks clicked on the doors.

I turned around. God! Now a huge truck was bearing down on us from behind: men were waving sticks, clubs, and scythes. Who were they? Thugs on the Big Man's payroll, out to terrorize the protestors?

Only two years before, almost everyone I met said with great enthusiasm, "Welcome to Egypt."

The truck from behind was getting closer, while a mob in front was playing chicken with the driver. Something had to give.

"*Nein. Nein.* Stop the car! Stop the car!" Gudrun shouted.

Instead, the driver speeded up and gunned for the boys. At the very last second, they jumped out of the way. The back window shattered, spraying glass throughout the limo. All of us instinctively covered our eyes. A red brick had landed on the trunks marked: "For Export Only." A whoosh of air enveloped the car.

Ramses turned around, saying, "*Hamdellah-assalama.* I'm glad we're safe."

"Anyone hurt?" I asked, gingerly picking up a large shard of glass and placing it behind me in the back seat.

"I say, this is not exactly the holiday I had in mind," Viscount Triksky said.

"This is war," the driver said in perfect English.

He was driving over a hundred and twenty kilometers an hour. The wind whipped Gudrun's red hair. No one said a word.

On the horizon, flames were shooting out of a high-rise building—the Big Man's headquarters.

Ramses el-Kibir moaned. "We must protect our national treasures. Go to the Museum immediately."

"The guests must be safe first," the driver said.

"Are you disobeying Dr Ramses? That is an order," Ramses said.

The driver drove at lightning speed, past whining ambulances. Packs of men stalked past us with clubs. Dawn was just starting to break, streaks of orange, like feathers in the sky.

Suddenly, the car slammed to a stop in front of the Conrad Hilton. Egyptian men in oversized suits fanned out around the entrance, clutching machine guns.

Gudrun begged us to stay in the hotel. "It's not safe out there," she said. But we couldn't be registered under our real names, anyway. I didn't have credit cards in my alias, and we didn't have much cash with us. We had to find Kharalombos's uncle. After we exchanged phone numbers with Gudrun, we set off for Garden City, my old neighborhood, further down the Nile.

The streets were empty. No taxis, even. We would have to walk a few kilometers up the Nile to Garden City from the Conrad Hilton. Outside the television building, tanks were mounting a siege. A soldier was stringing barbed wire directly in front of the building.

"No police on the street. Not even traffic cops," I said.

Kharalombos' eyes filled with tears. "I don't think I will get to see my son, ever."

I wanted to reassure him, but this looked like it might be the end for the Big Man.

We walked quickly down the Corniche by the Nile. Flames continued to shoot out from the top of the Big Man's party headquarters.

A kid about eighteen was taking a picture of his friend, who was sitting on top of a burned-out car in the parking lot in front of the headquarters.

"Don't speak," Kharalombos said. "Just keep moving."

The kid was holding up his phone as if he were a taking a picture of a castle in a distant land—a visit to the Louvre. An expensive jeep still smoked with burning embers.

Young men streamed out of the Big Man's headquarters, like frantic ants. Some were carrying leather office chairs over their heads. Others had their arms full of bars of Lindt duty-free chocolate—taking whatever they could carry from the building. A twelve-year-old boy was strapping boxes of Chivas Regal to a donkey.

"Keep walking," Kharalombos said.

Out of the corner of my eye, I saw another gang of men, armed with clubs and wooden planks.

"Stop!" one of the men called out. "Spies! Infiltrators!"

"Filth! Garbage!" Kharalombos spit on the ground. "Run now!"

For someone so large and heavy, Kharalombos was very light on his feet—all those years of teaching ballroom dancing. He could run as fast as a soccer player. Once I dared myself to look back; they were still chasing us, waving their clubs. I had a cramp in my side, but scarcely felt it.

At last, Kharalombos raised his hand. "You can stop now. They won't follow us into Garden City. Too many embassies. They think the CIA will get them."

"Are you crazy? Did you want to get us killed?"

"They are the dogs of the Interior Minister. *Baltagia.* Thugs."

A different breed than the men in the baggy suits, they had been kept discreetly out of sight. I had never seen them before.

"We have to avoid the American Embassy," I said. "Although I am sure they are under lockdown. They won't be looking for me."

Weaving our way through the back streets of Garden City, with its run-down villas and palaces, its battalions of pigeons and feral cats, I felt relieved to be back in my old neighborhood. Medieval-looking padlocks hung loosely from the wrought-iron gates in front of the old buildings. Many had magnificent wooden doors embossed with Islamic designs. Where embassies had taken over the villas, they were painted bright colors and renovated; otherwise, they had fallen into disrepair.

A group of men were huddled around a small fire in the middle of the street.

One of the men aimed a shotgun at us. We moved forward with our hands over our heads. "Please, don't shoot," I muttered under my breath. "That's not for killing rabbits."

"What?" Kharalombos said. "Just keep your hands up."

"That's *Amm* Sayed," I said. Uncle Sayed. "The *bawab*." The porter. Kharalombos needed glasses.

Another man with a shock of white hair advanced with Uncle Sayed. He was carrying a baseball bat. He had an odd-shaped body, very short legs with a long torso. He was wearing an Atlanta Braves tee-shirt. An American?

Kharalombos called out, "Ya, *Amm* Sayed. Uncle, it's me. *Ana* Kharalombos."

Amm Sayed squinted and then, slowly, lowered the shotgun. He must be blind since we were not that far away! Or maybe he didn't have money for glasses?

He ran forward and exclaimed: "Kharalombos! Kharalombos! We haven't seen you for such a long time. You light up our day." He kissed him on both cheeks. "Are you all right?"

Kharalombos asked, "How are your sons? Are they married yet?"

"Yes, thank God, they are all married. They are working as minibus drivers. It is not what we dreamed of," he said, sighing. "But we must earn our bread."

I had originally come to Cairo to earn my bread. But for young Egyptians without an education, there were few opportunities. Even with the second Iraq War, and as much as they disliked its policies, America was still the fantasy ranch on the television show *Dallas*. When people found out I was American, they begged me to help them emigrate. They never believed me when I said, "America isn't perfect, either. It's every man for himself!" In a society where much depended on *wasta*, or who you knew, they found it hard to imagine that I had no influence at the American Embassy, either, as a "*Doctor.*" Of course, afterward, I was on the Embassy's WANTED list, and maybe I was too wanted. I would never be invited to another Fourth of July party at the Embassy.

The informal citizen militia had dragged a La-Z-Boy chair out in front of the building. A man was fast asleep in it. His snore sounded like the wheezing of an elephant. He was clearly ancient—maybe about eighty-five. When I looked closer, I could see that he had a great many medals pinned to his green Izod cardigan. He was clutching an old-fashioned Saladin sword.

Kharalombos said, "Who is that?"

Amm Sayed smiled. "The landlord's uncle. A general. He wanted to help us guard the building. He has been telling us jokes and stories all night. He told us how he ate snake for breakfast in Sinai during the '73 war."

Kharalombos brightened. "Where is my uncle?"

"At the mental hospital with the patients," *Amm* Sayed said. "No one else would go. What a hero!"

Amm Sayed shook his head, sadly.

"What's wrong?" Kharalombos asked.

Why did *Amm* Sayed look so forlorn? I panicked, gritty from lack of sleep. Had something happened to Kharalombos' uncle?

"You can't believe the chaos. Someone stole the plant," *Amm* Sayed said. "Thieves have become bolder."

"The plant?" What was he talking about?

"My uncle keeps the spare key in a plant," Kharalombos said. "It was always safe before. That was our hiding place for years."

"*Salamtak*. Get well, Dr Gary," *Amm* Sayed said, turning to me. He kept shaking my hand. We had never kissed on the cheeks—I had never felt comfortable with that. "How is your health?"

He meant, are you still cuckoo? Of course, *Amm* Sayed had been there at the apartment building the day I had been sedated by the university doctor and taken away to the mental hospital. It was an ugly scene that I wanted to forget. And what a convenient way for the university administration to get rid of a rebel!

"Wonderful," I said. "I've fully recovered." I wondered what else he knew about me. The porters in Cairo seemed to know every morsel of gossip for miles around their buildings.

"Where are we going to stay?" I asked Kharalombos. "What now?"

The man with white hair stepped toward me and offered his hand. "The name's Bill…I'm a visiting professor in human rights law. You're quite a character." He chuckled. "Legendary, in fact."

"Have we met before?" I asked, pretending that I didn't know what he was talking about. "I'm a vacuum-cleaner salesman from Ames, Iowa."

Surely, he didn't believe such an outrageous fib.

"By the way, Gary," he said, as if he already knew all about me, "we are living in your old flat."

Had they found my novel? Helicopters roared overhead, zigzagging in the sky. Despite the chaos, I still clung to the hope that I might find my manuscript.

Amm Sayed pointed upward. "People want justice."

A wave of protests had started the month before in Tunisia, when Mohamed Bouazizi, a fruit and vegetable seller, had set himself on fire when he was humiliated and mistreated by the police. If the Tunisians can protest against their Big Man, the Egyptians had reasoned, then why not us? When Khaled Sa'id, the boy from Alexandria, had been tortured by the police, the image of his disfigured face had gone viral on the internet—years of abuse had fueled public rage. This was the boy we had seen on the video monitor at the Valletta airport.

My own anger seemed small. I had been so angry when the nurse had jabbed me in the rump and the two security officers from the university had dragged me off to a van, out of my apartment building in Garden City. A number of my neighbors had witnessed the scene, as I was shoved into the elevator and taken away. When I woke up, I was in a pure white room with twin beds, covered with light blue cotton coverlets with a floral design. A copy of the nineteenth-century painting by David Roberts hung on the wall—the bazaar in Cairo in pastel colors: pure romance.

There was little oriental romance in the noisy helicopters hovering above, a reminder of the modern, aggressive army. All of us looked up at the sky—one couldn't help but feel a sense of doom.

"Do you remember what happened in 1986? When the police recruits burned down the Holiday Inn? Many died," Kharalombos said, shaking his head. "Someone spread a rumor that their salaries would be lowered."

Amm Sayed sighed with a sense of resignation. "This is much, much bigger. I hope it doesn't get bloody. People want their rights."

I heard the voice of my yoga teacher from the mental hospital, saying, "Imagine you are at a peaceful lake." Even with my vivid imagination, I was finding that a stretch.

Bill was saying, "Y'all come on up and have a cup of coffee. Sample some good ol' pee-can pie. Meet my wife, Rose."

We left *Amm* Sayed and the snoring general to guard the building and followed Bill inside.

He waved at the old-fashioned cage elevator. "Elevator's broken most of the time. Our apartment's on the fourth floor."

We trooped behind him, every stair of the way.

When we reached the landing of the fourth floor, the door suddenly swung open. Rose said, "Now, Scarlett O'Hara, darlin', don't be a wart." A tiny Chihuahua was barking ferociously, as if she were a lion. Rose was in her late thirties or early forties—tall and svelte. She had terrific, tanned legs. She was wearing a pair of flimsy shorts with a red Alabama football tee-shirt: the CRIMSON TIDE. She had eschewed the cheerleader look; instead of long blonde hair, hers was cropped short in a spiky cut. What surprised me even more was the tattoo of a blue beluga on her upper arm and, beneath it, a slogan in caps: "SAVE THE WHALES."

Was the dramatic protest I had initiated at the university the best way to save the Nile? Or was it more that I relished the spotlight in leading the charge? Dr Gary Watson, the environmental crusader . . . In every situation, seeing myself as the hero.

"Baby, we have visitors," Bill said. "Put on the coffee. She makes the best pee-can pie."

Kharalombos reached down to stroke Scarlett with one of his giant hands.

"I wouldn't do that, if I were you . . . She hates men!"

But the advice came too late.

"Aaaaawww!" Kharalombos cried out, jumping back from the tiny dog. He almost knocked me over.

Bill was embarrassed. "Baby, could you put her in the back room?"

Drops of blood were oozing from Kharalombos's hand.

After she had left the room, Bill said, through clenched teeth, "Damn dog goes with us everywhere. We even had to take Scarlett on a Nile cruise. She jumped into the river. They had to stop the boat!"

Was the sex with Rose so great that he tolerated this spiteful dog? My problem with women was that I never wanted to commit—I had been engaged twice, each time for seven years. Gayle had pushed hard for marriage because of our research on "High Rates of Ammonia and Lead in the Nile." Was research on ammonia and lead the basis for a healthy marriage? On the other hand, Rachel was close to forty and kept showing me a *Ladies' Home Journal* article with a picture of a womb in the shape of a clock, TICK-TOCK—it made me limp. My romance with the Bulgarian acrobat, Boriana, had lasted six months—I would have to decide soon.

Rose suddenly appeared with peroxide and a long bandage. "You won't die from one of Scarlett's bites. You sit down right there and let me doctor you."

Kharalombos sank down in the formal straight-back chair, next to the dining room table.

I was dying to snoop around. I couldn't just barge into their bedroom and peer under the bed. Why not?

"Sit down, honey," Rose said, pulling out the dining chair next to Kharalombos. "Stay awhile."

"I need to use your bathroom," I said.

Bill disappeared into the kitchen.

"That way," Rose said, nodding toward the hall. She took Kharalombos's hand and was spraying it with disinfectant.

Kharalombos winced. "AAAAAAyyy!"

I sauntered as casually as I could toward the bathroom. But my old bedroom door was closed tightly.

A few minutes later, Bill was bringing in two mugs of steaming coffee. "I didn't introduce Gary. He used to live in this flat."

"You don't say!" Rose said.

Bill set the coffee mugs down on the dining room table. "Take milk in your coffee, buddy?"

"Milk. No sugar," I said. "You didn't by any chance find my novel when you moved in? It was called *Pure Water*."

The *Chronicle* headline: "Computer Virus Called Pure Water." Maybe I should change the title of my novel? It really wasn't catchy enough. *Pristine Water? Clear Water* sounded banal. *The Story of Fresh Spring?*

"No," Rose said. "Don't believe we did. Our maid, Zannuba, cleaned the place when we moved in. She probably threw it away. Bill, sweetie, did you see a novel anywhere? Under our bed?"

How did she know that's where I had left it?

"Naw," Bill said. "Never saw a novel. No siree."

Rose wrapped a long bandage around Kharalombos's hand. "That okay?"

Kharalombos grunted.

"Why don't you tell us about your novel?" Rose said, batting her eyelashes.

"Thank you for your consideration," Kharalombos said. "I am not harmed."

Rose winked at him. "I like to play nursi-poo. Know what I mean?" She fondled the brass ring in her nose.

"What?" Kharalombos said, blinked. "Nursi-poo?"

I surged on, describing the plot, "An American scientist is thrown into the Nile by the Egyptian secret police for exposing corrupt water companies. They're selling contaminated well water."

"Sounds like a real page-turner. Don't you think, Bill?" Rose said, plopping down in a chair at the head of the table.

Bill cleared his throat. "I don't mean to knock your idea, buddy. But don't you think that's a little paranoid?"

"Why not? Egyptians believe Souad Hosni, an Egyptian movie star, was thrown off a balcony in London by the Egyptian secret police."

Kharalombos's face had turned white—this was going to make him feel that his time had come. Sometimes I couldn't resist showing off my knowledge.

"Rose is a writer in her own right. She is working on a novel about snake handlers in Alabama," Bill said.

I laughed. "That sounds bizarre. Fantastic. What an original idea! I wish I had thought of that."

At the time, I thought I had done enough research on the issues of clean water in Egypt. But maybe, just maybe, it had also been a mistake to write a realistic novel about the country!

A single, thunderous shot rang out nearby. Had something happened to the porter? The group guarding the building?

Kharalombos asked, "Where is Alabama in America? Wasn't that part of what they called the Confederacy? They lost the Civil War. Thousands died."

"It was bloody," Bill said, "Over six hundred thousand men from both sides, I believe."

The phone rang. Rose got up to answer the phone, which was on a little wooden pedestal close to the dining room table. "Rose's Bar and Grill," she said, cheerfully. Suddenly she frowned and covered the mouthpiece announcing to us, "Citibank's being looted."

"The worst battle was Gettysburg," Bill was saying. "Fifty-one thousand men died on that battlefield alone."

Scarlett was barking.

"What? I can't hear you. Can you speak louder? No shit!"

She covered the mouthpiece again and shouted, "A shootout at the prison in Maadi."

She slammed down the phone. "Well, anyone for a little pie?" Her voice sounded false. She was acting like we were sitting on a porch swing in Alabama, not a care in the world. She ducked into the kitchen. Was she crying?

Bill led us into the living room. The atmosphere was somber.

"Please," Bill said, gesturing to the huge chairs. "Have a seat. Rose has done a real nice job of decorating the place. She put her heart and soul into making it a home."

Kharalombos settled into one of the giant chairs next to the sofa. I sat on the couch. To my surprise, Bill sat on the floor in an Indian-style pose, facing us.

"I'm an old hippie. Smoked a lot of dope in my time. Vietnam vet," he said, waving his hand.

Rose had hung orange tent work material on every wall. I felt as if I were hallucinating again—too many vivid colors and geometric shapes. And yet it wasn't unpleasant: Oriental fantasy—geometric designs of reds, greens, yellow, and blue. When I had lived in the flat, I had done nothing to decorate the place; the walls were a plain white. I was focused on my research and teaching and had not paid much attention to domestic details.

Kharalombos gestured with his bandaged hand. "That material is usually used for funeral tents."

Rose returned from the kitchen, plunking down a bottle of Maker's Mark in the middle of the coffee table. Plopping down next to me on the couch, she tucked her tanned, nimble legs underneath her, like a mermaid. I caught Kharalombos staring, too.

Bill asked, "Did you forget the pee-can pie?"

But Rose ignored him.

Kharalombos poured himself half a glass. He rarely drank.

Bill looked serious. "Baby, you know what we agreed. We shouldn't even have it in the house. Where did you hide it?"

"That's for me to know and you to find out," Rose said, filling her glass to the brim. "Rome is burning! You want me to drink lemonade?"

"Are you sure you didn't find a manuscript when you moved in? It was my last copy," I said.

"You kidding?" Bill said, aghast. "Everyone knows you make back-ups in this day and age."

I shrugged. "Live and learn!" I couldn't tell him why I didn't have an elec-tronic copy. And I couldn't tell him how I had dropped the flash drive down the elevator shaft, on the day I escaped from Cairo. I was hitching up the black robe, and the flash drive had slipped between the cracks and fallen down the shaft.

Rose took a swig of bourbon. "Let me tell you about our maid, Zannuba. Dumb as a bucket of rocks. She used to bake chicken with the head still on it. Gross! How does she expect us to eat that? It would be easier to fry the chicken myself. Except I'm trying to write a novel."

"Rose, he is asking about his book." Bill said. "Could you just answer?"

Rose threw her hands up in the air. "I told you there's no fuckin' book!"

"Just calm down," Bill said.

"You lied like a legless dog. Said Cairo was safe," Rose said, gulping the bourbon. "I don't know why I let you talk me into coming to this godforsaken place. It would have been much easier to stay in Tuscaloosa. Now I'm never gonna make Huff & Huff's deadline!"

"Maybe it'll turn up." I felt a little queasy. I imagined my novel being carted away to be recycled at Moqattam Hills, with all the gargantuan mounds of trash. I had slaved away on that book for eight years on every single university vacation—and not a single trace of it was left. Gone. Poof. I imagined myself in Moqattam Hills, rooting around like one of the few remaining pigs there who had escaped the government purge, through Pepsi cans, Kotex, bits of gristle, pizza boxes, leftover macaroni—desperately searching for those six hundred pages. Say, cowboy, do you think you've written *Moby Dick?* Even if I found the greasy manuscript, stained with tomato sauce, among the trash, no publisher would take me on—I was a pariah. Just who had gotten into my computer and created that nasty virus? Who had set me up?

Bill said, "Well, hell, I'm writing a book, too. About how Bush had anyone he suspected extradited to foreign countries. Where they were tortured. A clear violation of human rights. Let me tell you, plenty of people were tortured."

"Please spare us," Rose said. "TMI. This is clearly not the right time."

Kharalombos's face had turned green. "I am tired. Do you think I can rest somewhere?"

"Of course you have the master bedroom," Rose said. "Come with me."

Chapter 2

Animals Reign

OVER THE NEXT THREE DAYS, WE HAD TO ADJUST to long curfews. Four hours a day, we were allowed out. I walked in circles in the neighborhood, very close to the building—in fact, I circled one block thirty times. Kharalombos spent most of his time outdoors with the group guarding the building: he was entranced by the general's stories. Without any internet, we floated between rumors and phone calls.

Rose always had a drink in her hand and was always on the phone. She announced: "They are saying we better have a bag packed." Or: "They let all the convicts out of jail."

At first, Bill seemed to be unconcerned. "I was in Saigon when it fell." He sat cross-legged on the living room floor, cracking pistachios with his teeth and drinking Big Gulp glasses of Pepsi with ice.

But then, Bill started to behave strangely, too. As soon as you sat down in the living room, he talked compulsively about the different ways victims could be tortured—hung from the balls, pointy objects stuck up the anus, feet roasted over a fire, heads dunked in water. On the third day, he started telling me about how they used rat torture in the Elizabethan era. "They used to encourage the rats to eat the flesh of the prisoners. Hung the prisoners near the river Thames so the rats would eat them."

I started reading Rose's copy of *The History of Alabama Football* in the bathroom to escape.

Suddenly, the networks came back on. Mammoth throngs were boiling in Tahrir Square, less than a mile away from where we were. Citizens raised their fists, shouting at the Big Man: "Boo-hoo, we don't want you! Boo-hoo, we don't want you!"

One afternoon, fighter jets shrieked across the blue sky.

Whenever the living room was empty, Kharalombos sneaked phone calls to the Big Man's daughter.

I said in a low voice, "Are you calling the landline of the royal palace? They've split. Left town. 'Hit the road, Jack.'"

Kharalombos was despondent. "It's not funny. I'll never get to see my son Nunu now."

When he called Yasmine's mobile number, someone seized the phone and said, "This is her father speaking. Who are you?"

"Are you sure you have the right phone number?" I said. "Maybe it was the Big Man himself!"

We stood fixated, like zombies, in front of the television in the living room. Rose became more and more anxious as she watched the crowds teeming into the Square, elbow to elbow. She became feverish from lack of sleep and too much booze. "Y'all, I'm predictin' a massacre."

"I have an idea," I said. "Why don't we turn off the television? Kharalombos will teach us how to waltz this evening."

Bill chuckled. "That's a fine idea, Gary. Good thinking. Pretend we're going to a ball."

Kharalombos looked at me as if I were crazy. Then he started singing, "*Kelma helwa wi kelmetein. Helwa ya baladi!*"[1] He exhorted us to sing, lifting his huge hands in the air.

Rose said, "What's he saying?"

Kharalombos pushed the couch against the wall so we had a space. "Sing! Sing! Just listen to the words. After me."

Bill bellowed, "*Kelma helwa wi kelmetein. Helwa ya baladi!*"

"But what does it mean?" Rose huffed. "Speak English."

"It's a little like the song 'This Land Is Your Land, This Land Is My Land,'" I said. "'How beautiful my country is.' An Italian who grew up in Egypt, Dalida, made the song famous. It will bring Egyptians to tears."

Kharalombos put his arm around Rose and said, "And a one and a two and a three, sing: *Helwa ya baladi!* We sing first, then we dance."

We sang with gusto, "*Helwa ya baladi!*" How beautiful my country is. Kharalombos's eyes became watery.

Rose giggled. Kharalombos put his arm firmly around her waist, "Now, the first thing to remember if you are dancing a waltz is to count…"

We waltzed the evening away until late into the night. And that was the only night we slept.

—⁕—

The doorbell rang at 6:30 the next morning.

"Ah, *que bueno*," the short, petite woman said when I opened the door. "I am Abril."

Rose shuffled to the door, rubbing her eyes and yawning.

Rose and Abril kissed each other on both cheeks. "I am only going to Madrid. Not to America." But Abril's eyes filled with tears, "In case I don't come back, I want you to have my only copy of *Don Quixote*. My drying rack. And Blanca."

I had promised Boriana I would return to Malta after I found my novel. But would I wiggle out again?

---

[1] From Salah Jahin's lyrics.

Abril set the purple drying rack against the wall. Bill took the copy of *Don Quixote* and hugged Abril. Rose kissed Abril again.

"Now don't you worry, Blanca is in good hands," Rose said, taking the metal cage. With her other hand, she wiped away the tears.

A tiny, white fluff of a rabbit, curled up in a ball, was inside.

Bill called out, "*Hasta luego!*"

I shut the door.

"Who . . ?" I asked.

"A translator," Rose said. "Fluent in three languages. Puts us to shame. She helped me buy my microwave. I don't know a word of Arabic, except *shukran*! Thank you!"

Bill waved the fat copy of *Don Quixote* at me. The cover was torn almost in half. "You ever read this, buddy?"

"Long time ago," I said. "Wonderful story. Don Quixote and Sancho Panza chasing windmills. A spoof on chivalrous romance."

He handed me the tome. "It's yours. I actually prefer biographies, history. Real life!"

The dedication in Spanish said: "For Abril, for the love of adventure…"

Unless the adventure went south, or sour.

"Bill, honey," Rose called out, panicked. "We better find out what's happening."

Bill, who was bowlegged, ran like a duck toward the television in the living room. "Baby, come look at this."

The three of us gaped at the screen: thousands of people were leaving Egypt in droves. The deserted airport where we had been five or six days ago was now clogged with people.

The announcer's voice on CNN didn't wake Kharalombos, who was curled up on the couch in a fetal position, smiling, in a peaceful slumber, with a whistling snore.

The next morning Bill cornered me in the dining room when Rose was in the shower. "Gary, can I talk to you privately?" he whispered.

"Why are you whispering?" Kharalombos was snoring away on the couch, a few yards away.

"Well, buddy, I know we just met. I was wondering if you would do us a real big favor. Maybe in exchange...? You need a place to crash. We need a pet-sitter."

"You're not taking Scarlett?"

Bill shook his head. "Embassy's orders. One carry-on. No pets."

"I thought she couldn't be separated from Scarlett," I said.

He put his hand on my shoulder. "I've arranged for us to go on an Embassy plane to Cyprus. You can see what kind of shape Rose is in. Acting like a chicken with its head cut off. I have to get her out."

I was stunned. "You're coming back?"

"I wish I could say we were. We've had a great year here," Bill said. "But you can see for yourself that things are getting bad."

"When are you leaving?" I asked. I had really thought Bill would stick it out for the long haul, especially since he kept bragging about his bravery during the fall of Saigon.

"A few hours," Bill said. "The last seats on the plane."

"Rose doesn't know?" I asked.

When she got out of the shower, she yelled, "You're not my daddy. How dare you! I won't go!"

She slammed the bedroom door, with a viciousness I admired.

But, in the end, she emerged from the bedroom, with a tiny bag over her shoulder and her computer bag. She was sobbing. "Scarlett, I'm so sorry. But momma'll be back real soon. In a jiffy. You behave for your Uncle Gary. Let me show you."

I followed her into the kitchen. She flung open the refrigerator door.

An absurd number of packets of insulin took up the entire second shelf of the refrigerator. The third shelf was entirely devoted to Stella beer, the local brew.

She inserted the insulin into the hypodermic needle, scooped up Scarlett, and gave her the shot in the rump before I could blink. "See, easy as pie." Scarlett whimpered.

Bill called out, "Baby, driver's honking. Gotta go. We're gonna miss the plane. Stop dillydallying."

Kharalombos woke up an hour later. He stretched his long arms and yawned. "Where is everybody?"

"Flew the coop," I said.

—⚍—

I started combing the flat for my novel. First, I would start with the place I was sure I had left it—under the king-sized bed in the master bedroom. Throwing the bedspread over the side of the bed, I peered underneath. The first find was a pair of shiny, silver handcuffs. Then a black studded collar. A leather whip. Please spank me! Bubble wrap. Oh, Big Daddy, wrap me tight! Now, I'll put some pepper in your gumbo! Maybe I should suggest this to Boriana.

Kharalombos poked his head through the door. "Do you think it's proper to go through their belongings?"

I threw the handcuffs at him. "Need some cuffs for Gudrun?"

He caught the cuffs and tossed them on the bed. "Very funny," he said. Then he began to sing along with Asmahan's "*Ya Toyoor Ghanni*" on YouTube. "O Birds, Sing." He adored the glamorous Syrian singer, rumored to be a German spy, who had died in mysterious circumstances in 1944.

A sonic boom. What was that?

"Do you think anybody knows we're here?" I asked.

"Somebody could have easily followed us," Kharalombos said. "Traced the phone call."

The baby rabbit was thumping her back paws. Hungry? Scared? I had no experience with rabbits. When I was six, I had wanted a beagle. But Dad only allowed pit bulls and he named them after captains of industry: J.P. Morgan, Henry Ford, and Andrew Carnegie. My father thought he was grooming me to be the captain of his ship, Creamy Freeze. But I felt suffocated and had escaped to graduate school (or I had thought it was an escape.) But after a few dull appointments in academia, I had escaped to Cairo in my late forties—hungry for a little adventure. Of course, no one in Cairo knew that I had been denied tenure because of my activities with the Anti-Capitalism Front. But being sequestered in a mental hospital, and then living under the radar as a fugitive, pursued by the Egyptian secret police and Interpol, was a little more than I had bargained for.

"Do you think you could get some lettuce for Blanca?"

But Kharalombos was singing "*Ya Toyoor*" and staring at the video on his phone. He imitated Asmahan's operatic "Ha, ha, ha, ha." He waved, heading to the door.

Maybe Blanca wanted out. I gingerly lifted the latch on the cage, and she hopped out.

I stuck my head under the bed again: here's a copy of Rose's novel. The jacket cover: A dwarf in rural Alabama takes revenge on his lover in a story of betrayal and passion. A thrilling who-done-it in a carnival camp. A blurb from *Publishers Weekly*: "An exciting voice from the New South." Where was my novel? Give me mine! "An imaginative creator of a universe." That's me! "In the footsteps of Carson McCullers." Is that so? I tossed the book aside. I patted Blanca.

"You know, Blanca, there are so many nasty creatures in this world. You have to be careful!"

Just how long could we hole up here, taking care of other people's pets? Were the secret police on our trail?

At some point, I would have to give Scarlett a second shot of insulin. A dog outside was yelping. I remembered embracing Boriana when she was sobbing, the day I had saved her from her violent husband, Dragomir. Her sobbing had almost sounded like yelping. "You're safe now," I had said, embracing her.

The building vibrated and shook. Running into the living room, I switched the channel to Al-Jazeera. BREAKING: The local Carrefour superstore had been looted. A thug was carrying out a mannequin. The jewelry store in the mall had been stripped completely—even the cases were gone. Had the whole city gone haywire? Al-Jazeera showed a series of clips: police stations on fire across the country. EVEN MORE BREAKING NEWS: Ten thousand convicts were released from three prisons in Egypt. God! Maybe we should have gotten on the plane.

My hands were shaking, but I managed to put the insulin into Scarlett's shot. I chased her around the coffee table, up on the couch, off the couch, through the dining room, and finally cornered her in the kitchen.

"You die without this sugar, Scarlett!" I shouted.

During the week, we rationed the television, especially when we were eating. Images of looted grocery stores and banks, burned-out cars, and bleeding people poisoned your appetite.

Kharalombos often burst into the flat, breathless, to tell me what was happening in the street. "*Amm* Sayed stopped a minibus full of thugs with his shotgun. They had Molotov cocktails. They were going to throw them at our building! The Old General made them break the bottles and told them they should be ashamed of themselves."

Another night, *Amm* Sayed shot out the tires of a motorcycle that tried to break through the barricaded street.

The searing tear gas floated in from the Square and seeped into the flat. Dousing my face under the showerhead did not help. Pepsi worked well to neutralize the burning.

The images of the Big Man on television hinted that his reign was waning. Even the dyed black hair and the pancake makeup did not hide his weariness and fatigue—he looked rather sad, like an aging actor who insists on playing the part of a much younger Marlon Brando. His lofty speech about his love for the people and his own heroism in many wars, meant to soothe the crowd, provoked them instead.

A sonorous "BOOOOOOO!" of a million people carried from the Square, less than one mile away, straight into the living room. Soon after, incensed chants started: "WE DON'T WANT YOU." Or: "HEY, HEY, DEAD TREE, WE WILL BE FREE."

Another visual snapshot from the television: reptilian vehicles and tanks crawled toward the street corners, surrounding the masses of people who had gathered inside the Square.

"What are they going to do? You don't think they...?" I rested my head against the soft cushion of the couch.

Kharalombos waved his hand. "The army will always protect the people. This is the tradition of our country."

Rose's voice drawled in my head, "Y'all, I'm telling you, it's going to be a..."

At night, someone kept calling the flat. Deep breathing. Was it the Big Man's men? But weren't they too busy to worry about small-time imposters like us?

Besides the anonymous phone calls, someone kept ringing the tweety Chinese doorbell in the middle of the night. When I peered out the peephole, no one was there.

My novel might be in Scarlett's bedroom. On the bedside table was a stack of coffee-table books on Egyptology. Ramses el-Kibir in his Indiana Jones hat smiled back; he pointed a finger at me: "Gotcha!" The title of the book: *Explore One of the Seven Wonders of the World* with Ramses el-Kibir.

My stomach rumbled. Maybe I should cook something. I wandered into the kitchen and half-heartedly picked up a recipe book: *Southern Living: Home-style Cooking*. A piece of scrap paper marked the page: Mississippi Mud Pie. I turned it over—the title page to my novel, *Pure Water*. Eureka! At last! And yet... On the other side, scribbled cursive: sponges, toilet paper, Dettol, garlic, lemon, Coca-Cola.

The phone rang. "Hello. Hello?" An Egyptian kid giggled. "What's your name? What's your name?"

Next to the phone were scraps of papers with delivery orders or important phone numbers. DRINKIES: Two bottles of rum. VET in red magic marker. IRON PRESSER: Two ironed shirts. I turned over each random piece of paper from my novel, shocked. How could she? Didn't she have the slightest curiosity about the book? Nope! I read on Page 13: "Industrial wastewater discharge, pesticidal and chemical fertilizers, radioactive waste have an effect on life forms and may cause kidney dysfunction in humans. Fish routinely expire from high levels of ammonia and lead." Line after line of scientific jargon. What?! Why had I left that in? I skimmed Page 599: "Two men in dark sunglasses and oversized suits shoved me into an unmarked car. 'Boys,' I said, 'as Raymond Chandler would say, 'You are about as inconspicuous as two tarantulas on a slice of angel food cake.'" Pheweee! It stunk. Stagey and self-conscious. And was the plot, like the corpse of a bloated, decomposing cow, floating slowly down a murky, green Nile?

I was crushed—my novel served as scrap paper for grocery lists!

And yet . . .

When I'd finished it, I had thought: what could be a better who-done-it than an American scientist dumped into the Nile for his exposure of a grand conspiracy by water companies? Now, I was not so sure. Page 600, The End: "It looked like the end for yours truly!" Maybe my darling might have a few warts, or a pimple here and there, or, God forbid, a disfigured face.

I had a better idea. A grand epic: a man on the run who hides from Interpol dressed as a Crusader knight in a Hospitaller museum in Valletta. A man who finds his genuine calling when he walks away from his ambitious career. A man who was so driven that he never allowed himself to fully commit—who finds true love with a beautiful Bulgarian acrobat from Sofia. Anyway, if I wrote my autobiography I would surely be caught by Interpol! Why hadn't I called Boriana? Shouldn't I be worried about Dragomir?

I wandered back to the bedroom. Blanca was hopping back and forth in her cage. She sniffed the air, her white whiskers shaking. "Aaah, good girl. Come with me and we'll see if we can find you something decent to eat."

I picked up the cage and carried it to the kitchen.

No carrots, but I rescued a shred of shriveled cabbage. She nibbled at it and then looked at me with darting brown eyes, as if to say: Seriously, you expect me to eat this?

I opened the trap door and she hopped out, jumping back and forth, the length of the linoleum floor.

In the cupboards, there was an eclectic assortment of canned goods: pumpkin, sardines, Hormel Chili, baked beans. You must be kidding!

Without thinking, I tied up the trash, and opened the back door, leaving the bag for the garbage man.

"No! No!" I shouted. "That's the jungle! Stay inside!"

Rushing down the spiral staircase, I caught a glimpse of white.

A few minutes after I returned, Kharalombos peered into the kitchen. "What happened, my friend?"

"Blanca escaped. She's just a tyke. She'll get eaten by a street cat!"

Kharalombos was holding a newspaper cone. "Should we search for her?"

"She's gone. I looked everywhere!"

"Fried brains?" he said, opening up the greasy packet.

A curly, fried mass nestled between the folds of the newspaper.

"Thanks, but no thanks." I had one last Bounty, the Egyptian version of Almond Joy.

We broke our rule about eating in front of the television: the Big Man and his family had fled to Morocco. He was embracing the young king.

Kharalombos gasped. "It's so far away."

"Well," I said, using one of my mother's sayings, "look on the bright side. Nunu will be safe there."

"Asylum has been offered to the Big Man's family by the king of Morocco," the announcer on state television said, smiling.

The scene flashed to the immense crowd, raising their placards, "Justice Now!" in the Square. Then, a picture of the Big Man and his family—willowy Yasmine was standing next to a handsome young man. A small boy held her hand.

"That's Nunu!" Kharalombos shouted. "Yasmine! I will never see my son. It's over. Morocco is so far away!"

The announcer said, "The Big Man is accompanied by his wife, the Dragon Lady, his two sons, his daughter, her husband, and his first grandson."

Tears were streaming down Kharalombos's face. He set the fried brains on the coffee table. This was much, much sadder than watching him cry about all the dead pigs in Cairo. He was distraught, understandably. How could I console him?

The phone rang.

"If you make it out alive" reverberated in my brain. We couldn't feed on other people's hysteria. But how to remain calm? My stomach was disturbed.

"You get the phone," I said, making a dash for the toilet.

When I returned from the bathroom, Kharalombos was saying, "Of course, we'll be there as soon as possible. Don't worry."

"Who?"

"Gudrun. She wants us to come to the Conrad Hilton immediately."

"Is it an emergency? What happened? Is she all right?"

"She didn't say," Kharalombos said. "She said she must see us. We should hurry."

I was suffering from cabin fever and I needed a break.

On our way out of the building, *Amm* Sayed offered us some rabbit with *molokheyya*[2] and rice.

Kharalombos gave me a knowing look.

"Couldn't be," I said. "He wouldn't."

Then he asked, "Should we tell *Amm* Sayed to feed Scarlett?"

"Oh," I said, confidently. "I'm sure we'll be back."

Chapter 3

Antony and Cleopatra

WHEN WE ARRIVED AT THE CONRAD HILTON, THERE WAS a huge entourage waiting for us in the lobby. Many of them were carrying cameras and other filming equipment. Gudrun was wearing a red *galabeyya* embroidered with gold thread. An oversized black wig obscured her face.

---

[2] A plant/vegetable soup dish on Middle Eastern tables.

Kharalombos hugged and kissed Gudrun. "I will never get to see Nunu," he murmured.

"Nunu? Who is the Nunu?" Gudrun asked. She pinched Kharalombos's cheek.

"It's a long story," I said. "We thought you were in trouble. Knights to the rescue."

"His Majesty demands your presence," Gudrun snorted. "He wants you to play in his television show. Don't laugh. I am the great Cleopatra!"

Gudrun pinched Kharalombos's other cheek. "Kharalombos will be the perfect Marc Antony. You will be a servant. Or maybe Cleopatra's son. All the foreign actors flew the nest."

"I was handsome Hal, the playboy prince in *King Henry IV, Part I*, in high school," I said. "My theatre teacher said I wasn't half bad. Thought I had some talent. Even urged me to continue acting."

But Kharalombos was mesmerized by Gudrun. "As long as I get to dance with you." God, he was a sap. But who was I to talk? I had given Boriana a dozen red roses the night before I left Valletta. I had introduced her to the staff at the Knights Templar Museum in Malta, and they had agreed to let her take my job in the back, making wax knights. An acrobat; how long could she do this kind of work?

"What have you been doing all these days? I thought I might never see you two alive. It's good you are still ticking," Gudrun said, smiling.

"I was a vet," I said. "Kharalombos was a security guard."

Gudrun said, "I thought you sold vacuum cleaners at Walmart. That's what Kharalombos told me. Best salesman of the year!"

"Oh," I said, trying to sound as if I were a self-made man. "I have worked all sorts of jobs."

"Such a brave man," Gudrun said, adjusting the gold tiara on her black wig.

"Why, thank you," I said. "In another play, I also acted as the great Harry Houdini."

But Gudrun pointed at Kharalombos, who stood tall, as if he were a knight from the Middle Ages. Only one hour before, he had crumpled before my very eyes. He had so much emotional elasticity—I envied him.

Ramses el-Kibir suddenly appeared in front of us with a retinue of ten minions. He clapped his hands. "Silence! Silence! I must finish my current obligations to the BBC. That is why we must film the final episode today."

Gudrun winked at me, whispering, "I have never seen such tantrums as this man can throw. He is a baby. Don't take him serious. *Nein.*"

I raised my hand. "Is it okay to be out at the Pyramids? I mean, is it safe for *you?*"

"No problem. The army gave me permission to film." Ramses clapped his hands again. The entourage headed out of the lobby to their vehicles—a crazy mélange of black and white taxis, a blue American Chevrolet, film trucks, tanks, jeeps, and Datsun pickups.

Gudrun, Kharalombos, and I were crammed into one of the little Datsun pickups, next to the driver. I was sitting on Gudrun's lap; Kharalombos's head hit the roof. Our convoy, headed by a tank, made its way down the empty streets toward the Pyramids. Something strange: we saw a huge posse of camels and horses riding in the opposite direction.

"Where is Viscount Triksky? I thought he was a film consultant," I asked.

Gudrun snorted. "He drinks too much. Almost a bottle. Snoring on the couch like the Kaiser when I left."

Once we arrived at the Pyramids, it took hours to get dressed. The make-up artist spent over an hour, curling the hair on my wig and painting black kohl on my eyes. I was wearing a skimpy Roman toga—not exactly what I had in mind for myself!

Ramses waved me away, as if I were a fly. He pulled his Stetson over his eyes. "Improvise. I hear you are good at it." He bellowed, "Mustafa! Mustafa! Where is my camel?"

Did he know who I was? Or was he just bluffing?

The small thin man coughed, a bad smoker's cough. Finally, he said, "There are no camels, *ya fandem!*"

"Speak, man," Ramses said, furious. "What is it?"

"There are no camels and horses today," the small thin man sputtered. "They went to the Square."

"Why? I demand to know!" Ramses shouted, stamping his foot. I suppressed a desire to laugh. Gudrun guffawed. "A big baby," she said.

One of the cameramen offered the small thin man a wooden stool. He started to sit down. "You will not sit in my presence, Mustafa. Why are the camels and horses at the Square?"

He looked as if he might collapse from emphysema. He looked up and around to see if anyone was looking, and then whispered, "Someone paid."

Ramses said, "Ramses el-Kibir will not be defeated! Instead of the battle scene with the camels and horses, we will film Marc Antony killing himself. And then, Cleopatra killing herself. Gary, you will deliver the snake in a basket!"

A huge crowd of people from the nearby village had appeared to watch the shooting of the scene. Small children from the stables skittered around the cameras. Sellers had set up carts: they were selling water, KFC dinner boxes, peanuts, Egyptian flags, and postcards of the Pyramids, even though there were no foreign tourists. A few of the army soldiers who had escorted us to the Pyramids leaned against their tanks, chowing down on crispy drumsticks.

Ramses el-Kibir clapped his hands. The cameramen stood at attention. "Kharalombos, you will fall on your sword when you realize that you have lost the battle."

Kharalombos was imposing in his Roman toga and breastplate. He had a spear and a sword.

"I thought this show was about your discovery of ancient pharaonic treasures?" I asked.

Ramses laughed. "Of course, it is. I will point out Cleopatra and Marc Antony's grave at the end of the re-enactment. We are wasting Ramses el-Kibir's valuable time." He clapped his hands. "Move."

Ramses was never satisfied with the way Kharalombos fell on his sword, so we did the scene over and over again for two hours. "NO! NO! Just look like you've lost everything! You look too cheerful." It was true—Kharalombos looked like he was having fun. Every time he plunged the sword into his side, he grinned impishly. How I had loved playing the great Harry Houdini, escaping from a straitjacket when I was a junior in high school! But Dad had growled, "There's no future in art, son."

Finally, Ramses exploded. "Cut. Cut. We will do Cleopatra's scene. Gudrun, you lie there. Look sad. Gary, you will bring in the basket with the snake."

Of course, even the great Harry Houdini could take on a real cobra! Even with the bravado, my stomach churned.

Gudrun said. "*Ja-aa*, we will not endanger our lives! What kind of snake do you have in that basket? I demand to know."

"It's a cobra," Ramses said. "Don't be scared, though. He doesn't have any teeth."

One of the children from the crowd flicked open the basket. He poked the huge snake with a stick. The cobra reared its head. The crowd roared.

"Has the cobra been milked?" I asked. "Otherwise . . . "

Ramses el-Kibir shouted to the crowd. "Silence! This is serious. I'm warning you. Get that boy off the set. Not another word."

Kharalombos towered over Ramses el-Kibir, clenching his spear. "I swear to God, on my honor you will not endanger the life of this visitor to our country. This is against our tradition of hospitality."

The crowd hooted and hollered.

Ramses el-Kibir's nostrils flared. "Out of my way. We will shoot the scene. Gudrun, lie down on the couch. That is an order."

She snorted. "Do you think I am a fool? A nincompoop, as the Americans would say. Get another Cleopatra!"

Someone in the crowd shouted, "Look, the cobra has teeth!" The sleek, black cobra was swaying, rearing its head.

The sellers wheeled their carts away. The Bedouins, who had been lying on their carpets, packed them up.

But before I could sprint off, I felt a heave. I started to throw up—bits of fried stuff. One of the soldiers had offered me a drumstick.

Ramses shouted, "At your places. Get ready to shoot."

But the cameramen were lugging their heavy cameras to the film trailers. The soldiers were revving their tank engines.

Gudrun was saying to Kharalombos, "Sometimes, God is merciful. Kharalombos, my *Liebchen*, you are so brave. How can we ever thank you?"

What about me? I was the one who was being filmed with a live cobra!

Ramses' phone rang. He said, "What? I am coming at once! Defend our national treasures!"

Ramses rushed off the set with a troop of minions.

When I finally finished throwing up, the desert was empty except for two lone figures, Gudrun and Kharalombos.

"Where is everyone?" I asked. "I feel lousy."

Gudrun dabbed my forehead with a wet handkerchief. "*Ja-aa*, this is awful. Poor man. At least, we didn't have to film with the cobra."

I wiped my mouth with the back of my hand. Kharalombos handed me a bottle of water. "What happened to the cobra?"

Gudrun chortled. "Some fearless man killed him with a club."

I took a swig of water. Then, I started throwing up again—dry heaves this time. Kharalombos patted my shoulder. "Maybe the chicken was off."

"Ramses went to the Square. Camels are riding through the Egyptian Museum," Kharalombos said.

"No kidding," I said.

Gudrun threw her black wig down in the sand. She put the gold tiara in her purse. We headed back to the main road. The streets were empty. We walked about seven kilometers before we got a ride back to the Conrad Hilton. A man in a red Toyota with bananas piled high in the back stopped for us. Gudrun and Kharalombos crammed in the front; I balanced on top of the mountain of bananas in the back, hoping the driver did not cut the corners too sharply. Instead of dying from a cobra bite, I would split open my head in a car accident. Kharalombos tried to pay the driver, but he shook his head. "*Rabbena yekhalleek,*" he said. May God keep you.

Viscount Triksky was not asleep when we returned to the Conrad Hilton. He was watching something on television—it sounded like an American football game. He was sprawled on the sofa with his feet on the coffee table. When he saw us trooping into the suite, he quickly switched the channel to BBC News. He was drinking a Corona.

"It doesn't look like it was a blinding success," he said.

"You don't have to gloat," I said.

Gudrun said, "*Ja-aa,* I have never seen such a fiasco. This was why you came to the Egypt for that Ramses el-Kibir. We can forget the Nile. Tomorrow I am making my reservations to leave for the Taj Mahal."

"Well, he is a bit of a barmpot. Tell me. I am dying to know what transpired," Viscount Triksky said, his eyes glittering.

Kharalombos sank into a large chair. He closed his eyes.

Gudrun said, "Kharalombos was Marc Antony. Gary was one of Cleopatra's servants. He was going to bring me a cobra in a basket so I could kill myself." The Viscount smiled at me. "Nice kit." He winked at me. He must swing the other way.

"Think I ate something spoiled."

"Sorry, old chap. Should we order a boiled potato for you from room service?" Viscount Triksky said. "Maybe a fizzy drink?"

"No, thanks. I'll tough it out," I said, as if I were John Wayne.

Gudrun waved her hands. "There was no script! Weren't you talking about the script on the way from the airport? You are always talking the nonsense."

"There was a script," Viscount Triksky said. "But everything went a bit pear-shaped. You know, he's a prat. He changes his mind all the time."

Kharalombos said, "We walked back to the hotel. Almost twenty kilometers. They left us there."

"Bollocks!" Viscount Triksy said. "Ramses is a cad. What can we do to cheer you all up? What about a game of Snakes and Ladders?"

Gudrun snorted. "*Nein*. You play the Snake and Ladder. I want a glass of your whiskey."

Viscount Triksky's beady eyes narrowed. "I am afraid to say, someone nicked every bottle."

"You are telling us a story," Gudrun said. "You had ten bottles a few days ago. We didn't even have room for our feet in Ramses' car."

Kharalombos was playing with the remote control, flipping through the channels. On the screen, an officer in a green beret was reading a communiqué. "While the Army acknowledges the heroism of the Big Man for the Nation, they accept his honorable resignation. The General will now head the Nation. The good people at the Square are kindly urged to go back to their nests."

Gudrun said, "What is the man saying in the Arabic language? What does it mean?"

"The Big Man is out," I said.

Kharalombos sighed. "The Big Man's men will take over. There will be another Big Man."

Gudrun yawned. "There will always be a Big Man. I slept very bad for three nights."

"Can we stay here?" I asked. "Maybe we should call *Amm* Sayed to feed Scarlett. What about her shots?"

But Kharalombos's eyes were closed. He didn't answer.

"The Viscount will give you his room," Gudrun said.

"Well," the Viscount laughed lightly. "You are making the arrangements. In '74, when Haile Selassie was deposed, I got some kip on a bar table. Good night."

"What were you doing in Ethiopia in 1974?"

"A little work on the side," he said. "If you know what I mean."

No one wanted to talk and everyone went to bed.

In the middle of the night, I woke up, thirsty. A small hall light illuminated the hallway on the way to the bathroom.

A huge duffel bag tucked under his arm, the Viscount was tiptoeing toward the door.

—॥॥—

Gudrun rubbed her eyes. "So maybe the Viscount is downstairs having his breakfast."

"'Fraid not," I said. "I think he's cleared out."

Kharalombos said, "I was never convinced by his English accent. It reminded me of P.G. Wodehouse. I used to read those books when I was a boy."

I laughed. Triksky's accent didn't ring true. Brits usually followed soccer, not American football.

Gudrun said, "He's a rat. I wasn't sure of him from the beginning, but I was lonely at the camp. He came to pick up his niece at our camp. He kept hanging around."

"Did he rob you?" Kharalombos asked.

She sighed. "Only the price of a ticket to Egypt and a Nile cruise. I wanted a companion."

"You could have lost more," I said. "What are you going to do now?"

Gudrun smiled at Kharalombos. "Could I have this dance?"

Kharalombos bowed. Gudrun and Kharalombos started waltzing around the small living room. One night, Boriana had fed me grilled octopus on the balcony. Later, we had cognac and gazed at the stars. And then I had led her to the wrought-iron poster bed.

After the short dance, Gudrun said, "I'm hungry. Maybe we should have the breakfast downstairs and celebrate."

"What are we celebrating?" I asked.

"You are invited to America as my guests," Gudrun said.

Gudrun described her girls' camp, Clover Flower, in Texas. We would float on tubes and rafts for hours in a cool river, drink beer, and eat barbecue.

We both agreed to go to America soon, provided we could sneak out of Egypt. Why didn't I tell them I was going to return to Malta? I couldn't resist another adventure?

Kharalombos said, "What happens when the holiday is over?"

Gudrun shrugged, "We will see. You can teach the salsa or the cha-cha-cha to the girls. And Gary can teach the yoga?"

It sounded like a plan.

Part II

Paradise

Chapter 4

Homeward Bound

I WAS NOW ZOLTAN ANGHELESCU, a Romanian jeweler.

Kharalombos had gotten me another false passport. Would it work again? Of course, it had worked on January 28th in Cairo, but in the United States, post-9/11, I had my doubts.

The beefy officer with the Pancho Villa moustache said, "Welcome to the United States of America, Mr Anghelescu." We had flown into Houston.

I smiled and bowed in an old-fashioned way. I was wearing a brown plaid suit with a fedora. The officer was now swiping the passport through the computer. A drop of sweat rolled down the back of my neck.

"That rig is a little hot for Houston," the officer said. "For May."

I shrugged. "So colt in my country. You do not know." I was just imitating Boriana's accent. In school, my classmates begged me over and over again to do my imitations of teachers—I could mimic their accents and mannerisms perfectly.

A voice shouted in my ear, "Don't overdo it! Just smile and shrug."

"You're all set, Mr Anghelescu," the officer said, handing me the passport. Just like that? My frustrated theatrical ambitions were coming in very handy. Dad had always insisted that theatre was impractical!

Kharalombos took a Kleenex from his pocket and wiped his forehead. The officer was saying, "So the Egyptians had a revolution? What was it like over there?"

Kharalombos said, "Egyptians want their rights. They want freedom after thirty years of tyranny. A corrupt regime."

"Of course. Welcome to America," the officer said. "Home of the free and the brave. Have a nice day!"

We got through easily, but of course, Gudrun, with her orange hair, muu-muu, and purple basketball sneakers, threw the officer for a loop. She was saying, "I have had my citizenship for six years now. I am a pure citizen. A pure American. You can't imagine. Schulenburg is much better than Berlin. The only thing bad about America is the sausages."

The officer smiled. "Are you employed?"

Gudrun snorted. "I own the biggest camp for girls near Schulenburg, Texas on the river. You know it? Clover Flower? I have all the activities for the girls. The salsa, bows and arrows, discipline, marshmallows over the fire. Canoes. Maybe you want to send your daughter there?"

"Those camps cost a fortune," he said, examining the stamps on her blue passport. "It's a little weird that you went to Egypt during a revolution."

"What a dumbo idea. I should have gone to see the Taj Mahal. I told Viscount Triksky that India was better, but he never listens."

Kharalombos elbowed me. "I know," I said, under my breath.

The officer suddenly became serious. "Your husband is Russian?"

Gudrun sighed. "No husband, *nein*. There is no husband in my picture. As you Americans would say, he's a loser."

I cringed. My dad used that word to describe anyone who was not in the Fortune 500.

He studied her passport more intently. "What were you doing in Kazakhstan?"

Kazakhstan?!

"*Ja-aa*, before I had the Clover Flower, I was buying rugs from these countries. I was no good at the rug business. They are big cheaters. Liars."

"Mrs Grünewald, do you speak Russian?"

"I studied it in the *gymnasium*. But my Russian is now so bad, much worse than my English. I forgot everything. Is this a problem? I am a pure American. I love this country. Otherwise, I would never have said bye-bye to Germany."

Yes, why had she immigrated? It was unusual for Germans to become citizens.

"Please step aside," the officer said.

"She is blabbing too much," Kharalombos murmured.

"Are you still charmed?" I whispered.

She had never told us she was in the rug business. Were there other things that she had not told us about the camp?

Two hours later, we were still waiting for Gudrun to emerge from the grilling room. When she finally emerged, her face was pale.

"They are looking for Russians. Human traffic people. Slave and drug trade. This never happened to me in America. You have never seen such a long list of Russian names. You should have seen what they did to us during the War! My mother told me how they came into villages and raped women. And then, how they took Berlin!"

Kharalombos put his huge arm around her, "*Habibti*, don't talk so much. You shouldn't mention Viscount Triksky."

"That huckster," I said. I had squeaked past Immigration, but I was sure I was still on the Interpol Wanted List. I really would have to be under the radar—this was no joke.

—ɯɯ—

Once we left the big expressway, we drove on small, curvy roads, which wound near a rollicking, green river. Gudrun drove incredibly fast and the big Suburban tilted as we barely made each turn.

Kharalombos was sitting in the front. Even he said, "Take care, Gudrun. Maybe you could go a little slower. What's the hurry, *habibti*?"

Gudrun chuckled. "You live in Cairo where the people drive like maniacs! You don't know what you are saying, my bonbon." Then she giggled. "We have so much to do. Tomorrow is the first day of camp."

I was sitting in the backseat and leaned forward. "What?" All those years in noisy Cairo had ruined my hearing.

Willie Nelson crooned in the background, "Let's go to Luckenbach, Texas with Waylon and Willie and the boys. This successful life we're living got us feuding like the Hatfields and McCoys."

Gudrun tapped her jeweled hands against the steering wheel. She bellowed, "Let's go to Luckenbach, Texas." She had a huge ruby on her third finger. Just how wealthy was she?

Kharalombos stared at the landscape. "Texas is beautiful. I had no idea. We just hear about New York and California."

Sun rays shimmered on the luminous water, promising happiness. On each side of the river was lush green grass and enormous oak trees—such a contrast to the visual landscape of Cairo: brown, dusty buildings; honking cars; black plumes of exhaust.

"Could you turn that down?" Willie Nelson was screaming in my ear: "This successful life we're living."

I was not sure that my Dad would have considered me a resounding success, if he could see me beyond the grave.

Gudrun kept singing, "Let's go to Luckenbach, Texas."

"Tomorrow is the first day of camp?"

"We have three hundred little munchkins coming to the gate tomorrow with their cases. Are you ready to teach the salsa?"

Gudrun pinched Kharalombos on the cheek. "My *Liebchen.*" She kept singing, "Between Hank Williams's pain songs and Newberry's train songs and Blue Eye's Crying in the Rain…"

Kharalombos smiled distractedly, gazing at people in inner tubes who were floating in the water. They raised their beers to us as we drove past. Hail, to pleasure!

Kharalombos waved to them.

"Do you think any of the campers will want to take yoga?" I asked.

Gudrun smiled. "*Nein. Nein.* But don't worry, Gary. We will make you work! Inventory. Kitchen. There are plenty of jobs!"

I was alarmed—this was not what I had in mind. I had something grander in mind. Director of theatre? Storytelling? Even managing the art room.

"Here we go," Gudrun said, suddenly making a sharp turn. Behind the bush was a tiny sign that said, "Clover Flower Christian Girls' Camp."

Gudrun suddenly floored the Suburban up the side of a rather steep hill; at the top was a large house with a porch. A rather odd-looking contraption was rigged up in the front yard. Deer paid no attention to our arrival; they continued eating the corn. When the car rolled to a stop, they scattered into the trees.

Lacy ferns decorated the front porch. Several rocking chairs beckoned. An empty hammock swayed on the porch. I imagined myself lying there reading a thriller like *The Boys from Brazil.* Or even scribbling down notes for my new novel while I guzzled beer. Browsing through a guidebook to animals and birds of the Lone Star State. The possibilities seemed endless.

Kharalombos and I dragged our suitcases and Gudrun's steamer trunks into the "big house." Neither of us had brought swimsuits; we had left Egypt in a hurry. Gudrun disappeared.

Kharalombos sank into the couch. "Are you all right?" I asked. "Jet-lagged? Tired from the trip?"

"I wonder what will happen to Nunu. Will he grow up in Morocco?" The romance with Gudrun was a distraction from this sad fact.

"When are you going to tell her?" I asked.

"Tell me what?" Gudrun threw four or five bathing suits of all sizes at us. Plaid, Hawaiian, red-white-and-blue flag. One said: Don't Mess with Texas.

"That I also can teach merengue? Cha. Cha. Cha."

The Hawaiian print swimsuit barely fit me. When Kharalombos emerged from the bathroom, he was wearing the red Speedo.

I laughed. "Is that the only one that fits?"

His equipment was barely contained. He had a huge belly. Gudrun's bathing suit was a purple tutu with frills. Her legs were the size of tree trunks. The bra bodice had tassels on the nipples, like a belly dancing costume. She was wearing a white swimming cap.

"I know I am not Angelina Jolie. But if I go worrying about that foolishness, I will never enjoy my life. Do you want Heineken or the Blue Moon?"

We crossed the busy road with our icebox full of beer. Pickup trucks and cars zipped around the curve, as if they were in a race.

The river smelled of earth. The huge roots of the oak tree snaked into the water. In the distance, jet skis buzzed.

Gudrun threw a few yellow rafts into the water. Kharalombos jumped in, making a huge splash. We floated around for an hour, drinking beer.

Hours later, after a sumptuous supper of barbecued brisket, corn on the cob, and watermelon, Gudrun turned to me and said, "You will want to have some quiet after the long trip. I will put you in one of the counselors' cabins in the back."

"I don't mind sleeping in the big house," I said.

"This is good preparation for the session. You will be in the counselors' cabins when camp starts tomorrow."

Gudrun handed me a huge miner's flashlight. "Let's see. I think Aengus put out traps."

She led me down the pitch-black road—not a light anywhere. The locusts hummed. Could it be that bad? Kharalombos had already retired to Gudrun's master bedroom.

"There are a lot of varieties of rattlesnakes in Texas," I said.

"*Aaach*, we have never seen one. You have to worry about the cottonmouths," Gudrun said. "But they're in the river."

"The blacktail rattlesnake is the most common in this area," I said. "Of course, snakes are more afraid of humans and will retreat unless cornered. They don't deliberately stalk people. Anyway, they don't come out at night."

"*Aaach*, don't be a pussycat," she said. "You did well with the cobra."

"Of course, the Great Harry Houdini could easily kill a little ol' rattler," I said. "Just as easy as escaping from a locked coffin."

"Who?"

"He was a great American magician and illusionist."

"*Aacch*," she said, flipping on the light switch. "Whoever that is." She sighed. "So you see."

Boxes of industrial supplies were stacked against one wall. Heinz ketchup. Mustard. On another wall, huge sacks of corn. A small canoe in the middle of the room. I tripped over an oar.

In the corner was a single bed. I picked up the scratchy gray blanket with holes—it was too hot for blankets. I'd sleep nude. The pillow had been chewed around the edges.

"Is there a bathroom out here?"

Gudrun flipped on the switch. "The toilet." A single light bulb illuminated a very bare-looking toilet. A rather intricate cobweb dangled from the single bulb.

Gudrun clicked her tongue. "Emma didn't clean, *nein. Nein.* But you had a good dinner. We will fix up everything in the morning. Okay?"

Before I could say no, she closed the door and yelled out, "Nightie-night. Sleep tight."

I stripped off my clothes and plopped onto the lumpy mattress. Under the gray blanket was a filthy, stained sheet.

As soon as I lay my head on the foam pillow, a squadron of mosquitoes zeroed in for the assault, nipping my ankles, nose diving between my legs, and circling around my ears. Other invisible insects chewed on me as well. Fleas? Chiggers? Maybe my ideas about the camp had been a little glamorous.

Of course, I was not going to stay out here all summer. A voice sang, "The sun'll come out tomorrow. Bet your bottom dollar." I swatted another mosquito. In another high-school production, I had acted in *Annie*. Everything was BIGGER IN TEXAS. Anyway, Texans always thought they were better than Okies. "There'll be sun just thinkin' about tomorrow." I had played the part of Rooster, Annie's younger brother, a convict who had escaped from jail—along with two other accomplices, the plan was to rob Annie, who had been saved by "Daddy" Warbucks, a millionaire. A mosquito bit me in the groin. "Clears away the cobwebs and the sorrow." I couldn't stop scratching.

Tomorrow. Tomorrow. A creature was making a racket—too big for a rat! Where was the flashlight?

The creature had torn open one of the huge bags stacked relatively close to the cot. Harry Houdini would not have to kill a snake. But what was in the bag? I shined the flashlight at the bag: CORN FOR DEER ONLY. NOT FOR HUMAN CONSUMPTION. How was I going to get rid of him?

5 a.m. Too early to knock on the door of the big house. Gudrun would have no patience with me. On the other hand, was this a nice way to treat your guests who had traveled all the way from Egypt? Or did Gudrun just think of me as one of her minions?

Kharalombos was sleeping in a king-sized bed. I couldn't help but feel jealous. I wished I were back in Malta in my comfy bed with the feather pillows, Boriana snuggled against me. I had paid for the room at the Roma so she could stay there for another few months. This was why I had no cash left.

I made a dash for the toilet in search of a broom—no Saladin sword! Grasping the broom as if I were a caveman clutching a club, I wondered what to do next.

A bushy, striped tail was visible. "Ring-tailed raccoon," I said to myself. I had never seen one this close. Now what? The creature suddenly backed out of the bag. With the dark fur around his eyes, he looked like a train robber, a black bandanna tied around his head hiding the rest of his face. I poked him with the broom. His brown eyes gleamed and he growled at me, as if he were a bear, moving forward and backward, guarding that sack of corn.

An academic belief in the integrity of creatures was different from dealing with them in the flesh!

"Little outlaw, how did you get in here?"

The raccoon whinnied and growled, guarding his loot.

A line from a scholarly article appeared from past study: *Humans should be wary of raccoons. They are carriers of rabies, roundworms, and leptospirosis.*

Walking backward to the door, I unlatched it. My goal was to shoo Outlaw out of the cabin.

Ignoring me, Outlaw tucked his head inside the bag of corn and continued to chew.

I tapped his tail with the broom. He backed out of the bag and spun around, hissing at me. The claws were fearsome.

A word of advice about raccoons: if you try to chase away the raccoon and confront him, he may attack in self-defense.

Did I have to shoo him out? Wouldn't he leave eventually? I set down the broom and left the cabin door ajar. Why pick a fight?

It was now 7 a.m. Time to face the day. My ankles and groin itched. I was badly jet-lagged.

Chapter 5

The First Day of Camp

"SLEEP WELL? READY TO VORK?" Gudrun asked.

"There's a raccoon in my cabin," I said.

Gudrun was completely unfazed. "Welcome to the natural world! Care for coffee? Strudel? Doughnut?"

Gudrun gestured toward the breakfast table. Kharalombos was already wolfing down a chocolate-glazed doughnut. As soon as he finished one, he grabbed another from the tray with his large paw. He had purple hickeys all over his neck, which he had tried to cover with a blue bandanna. But even bandannas were not big enough to cover Kharalombos's massive neck.

I was dying to scratch my groin, but a gaggle of slim blonde-haired girls were congregated in the office—they were lounging on a brown leather couch.

One of the blonde girls squealed, "Awesome. You got into Yale? No way! What did you get on your SAT?"

Was I like that when I was a graduate student at Yale? Now that I was outside of the academic rat race, I could see that I had made the wrong choice for graduate study. Instead of literature and theatre, I had convinced myself that I was passionate about science. How could I have forced myself to spend all those years studying contaminated water?! More titillating than business, but still, not what I really craved. I read obsessively about the destruction of the Amazon rain forest, the endangered mountain gorilla in Uganda, and the baleen whale. A world-famous biologist, Dr Jakob Looke, an expert on water issues, took me under his wing. He was an Estonian who had met his wife in a displaced persons' camp in Berlin during the Second World War. Once he had confided to me, "Arriving in Hartford, Connecticut was the happiest day of my life. After all those years of being afraid of the Russians."

Water issues were a more tempting option than Dad's ice cream company, Creamy Freeze in Oklahoma City. Too many summers of driving refrigerator trucks and monitoring huge vats had turned me off. But even the default option I had chosen was not good enough. When I got a Ph.D. from Yale, he had shouted, "He'll never make a penny! Who will take over the company?" Mom had said, "But honey, not everyone can get a Ph.D. from Yale! You should be proud of him." The script was supposed to be an M.B.A., and then a lifetime of Creamy Freeze. Many of my Egyptian male students had confided to me in my office, "But *Doctoor*, my father insists on engineering! You don't know how much I hate it!" At fifty, would they have a midlife crisis, like me?

A very short, squat lady stood beside Gudrun. A pair of yellow half-glasses was perched on her nose. She was holding a clipboard. She scrutinized me. "Sorry, but yoga was not a big draw. You're on K.P. duty."

"Gary Smith. Nice to meet you," I said.

"Mary Alice Bodewell," she said. Her blue eyes twinkled. "Retired missionary. Presbyterian Church. I was in Tehran when it fell."

"Really?" That was a much more original introduction than mine.

"Mary Alice, he can be a Shawnee chief," Gudrun said, handing me a feathered headdress and a pair of Bermuda shorts. "Wear the costume. There is the toilet."

"Ready to join the ship?" Mary Alice said, studying her clipboard. "We run a tight one around here. Gudrun tells me you were an actor in Egypt."

"I just played Marc Antony in a BBC re-enactment," I said. "It will be aired on PBS soon." Maybe she didn't know I had been cast as one of Cleopatra's slaves. And really, who cared about such a tiny fib?

Mary Alice laughed heartily. "That's a good one."

"By the way, do you have any antibiotic ointment?" I asked. "I have some bad mosquito bites."

The group of blonde girls started singing: "Three blind mice. Three blind mice. See how they run. See how they run."

Mary Alice bellowed, "Ashley. Bring me the first-aid kit. On the double. Who is taking the eight-year-olds? Twelve-year-olds?"

I circled back to the breakfast table. Kharalombos handed me a cup of coffee, black, and murmured, "I'm teaching seven classes. We are *not* on holiday."

"I thought it was only salsa?" I said, elbowing him. "Do the tango?"

He yawned. "Look," he said, pointing with his index finger, which was coated with strawberry jelly. He read off his schedule. "Step aerobics. That is *not* dance."

"Don't you just go up and down on a box?"

"I don't work in the morning! I have a class at 8 a.m. No movie star in Cairo ever…" He took a bite of the doughnut.

I chuckled. "That's called the Protestant work ethic."

He chewed and stared glumly at the ceiling. "In Cairo, no movie star ever wanted a lesson before four o'clock in the afternoon."

One of the blondies batted her eyelashes at Kharalombos and simpered, "Do you know Omar Sharif? Listen to this. Do you think I have a chance on *Teen Idol*?"

Kharalombos ignored her and took another bite of his doughnut. She flounced off and threw herself on the couch with the other counselors.

Sleep-deprived, hungry, and desperate to scratch those bites, I took a swig of black coffee. I congratulated myself on my stoicism.

Mary Alice handed me a slick green book. A smiley face was drawn on the cover. "Hand them the rule book. Make them sign the liability agreement. Give them their tribal symbol. Got it?"

"Aye-aye, captain," I said. At least, my work as an environmental activist had some kind of value for society. Or was I just being a pompous ass?

Mary Alice cleared her throat. "You've got that right. I'm the captain of Clover Flower."

"Why the liability agreement? Have you been sued?"

Gudrun adjusted her Indian headpiece. "*Aaach.* A little devil's tongue got burnt by the macaroni and cheese! You can't imagine the nightmares we have been through. Twenty thousand to settle the case. *Ja-aa,* we are not taking any chances this summer!"

Mary Alice said, "Once the campers are signed in, they will be escorted to their cabins," she barked. "Two hours until supper."

The counselors' faces were hidden by huge cowboy hats. Thumbs were busy with iPhones.

Gudrun swooped down upon them, grabbing their phones and tossing them in a straw basket on the huge mahogany desk.

They yelped, like puppies:

"Guuuudrunn, I was right in the middle of a text message to my boyfriend, Joey...."

"Hey, that's not fair. That's mean. I'm waiting to hear what university I got into. Give it back."

Gudrun shook her finger at them, "*Ja-aa,* no monkey business this year. Or we will sell you to the zoo."

I flipped through the rule book: Clover Flower is a Christian summer camp for girls, founded in 1928. Devotionals are REQUIRED FOR ALL CAMPERS AND STAFF. Really? I had successfully escaped from church for fifteen years!

Guidelines for Clean Living:

1. No alcohol or marijuana. (Not even beer?)
2. No pocketknives.
3. No firearms or fireworks. (Fair enough.)
4. Absolutely no smoking. (Not a temptation.)
5. No fraternizing with or visits from the opposite sex. (And who had been doing the deed in my bed?)
6. No shaving cream or balloons. (Guess?)
7. No iPods, iPads, mobile phones, or computers. (Sure! Try to enforce that one.)

8. No string bikinis. No thong underwear. No spaghetti straps.

9. All girls are required to wear bras.

The girls might not be wearing spaghetti straps, but they were wearing white cotton shirts with plunging necklines. Some of them had even worn black bras under their shirts. The shorts caught the flesh of their bottoms. Had they had implants? Surely not. Having lived abroad for so long, I was out of touch with American culture.

10. Malicious gossip will not be tolerated. (Gudrun still did not know Kharalombos' secret.)

Suddenly, the door was flung open and masses of parents with tiny tots entered the office. Gudrun was standing next to the door. "So nice to meet you. Your darling will be a Shawnee. That way, please." She pointed to one of the girls in a Stetson. "Ready for fun?" Gudrun said, pinching the cheek of a cute little girl. "That way, please. She is a Comanche."

Mary Alice caught me scratching my groin. "We are a wholesome camp for Protestant girls!" Then she softened her tone, handing me a tube of anti-biotic ointment. "The chiggers are a killer here. You're the Shawnee chief. The bathroom."

"You ever hear of the Trail of Tears?"

Were they trivializing a serious issue? Yet Native American dress had already been appropriated by Hollywood. When I was small, I put my hand over my mouth and started whooping, as an elderly Cherokee gentleman passed in front of my grandfather's soda fountain. Granddaddy Watson, who was putting away a tub of Good Old-Fashioned Vanilla, said, "I'll take down yer britches right here and give you the belt if you don't stop it. Those folks were not treated right. It's not a game." And then he had told me the story of how the Cherokees had been rounded up in 1838 onto boats on the Tennessee, Ohio, Mississippi, and Arkansas rivers and shipped further west to internment camps. That journey alone killed four thousand Cherokees and members of other tribes—they had died from hunger, cold, and sickness on "The Trail of Tears."

Mary Alice said. "This isn't a university. Just put on the outfit." How much did Mary Alice know about me?

When I emerged as a Shawnee chief, Kharalombos had disappeared.

The shorts were extremely tight around the crotch. I had to resist rearranging my equipment. A steady stream of mothers with highlighted blonde hair in sleeveless pastel dresses mobbed me. Not one of them had a single wrinkle on her face, as if they were perpetually twenty years old. They wore expensive-looking sandals with rhinestones.

"Welcome to Clover Flower," I said. "Please sign here." I pointed to the dotted line of the liability agreement.

A mother shrieked. "You're a riot! Where did they get you? Are you Mary Alice's cousin? Can I take a picture of you?"

Might as well ham it up as a Shawnee chief. One part of me yearned for stardom.

"McKenzie, come on. Get in the picture with the man," the girl's mother said.

The kid shook her head. She stuck out her tongue at me. "He's not real. I want a picture with a real Indian."

"Now, McKenzie, darling. Can you say you're sorry?"

The little girl shook her head vigorously. "Not sorry," she whispered. "Ever."

"Come on, McKenzie. Be a doll. Why don't you get in the picture? Daddy will want to see how happy you are."

"I want to ride my horse, Star," she declared, sticking her thumb in her mouth.

Mary Alice had taken over handing out the liability agreements and the rule books. A stream of girls was being led out by the camp counselors, who were wearing Stetson hats.

Gudrun took the camera from the mother so we could all three be in the picture. "But Gudrun, my hair looks hideous!"

Gudrun chortled. "*Aacch*, Dixie, you always say that! You are beyond the beauty."

And was I beyond the handsome?!

The little kid pinched me hard on the butt.

"Hey! What do you think you're doing? Cut it out!"

The mother noticed, but ignored it. She said, "Daddy will be so happy with the picture."

I handed the kid a green rule book. Frowning, she unzipped her pink Snow White and the Seven Dwarves backpack and tossed it in. Ashley dragged her away.

Mary Alice said, "Sorry you had to put up with that. That kid is a monster. She'll spend most of her time at time-out. I didn't want to accept her again after what happened last year. But they donated money for an Olympic-sized swimming pool."

"What happened?" I asked.

"She burned down one of the cabins," Mary Alice said. "Pyromaniac."

"But she's seven years old!"

"You' ll earn your money here," Mary Alice said. "Working in Iran under SAVAK's surveillance was a piece of cake."

I peeked out the office door. The curved driveway was lined with fancy cars: BMWs, Mercedes, Land Rovers, and Jeep Cherokees. Were these little girls excited about summer camp? I remember the long, tense ride in a white Cadillac from Oklahoma all the way to Idaho for wolf-tracking camp when I was seventeen. Since I had quit track and football, Dad insisted it would "make a man out of me." How I had hated that camp—ranch boys from Montana had bullied me on the trek and planted moose turds in my tent. When they tried to drown me in a stream, I hitchhiked to Alaska and worked in a ticket booth at Denali National Park. Despite the many phone calls from Mom about how I had broken Dad's heart and his checkbook, I had a breakthrough that summer. An Eskimo girl named Chikuk, with fervent brown eyes, took me on treks to see owls and bald eagles. Our expeditions also led to thrilling explorations in her cabin, late at night.

I learned how to fight back. Things became increasingly strained with Dad, though. But, in the end, I had not really gone out far enough on a limb—the academic work I had chosen was still within a safe framework. I was avoiding the uncertainty and freedom of the creative life I secretly desired. Like Dad, I was driven and put my energy into work—contaminated water, instead of ice cream!

At Yale, I was awarded a grant to study the wildlife in the Amazon rain forest one summer. After I returned from my trip, I couldn't wait to tell my parents about my experiences. "Dad, I saw some amazing animals. The three-toed sloth is an endangered species!"

Mom said, "Honey, aren't you curious? Don't you want to see his pictures of blue frogs?"

"They're fluorescent, Dad. I've never seen anything like it."

Poker-faced, Dad droned on about Creamy Freeze. "Amaretto Swirl with Toffee is one of our most exciting tastes yet."

I almost choked on Mom's chicken casserole. She made it with Campbell's mushroom soup following the recipes in Grandmother Grace's *Presbyterian Wives' Cookbook*. He still forced us to listen to a two-hour monologue about the virtues of a new brand of ice cream at his company—it was my first disillusioning experience with re-entry to the United States after travels elsewhere. An only child, all I could do was complain to Mom. She always defended Dad, saying, "He means well. He just doesn't know how to show it." When I fell into depression in my late twenties, Mom parroted Norman Vincent Peale's wisdom: "Find the upside of problems." Or: "Practice happy thinking every day."

But the one gem I should have heard: "Throw your heart over the fence and the rest will follow."

In his seventies, Dad became diabetic and couldn't even sample the marvelous tastes: Rum Raisin, Black Cherry with Chocolate Swirl, and Blueberry Cheesecake. Even when I landed a university appointment in my thirties, Dad only asked about my retirement plan. "Now, son, the main thing is to secure your retirement." (On that point, he was right.) Mother gently suggested that he play more golf, but his high score made him so miserable that he quit. If he didn't make par, he swore so much and threw his clubs into the lake; even his close friends fled. Ice cream and business were his only two hobbies. The final straw was when Velvet Red Bucket bought out our family business. Dad might have developed new brands, but he had not kept up to date with technology: the accounts were still noted in pink ledgers. At the end of his life, all he did was read biographies of generals from the Second World War, like Douglas Macarthur and George Patton. After he died, my mother took up painting and became known for her abstract watercolors. She sold the house and moved to Taos, New Mexico.

When the rush was over, Mary Alice swirled around in the executive office chair. She tapped her pencil on the desk. "Now, let's see. I need your Social Security number so I can get you on the payroll."

"That's a problem," I said.

Mary Alice chortled. "What do you mean? Every American has a Social Security number."

"I can't use it," I said.

Gudrun was over at the breakfast table, grazing on doughnuts. "Aren't you hungry? We have to feed you after that terrible raccoon. How about a cruller?"

Mary Alice asked, "Are you a WANTED MAN? That's all we need now."

I laughed. "No, of course not," I said. "You might say Buffalo Bill Cody, part of a Wild West show."

"What do you mean?" Mary Alice's lips were pursed into an intimidating frown.

"Gudrun," I pleaded. "Can I talk to you outside?"

"*Nein,*" Gudrun said. "*Nein. Nein.*" She bit into the cruller. Syrup dripped down her chin. "Give us the bad news. You are *child molester.*"

"I am not a child molester," I said.

"A thief?" Gudrun said, her eyes narrowing. I imagined her hitting me over the head with a canoe paddle.

Mary Alice chimed in, "A swindler? Like Triksky."

Gudrun said, "Triko."

"Met him in Cairo. Hey, that rhymes!" I said.

Mary Alice said, "That's not funny."

"I think I might audition for *Saturday Night Live!*" I added, trying to lighten up the tense atmosphere.

"If you don't tell us the truth, we will call the Schulenburg Police." Gudrun held up the black phone receiver. "After all we went through in Egypt, I can't believe you are doing this to me."

"It's not that clear-cut," I said. "I'm accused of something I didn't do. And now, I am in too deep…"

"We live in the United States of America. Innocent until proven guilty," Mary Alice said. "Why don't you hire yourself a lawyer and get your name cleared? Simple as that. That's what we did with that macaroni and cheese case, although it cost us an arm and a leg."

Had she been living under a rock? Prisoners had languished in Guantánamo Bay for years. The Patriot Act, hastily passed after 9/11, had given the American government broad powers to detain anyone "suspicious." What had happened to that beloved chestnut of American democracy, "innocent until proven guilty?"

Gudrun kept munching on her cruller. "A pretty coin of gold. Like some fairy tale. We have to spin the straw into gold this summer."

"'Fess up," Mary Alice said. "Or we will put you in time-out with that brat McKenzie. Make you ride Star, the wild stallion."

"Okay, okay, okay," I said. "You've got me over a barrel. The short version of a very long shaggy-dog story is that somebody in Cairo sent my publisher a nasty virus, which destroyed all of the new books at Zadorf Publishers for the year. I denied it, of course."

Mary Alice bellowed. She kept laughing and laughing, until tears streamed down her cheeks.

"What's so funny?" I asked.

"No earthly way," Mary Alice. "Everything is written on your baby face. You look so innocent."

It had never occurred to me before. Maybe that was why I could carry off disguise! Man, oh man, why didn't I look in the mirror and keep complimenting myself!

"So you are a liar?" Gudrun said. "I am disappointed. So many men are liars. Is Kharalombos in this basket of trouble, too?"

Her disappointment did not diminish her interest in wolfing down the cruller.

Mary Alice chewed on her pencil. "We'll have to pay you under the table. Like we do with the kitchen help. I get tipped off by Charlie when Immigration will come around. Everyone hides in the stable. They don't have their citizenship."

So Mary Alice and Gudrun were working the system, too. They hired illegal immigrants to save money.

"Who's Charlie?" I asked.

But Mary Alice ignored me and looked down at her clipboard.

"What is Kharalombos's secret? He has one," Gudrun said. "I know it. Men are all liars!" She licked the syrup off her fingers.

"Everyone has secrets," I said.

Mary Alice leaned back in her office chair. Suddenly, her mood changed. She drew her forefinger across her neck. "I remember those last days under the Shah. We knew so many who disappeared….If you blabbed a secret, someone just might disappear." And then, she whispered, "Executed."

Gudrun said, "Aacch, you tell that story too much. That was a long time ago! No one is going to disappear here! We are in Schulenburg!"

Mary Alice cleared her throat. "One thing's for sure. You will have to sing for your supper on this ship. Is Gary your real first name?"

"Yes," I said.

"That's true, at least, then. Clover Flower is not a bad place to be."

Chapter 6

Too Many Cooks Spoil the Broth

GUDRUN BURST THROUGH THE DOORS OF THE ENORMOUS, industrial-sized kitchen. I followed her. Cauldrons were boiling on several of the black burners. A red-haired woman in a blue-checked apron stood at the counter spooning tomato sauce onto a pizza. A Mexican woman was saying, "*Yo creo que sí.*" She gestured to the other women to keep chopping green peppers.

"Ah, there ya are. Are you grand now, Gudrun?" the woman asked. "Did you get all the wee tots settled in their cabins?"

"*Ja-aa,*" Gudrun said. "I want to introduce…"

"Well, who's your man?" the woman interrupted. She raised her eyebrows. "A health inspector?"

"Gary," I said, confidently. What about changing the last name?

Despite the long apron, the Irish woman had a voluptuous figure and a full head of red ringlets, like a queen.

"Gary Cooper," I said, winking at her.

The Irish woman said, "*Ha!* You're trying me on! My favorite is *Man of the West*. A rogue is stranded after a train robbery."

I didn't recall that one, but I was saved by Gudrun's garrulousness.

"The two who came back with me from Egypt," Gudrun said. "They saved me during the Revolution."

"Aaah, well, then he's a hero, is he?" the woman said. "You must have an exciting life out there? I always wanted to visit the Pyramids, but then after the Celtic Tiger, all the work dried up. I'm Sinead." She extended her hand, which was covered with flour.

"It's wild," I said, giving her hand a squeeze. "*A Thousand and One Nights* is not far off."

"Have ya ever worked in a restaurant before, Gary?" Sinead asked. "Just to know what I should have ya do."

"I managed a Domino's Pizza parlor in New Haven for a few summers," I said. "Made the occasional pizza."

It was a rather short-lived career: three weeks as a delivery driver. After a Harley-Davidson motorcycle gang stripped me of my clothes at a Motel 6, I ran back to the shop—starkers, except for the red Domino's golf cap.

Sinead looked me over. There was a shrewd glint in her breathtaking green eyes—she was very street-smart.

"You have beautiful green eyes!" I blurted out. "Such an unusual color."

"Gary Cooper, yer a rogue!"

A huge Mexican-American woman handed me a hairnet and plastic gloves. Her black hair was stuffed under a tight hairnet of her own.

"Anyway, *watchale*," she said. "You have to wear the hairnet 'cuz those *pinche cabron* gringo inspectors'll be coming around. If there's one single violation on their list, Gudrun'll get fined. One single *pendejo* roach, they'll close the place down."

"When I'm not around, Letty here's in charge. We had a few inspections that went arseways on us. Got a kick in the bollocks from the health inspector."

Sinead rolled her eyes.

Letty waved her finger at me. "No *chingazos* in this kitchen. Where're you from?"

"Oklahoma."

"I heard somethin' about you bein' an actor? Is that true?" Letty asked.

"I was in the TV show *Twin Peaks* awhile ago in Hollywood. I played FBI Dale Cooper who investigates the murder of the homecoming queen Laura Palmer." Why did I say that? So far from my normal life in academia, did every repressed wish become my story? If I couldn't publish my novel, I could live it.

Sinead popped me with a kitchen towel. "So yous knows how to tell a tale or two!"

Letty sighed. "Don't remember that show. My favorite is *I Love Lucy*. Anyway, my dad knew Freddy Fender. Ya know," she sang, "Wasted Days and Wasted Nights."

Unlike Letty, her husband, Speedy, was tall and thin. He sported a handlebar moustache. On second glance, he had a small paunch. Even though it was hot, he was wearing Wranglers jeans and cowboy boots. He had on a Houston Astros baseball hat backward, like an umpire. He was chomping on a big wad of gum.

A bright red pickup with jacked-up monster tires was backed up to the entrance of the kitchen. "*Amigo*," he motioned to me. "The word is that you're a hero. Saved Gudrun during the Egyptian Revolution."

"Sure," I said. "I slung her over my back and carried her to safety. She was in the middle of a huge protest in Tahrir Square."

Speedy didn't blink. "Mary Alice is the one who'll kick your ass. Can you give me a hand with these eggs?"

As we were carrying in crates of eggs to the kitchen, Speedy said, "*Compadre*, you play poker? We need another guy to make our table tonight. Aengus, Sinead's husband, is always beezy. Always workin'."

"Why not? I'm game," I said.

I set the crate of eggs down and opened the walk-in refrigerator. The cold was almost electric. He didn't take anything, but he scanned through the shelves, stuffed with chickens. His eye lingered over a huge cut of roast.

"Those *pendejas* can be *pinche*," Speedy said. "They don't pay us enough. How much are they paying you?"

"I am a little vague on the details," I said. "We just got here."

"Man, you're crazy. Are they paying you minimum wage? Those gringas in this outfit are gettin' richer and richer."

Out of the country for so many years, I was ashamed to say that I didn't even know what minimum wage was these days. He would think I was dumb. Many Mexicans without their papers worked menial jobs and were paid under the table. Yet Texas was still the lush dream of palm trees and orange groves— and Mexicans sent small gold nuggets back to families, huddled over fires in dusty ranchitos.

"Do you need anything else?" I asked. "Sinead said we had to be careful about the door."

Speedy laughed. "Sinead, the new *cocinera*. The new cook. Letty is much better," he said, closing the door carefully. "Don't tell anybody, but Sinead's tacos taste like dog sheet."

—m—

Mary Alice pushed open the kitchen doors as if she were pushing open the doors to a saloon. She was wearing a blue captain's cap. Tufts of her white hair stuck out the sides, like wings.

She set her clipboard on the shiny silver counter. She studied the floor and then tiptoed, as if she were following a trail of blood at a crime scene. She pushed through the doors and approached the refrigerator in the back.

I was standing at the counter, chopping apples.

She looked at me and said grimly, "Roach feces. They look like crushed red pepper. Where's Sinead?"

The floor looked clean to me.

"She was here a minute ago," I said. "Maybe she stepped out." I kept chopping apples. We were preparing ten pounds of tuna salad for lunch.

Mary Alice's eagle eye surveyed the kitchen. She headed for a wet mop, leaning against the doorjamb.

"Roaches like wet mops," Mary Alice said. "This is no joke. We have to be ready for the FDA inspector all the time."

"I heard about the inspector," I said. "A right divil, he is." I couldn't resist imitating Sinead's accent. "He'll give us a kick in the bollocks."

Mary Alice barked, "That's not funny. The fine could be a thousand dollars. You're not wearing your hairnet!"

I felt my bald head. Where was my hairnet? How had I forgotten that? I was jealous of Sinead's husband's full head of blonde hair. If I had more hair, would it be easier to seduce Sinead?

Mary Alice ticked something on her clipboard with her red pen. Quickly, I fastened the hairnet over my head. It was very tight, and the elastic burned around the edges of my scalp.

"Did you run a school when you were in Iran?" I asked.

She was in a foul mood. Why didn't I keep my head down and keep chopping apples? But I saw this as a chance to collect more stories.

"I've been captain of a lot of operations. Hospitals. Schools. When I was in college, I ran a funeral parlor," Mary Alice said. "Why do you want to know?"

One morning, Speedy lurched into the kitchen with a bottle of tequila. The Mexican ladies were busy making their morning hot sauce. A food processor whirred. The pungent smell of cilantro lingered in the air.

He pulled up a chair to the large round table in the center of the kitchen and plunked down the bottle. I was seated there, cracking dozens of eggs into a mixing bowl.

He hiccupped. "Have some *cojones*, *amigo*. Drink. Be a man. Be a man!" he roared.

"One spring break in college at South Padre Island, I got tanked on tequila," I said. "I threw a couch off a balcony. My dad was furious! The owner of the hotel filed a lawsuit against me for destroying his property. Dad had to bail me out. It took me three summers to pay him back."

But I was talking to myself. Speedy was three sheets to the wind.

He snorted, then hee-hawed, as if he were a donkey. Just as suddenly, he started crying. "On this day, ten years ago, my papa died in Mexico." He pronounced it May-Hee-Co. "And believe me, I wanted to be there, but I was workin' at this sheety construction company in Brownsville. Laying pipe for the port of Brownsville. Those gringos wouldn't let me go."

Did he miss home? I couldn't imagine not being able to return to Oklahoma City if I wanted to. It wasn't because the boss had forbidden me. I wanted to protect Mom from being harassed by federal agents.

Speedy shouted something in Spanish at the ladies and banged on the table with his fist. One of them shook a spatula at him. Another swung around, her braids flying, and cursed him.

Suddenly, Sinead was standing in front of us with her hands on her hips. "Yer blutered… Go on home and sleep it off, bad boy."

"I just got here!" I said.

"Shush," Sinead said, waving me off.

Speedy swayed. "I want to speak to my woman. *Mi mujere*. Where are you hiding her? Did you tie her up in the supply room?"

Sinead shouted, "Jesus, Mary, and Joseph. Get on home now before Mary Alice sees ya. She'll go mad, she will."

Speedy had grabbed Sinead by the wrist. "You have to call KFC! I'm fuckin' starvin'. I can't live without fried chicken. Call those *gatos*! Now!"

"I'm askin' you nicely the first time, Speedy," Sinead said, through clenched teeth. "Take your feckin' hands off of me. You've already got two warnings in your file."

I tickled Speedy's tummy and he giggled. He let go of Sinead's arm, but then he reeled toward the other ladies.

One of them grabbed an egg from the table and broke it on Speedy's head. Yolk dripped down his face, over his eyes. He started bawling and babbling in Spanish. "*Mi papi…*"

"*Ándale, ándale*," Letty said, whisking him away from the ladies, who were busy at the griddle.

"What's going on?" I was bewildered. I really should have invested more time in learning Spanish.

Letty said, "His father died when he was twenty. He owned his own fishing boat near Veracruz. He was lost in a bad storm. *Muy triste.* He's sad. This is his father's death day and we're so far from the grave. Too far to light a candle."

"Right," Sinead said. "Letty, can you take him back to the cabin? He'll probably pass out. Gary, thanks for covering me back."

"Always ready to assist anyone in distress," I said.

Letty led Speedy away, as if he were a small child. He turned his head around and sang, "Wasted Days and Wasted Nights! Why can't you be loving *meeeee*?"

"Nobody's perfect," I said. Everyone had a flaw. What was mine? My desire for attention? Embroidering the truth? Selfishness?

"Well, the love of drink is a big one, I'd say," Sinead said. "Big problem in Ireland, it is." She continued cracking eggs.

—m—

Speedy poked his head into the kitchen. He was whistling, "Wasted Days and Wasted Nights."

"Hello there, *amigo*. Give me a hand!" he said. "We've got a load of Hormel chili. After that, enough paper towels for Mexico City!"

"I thought everything was homemade here," I said, throwing down the dish towel.

"Don't tell me you believe that bull!" he said, smiling. "When are you going to shoot pool with me? There's a *cantina* called Roy's in Schulenburg."

"Love to. Hey, are you all right?" I asked. He acted as if nothing had happened. Maybe he didn't remember.

"Busted," he said. "Am sleeping on the couch."

"You're kind of walking on the edge," I said. I was one to be talking. But obviously, I couldn't confide in Speedy.

"Is Sinead here?" Speedy said. "You know, sometimes I don't even remember what I say. I can be a real *pendejo*. I do remember feeling sheety about my dad. We never found his body. His boat washed up on the shore. I think we put his watch in his coffin."

"I'm sorry, Speedy," I said.

"It happened a while ago. But you know, man, I still have dreams about him. He's bringing in nets under the full moon. Is your dad still alive?"

"No," I said. "My dad's gone." If I explained who my dad was, he would think I was bragging. And then, of course, my Ivy League background was always a conversation stopper with working people. They were either overly deferential or hated me for my privilege. Did we believe we were more egalitarian in this country than we actually were?

Sinead interrupted, "Well, there's yer man. Been doing any Hail Marys?" Sinead was wearing long plastic gloves.

"I'm real sorry, Sinead. I was thinking that I could make a barbecue for you one night. Make it up to you. South Texas barbecue. Special recipe. How about this weekend? The kids are going on a hike on Friday. Aren't you doing packed lunches?"

"Ah, well… Visitors' day is coming up soon. I have to work on the menu."

Speedy smiled. "You're living in Texas. And you never even had real barbecue!"

"Well…" Sinead said. "I'll have to get a sitter."

"Letty's cousin will do it. Or you can bring your kids. We don't care. See you Friday!" He motioned to me. "We've still got fresh corn to unload."

Once we hauled the last batch of corn into the kitchen, I closed the back flap to his truck. "See you around."

"*Amigo*," Speedy said. "You're coming?"

Thumbs up.

When I went back into the kitchen, Sinead had started making a huge tray of brownies. "Well, yer man is all contrite now. Wonder how long that will last." She sighed. "Are you going, Gary?"

"Why not?" I said. "Kharalomobos is tied up."

—∾—

In the end, Sinead and I went to Letty and Speedy's for the barbecue. Aengus had gotten extra work on the weekends at a fracking site in West Texas. Letty and Speedy were living in a tiny cabin on the property—two small bedrooms, a galley kitchen, and one single rocking chair in the living room. So what Speedy said about Gudrun seemed to be true: "She's stingy." Were they vastly underpaid? Had my dad underpaid his employees at Creamy Freeze to boost his own profits? Why had I never thought of this before? Was I also living in my own bubble?

A toddler waddled toward us, screaming. A fourteen-year-old with a mohawk grabbed the kid a bit roughly before he fell. "*Cuidado!*" Letty shouted. "*Watchale.*" She placed dough for tortillas in a silver press. A young girl about sixteen, in a halter top, was sitting at the kitchen table painting her fingernails a bright red.

The kid with the mohawk asked, "Are you a new cook?"

"You could say that," I said.

Sinead giggled. "Ah, yer a man with some kind of past life, ya are. But, surely, not a cook!"

At first, I ignored the invitation to talk. But how long could we keep things a secret?

Letty gestured to the fridge. "*Cerveza?* Help yourself. I'm almost finished with the tortillas. Where's Aengus?"

"Workin' as a fracker," Sinead said. "West Texas." She ruffled her hand through her unruly red hair, tucking a rebellious curl behind her ear.

"Too bad," Letty said. "Too busy to party."

Sinead opened the fridge and grabbed two beers. She handed me one, and then popped open her own.

She licked the foam off of her lips and smiled at me. There was a wicked flicker in her eyes. "Need the dosh," she said. "Always too busy to…"

Sinead was wearing short blue jean cutoffs that showed off her firm legs. Underneath the white cotton Guinness tee-shirt, she wore a plunging, lacy black bra. She leaned lazily on her elbow.

Letty sighed. "Speedy could work extra, too. He always says he's too beezy." Then, she smiled. "Homemade hot sauce and homemade chips?"

The tortilla chips were hot and crispy from the hot oil. "Delicious!"

A pot of beans bubbled on the small stove. The unmistakable whiff of cilantro filled the cabin.

"Where's Speedy?" I asked.

"You didn't see him?" Letty asked. "He's on the other side of the hill, making the fire."

—ɯ—

Speedy was tying a skinned animal to a homemade spit. He raised a beer and shouted, "Let's party!"

"What are you barbecuing?" I asked. The animal was not huge—it was obviously not a pig.

He sat down on the ground next to a huge icebox. "Goat," he said. "Soaked it overnight in vinegar. Special Mexican recipe. Promise you won't tell."

"They don't sell goat in the grocery store."

Speedy winked at me. "The anglos are so rich around here, they won't notice one *cabrito*. Man, the way I figure it, *con poco poco*. A little here and there. The guy next to the camp is filthy rich. And Gudrun is so *pinche*, we are about to go on food stamps."

"You stole it?"

Speedy raised his finger to his lips. "Sssh… He came through a hole in the fence. Let's say he was lost. And then was found."

"I thought you wanted to keep your job?"

Speedy laughed. "Sure, man, we're trying to butter up Sinead. But then, we've got no money. Be a man! Don't tell me you don't eat sweetbreads!"

The cold beer was refreshing. Speedy opened the icebox. I had also heard that Mexicans ate testicles. This guy wouldn't respect me unless I acted tough.

"Sure do," I said.

Speedy was opening his third beer. "Man, what world are you from?" He suddenly eyed me suspiciously. "Are you hiding from the cops here?"

I was tempted to tell him the story, but another voice screamed in my ear, "No!" When he got drunk, he'd blab everything.

"Are you one of the guys who scammed Wall Street? No one would ever find you at Clover Flower, unless, unless….Man, what's a *chiquito cabrito* to millions…."

"I didn't steal anything," I said. But I sounded a tad defensive.

"This is a *puebla*. Everyone will find out sooner or later. So you might as well tell me."

"Does everyone know that you served time?" I raised my bottle of Corona. My high-school theatre teacher's coaching came back to me: "Be bold. Go inside your character's skin." Was I now Philip Marlowe in *The Big Sleep*?

Speedy gasped. "Man. *Chingauzos*. How did you know? Pleez. Be eazy on me. You're undercover, ATF. Drugs and firearms. Sheet!"

I imitated my father's voice when he was displeased with me. "I'd appreciate it if you don't broadcast the FACT around."

Speedy laughed nervously. "Well," he said, changing the topic. "Did Aengus show up? He doesn't like me. He's always too busy to party. When he first came, we had a lot of fun. Then he started getting his ass whipped by Sinead."

His sixteen-year-old daughter was waving in the distance. "Dad! Dad!"

Speedy sighed. "She can't go out to the mall looking like that. She'll get knocked up in no time. Can you turn the spit? I'll be back. Keep putting the sauce on."

Taking the brush, I basted the goat with some kind of dark sauce—Worcestershire with cayenne pepper. The goat looked a little like a skinned dog.

A few hours later, we brought the goat, along with the sweetbreads, the plump glands, into the cabin. Letty had put out a huge spread: homemade tortillas, hot sauce, pinto beans, guacamole, fresh corn on the cob. And for dessert, fresh flan, a crème caramel with brown sugar caramelized on top.

After we'd gorged ourselves, Sinead licked her fingers and gave me a sly wink. "Yer a better cook than I am, Letty, so yer are. I haven't had so much fun fer a long time. The dessert is to die for, it is."

Letty exchanged a look with Speedy, but Sinead seemed not to notice. Had I landed in the middle of huge resentments from the past that I knew nothing about? Did they secretly hate Sinead?

We started a game of poker, just a simple limit Texas Hold 'em betting with quarters. Everyone was drinking ice-cold Corona.

"Mom, Juan José is annoying," Pepe said.

Letty got up to prepare him another bottle of milk. "Hey, Gary," Letty called out from the kitchen. "You ever been married? Got kids?"

Speedy handed me the cards. "You deal, mystery man."

I shuffled the cards. "Divorced. Have a grown daughter, name of Allie. She's a white-water rafting guide in Alaska."

In a few minutes, Letty returned with the bottle and gave it to Pepe. "Feed your brother."

In my fifties, there was no going back. Why hadn't I married Gayle, my lab partner at Yale? I had felt hemmed in by her agenda, a lifetime of research on contaminated water. Then Mom suggested a friend's daughter. "Rachel is a nice girl. Good family. Why don't you call her?" Dad chimed in behind his newspaper: "Her father owns Oklahoma Lightning Energy, Oil, and Gas." But I also dreaded a relationship—it was too domestic; it felt like a strait-jacket. Rachel would want to buy baby clothes the day after our engagement. I loved Boriana's spontaneity, but I knew almost nothing about her family. Were they gypsies? Her English wasn't terrible, but would I really be able to communicate with her?

"I worked for an organization called WildEarth Guardians for a long time in Alaska," I said, improvising while dealing the hand. "Tried to save the North Pacific whale. It's an endangered species. There are probably only forty left in the world."

Speedy roared. "You're one of those crazy environmentalists!"

This was the wrong story to impress the group.

Sinead drummed her hands on the table. "We want something juicy!"

Letty was munching on one of the greasy chips. "Well," she said, leaning forward. "I heard that Gudrun was doing it last year with the famous Egyptian archaeologist, Ramses el-Kibir. You know, the *muchacho* with the big hat. That's why she went to Egypt."

What? She never told us that. She never acted as if she knew him. But then, why had he picked her up at the airport?

"She gets tired of 'em, quickly, all right. How long do you think Kharalom-bos will last?" Sinead hiccupped. "Gudrun is right bossy. A man might think she is taking his pants away."

Speedy poured more beer into my glass. "Don't be a sissy drinker. Drink like a man!"

Sinead started laughing so hard, tears appeared in her eyes. "Can you imagine the two of them doing the deed? Can ya? Which one gets on top? They're so big, one'll mash the other."

Speedy dealt the next hand. For a few minutes, it was quiet, except for the slapping of the cards.

"Fold," Sinead said.

"Me, too," Letty said, sighing.

I set down my cards. "Two pair of Big Slick. A pair of aces on the flop and a pair of kings on the turn amidst the four, five, six of clubs. What do you say to that?"

I thought I was trapping Speedy.

Then Speedy shouted, "I won! I won!," showing his two whole cards of seven and eight of clubs. "Straight flush." He reached into the center of the table and dragged masses of quarters to his chest.

"*Que chulo*," Letty said, pinching Speedy's cheek. "Aah, *Mamacita*. The new Egyptian dance teacher, he likes the young ones. They better watch it or they will have another lawsuit. Purty soon, we are gonna have trouble."

At last, at three in the morning, Sinead and I left swaying, arm in arm, down the dark trail toward her cabin. We sang at the top of our lungs, "And it's no, nay, never no nay never no more." Sinead hiccupped. "Will I play the Wild Rover, no nay never no more," she sang squeezing my hand.

When we reached her cabin, I kissed her on the mouth. "It was a fun..." I said, but didn't finish. We were soon rubbing against each other, as if we were two sixteen-year-olds. "Do it to me, mystery man," she moaned. "I'm yer bitch!" She licked my ear. "Be a man!" she whispered. "Yer my man!"

The rocking back and forth spiraled into a desperate, pleasurable frenzy. At last, the snap on her lacy black bra popped open, and I cupped one of her creamy breasts in my palm. Sinead's bold hand hunted for the zipper on my shorts.

Suddenly, a child wailed from inside the cabin.

As if she had woken up from a dream, Sinead abruptly pulled down her tee-shirt. Backing away from me, she said, "Gary, you divil! I'm married! And I've got my two wee men!"

"But..."

The door slammed. A gust of wind tinkled the chimes.

My flashlight bobbed in the dark. Where was I? A coyote howled nearby. I staggered toward my cabin, hoping that I did not meet the creature face to face. Struggling with the key, I finally jimmied open the door. I plunked down onto the bed, fully clothed, face down.

When I woke a few hours later, I imagined Boriana when she was angry—how her mouth curled into a nasty frown. What the hell was I doing?

In the morning, Sinead's face was green when she came into the kitchen. The Mexican ladies were having a relaxed breakfast outside at the picnic tables. Letty had not shown up.

"Are you okay?" I asked, handing her a cup of steaming coffee. Sinead's boldness reminded me of the Indian girl, Chikuk, who had invited me to her cabin every night that summer in high school—not afraid one bit of her own sexuality.

"Feel like *shiiit*," she said. She gulped the coffee. "Think I had about twelve beers. Where's Letty?"

"Not here."

"Ah, well," Sinead said. "Let's muddle through."

She summoned me to the back with her forefinger. Her voice from last night teased me, "I'm yer bitch." What had happened to my great resolve to resist her?

She closed the freezer door firmly. "That's sorted."

I stroked her arm. But she pulled back, waving me off. "Don't be daft." She abruptly turned around and stared at the supplies, stacked on the shelves.

"Take these," she said, thrusting bag after bag of fish fingers and French fries into my arms until they reached my chin. "One more thing, let's just keep what happened last night between us. If you know what I mean."

"You're the cook," I said, winking at her. Instead of Sinead wrapped in a tight starched white apron, I imagined her posing before me scantily clad in a black lacy corset, her red ringlets wild, her freckled breasts bulging out, like the wife in *The Cook, the Thief, His Wife, and Her Lover*. I imagined myself slowly unsnapping the garters strapped to her smooth legs.

Sinead's green eyes burned. "I'm not feckin' jokin'. We were hammered last night. It can't happen again. Aengus'll kill you."

I imagined Aengus's fist plowing through my nose.

"Okay, okay. I get the message," I said, feeling a little disappointed. Why was she sending me these mixed signals?

As if she had read my mind, she said, "Won't just belt ya. He'll chop ya up and have ya for lunch."

Was I falling for a gangster's wife? And was she much tougher than she let on?

Later in the day, Sinead said, "So, Gary, you'll turn off the lights when you've got everything sorted?"

A huge stack of dirty platters was heaped on the counter. "Sure," I said, but I didn't look up.

"Ah, Gary," Sinead said, looking around to see if anyone was within ear-shot. "I don't want to be leadin' ya on, like. It's not like I don't want to. Ya might think I'm a floozie, but I swear on my ma's grave, I've never been tempted by anyone before, except Aengus."

"You've made yourself clear," I said. Was this a game she frequently played?

She giggled. "Gary, you divil!" she said, lightly touching my shoulder. "You rogue." Just the slightest touch sent a surge of electricity to my crotch.

She sauntered toward the laundry bin, her hips swaying. As if she knew I was watching, she slowly untied the string on her apron, lifted the loop over her head, and tossed the apron into the bin.

The rusty hinges on the doors squealed as she went out. I felt relieved. In the time I had been at the camp, I had rarely been alone. A few times late at night before I collapsed, I scribbled down descriptions of the camp and some of the more colorful characters in a torn spiral notebook. If I had time, I studied my guidebook to the animals and birds of Texas. I was hoping to see an East-ern bluebird. But when? I had little time to watch birds. An affair with Sinead would be reckless. And I had promised to return to Boriana.

A big mixing bowl was left in the sink. Thick, creamy chocolate icing dripped off the beaters. The secret of Sinead's baking was that she used the most expen-sive butter and cream—defying the "healthy food" propaganda of the camp. I ran my finger through one of the beaters and licked off the chocolate icing—remembering Sinead licking my ear. What else might she do with her tongue?

When I was a small child, my Grandmother Grace had let me lick the bowl when she was making her famous Whiskey Lizzies with nuts and raisins for Christmas. Later, when I was in high school, we smoked cigarettes and drank black coffee together at her round oak table. One could always count on her for frankness, although sometimes it stung. "Look, pumpkin, you're gonna have to fight like a Trojan, if you're my size," she would say. "Just tell your father straight out if you don't want to fool with football. You've got a good mind." During the Depression, Grandmother Grace had taught Latin and Spanish in Lubbock, Texas.

Kharalombos moseyed into the kitchen with three packages of smoked bacon tucked under his arm.

"Hey, Sinead needs that for her recipe tomorrow! I think she's doing something with quail."

He lit the griddle and started pulling strips of bacon out of the package. It seemed that Kharalombos, stressed and homesick, was finding comfort in food. During the revolution in Cairo, we had the opposite problem—we ate whatever we could forage, chocolate bars or canned baked beans. But even then, we had little appetite because of our anxiety.

"*Ayiz takol haga?*" he said, flipping the sizzling bacon.

"Why are you speaking in Arabic?"

"*Andi haneen lil-balad*, Gary. Homesick. America is only about work."

"Yeah," I said. "That's the downside. Foreigners never realize this until they live here. So you miss Egypt?" I felt low, too. I missed the place as well. Would I ever go back? And do what?

Kharalombos turned on a small cassette recorder. He started singing along with Dalida. "*Kelma helwa wi kelmetein. Helwa ya baladi!*" How beautiful my country is![1]

Helwa ya baladi! Dalida crooned. *Helwa ya baladi!*

We sang along, *Helwa ya baladi!* I was reminded of that night we sang and danced with Rose and Bill when we felt panicked during the revolution. What had happened to them? Scarlett O'Hara?

He switched off the tape and sighed.

"How are things going with Gudrun?" I asked. "I haven't seen you for days."

He put his large hand around his throat. "*Khan'ani.* She's suffocating me. Follows me everywhere. Attends almost every dance class. We have to do it every night. My only time alone is bacon and eggs in the middle of the night."

"No hanky-panky with the girls?" I said, testing the waters. I wondered if the rumor I had heard about him at Letty's was true.

"What? *Tafheen.* Those trivial little girls. No way. Why?"

He was so surprised that I was sure he was telling the truth. "No reason," I said, but I wasn't sure Kharalombos bought my bluff.

---

[1] Sung by Dalida, an Italian-Egyptian singer who lived and sang in France.

"You're not having an affair with Sinead?" Kharalombos said, as he gobbled the bacon. "That's the talk of the people."

I acted indignant. "She's married!"

Kharalombos chortled. "Don't tell me you are a puritan! She's a sweetness. *Asal.* Those hips! Have you ever seen such beautiful eyes?"

"Look, we can't leave this place a mess," I said. "Wash the pans."

"Gary," Kharalombos, said, offering me a greasy strip of bacon. "You know I don't do dishes."

"For crying out loud, Kharalombos," I said, slapping a dish towel against the counter. "You're not in Egypt. You might have to do a chore or two!"

Kharalombos shrugged. "Only maids and women wash dishes."

I felt lousy. "Do what you want!"

"Burning the candle at both ends," as my grandmother would say. She had died my first year of graduate school at Yale. I still missed her. She always listened when I needed an ear. Mary Alice reminded me a little of Grandmother Grace.

Chapter 7

Visitors

SOMEONE WAS BANGING AT THE DOOR OF MY CABIN. I sneezed. Then I grabbed my shorts and zipped up quickly. I didn't bother with a tee-shirt. A muscular-looking man in a sleeveless white tee-shirt was standing next to Mary Alice outside the door. A large blue swallow was tattooed on his forearm. He looked like a boxer. Or maybe he was a soldier? He had a buzz cut—about forty-five years old.

Mary Alice cleared her throat. "I've got to get back before our visitors arrive. This is our new neighbor, Azzurro Agua."

"No relation to the Capones…?"

Azzurro snorted. "I can walk the walk and talk the talk. Say, you haven't seen my goat, Leo? Like someone threw him in the rivah, the Guadalupe."

"I saw a little fawn pass by yesterday morning at dawn. But no goat. But deer don't eat goat, do they?"

"You on the Johnny Carson show or what?" he said, folding his muscular arms.

"Name's Billy the Kid," I said, extending my hand. I could play the tough guy as well. "Look, you don't look like the kind of guy who would have a pet goat."

"Maybe I'm a softie at heart. Know what I'm sayin'? It cost me a fortune to ship Leo back from Libya."

"Softies don't make it in Libya. I guess Mary Alice told you that Kharalombos and I just returned from Egypt."

Azzurro smiled. There was a glimmer of malice in his eyes. "Heroes of the revolution."

What? He'd already heard the stories? If he'd heard the gossip, it wouldn't be wise to spread a rumor about myself.

Mary Alice was tapping her foot. "Gary, we don't have all day. You can get acquainted with Azzurro later."

I didn't relish this suggestion. She wasn't serious? Although he didn't seem like a bad guy.

"Thanks, anyway, Billy the Kid," Azzurro said, heading back up the dirt road. A scorpion was tattooed on the back of his calf.

"Hey, what were you doing in Libya?" I called out.

He answered, but I didn't hear him.

Mary Alice said, "What did he say?"

"He was a mercenary for the Clown Man," I said. Why did I say that?

Mary Alice whispered, "The word is he just bought that house with cash. Seems a little fishy. We don't want him anywhere near our girls. What really worries me is that we share a septic tank with him. I told Gudrun it was better to have our own. But she's always so stingy!"

—◊◊◊—

We barely finished in time for service. When I was laying out the enchiladas on the serving line, I spotted the seven-year-old McKenzie, who had burned down a cabin. Her mother, Miss Ex-Universe with the platinum blonde hair, was holding her hand. A man with granny glasses and a white goatee walked beside them. Mary Alice was showing them to their seats at the head table.

Sinead was just putting the crème caramel into the huge oven.

"Who are the bigwigs?"

"Your man, Cameron Wiley the Third, is one of the biggest oil frackers in West Texas. Aengus is working for him," Sinead said, putting a strand of her red hair behind her ear. "He's made a heap. Aengus says he spends the dosh on Greek statues. Antiques. Expensive art. His house looks like a right museum."

Cameron looked like a preppy university professor. He was wearing khaki pants with a white oxford cloth shirt—the sleeves were rolled up to his elbows. No cowboy hat. No boots. No Wranglers. No hint of the Old West. He defied the stereotype of an oil man.

Sinead said, "Mary Alice wants you serve 'em direct at the big table. The wee tots will go through the serving line. Don't forget your Indian headdress."

"Can't someone else do it?" I said, rubbing my wet hands on my apron. "I prefer backstage. It's more fun."

"You're the only one who speaks English 'round here. Quit being a gimp."

"I'm not your mystery man?"

But she didn't reply. "Letty saved the day, she did. Somebody nicked my bacon. No way I could do the quail. There ya go, easy does it." Sinead handed me a full tray. Her breasts were well covered now by a white apron. "Heed yerself."

The campers twittered. They were lining up. I walked slowly with the heavy tray. I felt as if I were in high school again, working summer jobs. Except for the foray to Alaska, however, my only summer jobs growing up had been at Creamy Freeze: driving the company truck, monitoring vats, spying on pilferers, and filing invoices. On the other hand, this enforced sabbatical from the university had given me the chance to interact with a wide range of people that I might not ordinarily get to know.

Setting down the tray on the red-checkered tablecloth, I said, "Gourmet enchiladas with homemade guacamole and beans. Hope you enjoy it."

"Daddy, he's not a real Indian," McKenzie said. "Hey, mister, are you a loser?"

The man with the goatee said, "McKenzie, that's not nice. Say you're sorry."

The little girl shook her head vigorously. "Not sorry. Ever."

That seemed to be the only thing this little girl could ever say: "Not sorry. Ever." Woe to the unlucky man who pledged to take her for better or for worse.

He said to the woman with the platinum hair, "We need to work on her manners. This is not the way I was brought up in West Texas."

Mary Alice stepped up to the microphone. "Ladies and gentleman, girls of Clover Flower, we are fortunate to have the famous biblical scholar, Dr Klaus Kaiser, with us today. He'll lead us in prayer."

The platinum-haired mother said, "You're the Shawnee Chief! Be a doll and get me some Starkist in water!"

"Well, I was…" I waved. "I'm now a waiter." My identity changed frequently.

Dr Kaiser stepped up to the microphone. It suddenly started to squeal, as if it were rebelling. He tapped it with his forefinger. "I never know how to use these things. Well," he said. "*Kleine Lieblinge*. Which is to say, My little darlings…. Are any of you little darlings learning German?"

Not a single girl raised her hand. They were giggling. Dr Kaiser was wearing a checkered blue wool flat cap—a bit old-fashioned and hot for a summer in Texas. Long khaki Bermuda shorts with brown socks, which almost reached his knees. He was wearing leather sandals with the socks. The most incongruous piece of his outfit was a green tee-shirt with the slogan: "Go Baylor Bears." A smiling yellow bear was embossed on his chest. I made a mental note to jot down these details in my ragged spiral notebook.

Mary Alice stood with her arms folded. She was staring at the girls, but they continued giggling. She blew her silver whistle. She moved toward the mike. "Those who don't behave won't swim for a week."

The place went silent, not even a peep.

Dr Kaiser was an older gentleman in his late sixties. "So, we will start with a short prayer said in the home in Germany before meals. You can repeat after me if you like: 'All creatures great and small have their food, each little flower drinks from you. You have not forgotten us, dear Lord, thank you for that.'"

What was the prayer that Dad used to say before meals? I only remembered, "God is great. God is good…" A phrase of the Lord's Prayer floated in my consciousness: "Our Father Who art in Heaven." Did I feel hemmed in by church suppers and Sunday school at the Presbyterian church? All of the social niceties? And yet, on some level, I was a believer. Do unto others. Had I behaved selfishly with my two fiancées? Would things be different with Boriana? Did you have the power to change yourself? Or did you keep making the same mistakes over and over again in your life?

Mary Alice stepped up to the microphone. "Thank you, Dr Kaiser. Maybe you want to say something about your important work to the girls."

"*Aacch*," Dr Kaiser said. "I am sure that the little darlings are hungry and want to eat this marvelous, exotic food. Another time."

Mary Alice's voice boomed over the microphone: "Girls, Dr Kaiser reads ancient languages and has discovered many exciting things about our Bible. Any questions?"

Silverware clinked. The girls tittered.

When I got back to the kitchen, Sinead was turning over the trays of crème caramel onto a large platter. The brown sugar on the bottom made a crust on the top when you flipped over the pan. Her cheeks were red from the heat of the oven.

"Did they like it?" she said. She was cutting out small squares and putting them on plates. "Just finishing the afters."

"Miss Universe wants tuna," I said. "She's afraid of getting fat."

"Lady Muck wants tuna, does she? And here we are, running around like blue-arsed flies. Might be some in back." She nodded toward the supply room.

I went to the huge cupboard where the canned goods were kept. The stock was disorganized: canned herring, sardines, salmon, mackerel, anchovies, crab, shrimp. Canned franks and beans. Canned spaghetti. Campbell's soup. The odd cans reminded me of Bill and Rose's cupboard in Cairo. I would never see them again. One single can. I looked at the side: In Briny Oil.

When I came back, Sinead was sitting on a little wooden stool. "I'm wrecked," she said. "Did you find any?"

"Mongol Tuna?" I said, waving the can.

Sinead chortled. "Aye, we feed that to the stray cats."

I chuckled. "How should I serve it?"

"Rinse off the oil," Sinead said. "Squeeze a little lemon on it. We've got some fresh dill somewhere. Cut up a wee carrot. We've got some leftover tomatoes. Lettuce. Don't bother yerself. Let her starve, like the English did with us during the Great Famine!"

Why was I so eager to break off my relationship with Boriana for this feisty Irish woman whom I barely knew? What kind of baggage was she carrying? Or did I just want a roll in the hay?

When I got the plate done, I took it out to the main table. The oilman and McKenzie had disappeared. Miss Platinum Universe was scrolling on her iPhone. Flies had started to feast on the cheese enchiladas.

"The flies are biting me," Miss Universe complained.

"Black horseflies. They're after your blood." I set the tuna plate in front of her. "Bon appétit!"

"It looks oily and dark. Gross," Miss Universe said. "Don't think I can choke it down, even if the nutritionist says it's good for me."

She was right—it didn't look very appetizing.

"Sorry," I said. "That was the best we could do under the circumstances."

She suddenly smiled. "Hey, Mr Shawnee Chief, would you like to see your picture? You look cute!" She scrolled down on her iPhone. A middle-aged bald man smiled goofily at the camera with plumes of orange feathers above his head. McKenzie was sticking out her tongue at him. Miss Universe's smile was forced. Was she happy?

"Should I send you a copy?" she asked. "What's your name? Are you on Facebook?"

"Buffalo Bill Cody," I said.

"That's not your name!"

I blew her a kiss and bowed, before moving to collect the plates from the other end of the table—nothing left, not even a single pinto bean.

Mary Alice murmured, "Thank you, Gary. Delicious."

She leaned her head back into the discussion with Gudrun and Dr Kaiser, as if they were plotting something. Gudrun was smoking a cigarette in a long black holder, as if she were a debutante from the twenties. She waved, but I wasn't going to be introduced to Dr Kaiser. Academic protocol—no one knew I was a professor at the camp. Did I enjoy being invisible or not? Was this my way of evading responsibility? I could act like a horny college kid and make out with Sinead, the Irish cook!

Suddenly, Kharalombos appeared on the makeshift stage in baggy blue jean overalls, three sizes too big for him. Where had he bought those? Walmart? A conical paper hat perched on his head. And he had glued on a black, bushy, Turkish-style moustache.

Kharalombos sang, "Baa-baa, Ali Baa-baa, have you any treasure? Yes sir, yes sir, three bags to measure." Then he shouted, "Sing after me."

The girls screamed, "One for my master, one for my dame, and one for the little girl down the lane."

Five young girls, wearing bikinis with sheer red scarves tied around their waists, danced around Kharalombos. They were carrying screwdrivers instead of knives and they moved around him in a circle, swaying their hips in a provocative way—a feeble attempt at belly dancing. It looked a little like a seventies' disco dance. Then, in pairs, they faced each other and dueled with their long screwdrivers. The teenage girls ran off the stage and another group of thin girls ran on. This group also wore bikinis but had covered their mouths and noses with red bandannas, like bandits. One of them shouted, "Open Sesame!" They were carrying loot into their cave: papier-mâché goblets spray-painted gold, Mardi Gras costume jewelry, and a small, sequined, silver shoebox. They set their treasure in a designated spot under one of the picnic tables. "Close Sesame!"

The small girls in the audience squealed with delight.

Kharalombos' moustache was lopsided—it looked as if it might fall off. His paper-cone hat blew away. He stood next to the picnic table and roared, "Open Sesame!"

Suddenly, Ramses el-Kibir marched into the middle of the makeshift stage. He was wearing his Indiana Jones hat with jeans and a short-sleeved cotton Oxford shirt.

"There he is!" one girl shouted. "Captain Mummy."

The children dropped their forks and stampeded toward him.

"Shit!" I moved as fast as I could with the heavy tray toward the kitchen before he could see me. I didn't want to have any more to do with him after the fiasco of the reality television show.

Sinead ran to the door of the kitchen to see what was happening. "Oh, that's Ramses el-Kibir. He comes to visit every year. My wee tots love his television show."

"No one told us he was going to visit."

Sinead was munching on a carrot. "Of course, you probably know everyone in Egypt. Is he dangerous?"

"If you call being filmed with a live cobra dangerous…"

Gudrun leapt up from the main table and ran to the mike. "*Aacch*, girls, please return to your seats. We are so happy to have Captain Mummy with us, but we must have order! Girls, please. Order! Order! Take your seats at once!"

The girls ignored her completely. They were tugging at his pants. Taking off his hat. He was smiling broadly and waving, as if he were Mick Jagger. Were they going to take off his clothes? He probably wouldn't mind. I felt slightly jealous of his stardom.

Mary Alice blew her silver whistle. Suddenly, just as quickly, they rushed back to their seats.

Gudrun was kissing Ramses on both cheeks. She was wearing the muumuu with large hibiscus flowers against a yellow cotton print—the same dress she was wearing when I met her on January 28th, Black Friday of the Egyptian Revolution. Did she have any other clothes? Letty had said she had had an affair with Ramses. Was that true, or just gossip?

Gudrun stood at the mike. Her face was flushed. "We are so delighted to have Captain Mummy with us today. Of course, it is a little unexpected, but that is the charm of… *Ja-aa*." She brushed her carrot-red hair out of her eyes, putting a strand behind her ear in a girlish way. She addressed Ramses el-Kibir, but her voice carried over the microphone, "My *Liebchen*, I thought you were coming tomorrow?"

The children were chanting, "We want Captain Mummy! We want Captain Mummy! We want Captain Mummy! We want…"

"Okay, children," Gudrun said. "*Nein, nein*, we will not have the chaos. Everyone who wants one of Captain Mummy's books must stand in line. The small children will go first." A long line formed instantly, curling around many of the picnic tables, almost to the camp's small lake—at least two hundred girls were waiting for autographs, or books. A huge tower of books teetered on one of the picnic tables.

Kharalombos burst into the kitchen. "*Khara!*" he shouted. "*Khara! Ahha, bent kalb, bent weskha, sharmuta! Heyyalli sharmuta! Ana itzalamt. Ithaanet karamti!*"

Sinead turned to me. "Too many languages fer me in this kitchen. What the feck? You speak Egyptian."

"Shit," I said. "I've been wronged. I've been humiliated." I didn't translate "She's a bitch" and the rest.

Kharalombos flopped onto a wooden chair, which snapped in two, as if it were made of matchsticks. "*Khara!*" he said. "She made a cuckold out of me." He gestured with his hands. "You can see how he spoiled my show. Utterly spoiled. Working here is impossible. *Mish mumkin!*"

"He sure did," I said. I wondered what Ramses el-Kibir was up to but didn't say anything more since Kharalombos was so upset. Why hadn't Gudrun told us Ramses el-Kibir was going to do a book signing?

In the distance, the oilman, Cameron Wiley the Third, was shaking hands with Ramses el-Kibir. McKenzie was hugging a book to her chest. Miss Universe was now chatting with Dr Klaus Kaiser. She looked animated and was laughing happily. She had seemed so unhappy a few minutes ago. Was it Dr Kaiser's charm?

Sinead shrugged. "Yer making too much of it, I'd say, Karalimpos. Think their relationship is strictly business, although he's probably got a roving eye. Are you hungry?"

Kharalombos growled. "Kharalombos, not Karalimpos! Do you have any sardines and onions? A cold beer?"

Kharalombos looked like a giant elf. The conical hat had been replaced with a tinier one. The bushy Turkish moustache dangled above his lip.

"The kids loved the show," I said. "It was very creative. Reminded me of Ismail Yassin's comedy, *Ali Baba and the Forty Thieves.* Is that where you got the idea?"

Kharalombos muttered, "*Ya khabar eswed.* I've come all the way to America to be a cuckold! And I have to get up early every morning. That is the real torture. For what?"

"Letty's enchiladas are dead good. Don't you want to try them? Should I make you a plate?" Sinead asked.

"I don't eat chicken," he said. "Bacon. Lamb and beef. Fish. No chicken! No rabbit!"

Sinead said, "Think there might be some sardines in the cupboard."

"There's plenty," I said. I didn't know who had a taste for sardines, but there were enough for a tornado storm cellar, like the kind we had in Oklahoma.

I made Kharalombos a full plate of chili sardines, shallots, potato salad, and a thick slice of homemade sourdough bread. Found some cold Corona beer in the industrial fridge in the back.

Kharalombos was chomping on a small shallot. He was not happy, but he was a little calmer.

"Cool it," I said. "Everything'll work out."

Kharalombos frowned. "How can a cuckold be optimistic? Should I just lie down like a coward, while my manhood is taken away? *La'. La'.*"

"You don't know that for sure," I said. "Maybe he was just flirting with her."

Or maybe he'd had a brief dalliance with her, like I had had with Sinead? And she had hoped for more?

Speedy, who was never fast unless it involved booze or beer, loped into the kitchen. "Man, you wouldn't believe it! CNN is outside! Prue Scoop is interviewing that Egyptian *gato*. What's his name?"

"What?!"

Speedy was breathless. "I'm not sheetin' you. CNN is outside! Look fer yerself! They're interviewing that *beeg gato* about the loot stolen from the Egyptian Museum during the Revolution."

"We have to hide!" I panicked. We couldn't be on national television—this was a disaster. "Kharalombos!"

"Have some *cojones*. Don't you guys want to be on TV? Be famous? Gudrun wants you to be interviewed," Speedy said. "She's telling Prue Scoop about how you saved a poor German lady during the Revolution."

Kharalombos set his beer down. "She forgot about my situation. We have to disappear. Please, help us…"

"I don't get it. Did you guys knock off somebody big in Egypt?" Speedy asked. He took a swig out of Kharalombos' Corona and leaned against the table.

Sinead said, "You're both mad. Barking."

"We're Wanted!"

"Nah," Speedy said. "You didn't. I have seen some mean mother-fuckers in my life. You're not mean enough to…"

"We didn't kill anyone," I quickly added.

Sinead nodded. "In the back. The supply closet. We'll cover fer ya."

The children were singing, "Oh, they built the ship *Titanic* to sail the ocean blue. And they said it was a ship that the waves would never go through….Oh, it was sad….It was sad when the great ship went down…"

—m—

CNN was gone. Ramses el-Kibir was on his way to Houston for the opening of a pharaonic exhibition at the Museum of Art.

"Thanks, Sinead," I said. "That was close."

"'Fess up," she said, when she opened the door to the supply closet. It was stuffy and hot. Just the opposite of being locked in the freezer.

"I'm accused of being a cyber-terrorist," I said.

Sinead hooted. "Some rogue. Since the moment you came here, you just tell one tale after another."

"Am not. I also got into the US on a false passport. Could go to jail on that alone. Identity theft. That's the truth."

I was in hot water. And it would cost me thousands in lawyer's fees to prove my innocence to the federal government. I had not touched my savings. But I was also unemployable now. No university would hire me. I could not spend the rest of my life working in the kitchen at Clover Flower. Or maybe I'd have to? That was a sobering thought—years and years of scrubbing charred pans! Cleaning toilets! Still, this was the fate of many, many people. So many Mexicans died crossing the Rio Grande—hoping for any job. On the other hand, did I also relish being a Wanted Man? It made me feel important. And there was the challenge of how to evade the authorities—I had to rely on my wits and disguises to survive. The story of how a hapless, maladroit professor had brought down the computer system of a major publishing company would have been amusing, if it were happening to someone else. Had the Egyptian Secret Service framed me because I had exposed companies who had dumped chemicals into the Nile? Just who had gotten into my apartment in Cairo and hacked my computer? Of course, before I was accused of hacking Zadorf Publishers, there had been the episode at the university. I had spearheaded the protest against contamination of the Nile, urging students to dump masses of spoiled fish at the entrance—that was a fact. And the other fact was my tree-sitting campaign, which was even too radical for the University of Oregon. Over one hundred days perched in a tree to block the logging companies. The stunt worked, but I also lost my bid for tenure.

"And Kharalombos?" Sinead said. "The accomplice?"

Kharalombos was breathing heavily. "I was teaching the President of Egypt's daughter how to waltz. And…"

"You got her in the family way," Sinead said.

"I have never seen my son, Nunu," Karalombos said. "He's not in Egypt. They fled to Morocco."

"Oh," Sinead said. "Right. Think I heard of him. The president is a dentist?"

I didn't correct her. That was Bashar el-Assad of Syria. Did she even read the newspaper? Was I being a snob or was this a good hunch?

"Gudrun persuaded us to come and work for her," I said.

Sinead giggled. "Both of ya are daft. Completely daft. But sound men all the same. Meantime, we have to finish the kitchen before Mary Alice turns up."

Entire plates of enchiladas were scraped into the garbage. So much waste!

"Seems a shame to throw it away," I said. "Are you using it for compost?"

"Brilliant! Suppose our gardener would appreciate that. Why don't you get 'er started? In this bin here."

Mary Alice marched in with her clipboard. "Great news about Ramses's interview at our camp! Prue Scoop, CNN's Chief Correspondent on the Middle East, mentioned Clover Flower three times in the interview. This will help us bounce back after being sued last year."

Kharalombos grunted. He was stuffing chili sardines into his mouth.

"Why are you two so sour?" asked Mary Alice. "You have a grudge against Ramses el-Kibir?"

Kharalombos grunted again. "He spoiled my show."

She stood in front of him, tapping her foot. She was tiny next to the huge Kharalombos. "So," Mary Alice said. "A little feedback. The screwdriver dance was too, uummm, you know what I mean? We are running a Christian girls' camp. Not a shoot for *Playboy*!"

Kharalombos had just downed his fifth beer. "*Ya salaam*! Did you want me to use real swords? Don't worry. There won't be a next time!"

Sinead was now sitting on a small wooden stool, studying a cookbook entitled *Fast, Healthy Meals from the Southwest*.

Mary Alice asked, "By the way, Sinead, have you seen a goat? Our new neighbor, Azzurro, has lost his pet goat, Leo. I want to stay on his good side. Our septic tank is on his property."

I avoided her eyes. That outlaw, Speedy! Well, at least we knew we hadn't eaten a dog!

Sinead curbed a giggle, which turned into a cough. "No, can't say that I have, but there are plenty of stray cats around here. Seen a baby armadillo the other day outside the kitchen. We don't have those in Ireland."

Mary Alice said, "It's no joke. I am sure you know what a goat looks like. Have you seen our new neighbor?"

"Heard he'd made a lot of quid," Sinead said, and waved. "Somewhere in the Middle East. Not sure which country?"

Was she being disingenuous?

"Looks like a tough guy," I said. "My wrestling skills from high school might come in handy."

I'd never put my toe in the ring!

Letty sidled up next to me so she wouldn't face Mary Alice. "Gary, this is how you rinse dishes. Fill up the sink with water. Not every single dish under the tap."

She rolled her eyes toward Mary Alice. "Oh, yeah," I said. "Sure, thanks for the tip, Letty."

Suddenly, Gudrun pushed through the swinging doors. She was exuberant. "We made CNN! That is something wondrous for us!"

"We never want to see Ramses el-Kibir again!" Kharalombos said. "*Da ragel nassab.*"

"What, my *Liebchen*?"

"He's a fraud," Kharalombos shouted. "Don't you see? After that stupid television show in Cairo, why do you still talk to him? I asked you not to talk to him! You went behind my back!"

Exactly what I had done to Aengus!

I still had to rinse quite a few more enchilada pans and a huge mixing bowl. I might have escaped to the supply room, but Mary Alice was standing behind me.

"Need to see if we've improved on the staff bathrooms," Mary Alice muttered. "Don't leave your post on deck."

As soon as she was out of sight, Letty whispered to me, "Whew! That was close. I am gonna kill him. That *pendejo* lied to me."

Sinead jumped up from her stool. "Letty, let's check the stock for the next week."

Gudrun's voice boomed, "My bonbon, you misunderstand. He had to stop in Houston to speak to the curator of the museum. A new exhibition of his latest discoveries. After that, to New York to visit his agent about his new book."

"Go to New York with your boyfriend! Forget about me! My life is not here. I don't like America. All you do is work. Talk about work. Breathe work. Eat work. It's duller than Switzerland!"

But that was exactly why so many came to the United States: in search of the dream. Who could fault anyone who wanted a better, safer home? At the same time, Kharalombos missed Cairo, his home: he ached for those leisurely afternoons or evenings, lounging at outdoor cafés, sucking on a hookah. He had time for all of his immense, entangling network of acquaintances and friends. There was always time for a chat in Cairo. No one would refuse to listen—that was the charm that tourists didn't see on a quick visit. Other charms were more obvious, like the brightly colored murals of the pharaonic tombs in Luxor, the sheer size of the Pyramids at Giza, or the turquoise water of the Red Sea.

"My bonbon, he is not my boyfriend," Gudrun said, pinching his cheek.

"I am not your baby!" Kharalombos shouted. "Take your hands off of me!"

"*Aaach*, my *Liebchen*," Gudrun said. "Don't be ridiculous. You are the only one for me."

"Gary, tell her Cairo is better!" Kharalombos shouted. "You lived there most of your life. Why aren't you defending me? You are my only friend here."

"Well," I said. I was about to get smashed in the middle of a lovers' quarrel. "It's another world."

How to convey the color of Cairo, that lively, crazy city, with its humor and esprit de corps?

"I have no rights here," Kharalombos said. "I am working day and night. *Inti bakheela awi, gelda.* You are miserly! I am always hungry here. And then you ask me to work ten hours a day for this foolish Ali Baba show. And we never got a salary! What is this *khara*—this shit? We are slaves!"

"Oh, my bonbon," Gudrun said. "What is *bakheela*?" She started talking baby talk. "You can have whatever you like. Would you like a pork chop? Pork ribs? Smoked bacon?"

"I am not a *kherati*. I don't mooch off tourists. I have my Greek nationality and I don't have to stay at this foolish camp. You have destroyed my manhood. I am leaving tonight!"

—w—

I sneaked away to my awful cabin. I would talk to Kharalombos later, when he cooled off. Pernicious chiggers burrowed into my skin. Even rubbing Off on my legs didn't help. In my chewed-up spiral notebook, I scribbled with a pencil nub: *Manliness. Manhood. Macho. "Be a man!"* Sinead whispered seductively in my ear, *"Be a man!"* For my Dad, that meant work, money, and football. For Kharalombos: Saving face. Dignity. Possession. For Aengus: Physical strength. Silence. Mechanical know-how. For Speedy: Drink. Cards. Pool. And for me? Knowledge. Respect. Bravado. Having an audience. Showing off. I had always thought of myself as modest. I was surprised to discover that I had a flair for bravado—seeing if I could pull off the next disguise.

Around midnight there were voices outside. The sound of footsteps crunched on the gravel road, from the direction leading up to Azzurro Agua's property. *"Aaach,"* a voice said. "It seems too strange to be doing business so late at the night." He laughed nervously. "Why wasn't the appointment in the light of day? What is the name of this gentleman? I only do business with respectable people."

"Dr Kaiser," another voice said, "Let me assure you, you are doing God's work. With your knowledge and our resources, we will."

"Viscount Triksky," Dr Kaiser said. "I don't want to be involved in anything nefarious."

"I say, old chap, the gentleman is first class. A1. Wait until you see."

Triksky? What was he doing here? God! First, Ramses el-Kibir and now Triksky! Was Ramses el-Kibir bluffing about going to Houston? Was he still in the area?

"This is just plain service, that's all there is to it," the voice said. "God's work." Who was the third voice?

Were they building a monastery on Azzurro Agua's property?

Chapter 8

Kharalombos on Strike

A T DAWN, KHARALOMBOS POUNDED ON THE DOOR TO my cabin. He was carrying a giant maroon Samsonite suitcase. Gudrun's little white and black terrier, Dagmar, had followed him. She yapped.

"We are in a harem," Kharalombos said. "We have been castrated. Unmanned. Deprived of our *rogula*! Our manhood."

"You'll make up with her," I said. "Did you sleep at her house last night?"

He yawned. "On a hard picnic table. I'm going back to Egypt if I can purchase a ticket. I am going to call my uncle to send me a thousand dollars through Western Union. These *sharameet* are making us work for free. We are enslaved. This is worse than the Russians."

Did Kharalombos have any experience with Russians? I wondered. He had never mentioned Russians before. If I had no other resources, I would be more alarmed about the money. Was I playing at work here?

Dagmar was yapping at him angrily. I scratched her head and she softened.

"I don't even know if they have Western Union in Schulenburg. Maybe the next town over, Fredericksburg? You'll have to get someone to drive you over. I am sure Gudrun won't take you."

Kharalombos sat down gloomily on my rickety bed; it collapsed onto the floor. "What is this *khara*? Why didn't you complain? I have never seen such a miserly woman in my life. How can you sleep in such a filthy place?"

I shrugged. "Never here."

There was nowhere else to sit so I sat on the concrete floor, next to the boxes full of Lysol disinfectant. Kharalombos sat on the ground next to me. "I thought America would be different," he said, sighing. "You hear so much about it and then, this? Even when they are having fun, Americans are such slaves to schedules. I am suffocating."

How different to live in a country, rather than experiencing it through Hollywood movies!

I suddenly remembered the conversation I had overheard at midnight. "Kharalombos, something strange is going on."

"You mean, how we have been unmanned by a German bitch? Men should find castration strange!"

If I laughed, he would think I was laughing at him.

"No," I said. "Listen, Triksky is here! I heard his voice last night. With Dr Kaiser and somebody else."

"What do you expect?" Kharalombos said. "What can you expect from such people? He is probably cheating someone. It has nothing to do with me. I just want to go back to Cairo. My old life. This place is dead for me."

Did I feel alive here, either? Of course, I felt exhilarated when I was kissing Sinead. But I couldn't pursue her. That was crazy! Did I want to be a Don Juan? Smash up lives? I must call Boriana. See how her job was going at the Knights Templar Museum. Out of sight, out of mind? Why did I find Sinead so alluring? Was I compatible with Sinead in any way, except that I lusted after her body? And she had two small children and a husband already!

"Did you ever see Azzurro Agua, the new neighbor?"

"*La*," Kharalombos said emphatically. "*La*. Why do you involve yourself? You sound like an Egyptian housewife who is interfering in her neighbor's affairs. Why do you care?"

In Cairo, Kharalombos namedropped and gossiped on the phone in Arabic about Omar Sharif—about how he had seen him at his son's expensive Italian restaurant, Zizi's in Zamalek. Since when were all of Kharlombos's conversations lofty, philosophical discourses?

"You should see Azzurro," I said. "He looks tough. Maybe he is doing something illegal. Something dangerous."

Kharalombos laughed. "Listen to yourself. You sound like a schoolboy. You are the one who is wanted by the American government and Interpol. Not me."

So in Kharalombos' mind I was either an Egyptian housewife or a naïve schoolboy? That should have made me furious. But was Kharalombos lashing out at me because he felt his manhood had been threatened here? Plus, he was also suffering from culture shock. Still, maybe Kharalombos was partly right. Leading impressionable students to dump a ton of rotten tilapia at the gates of the university had been an immature prank—it probably cost a fortune to clean up the mess. Had I used the dramatic protest as a way to get attention? Other faculty had also joined the demonstration. Had there been repercussions against them by the administration? I had never even thought of that before. Had anyone lost their jobs because of me? Writing an investigative article with concrete facts and statistics about the dire pollution of the Nile for the *New York Times* might have been more effective, if I were serious about clean water. And too much scientific jargon had spoiled my novel, *Pure Water*—which was why Rose and Bill used it for scrap paper. It deserved to be hurled in the trash.

"I wasn't the mastermind of the virus," I said. "On that front, I wasn't wrong."

"So this Azzurro Agua, the neighbor, probably doesn't think he is doing anything wrong, either. Who ever heard of keeping a goat for a pet? Americans are strange."

Dagmar yapped in agreement.

"He was working in Libya."

Kharalombos sighed. "So? Who cares? I'm hungry. Listen, *habibi*, I don't care about Azzurro and Leo. Can you help me get back to Cairo? I am like a fish out of the water here. I can't breathe."

In the next few days, there were flurries of phone calls to Cairo. Kharalombos's parents were dead, so he relied on his uncle, Dr Achilles Kharalombos, my old shrink. Kharalombos finally got word that his uncle was on holiday on Skopelos Island in Greece, and he tried unsuccessfully to call him there. The doctor's mobile was always turned off. His uncle was casual about the emergency. "No need to rush back to Cairo in summer," he said. "You will make up with your lady."

Kharalombos refused to teach his dance classes. He stayed up all night, making phone calls or singing, in Arabic, Asmahan's "*Ya Toyoor Ghanni*"—"O Birds, Sing." Dagmar refused to leave his side. So now I was not being kept awake by mosquitoes or chiggers, but by Kharalombos and a yapping Dagmar. When he was awake, he was noisy. And when he was asleep, he snored loudly. Tiny girls were knocking on the door for Kharalombos, begging him to come and teach his dance classes. "Please, can Mr Kharalombos come and teach us today?" They were tired of making bread boards and longed to continue with their dancing lessons.

I longed for a tiny bit of privacy and less drama. One afternoon, Ashley, the teen counselor, drove Kharalombos around in her red convertible MG, searching for fava beans, commonly eaten for breakfast in Egypt. He left his cell phone behind. I punched in Boriana's phone number.

To my surprise, she answered.

"It's me," I shouted.

"My sweet man," Boriana gushed. "Where are you calling from? Did you find your book?"

"I'm in Texas."

Boriana laughed. "Bang. Bang. Are you like John Wayne? When are you coming back?"

"I don't know," I said. "I miss you."

"I miss our dinners on the balcony of the Roma pension," Boriana said wistfully. "I will be leaving Malta soon."

"What happened with Dragomir?" I asked, suddenly alarmed. Was she going back to him? Unlike Gayle and Rachel, Boriana might not wait around for seven years.

But the line was suddenly cut. I tried for over an hour, but the overseas line was busy.

Whenever Gudrun called Kharalombos, he didn't answer his phone. He avoided all meals—either I had to bring him food or he sneaked into the kitchen at midnight.

"Don't you think you're being a little childish?" I asked. "Maybe Gudrun wants to apologize. Do you even remember why you're mad at her? It's been a week."

"I told her never to see Ramses el-Kibir again," Karalombos said, his arms crossed. "She is two-faced. She went behind my back."

"Are you jealous of Ramses el-Kibir?"

But Kharalombos ignored me and picked up his mobile phone. He was scanning his messages.

"Here's one from Boriana," he said, tipping the phone at me. Boriana had written: MY DEAR GARY: KISSES FROM MALTA. NOT SAME WITHOUT YOU. CIRCUS PLAYS IN MOROCCO FOR TWO MONTHS. BACK TO SOFIA AFTER. IF YOU LEARNED ARABIC, YOU CAN LEARN BULGARIAN! I STARTED DIVORCE PAPER AG. DRAGOMIR.

So she was serious! Maybe it would work this time. She was more creative than my other two fiancées and she had a sense of humor. How could anyone live without humor in this remorseless, dangerous world? It was as necessary as fresh oxygen.

"How does she know this is my number?" Kharalombos asked.

I shrugged. "I used your phone when you were driving around the state, looking for fava beans."

Kharalombos said, "Maybe you could get a job, working as a lion tamer in the circus!"

"I thought a clown might be more like it," I said. I didn't know what country we would live in, or if I could ever get a job again, but I still felt hopeful.

Another night, Kharalombos stayed at Speedy's all night, playing poker. He slept all the next day until six o'clock.

Just as he was waking up, Mary Alice showed up with her clipboard. After she had criticized him for the Ali Baba show, he had nothing but disparaging things to say about her. "The second *sharmuta*. Bitch. Castrator of men," he said.

"Don't you think that's a little harsh?" I asked. Mary Alice was salty as horseradish, but she wasn't mean.

Kharalombos only snorted. "They're castrators."

Mary Alice was not fazed that Kharalombos was standing there in his light-blue boxer shorts, his penis lolling through the slit.

"There has been an obvious breakdown in discipline. We are concerned that you're going around with Ashley. In terms of our liability. You are a forty-five-year-old man."

Kharalombos folded his burly arms. "I didn't touch her."

Mary Alice screwed up her nose with distaste. "It's not wholesome. We have a reputation to uphold in the community. We can't have another disaster this summer."

"It was completely harmless. You always talk about wholesome. Is your camp like white bread? Or they are all white flowers?" Kharalombos asked, and then chortled lewdly.

"She is a very well-developed young girl. One might be tempted. With those halter tops and blue jean cutoffs."

Mary Alice looked at me while she was saying this. Did she know about what had happened with Sinead? Maybe she suspected.

"I am preparing my departure so you will be free of me soon," he said. "Any other orders?"

"Dagmar," Mary Alice said. "Gudrun wants her back." Mary Alice reached down to pick up Dagmar. The dog growled and then scurried away behind a sack of corn.

"Come on, girl," Mary Alice said in a softer voice.

Dagmar made an ominous, low, growling sound, which sounded deadly for such a small dog.

Mary Alice sighed. "I don't have time for this. Go ahead and stay. Gary, we need to talk about a change in your assignment."

Following Mary Alice outside, I said, "Sinead says I'm a perfect sous-chef. I see no reason why I should move."

Mary Alice looked at me shrewdly but didn't betray anything. Instead, she said, "We are shorthanded in maintenance. Aengus is talking about working more hours for Cameron Wiley. He is making a lot more money in West Texas. We just can't pay him much more."

"We haven't been paid, either."

Mary Alice grimaced. "Believe me, I am working on that. You'll get paid tomorrow. Cash."

"I could organize a play for the girls. I was the president of the Thespian Club in high school. Our performance of *Twelfth Night* won first in the state competition." Now that I'd resolved to bluff, I couldn't stop! I was having fun revising the history of my life.

Mary Alice was unconcerned. "Aengus will teach you."

"No, I mean it," I said. "I have absolutely no talent for repairs. Anything I touch breaks. Murphy's law. I could supervise the art room. Take them on hikes and point out local wildlife. Birds."

"We need you," Mary Alice said. "You'll learn."

As soon as we got our salary the following day, Kharalombos asked Ashley to drive him over to Fredericksburg to pay for his ticket back to Cairo.

A carrot-red head peeked in the door. "Where is my *Liebchen*?"

Better to tell her the truth. "Ashley drove him over to Fredericksburg to pay for his ticket."

Dagmar barked at her, as if she were a stranger. Gudrun's face went white. "He is going off with that young girl."

"No, no, no," I said. "He's dying to go back to Cairo. He's restless."

"Cairo!" Gudrun said. "No one told me he was leaving! This is a calamity. *Ja-aa*, have you been watching the news? Cairo is not so good. Gary, please, what can I do?"

"I don't really know," I said. "He's homesick. He's determined to leave."

What was going on in Cairo? From here, it might as well be Mars. All this communication—and we still were focused on what happened in our local reality, wherever we were. When we were in Cairo, we were focused completely on the Square and had no idea what was happening in the rest of the world. Weren't most people the stars of their own empirical universes? Unless you were glued day and night to the television and the computer, living vicariously through the tragedies of others, through the news. Was that a healthy way to live your life? Or, for some people, had virtual reality become more real than the life they were supposed to be living?

Gudrun started weeping. "My *Liebchen*," she said. "I will never find another man my size. And he is so funny, although he has a bad temper."

Dagmar yapped in agreement.

"I'm no expert," I said. I remembered Boriana brushing her shiny, long hair in front of the mirror in our room at the Roma pension. After a shower, she had wrapped herself in a towel as if it were a toga—how regal she looked. I was lying on the bed, looking at her in the oval mirror with the gilded frame. She stuck out her tongue at me, playfully. Did I want to start from scratch in another country at fifty? That was assuming she divorced Dragomir!

"He feels like he doesn't have any power in his life," I said. Was I talking about Kharalombos or myself?

"*Aaach*," Gudrun said. "But all the little children of Clover Flower are following him like he is the Piped Piper."

"That's not exactly what I mean," I said. "If you want him, let him go."

Was that what I had done with Boriana? Or had I been more obsessed with my novel, which I now admitted was a flop? Hadn't I always put my scientific work and my writing ahead of my relationships?

"*Ja-aa,*" Gudrun said. "Dagmar, my *Liebchen*, don't you want to come home? You will get some doggy treats." Gudrun ventured to pick up Dagmar, but she squirmed out of her grasp and ran away. "So, you are punishing me, too."

"Who is Dr Kaiser?"

"My cousin from Berlin," Gudrun said. "He is a famous Coptic scholar. He can read all the ancient languages. I envy him. Even medieval Arabic. He's a genius. He was always better than me in the *gymnasium*. But when we were kids, he could not skate on the ice! And now, here we are in America!"

"What is he doing in the US?" I asked. "Is he teaching at Baylor?"

"*Ja-aa,* " Gudrun said. "They have a big project, collecting ancient manuscripts. And then they have conferences to study and talk about them."

"I thought I heard Count Triksky's voice last night," I said.

"No!" Gudrun said. "This is impossible. He would not dare come back to this place. He is a big thief! I will call the police immediately." She shook her forefinger at me, like a schoolteacher.

"Even if your cousin was with him?" I asked.

Gudrun looked at me in horror. "You are joking with me? How does he know the Triker? We have put the Triker behind us."

"They were walking up the gravel road to Azzurro's. I don't know who the third man was. He talked a lot about God."

Gudrun was disturbed. "The Italian man with the blue tattoo. He is no good. I must tell Mary Alice."

She left in a hurry.

—m—

Later in the afternoon, the blue summer sky turned gray and gloomy and the wind whipped through the trees. The place shook with thunder and rain pounded the ground hard, like beads. Occasional streaks of lightning illuminated the horizon. It continued raining for over two hours and showed no signs of stopping.

Soon we were running from cabin to cabin, to stop up the leaks. Mary Alice made me carry pans to catch the dripping rain that was leaking into the cabins. The younger children were crying and squealing. The teenage girls were playing cards in their cabins.

In the main office, the television blared with updates on the storm.

"Gary," Mary Alice said, "can you get a pot and put it on my desk? Our records can't get wet. That last roofer was a crook."

Gudrun said, "We find thieves everywhere we turn. And all our outdoor activities are going to be cancelled."

The rain continued for days. The ground became soggy. The children got into mud fights. The water of the river rose.

Mary Alice said, "Soon we'll be Rainbow Ark."

I felt a twinge of guilt for the animals I had been taking care of in Cairo. What had happened to Scarlett O'Hara?

On the day Kharalombos was supposed to leave for Cairo, he showed up in the office with his Samsonite suitcase. "Would you please give Ashley permission to drive me into town? I could get a taxi to San Antonio."

"Out of the question," Mary Alice said. "The little MG would be swept into the river. I am responsible for her safety."

He had not seen Gudrun for days. She was sitting at her desk, looking glumly at the television weather report.

"My bonbon, you cannot go," Gudrun said. "I cannot allow such a thing."

"I am not your slave," Kharalombos said. "You can't keep me here. I am asking politely if you will take me in your Suburban. Then I will start shouting."

Mary Alice grimaced. "The roads are closed. They have closed the bridges."

Kharalombos's face became red. "This is a conspiracy to keep me here!"

Gudrun offered him a damp doughnut. "*Aaach*, my *Liebchen*. Would you like a cruller?"

"She's telling the truth, Kharalombos," I said, pointing toward the small television. It listed all the roads in the area that were closed. A cheerful weatherman was saying, "We repeat. Under no circumstances should drivers be on the roads."

The door blew open with the wind. Aengus stomped in with his muddy boots. "Yer man. Need you. There's a wee snake in one of the cabins."

The mud squished beneath every footstep.

But when we arrived at the cabin, Aengus caught the snake easily and twisted its neck, as if he did this routinely. Did he want to show me what he could do to me for touching his wife? Was this a warning?

Some of the girls were squealing and screaming. Others continued on with their card games, completely unfazed.

"Just a wee garden snake, I'd say," Aengus said. "Nothing serious. The ones ya have to watch it fer are the water moccasins."

Aengus held up the lifeless snake, which now looked like a limp fan belt.

"That's a Speckled King Snake," I said, touching the sleek, scaly skin. "Non-venomous, but you must know that. Rat snakes. Brown snakes. Also nothing to be afraid of."

"So yer man studies snakes in his other life," Aengus said, shaking his head. I waited for him to confront me about Sinead, but he said nothing.

"Something along those lines," I said.

—⁜—

Kharalombos was so depressed he decided to sleep day and night. He slept so much that I wondered if he were still alive. Since I had nowhere to sleep, I slept on the wet concrete floor. There was another text message from Boriana: WRITE, DEAR GARY. KISS. KISS. I dreamed of Boriana's intense brown eyes. Would I ever see her again? Even if I wanted to go to Bulgaria, where would I get the money? As soon as I used my account, I would be tracked.

When Kharalombos was not sleeping, he was singing Sabah's song: "*Ana bakrahak ma ba'rasfh leih ana bakrahak.*" "I hate you, I hate you, I don't know why I hate you, and if they put a noose around my neck, I would still hate you. I hate the breeze…"

Furious that he had missed his plane to Cairo, he continued his strike.

—⁜—

Suddenly, the rain stopped. Aengus wanted me to work with him on a number of projects outside. I missed chatting with Sinead. Aengus rarely spoke. Did he know?

"Yer being trained to take over," Aengus said. "In case there's an emergency."

"What?" I said, following him out to the shed. Had they lost their minds?

"Aye," Aengus said. "Most of them weekends I'll be out in West Texas. The government says you'll be takin' over."

"The government?"

"Yer hens." Aengus rolled out an electric lawnmower. He frowned. "Yer ever started a lawnmower? You wore a lab coat in yer other life, didn't ya?"

He yanked it once and the motor roared. Then he shut it off. "Go on. Give 'er a try."

The machine barely whinnied. "I have an electric lawnmower at home," I said. I had never even bought a house! The only yard I had ever cut in my life was the front yard of our family home in Oklahoma City. Dad made me get up at seven on Saturdays and cut the grass: "Builds character, son!"

"No matter," he said, pulling the cord. The machine roared. "We're cutting near the property line."

He pushed the lawnmower down the dirt road. Near the property line was a huge garage. When he saw that the garage door was half open, he turned off the mower.

"Your man who owned this place before was into boats," Aengus said. He gestured to me. We peeked under. "Halloo," he called out. "Anybody home?"

"Have you met Azzurro?"

The place was deserted. He pushed the garage door upward. It moved forward and then rolled back. He shoved it up high so we could see inside.

"What the feck?"

It looked like the *Antiques Roadshow*. A Model A in perfect condition, painted red. There was also a tiny yellow Porsche. A blue Mustang convertible glistened with fresh paint: New York plates. Against the wall was a burgundy Louis XV sofa and matching high-backed chairs. Cardboard boxes were stacked against the wall next to the couch. On the boxes stenciled in Arabic: Baghdad Museum files. Why did he have the files?

"That belongs to the Baghdad Museum," I said, pointing to the cardboard boxes. I was dying to have a look.

"So yous is a scientist and reads Arabic, is it?"

I nodded. "Yeah." Wanted to avoid any more personal confessions. But Aengus looked at me with genuine admiration. "Hard language. You must have a good education. Left school early myself. Biggest mistake of my life. Wish my Da would have encouraged me. Was full of hate, he was."

Then he nodded toward the cars. "That's worth a fair bit. Wonder where he is. Even in the countryside, there are thieves." He pulled the garage door all the way to the ground. "We better get on with it."

The property line was only marked by a thin piece of cotton string. He watched while I mowed, then gestured for me to turn off the motor.

"Yer getting a wee close to the septic tank," he said. "I'm telling ya, a backed-up septic tank is a right mess. They were always dependin' before on the boat man to help 'em out. The tank's big enough, but the problem is, it's on his property."

"What do you do if it backs up?" I said.

"Yer man better be good," he said, shaking his head. "Emergency number's on the shed."

Maybe I should read up on septic tanks. As I was putting away the mower in the shed, I searched for the name of the company, but the print had faded.

A dog was barking nearby. We ran through the brush toward the yelping. A raccoon bared a ferocious set of teeth. Dagmar was backing away. Her paw was bleeding.

"Gary, give her a wide berth," Aengus said. "They're somethin' fierce." The raccoon turned around and ran off into the brush.

"Yes, I know," I said. Was it the same raccoon that had invaded my cabin on the first night?

Aengus scooped up Dagmar and cradled her as if she were a baby. "We'll have to get 'er to the vet." Blood smeared his white camp tee-shirt, which said: "Clover Flower: Wholesome Living."

I ran back to my cabin to tell Kharalombos that Dagmar was badly hurt. He was singing Abdel Wahab. "*Leh, leh, leh, ya ain leilee taawil? Leh, leh, leh, ya ain dam'ee saal?*" "Why is my night so long? Why do my tears flow?"

"Dagmar's hurt," I said.

Kharalombos stopped singing. "What happened?"

"Attacked by a raccoon."

"Is it serious? My poor Dagmar," Kharalombos said. He suddenly forgot he was pouting.

"There's a lot of blood. It's serious."

He rushed to the office to find out about Dagmar. And he insisted on going to the vet with Gudrun, who was crying.

She thought she might lose Dagmar.

Chapter 9

Overflow

ON THE FOURTH OF JULY WEEKEND, THE SEPTIC TANK backed up. I longed to be back in the kitchen. I might be better off working as a clown in the Bulgarian circus! Aengus was away in West Texas, working for Cameron Wiley's outfit. He was driving huge water trucks. The septic tank companies were closed for the weekend. Every company I called said, "Happy Fourth of July! We'll be working again on Monday. For emergencies, call..."

No one ever answered the emergency numbers. Instead, there were recorded songs. Robert Earl Keen: "The Road Goes on Forever and the Party Never Ends..." The tape played again and again. I slammed down the phone. Another: "Bye-bye, Miss American Pie, drove the Chevy to the levee, but the levee was dry..."

Water covered the bathroom floors and washed over my ankles. Instead of clear toilet water, brown sludge oozed through the entire system. A few toilet bowls were clear, but gross torpedo-shaped turds, swathed in mushy toilet paper, floated in most of the commodes. When I had escaped from Cairo, wearing the full veil, I had gone into the women's bathroom at the airport. The young attendant had wanted to chat about her brother, who was working as a carpenter in Saudi Arabia. I did not want to rebuff her, but if I uttered a word, I'd blow my cover. I giggled and gave her a hefty tip, wobbling out on those narrow yellow heels, which pinched my wide feet.

McKenzie, the fracker's seven-year-old daughter, stood with her hands on her hips. "Hey, mister, have you seen all the doo-doo? I'm gonna call my daddy and you'll be sorry."

I laughed.

A few girls were sitting on top of their bunk beds, playing gin rummy. They were still in their pajamas. One hooted.

An arch voice said, "We are paying a lot of money for this camp experience. Next year, we'll go to Diamond Head!" The little girl had a very unattractive little pug nose with freckles. She was thumbing away on her phone, sending someone a text message.

"Talk to the management."

"You are the management!" Pug Nose said.

Ashley, Kharalombos's friend, pinched her on the butt. "Go jump in the Guadalupe, Megan."

"I'm Gary," I said, holding out my hand.

Ashley smirked. "Oh, Gary, I know who you are!" She adjusted the thin strap of her red halter top. "Kharalombos talks about you all the time!" She winked at me.

"And?"

"He says…" Ashley was playing with the tiny flap of material that covered her supple breast. She stared at me provocatively.

I looked down at my Keds which were covered in mud and sludge. "He says?" They reeked of shit.

"How is he?" she giggled. "Is he going back to Cairo? Did he dump the Jolly Green Giant?"

How to let her down gently? "These are adult problems," I said.

"I'm grown-up. Just as grown-up as you are," Ashley said, sticking out her lip.

I hated to admit that might be true. How could you live more years on this earth but still remain immature? Rachel and I had broken off our engagement because of so many silly fights about the wedding: the napkins, the venue, the bar, the dress, the guest list. I had insisted on a small wedding in a chapel; she had insisted on a wedding in the biggest Presbyterian church in Oklahoma City. We had even quarreled about the honeymoon—she wanted to lie on a beach in Bermuda; I wanted to go birdwatching in the Galápagos.

"Go ahead. Tell me the truth," Ashley said, smiling. I imagined that she had gotten everything she always wanted.

"Well, he…"

"She was so mean to him." Ashley bit her lip. She burst into tears. "I never met anyone like him."

Of course, Kharalombos was an unusual character. But I had gotten to know him better at the camp—how he behaved when he didn't get his way. Of course, I had to admit that I, too, could throw tantrums if I didn't get my way. One day, after one of many fights with Rachel, I had slammed the front door of my apartment so hard it had shattered the glass.

Ashley ran to one of the bunk beds and threw herself on it, bawling. "I loved him. He only liked me for my car."

This sounded almost as melodramatic as an Egyptian movie!

One of the girls playing cards hung upside down from the bunk and said, "Hey, Ashley, why don't you play Go Fish with us?"

McKenzie glared at me and held out a tiny pink phone. "Talk to my daddy now."

"Hello?"

"To whom am I speaking?" a voice said.

"I'm Gary," I said. "The handyman." As the kids would say, "Not!"

The male voice said, "Is it true? Sometimes McKenzie fibs."

"We have a few plumbing problems," I said, countering with another fib. "But Mary Alice will call you later and explain everything."

I handed the diminutive pink phone back to McKenzie.

She stuck her tongue out at me and chanted, "Liar. Liar. Pants on fire."

When I returned to the main office, I read up on septic tanks on various websites. THE DAILY PLUMBER. GO SEPTIC. Really, how hard could it be, for crying out loud? First, identify what is wrong. How did you know? My respect for plumbers increased exponentially. Collapsed pipe. Surface water leaking into system. Pipes leading to septic tank are blocked. Percolation system. What's a soak pit?! Self-help guides were vastly overrated. No way around it, you needed an expert.

Mary Alice marched into the office with her clipboard. Gudrun was lumbering after her. "We need an action plan. Our ship is going down."

"For the first time, I am getting homesick for Germany. Black sausage. Wiener schnitzel." Gudrun said. She was breathing heavily. "Wish I had not bought Clover Flower."

What had made Gudrun see America as Shangri-la? When had she decided to sink her fortune into this camp? And why? What had been the turning point in her life? The rug business in Kazakhstan had gone bust?

"Gary," Mary Alice said, clearing her throat, "when will the septic company be on the scene? You have contacted them?"

I shook my head. "I've called ten companies. All closed. Holiday weekend."

Gudrun shook her red hair, as if she were a rag doll. "What about the American efficiency? We are hearing about this all the time in Germany! The Americans never take holidays."

Mary Alice sighed. "Fourth of July is bigger than Christmas Day."

"Have you seen the bathrooms?" I asked.

Mary Alice said, "Grimsville. We've just inspected all of them. If the inspectors don't get us on kitchen contamination, they'll get us on sanitation." She tapped her pencil on the desk. "Now, let me see. Maybe Azzurro can help us."

"Azzurro? Is he a plumber?" I asked. "He looks like he might know a thing or two about machine guns."

"People have hidden talents."

"I thought you said he was dangerous?"

Mary Alice glared at me. "Don't be a smart aleck. Do you have any better ideas?"

"No," I said. "Of course, as you know, I'm not a certified plumber. I've got a black belt in karate. But that's not very useful right now."

I did not even know the moves in karate! For someone so honest, I was turning into a perpetual liar.

Mary Alice barked, "Gudrun, you and Kharalombos come up with some entertainment for the kids. A belly dancing lesson?"

"*Ja-aa*," Gudrun said. She picked up a doughnut swathed in coconut and studied it as if it were an artifact. "My *Liebchen* is fast asleep now. I'd hate to…"

Mary Alice's voice boomed, "Wake him up! If you want to save your camp. Our ship." Mary Alice pointed the pencil at her. "Our investment."

A little while later, I walked down the dirt road with Mary Alice to the adjoining property. Mary Alice held the clipboard to her chest, tightly. Did she sleep with it? I remembered Boriana's leg intertwining with mine in the poster bed—that was another life!

Mary Alice's phone rang: "Strangers in the night, exchanging glances, wondering in the night, what were the chances?"

Sinatra's melodious voice was suddenly cut off.

"Clover Flower. Mary Alice Bodewell. How can I help you?" Mary Alice answered. She paused. "Did you try everywhere? Are you sure? Okay, thanks, Speedy. Swing by the office, anyway. I'll cut you a check."

Mary Alice's face was grave. "No port-a-potties in the three counties. There's a Willie Nelson concert on the LBJ Ranch."

"Oh," I said. "What does that mean?"

"Our backup plan," Mary Alice said. "We have to get that septic tank fixed."

"I forgot to tell you that Cameron Wiley called when I was inspecting the bathrooms. McKenzie called him."

She waved her hand. "She needs a good spanking. It's not urgent. The ship is adrift."

The garage door was half mast again. Mary Alice poked her head under and shouted, "Azzurro? Yoo-hoo, anybody home?"

A song was playing on a radio: "I hear the train a-comin', it's rolling round the bend, and I ain't see the sunshine since I don't know when…"

With a single push, the door rolled upward.

"Johnny Cash?" Mary Alice said. "Thought he might be listening to….I don't know? José Iglesia? That's quite a collection of cars."

"Aengus and I saw them the other day," I said.

"Why didn't you tell me?"

I shrugged. "Can't keep up. Too many things going on."

Johnny Cash sang, "But I shot a man in Reno just to watch him die. When I hear that whistle blowing, I hang my head and cry…"

"Look," I said, pointing to the cardboard boxes, stacked knee-deep next to the red Louis XV sofa. Funny that such a macho-looking guy would have a formal couch like that: the sofa of an old-fashioned Egyptian parlor. Why would someone ship that all the way back to the US? A real waste of money.

Mary Alice read the Arabic script perfectly with the correct accent. "*Men Mat'haf Baghdad.*"

"You speak Arabic?"

"Arabic and Farsi," Mary Alice said. "Spent ten years in Cairo, running a girls' school."

"Thought you were only in Iran," I said.

"Finished out my career in the church in Cairo. It was relatively tame compared to…" She waved her small hand. "…Iran under the Shah." She pulled out a pair of new dishwashing gloves from her windbreaker pocket. "These were for Sinead."

"What are you doing?"

Mary Alice grunted. "Put them on."

"Why?"

"We don't want any fingerprints on the boxes or the documents. We don't have much time."

"Do you think Azzurro is CIA?" I had become infected by Cairene paranoia. Wasn't that preposterous? Why would he be living here?

"Something nefarious," Mary Alice said, ominously. "I can't put my finger on it."

I put on the long dishwashing gloves. This felt amateurish. Was I living out my fantasy as the detective Philip Marlowe? I pulled the top box off. The flap was loose.

Even though the boxes were labeled in Arabic, the documents inside were in English: *Special Report from the Antiquities Task Force on the Baghdad Museum, Prepared by Lt. Colonel Baldo Durante.* Who was that?

Objects Looted: Named. Objects Recovered: Named. Treasures of Nineveh. The Treasures of Nineveh! Lists and lists of antiquities.

I shook my head. "It doesn't look like anything secret. They were try-ing to recover objects looted from the museum. But why does he have all the documents?"

An engine rumbled nearby. Missing a muffler.

Mary Alice said, "Quick. Put the box back. He's coming."

I heaved the box back against the wall.

The door of the battered lime-green pickup slammed.

Mary Alice stood there, looking stern with her clipboard.

"What the fuck? Are you planning to drive away the Model T?" the man asked. He had beady brown eyes with huge ears, like E.T. "Should I call the cops?"

Mary Alice barked, "Who are you?"

"Hey, lady, I was going to ask you the same thing." His fingers were coated with black grease. He was holding a paper sack, soaked through with oil. His guffaw sounded like a hyena. "Had the munchies."

"I am Mary Alice Bodewell, the owner of the camp next door. We were looking for Azzurro Agua."

"Name's Josiah," he said, but he didn't offer his hand. "Azzurro hired me to work on his cars." He had one roving eye. A mustache with only a few hairs made him look like a feral rat. He was wearing a faded orange tee-shirt that said "Nirvana" and a pair of Levi cutoffs.

"Where's Azzurro?" Mary Alice asked.

"Look," Josiah said. "I'm not his old lady. He told me he was going on a trip. He just asked me to work on his cars while he was away."

"Did he say when he was coming back?"

Josiah coughed. His eyes were red. "A few weeks. I dunno. He didn't give me many details. Who's your pal?"

"Gary," I said.

"What's with the gloves?" he asked. The one good eye winked. I was alarmed. He looked like a creep.

Mary Alice said, "He works in the kitchen. Josiah, have I met you before?"

In the background, Johnny Cash crooned, "I had a friend named Ramblin' Rob who used to steal, gamble, and rob…"

"Dunno. I deliver firewood sometimes," he said. "But don't think you would've met me before. I've been living with my auntie over yonder near Huntsville."

"Let us know when Azzurro comes back," Mary Alice said.

Josiah smiled, but his one eye was focused on the barbecue sandwich. "Sure." He peeled away the greasy paper and wolfed down a bite. "Cal Bob's Smoke Shack," he said, but the words were muffled. His mouth was full of huge chunks of meat.

As we were walking away, Mary Alice said under her breath, "I don't like him one bit. We can't count on him to help us with the tank. Of course, maybe if Azzurro is CIA or doing something secret, he wouldn't be telling anyone where he's going."

"Really?" I asked. "Sounds like that movie, *Syriana*. I don't believe it!" George Clooney is a CIA agent trying to stop illegal arms trafficking in the Middle East. I couldn't remember the rest of the byzantine plot—oil, emirs, arms dealers, Hezbollah, assassination—the threads never came together.

Who would believe Interpol had a warrant out for me? And to add to that, traveling on a false passport.

"Precisely," Mary Alice said, as if she had read my mind. "What better place to hide out. Small country town. Middle of nowhere."

—∞—

We headed back to the office.

Mary Alice tapped her pencil on the huge calendar on the desk. "I'm worried," she said.

Speedy rushed into the office. "I came as soon as I heard."

Mary Alice sighed, gloomily. "Josiah is bad news."

Speedy turned white, as if he had seen a ghost. "Josiah? That *gato*? Maybe it's not the same dude. What's he look like?"

"Seriously, Speedy, how many guys have the name Josiah?" I asked.

"He's down at Azzurro's garage. Working on his cars," Mary Alice said. "Long hair. Big ears. A real hillbilly."

"A wandering eye," I said.

"He's…" Speedy said, as if he were about to say something significant, but then stopped.

Mary Alice looked at me. "You think he's on drugs?"

"Maybe he was stoned," I said. "Or on something else?"

Mary Alice cleared her throat. "We can't worry about Josiah right now. We've got bigger fish to fry. Speedy, know of any plumbers?"

Speedy sat down at the office phone. His hand was shaking. Mary Alice didn't notice. "My cousin, Armando. He's good. But he's a little expensive."

Mary Alice hooted. "Now we're in business. Why didn't you tell me before?"

Part III

A Dagger or Two
in Paradise

Chapter 10

Helicopters Overhead

A HELICOPTER ROARED ABOVE THE CABIN, REMINDING me of the days of the Egyptian revolution. I imagined myself being led away in handcuffs in front of that brat McKenzie, while she shouted, "Loser!" Seriously, Gary! Why did I care what some little brat said about me? Being on the run for so long was making me paranoid! Kharalombos had made up with Gudrun and was sleeping in the big house—Dagmar's almost fatal injury with the raccoon had brought them back together again. They had made up in the vet's office during the hour when Dagmar was getting her stitches.

A police cruiser sped up the road to Azzurro's property, dust in its wake.

Dry twigs snapped under my feet. Walkie-talkies hummed. A beefy-looking blonde cop was securing the garage with a heavy lock. A frail man in his seventies with snow-white hair was sealing off the entire backyard with a cordon of yellow tape. He was not in uniform, but he was wearing plastic baggies on his feet.

Better not to draw attention to myself. But I was dying to know what was going on. I crept back to my cabin and put the sheet over my head—dreamed of a mug of hot, steaming coffee.

Someone was pounding hard on the door. It sounded as if he might kick it in. Aengus was shouting, "Eh, Gary, I know yer in there. Open up or I'm comin' in."

I crawled out of bed and threw open the door.

"Thank God yer alive." I had never seen Aengus this emotional. "Jesus, Mary, and Joseph, yer gave me a right scare."

"Of course, I'm alive," I said. "What are you talking about?"

Aengus said, "I thought I'd get a start on the mowing, like. Before it gets hot. And just as I'm rolling the mower toward the property line, I see the yellow tape. Yer man says, yer not allowed to come any further."

"I saw the police."

Aengus said, "They've found a body."

"What?"

"Someone's been murdered!" Aengus said.

"Murdered!"

"Since the supply cabin was close to the site where they're digging, I thought maybe…"

"You thought it was me?"

"They wouldn't give anything away. Just said we'll be interviewing everyone shortly," Aengus said. "Taking statements."

If I gave a statement, then I would have to give my full legal name. I would have to go underground. But, where? And then, if I were hiding from the police, it would look like I was implicated in a murder. Maybe I could hide in the kitchen again. I couldn't hide forever. The FBI would find me sooner or later—how many counts of fraud? Identity theft. Cyber-terrorism. I would spend the rest of my life in the penitentiary.

"I'd like some coffee," I said. "We can't do any work right now."

"Aye," Aengus said. "I've had my oats, but Sinead'll have to know."

But Sinead had already heard. Letty's cousins from Mexico had fled, afraid the police would tip off Immigration. Dagmar was hanging around the kitchen door, barking, aware of the panic.

A lock of Sinead's red hair had fallen into her eye. She wasn't wearing a hairnet. "Letty, finish up the rashers. I'll be doin' the batter for the cakes."

"There's been a murder up the wee road," Aengus said. "Right under our noses."

Dagmar yapped.

"We know," Sinead said. "Can ya tie on an apron and pitch in, like? Ya can see we're short-handed, luv."

"Where are the ladies?" Aengus asked, surprised. The kitchen was empty except for Sinead and Letty.

"Aaah, what planet are ya on? They're working without their papers, they are." Sinead was vigorously stirring the batter for the pancakes. "Gary, can ya give a hand?"

"Sure," I said, pulling a long white apron off one of the hooks.

"Yogurt. Cereals. In the back." She nodded toward the supply room. "Ya can do it with yer eyes closed. Don't get locked in the wee freezer."

Letty was moving the sizzling, spitting bacon back and forth across the griddle, as if she were in slow motion. "We have the cartels on the border. You wouldn't believe those mean *cabrons*. One time, the sheriff of Laredo didn't even last a day. Those *cabrons* shot him in the face in front of his children. *Watchale*, if you ask me, it's a drug murder."

I remembered the chilling headline: "Creamy Freeze Foreman Dies in Drug-Related Murder." When I was in high school, one of Dad's most trusted foremen, Weddo (Blondie) Silva, was shot in the face by a Mexican drug gang. He was smuggling cocaine that had come from Colombia and traveled through Mexico, up across the border of Texas, and into Oklahoma. When a shipment arrived, Weddo packed the cocaine in vanilla Creamy Freeze ice-cream cartons and used the company trucks to distribute the loot. The drug pickups were tied in with the regular distribution of Creamy Freeze ice cream through several neighboring states. Dad was deeply upset about the murder, and after that, he started to have problems with his blood sugar. Did Dad feel responsible for Weddo's death?

"What a way to start the mornin'. It'll take away yer appetite," Sinead said. "It will. How ya getting' on there, Letty? So you met 'em?"

"Azzurro," Letty said. Her neck wobbled when she giggled. "He was reel buff. He had this little scorpion on the back of his calf."

"Letty," Sinead said. "How da ya know all that, eh? Wadda ya say if Aengus takes over fer ya? Take a rest on the stool. Only fifteen minutes until service."

"Letty, set there on yer stool and tell us about murder in South Texas," Aengus said, as he was tying on the apron. "Give us a tale or two."

Was Aengus making fun of Letty? Surely not. Maybe he was just curious. How could someone's murder be casual entertainment for others?

Letty's fanny was so large that her fat overflowed the stool. "They're not happy stories," she said glumly, holding her chin in one hand. "Especially if you know the *muchachos*."

"Eh," Aengus said, swooping up a number of pieces of bacon with a spatula and putting them on a paper towel to dry. "It's a right pity. So you knew a few?"

Sinead hissed, "Give it a rest." Then she continued on in an artificially sympathetic voice, "We know what yer talking about, Letty. As I mentioned before, there was the kneecappin' in Belfast—ya never could walk again."

"Aye," Aengus said. "Informers just disappeared. Have you heard of The Disappeared?"

Sinead was pouring pancake batter onto the griddle. "I said, 'Give it a rest.'"

"I was just makin' conversation," Aengus said, heaping up the rest of the bacon on a plate. "No need to jump on me back."

"This isn't a tea party, if ya haven't noticed," Sinead said.

I was setting small boxes of cereal on trays. "I always thought you were from Dublin."

Aengus was untying his apron. "The North and proud of it," he said, throwing the apron in the laundry hamper. "Enniskillen."

"Did ya ever meet yer man Azzurro, Gary?" Sinead did not want to talk about where they were from or the past. Did they have something to hide? Maybe I was not the only one with secrets.

"I thought he was a mercenary," I said. "Worked for the Clown Man in Libya."

My hearing had been destroyed by noise pollution in Cairo. That day Azzurro told me what he was doing in Libya, I had not heard exactly what he said. Why was I exaggerating? After living in Egypt for so many years, had I adopted this cultural habit?

Aengus said, "Eh, you don't say. I never had that impression at all. Thought he was a decent enough fella." He lingered at the door. "But maybe he's not the one. Maybe it's someone else who's buried over there."

"Azzurro was reel nice!" Letty shifted her weight on the stool. The legs snapped. Letty went down hard, straight onto the concrete floor, knocking the wind out of her. There were tears in her eyes. "I'm too fat," she said, starting to bawl.

"Ah, never mind, luv," Sinead said. "We all love our food. Don't be so hard on yerself, Letty. It's one of the pleasures in life."

I ran over and tried to pull her up, but she wouldn't budge, as if she were dead weight. She was at least fifty or sixty pounds heavier than me. "Can you give me a hand?"

"Ah, well, there you go," Aengus said, helping me lift her. "Uppsa-daisy."

Dagmar, who had been waiting at the door for her chance, jumped up on the counter and stole a piece of bacon.

"Yaaah, get down off there, ya little gouger," Sinead said, clapping her hands. The dog scurried out the door.

Speedy loped in, breathless. "Sheet, the place next door is crawling with cops."

"Ah, Speedy," Sinead said. "That's old news. Anything more to report?"

Mary Alice stood at the door with her hands behind her back, as if she were a general, surveying a battlefield. "Everything under control?"

Sinead smiled professionally. "Ready for service. You can ring the gong. Gary, would ya do the honors? Yer grand."

Mary Alice said, "Gary, before you go, I've got an announcement for all of you." She cleared her throat. "You've heard by now that Azzurro's property is a crime scene. I've talked with Charlie and they're coming in a few hours to take statements. Everyone stay close. There's nothing to be afraid of."

Really? A murderer on the loose? Federal prison?

Speedy followed me out to the gong.

Afterward, Speedy gestured toward the supply closet. As soon as the door was shut, I whispered, "Do you know Josiah?"

"He's mean," Speedy said. "I'm not kidding."

"How do you know him?" I asked.

Speedy whispered, "This is no fuckin' joke. Swear!"

"Sure," I said.

"No, Gary," he said. "I mean it. The guy is a *cabron*. Would cut off your balls."

I shuddered, tugging at my crotch to make sure they were still there. I thought of Boriana. If I were castrated, would she love me enough to pledge her undying love, for better or for worse, anyway?

"Did he kill somebody?"

Speedy sighed. "Yeah. He served time. Just got out on good behavior. He's been in Huntsville for twenty years."

I remembered he'd said he was "visiting his aunt." "Don't you have capital punishment in Texas?"

Speedy snorted. "New evidence in the case. He was just an accessory."

"Do you think he murdered Azzurro?"

"He could have," Speedy said.

"But why?"

Speedy said, "'Cuz he felt like it. Or maybe he wanted those cars. Or maybe he was on meth. He's a meth-head."

"Speedy, I'm on the run myself."

Speedy looked at me in disbelief. "So you're not undercover! Not part of a sting operation?"

"No," I said. "It's not like that."

Speedy guffawed. "Tax evasion? Cheated the feds?"

"No." I shook my head. "The government thinks I'm a cyber-terrorist."

He howled. "Naaaah. No way! You don't look like a hack!"

I was a little hurt that it seemed so unlikely that I was a computer genius. Why didn't the US government also see that this was a ludicrous accusation?

"Look, I need your help," I said. "I can't use my real identity. If I don't give a statement, it'll look suspicious."

Speedy said, "That's easy. I can get you a false driver's license. Don't think they'll check it. You look like an accountant."

"An accountant?" So much for my idea about myself—the environmental crusader! The radical! The novelist! Although maybe I was more of a scientist than a novelist...after looking at the scraps of *Pure Water*. Was it better to be inconspicuous? Or did I yearn to be "like a tarantula on a slice of angel food cake"?

"Shit, yeah. Doubt they'll run a check on you. Be natural."

"How can you be so sure?"

Speedy winked. "I know how cops think."

"I think you're underestimating them."

Speedy slipped me a false driver's license in less than an hour. Missouri. Expiry Date: 6/2/14. Birthdate: 10/08/60. Gary Joseph Smith. Address: 2011 Park Place, St Louis, Missouri. Height: 5 foot, 3 inches. Sex: M. Color of Eyes: Brown.

Charlie was taking statements in the main office of the camp. He was twirling around confidently in Mary Alice's office chair when I came in. He was the frail man in his seventies whom I had seen at the crime scene. But what I had not seen from afar were his canny blue eyes. He might be a police officer in a very small town, but he was not dumb. He just might run a check on me. At least I might have time to write my second novel in prison!

Charlie scratched his nose. "We have identified the victim as Patrick Quinn. Did you know him?"

"Patrick? He said his name was Azzurro Agua. He just bought the house next door. We heard he paid in cash."

"Where did you meet him?"

"Mary Alice brought him to my cabin. He was looking for his pet goat. It had disappeared."

Charlie's half-glasses were perched precariously on his nose. "You do realize this is a murder investigation. No monkey business. We don't take anything lightly."

"But he did have a pet goat. I've known people who had pet ferrets. Rabbits. Even a diabetic Chihuahua!"

Had Scarlett survived the Egyptian revolution? Or had the neighbors broken down the door when they smelled her corpse? That had happened once in Cairo, when a French woman was murdered by her Egyptian lover.

Charlie licked the lead on his pencil. "I believe we're getting off the track, Mr Smith. What did he look like?"

"To be honest, I thought he looked like a boxer. Or a wrestler. He had two tattoos."

"Where were they?"

"A scorpion on his calf. A bird on his forearm. Think it was a swallow."

"Uh-huh," Charlie said. His pencil scratched noisily on the reporter notepad. "What was he wearing?"

"Shorts. A tee-shirt," I said. "Some kind of muscle shirt. He sure fooled me. I thought he was an Italian by his accent. Do you think he might be connected to the Irish Mob?"

Charlie said, "I am not at liberty to divulge my opinions, Mr Smith. Could you just answer the questions?"

"Of course," I said. "I'm sorry." So he thought I was a crank.

But then he looked at me with real doubt. "When did you see him last?"

"Two weeks ago? When Mary Alice brought him to my cabin."

"Did you notice anything strange about him? Before or after the meeting? Think carefully. The smallest detail could be important."

"He was working in Libya," I said. "But when I asked him what he was doing there, I couldn't hear the answer. I lost my hearing in…"

Don't say it! Forget about Cairo. Forget you ever went there!

"Oh," Charlie said, furiously scribbling. "I see." Then he stopped suddenly. "How did you lose your hearing?"

"Ran a jackhammer on construction sites for years."

He glanced at my hands. "Where are you staying in the camp?"

"My cabin is close to Azzurro's property line. Or Patrick's property line."

Charlie looked me straight in the eye. "Did you see ever see anyone visiting him?"

Should I tell him about the three voices, going up the road to Azzurro's property? If I mentioned Triksky, then I'd have to mention Cairo and my own story. Should I tell him Mary Alice and I were snooping around in Azzurro's garage? No! He would find the Baghdad Museum files soon enough. But my conscience told me I should say something if a man had been murdered.

"I heard voices one evening."

"Yes," Charlie said. "Go on."

"Three men were walking up to his property. It was late at night. About midnight. But I think one of them was Dr Kaiser, Gudrun's cousin. I can't be sure. He has a strong German accent."

Charlie noted it down. "Is there anything else? Did you recognize the other two voices?"

If I told him about Triksky, then I'd have to tell him my story.

"No," I said.

"Are you absolutely sure?" He pursed his lips. His eye was as alert as an eagle's.

"Yes." If I didn't lie confidently, I was history.

"That'll be all, Mr Smith," Charlie said. "Can you send in the next person?"

When I returned from making my statement, Sinead said, "Now, Gary, don't go too far. The Mexican ladies have made themselves scarce, like."

Later in the afternoon, a van marked "Channel 5 San Antonio" was parked at the end of the driveway.

Mary Alice marched into the kitchen, clutching her clipboard. "If any reporters make it this far, you're to say, 'No comment.' It's bad publicity for Clover Flower. Understood?"

Sinead said, "Aye. Gary, can you get me some eggs in the back? I'm thinkin' I might make an orange cake for dinner."

Not more than five minutes later, a reporter stuck her nose into the kitchen, followed by a cameraman. I had to stay incognito—I absolutely could not be on television. A woman with a mike stuck it under Sinead's nose. "There's been a murder not far from here. Did you know the victim?"

Sinead said, "Yer trespassin', ya are. If ya don't get off Clover Flower Camp property, I'll be callin' the police. They're nearby, they are. Now go on, skid-daddle. We've work to do here."

I was in the back, getting eggs for Sinead's orange cake. Just as I was approaching the kitchen, I heard Sinead and Aengus talking in low voices.

"Jesus, Mary, and Joseph, yer getting careless, ya are," Sinead said, in a conspiratorial voice.

Aengus said, "Yanks haven't a clue about Northern Ireland, Sinead. It might as well be the moon. Do ya think it's even on their radar screen?"

"Ya gave me yer word. Yer not still involved, are ya? We're starting a new life here."

Involved in what? What had they left behind?

I coughed.

Sinead said, too cheerfully, "Did ya get the eggs I wanted, Gary? Yer grand."

She took the eggs without looking at me. The evening of the kiss had vanished.

When I entered the kitchen, Aengus had ducked out. Why had they come to this tiny town in central Texas?

Sinead said, "Gary, yer back in the kitchen fer now, like. We've got a right disaster on our hands."

Chapter 11

Fallout

THE TINY TELEVISION NEXT TO THE GRIDDLE WAS blaring. Letty was being interviewed: "*Que chulo*! I met him only once. He had this bird tattoo on his arm." The reporter asked, "Do you think the murderer might still be in the vicinity?" She shrugged. "I don't know. He might be. I'm just a cook."

Then a professional-sounding voice from the television continued: "A man with a mysterious past was murdered and buried on the property next to the famous Clover Flower Camp, a Christian camp for girls. Yesterday, the victim was identified as Captain Patrick Quinn from New York State, who was working on a special unit in Iraq. Local Schulenburg police refused to comment on the ongoing investigation."

"Azzurro wasn't Italian?" I asked, pointing to the television. "His name was Patrick Quinn?"

Sinead pushed a piece of her red hair under her hairnet and kept frying bacon. "We're in the thick of it, we are. Not good fer business, I'd say. Bombs and murders put people off."

Was she thinking of Northern Ireland? And yet we weren't in Northern Ireland, just a peaceful, isolated town in the central Texas hill country. I remembered those frightening days in Cairo, during the Egyptian Revolution, when millions had gone down to the Square.

"Where is everybody?" I asked, bewildered.

"The Mexican cooks are hiding," Sinead said. "We're shorthanded today. Get yer apron on." She had stopped flirting with me, or even calling me "Chancer" or "Rogue."

So I was not the only one hiding from the law! Those poor ladies were trying to earn enough bread to send back to their families in Mexico. What would happen to them?

Mary Alice marched into the kitchen. She barked, "Have you seen Letty? I'd like to wring her neck."

Sinead was frying as fast as she could. "Heard she'd gone to Hollywood, she has. Takin' up a new career!"

Mary Alice waved a white kitchen towel at me. "Is she hiding out in your cabin, Gary?"

"Why would you think that?" I asked.

"Palsy-walsy with Letty and Speedy," Mary Alice said.

What did she know about my friendship with them? Did she know about the barbecue? Surely not that Speedy had provided me with a false driver's license? Saved me from being hauled in by Interpol? Of course, Charlie might call me back for more questioning. But so far, so good. I wasn't sure he bought my story, though.

I tied the long white apron around my waist.

"Eh, Gary," Sinead said, "I know you've no talent for the cooker. Can you put out the cereal?"

Mary Alice was pacing around the kitchen with her hands behind her back. "I specifically told everyone not to talk to reporters. This is not good news for our ship."

Sinead said, "If ya ask me, some folk 'round here lack noggins. Did ya tell her directly, like?"

Sinead was two-faced and knew how to serve the boss. Was that why Speedy and Letty didn't like her? And she slathered her harshness in folk wisdom.

Letty came through the swinging door, buoyant. She was smiling. "I was just on Channel 5. Me! Letty Martinez on TV!"

Sinead rolled her eyes.

Mary Alice boomed, "We know. The phone is ringing off the wall in the office."

Letty was surprised. "Why?"

"The murderer could still be in the vicinity," Mary Alice said. "And I quote. Do you know what kind of panic that has created?"

"But..." Letty started. "She..."

"Don't sass me." Mary Alice said. "Young lady."

"I just..."

"And another thing. If you want to keep your job in this operation, and I assume you do, Charlie wants statements from your cousins."

"But I don't know where they are," Letty said, shrugging.

Mary Alice was tapping her foot. "You will be obstructing a murder investigation. You could go to jail for that."

Letty appealed to me. "What does obstruct mean?"

"They have to tell Charlie what they know," I said.

Letty giggled. "But they were in the kitchen, making hot sauce and tortillas. How stupid. How would they know anything about the murder?"

"It's not a laughing matter," Mary Alice said sternly. "They have to answer the questions of the police like everybody else."

"In Mejico, everyone is scared of the police," Letty said. "*Muy feo.* Very bad. My cousins are scared."

Dad had to testify in the murder trial of Weddo Silva. There was no evidence that he knew anything about Weddo's cocaine-smuggling operation.

"Charlie knows they don't have their papers," Mary Alice said.

Letty's face became hard. "You know the INS! Those *cabrones*. The round-ups."

"I have a deal with Charlie," Mary Alice said.

Was Dad implicated? Did he have a deal with Weddo? I didn't want to believe that. But why? Wasn't he making enough money on the ice cream? When did the desire for money become a sickness?

Letty sneered. "Sure! We've heard it before!"

I had never seen this side of Letty before. But maybe she felt as if Mary Alice had let her down. And she had been demoted when Sinead was hired. Was Mary Alice ruthless? Anything to make a profit?

"Stop tryin' it on there, Letty," Sinead said. "Do what she asks ya."

Mary Alice said, "Let me handle this, Sinead."

"I was just tryin' to help," Sinead said. "We've got no time a'tall before service. Don't know how we're gonna make it before eight. It's already half seven. Gary, do ya have any idea how to make pancakes?"

"Do you have a mix?" I asked.

"Don't believe we do," Sinead said, sighing. "Yer a star. Just pitch in where yer needed."

Dad had inherited Creamy Freeze from his father, a hard-working man of Scottish descent who had wanted to get out of small-time scratch farming during the Dust Bowl. (Of course, we couldn't boast that we had come over on the Mayflower, but we were distantly related to Robert Bruce, King of the Scots, who led the revolt for Scottish independence. Granddaddy Watson determined that there was a more direct link to Alexander Graham Bell, the inventor of the telephone, when he was tracing the family tree in Scotland.) In the beginning, Granddaddy sold ice cream at a soda fountain in downtown Oklahoma City, and then he bought a local truck. Granddaddy Watson had been more interested in civic-minded clubs and projects than in making money—like Rotary Club initiatives to establish college scholarships for Cherokees. Dad had expanded the business: ten, twenty, one hundred trucks. Dad had sold ice cream to schools, churches, and hospitals, expanding his operation to neighboring states. Creamy Freeze became known for its original flavors in bright, attractive cartons, with plastic prizes tucked inside. From the moment I arrived on this earth, I was heir apparent of Creamy Freeze.

"Charlie's down at your place," Mary Alice said. "He'll interview your cousins. He's got a translator. Try to reassure them."

Letty was wiping away her tears. "They can't go back to Mejico. The cartels are reel bad."

Five minutes later, Speedy loped into the kitchen. He pulled the apron off a hook and wrapped it around his waist. "I'm fillin' in for Letty," he said. "They're all wailing at my house. They think they're going to be deported."

I wondered if they had been terrorized like this before? Did overfed officers send them back across the border in trucks?

Sinead sighed. "We've no time a'tall before service. Can you perform miracles? Pancakes?"

Faster than I had ever seen him move, Speedy poured flour and milk into a mixing bowl. He cracked a few eggs. Formed a batter. Poured the batter onto the griddle. Soon there were little stacks of neat, round discs on a plate.

"Eh," Sinead said. "So you know how to cook, after all, ya do? You've been playing us all this time."

"Shoney's," Speedy said. "Had to find a way to pay for my weed in high school. *Comprendes?*"

"Could ya just speak English, like?"

Speedy nodded toward the plate of pancakes. "Charlie suspects me," he whispered. "He said, 'I know you're on probation.' I told him about the goat."

"Probation?" Why was I surprised? He had gotten the fake driver's license very quickly, as if he had a collection in his bedroom drawer.

"Keep your voice down," Speedy said. He gestured toward Sinead.

"For what?"

"A little weed. I stole a car once."

"You stole a car?!"

"Shhh. Once," Speedy said. "I was just a kid. Seventeen."

"Did you mention me?"

Charlie would know I had not told him about the stolen goat. There might be other things I was hiding.

"What's all the whispering about, there, like?" Sinead said. "You're like a bunch of wee schoolgirls. Eh, 'fess up."

The phone rang. "Aye," Sinead said. "Aye." She hung up the phone. "Mary Alice says you're wanted at the main office, like." She added, "To answer the phone."

When I arrived at the office, Gudrun and Mary Alice were sitting at the mahogany desk poring over their insurance agreement. They were both wearing their khaki Bermuda shorts with long red knee socks. They were also wearing their Indian headdresses. Reader half-glasses were perched on their noses. Gudrun's were purple.

Mary Alice was very grim. "Gary, please cover the phone."

I sat in the swivel chair. The same chair that Charlie had sat in yesterday. They still had a plain, black, old-fashioned telephone with a rotary dial. I really hoped he didn't call me back for more questioning.

"A word of advice," Mary Alice said. "Try to answer neutrally. Have you ever answered phones before?"

"Domino's and Creamy Freeze. That's it!"

"It's more money than the cost of a pizza or an ice cream. It's five grand for a session. We're not committing to refunds or half-refunds yet," Mary Alice said. "Say something, like, we're looking into the matter. Whatever they say, be polite."

"Whatever you do, Gary, don't tell them to jump into the river." Gudrun guffawed. "You might feel like it. They always tell me how bad my English is, *aaach*. I would like to see them, speaking German in a small village in the Black Forest."

"Look, Gudrun," Mary Alice said, "it's in the fine print." Mary Alice was holding a magnifying glass over the document. She read aloud, "Only cancellations due to natural disasters are covered: flood, snowstorms, mudflow, wildfire, heat waves, earthquake, volcanoes, and hurricanes. Cancellations due to allergies caused by rabid dogs, snakes, wasps, bees, scorpions are also covered."

"Gary, can you read this?" Mary Alice said, sliding the paper toward me.

The words were blurry. It was even smaller than the writing in Arabic newspapers. I pulled my reading glasses out of my pocket. In the tiniest print, which even an ant could not see, was written: "Cancellations due to man-made error or infractions, like an industrial accident (e.g., being run over by a forklift or a bulldozer) or malicious behavior which causes harm and could have been prevented (e.g., first-degree murder near the premises of the camp), are not covered by the policy. The insured is obliged to cover his own losses. Claims of this kind will *never* be considered. No exceptions."

Mary Alice muttered under her breath, "Lord." She staggered backward from the desk and sank into the sofa. Staring up at the ceiling as if it were a dark sky, she said, "How did I miss it? I could have sworn I had gone over it with a fine-toothed comb."

Gudrun plopped down beside her, rueful. "*Aaaccch*," Gudrun said. "This is like the *Titanic*. Worse than our problems last year. I think I want to sell and go back to Berlin. Forget about America."

Mary Alice looked as if she might cry. "You might not have a dime left." I had never seen Mary Alice so shaken.

Dad was shaken when he sold Creamy Freeze to Velvet Red Bucket—he waved the check at me. "I have to clear out my office in a week. That's the deal." He had made a bundle, but he had lost his life's work—and joy.

The phone rang. "Clover Flower Girls' Camp. How can I help you?" I swiveled in the chair, as if I were in charge.

"Is my daughter's cabin near the crime scene? The property line of the man who was murdered?"

"Rest assured," I said. "Your daughter is safe. She's having her breakfast."

"She's not answering her cell phone," the voice said.

"Cell phones are not allowed at Clover Flower," I said. "It's listed in the rule book which we handed out at orientation."

"What an asinine rule! Are you the one who thought up that stupid rule? You know what you can do with your rule book?"

"Thank you for calling!" I said, hanging up.

The phone rang again. "Clover Flower."

A gravelly baritone voice said, "Just what kind of operation are you running down there? We thought it was a wholesome Christian camp. We want a full refund or we'll sue!"

"We're looking into the matter. Thank you for calling!" I said.

"I'm driving over from Houston today to pick up my granddaughter. Have you closed the camp yet?"

"No, sir, we are still open," I said.

"Well, you oughta close if your outfit is the scene of a crime."

"Thank you for…"

Kharalombos trudged in with three sacks of doughnuts from Dunkin' Donuts. Dagmar followed him. Gudrun waved to him. Dagmar yapped.

"I want to talk to Mary Alice *now*," a voice on the phone said.

"My *Liebchen*, can you bring me a cruller? The coconut caramel," Gudrun said.

"Mary Alice has just stepped out. She will return your call shortly," I said.

"I'm Cameron Wiley, the CEO of Frackers International, based in Houston. I'd appreciate it if you put Mary Alice on the line. I don't have time for the runaround. I have a board meeting in fifteen minutes."

"Mary Alice," I said, covering the mouthpiece. "It's Mr Wiley from Frackers International."

Mary Alice had sunk so low into the couch that it was difficult for her to get up. She didn't exactly run to the phone.

I handed her the receiver.

"Hello, Cameron," Mary Alice said. "Everything is under control. Well, yes, it's a problem. Uh-huh. Yes. McKenzie is fine. We're cooperating with the police."

I peeked out the glass door. A convoy of expensive cars was just pulling into the circular driveway.

The door flew open. It was windy outside. A number of parents trooped in.

Amazingly, Mary Alice regained her composure. "All hands on," she said. "Gary, keep answering the phone."

She and Gudrun greeted the parents cordially, offering them coffee and doughnuts. The anorexic mothers might be tempted by good coffee. Instead of Nescafé, they had splurged on Lavazza Hazel—Italian coffee.

Mary Alice's voice boomed, "I can assure you that your children are safe. They are having breakfast right now. If you like, we can all go down to the camp."

A woman teetered in the door on Roman sandals with heels like spikes. She was wearing huge sunglasses and was dressed like a porn star: black leather pants too hot for the climate and a flimsy white chemise—really an undershirt. Nipples the size of silver dollars were visible through the transparent top. Her hair had been dyed pink on one side; the other side was peroxide blonde. Besides the diamond piercing in her nose, she had even more piercings in her ears than she had had before.

Some of the other mothers, in their tasteful, colored, sleeveless sundresses and rhinestone sandals, gaped at her. One murmured, "There was an article about her in *Texas Monthly*. Did you read her novel, *The Last Roller-Coaster Ride*?"

She stood with her hands on her hips, facing Mary Alice and Gudrun. "Are you ladies the captains of this rodeo? Our niece is in imminent danger."

Mary Alice cleared her throat. "She's not in any danger. Would you like a cup of freshly brewed Italian coffee to start this fine summer morning?"

One of the mothers said, "We've come for a refund. To take our babies home."

Another echoed, "Yes! We don't want anything to happen to our children if you have a serial killer on the loose!"

Bill was right behind Rose. "Baby, maybe you'd better cool it and find out the whole story."

But Rose ignored him and stood at the doughnut table. "You!" Rose stood in front of Kharalombos and tapped her long red fingernails on his chest. "You didn't take care of my baby like you said you would! Do you know how much money it cost us to get her out of Egypt? Thousands. Thousands. Where's your confederate?"

Kharalombos shrank back. *"Mesh fahim.* Madam, can you kindly take your hands off of me. You did not understand the circumstances."

"Why, I never." Rose set a small wicker basket on the ground. A tiny snout peeked out.

An anorexic blonde in a pink sundress exclaimed, "Were you in Egypt during the Revolution? How interesting."

Bill was saying, "I posted something about our experiences on my blog if you're interested in reading about the revolution. Kharalombos is the one you want to talk to. He's Egyptian."

"It's a miracle Scarlett O'Hara is still alive," Rose said. Scarlett yapped. Dagmar, who was sitting on a chair next to Kharalombos, growled.

"Clover Flower," I said mechanically into the phone. I was dying to escape this unpleasant chore.

Bill got his information from CNN's Prue Scoop and posted it on his blog.

A voice on the phone said: "I am gonna sue you for every penny you're worth if something happens to my daughter Charlene. I promise you, mister. You won't even have a pot to pee in."

"Uh-huh," I said. "Have a nice day!" I left the phone slightly off the cradle. Take that!

Bill extended his hand across the desk. "Buddy, we meet again."

"Hello, Bill," I said, trying to extract myself from his crippling handshake. "I trust you got home safely from Cyprus." Planes leaving Egypt during the revolution had gone first to Cyprus. From there, travelers had to make their own arrangements to get to the US

"Sure thing. We landed on our feet. Got to Atlanta and then on in to Alabama. I'm a visiting professor at the University of Texas this fall. And my book on torture just came out. Got good reviews. Of course, George W. started all those initiatives after 9/11 that violate human rights. Waterboarding. Where you dunk the victim's face in…"

The room went quiet for a minute.

One of the fathers huffed, "Yes, sir, we've got to protect our way of life from terrorists." He was wearing a white oxford-cloth shirt, light khaki pants, and leather Topsiders. Did this bland outfit define the "American way of life?"

Could anyone tell, from the way I looked in my Indian headdress and camp uniform, that I was a committed environmentalist who wanted to protect our natural world? A staunch member of United Socialists of America? Or an aspiring novelist? What did writers look like? Did clothes make the man? Or woman, if you wanted to be politically correct. Of course, a man could also pass for a woman, as I had discovered when I successfully swathed myself in black cloth and donned yellow high heels.

Gudrun sat down heavily on the couch. "*Aaacch*," she said. "Have you ever visited the Egypt, ladies and gentleman? You never met nicer, goot people, who would give you their last disc of bread. And the Pyramids are something out of this world! *Ja-aa*. My only regret was that the Nile cruise was canceled. Maybe next year if I…"

The parents clustered around Gudrun. One gushed, "I've always wanted to take a Nile cruise. When do you think it will be safe to travel there again?"

"Well, getting Scarlett shipped to Alabama was a cause of some concern and anguish, as you can imagine," Bill was saying. "But we've got to count our blessings. It was nothing like the time I left Saigon before it fell…"

Rose caught my eye. Her eyes narrowed, as if she were looking at a cockroach.

"Anyhow, we appreciate everything," Bill said, gesturing with his large hands. The knuckles looked swollen. "You tried."

Rose snorted. "What in the Sam Hill are you talkin' about? Gary promised to give Scarlett her insulin shots and he reneged on the deal. Plain and simple!" She pointed a red fingernail at me. "Left Scarlett to *rot!*"

"I am really sorry, Rose," I said. Once in graduate school in New Haven, I had offered to pet-sit for the chair of the chemistry department. While I was putting a leash on one of the dogs, the cat, Marie Curie, escaped through the door and was run over in front of my very eyes. Telling the owner had been excruciating, especially since she was on my dissertation committee.

"Baby," Bill said. "No need to get madder than a wet hen. Maybe you don't have the full story."

"Well," I said. "Bill's right. That's not the full story."

Could I tell her the real story? We had abandoned Scarlett because we thought Gudrun needed to be rescued and saw ourselves as Knights of the Round Table! We were starring in a pharaonic reality television show!

"Our neighbors told us you just disappeared into thin air!" she said, snapping her fingers. "That you'd sold some of the animals to a pet shop. You even ate one!"

"I wasn't a bad vet," I said. "Considering."

She was right to blame me. On the other hand, we had intended to return. But were good intentions ever enough?

"Baby, I told you there was a logical explanation. You don't need to go believin' every rumor you hear. You're puttin' Gary on the spot."

"How can this man be trusted with my niece? He can't even be trusted with animals! We're pulling my niece out of this godforsaken camp," Rose said. "This hellhole."

"Well, now, Rose," Bill said, placing his hand on her shoulder. "Don't go off like a pistol half-cocked."

Mary Alice cleared her throat. "We can bring her up to the main office," she said. "Don't think she'll want to go home, though. She's having a ball." She frowned and spoke into her walkie-talkie, "Handyman on deck. Handyman on deck. Can you bring Miss Leigh to the front office?"

"What's the situation in Egypt now?" a mother asked Kharalombos. "Is it getting any better?"

Before Kharalombos could answer, Bill jumped in. "Military junta. More violations of human rights. God willin' and the creek don't rise, there won't be any real change with the army in charge. The whole region is in a state of chaos. Did you hear what happened today in Libya? The Clown Man was hunted down by his own people and murdered in cold blood. They found him hiding in a ditch."

It sounded bad. I wondered what had happened to the Big Man. And what would happen with the New General who had taken over in Egypt? Would inequities be redressed? Would Egyptian citizens find the justice they dreamed of? Bread, Dignity, Freedom, Social Justice.

"They say the Big Man from Egypt and his family have also been murdered," Bill said, casually. "But you should ask Kharalombos. He would probably have the latest news on Egypt. What's happening there, bud?"

"*La'. La',*" Kharalombos said, but could say no more. "*Ya rabbi. Ya rabbi.*" He looked as if might start sobbing. He had never even seen his son, Nunu.

Could it be true that the Big Man and his family had been killed? Every day brought turbulent news from Tunisia, Egypt, and Libya—they were calling it "The Arab Spring." Citizens were demanding freedom and social justice. And there were even rumblings in Syria now.

"Well, good riddance, I say," Rose said. "All those dictators in the Middle East should be taken out and shot. Put that in your pipe, darlin', and smoke it."

"Rose, baby," Bill said. "How can you say that? That's not the kind of principles liberal democracies are based on."

"I don't give a fat rat's ass if it's not politically correct," Rose said. "They're monsters. What goes 'round, comes 'round. They deserve whatever they get."

I didn't exactly agree with her—but it was hard to sympathize with the Big Men and their thugs, who were responsible for blood-curdling atrocities. Even though the Clown Man wore a jester outfit and made outlandish, wacky statements that were parodied in the Arabic newspapers, he was still dangerous. Thousands in his country were chained up in dark, underground prisons that were no different than medieval dungeons out of an Alexandre Dumas novel.

Gudrun patted a place on the couch. "Rose, *Liebchen*," she said. "Why don't you sit down here while you wait for your niece? Do you like the milk in your coffee? Kharalombos…"

But Kharalombos was bawling in the bathroom. He would never cry in front of women.

Rose waved at me. "I take it black." If I had had any strychnine, I would have put it in her coffee.

"There you go," I said, handing Rose a steaming cup.

One of the mothers said, "Aren't you Rose Leigh? Didn't you just have a novel published? You were the featured writer at the Austin Writers' Festival."

Rose flopped onto the sofa, as if she were thirteen. "That's right. My new novel is called *Murder among the Serpents.*"

Bill beamed. "I'm real proud of her. She persevered when she was in Cairo. It wasn't an easy place to write, with a revolution and all. *Publishers Weekly* said, 'Even more brilliant than her first.'"

He didn't mention that he was hiding the Maker's Mark from her. Keeping hysteria and madness at bay.

"Well, darlin'," Rose said, without any further prompting, "it's a novel about a preacher who murders his wife with a rattlesnake. The Church with Signs Following believes in the letter of the law, rather than the spirit. All cock 'n' bull. If you raise the snake to the sky and he doesn't bite you, it's proof of your faith. God will save you from harm."

Was Bill ever tempted to get rid of her?

The mothers stared at her with their mouths agape.

Gudrun said, "It sounds very exotic." Then she laughed. "I can't imagine the Lutherans doing that in our church. So strange. What is the cock 'n' bull?"

"A lot of hooey," Rose said.

Gudrun's face was blank.

Rose turned toward me. "By the way, did you find your novel, *Pure Water*? You had all that time during the Revolution to search for it. Looking under my bed. Tell me, what did you find? Anything to tit-till-ate you?"

How did she know? Or was she bluffing?

"I didn't know you were a writer," Mary Alice said, biting into a chocolate-glazed doughnut. "You're a man of many talents."

"It's only a matter of time before my agent sells it. I've written a thriller on a hot topic," I said. "Water in Egypt."

I was forced to admit that the manuscript was foul and stank to high heaven! Bill was staring at the doughnuts. Was he embarrassed that they had torn the manuscript up and used it for scrap paper? I imagined Rose reading it to Bill in bed after a bondage session using the handcuffs, or maybe even the whip: "Listen to this, darlin': 'I was a man on a mission. I would get to the bottom of all the lies about clean water. I was neat, shaved, and sober, and I hailed a black and white taxi in Cairo. The driver opened the door with a screwdriver.'"

Rose laughed lightly. "Well, I wrote three novels before I ever published anything. Don't despair! Don't despair! Of course, after *The Last Roller Coaster Ride*, I was picked up by Huff & Huff as part of their 'Emerging Voices from the South' series when I was just thirty-five."

"Rose," Bill said, clearing his throat, "I think you might be pourin' it on a tad thick now."

Gudrun looked at me. "I am getting a headache. Is there any Tylenol in the first-aid kit, Gary? Do you understand what they are saying?"

"More or less." I sympathized with her. All those years of missing jokes or idiomatic expressions in Arabic could throw you off in conversation. And then people raced on to the next topic.

An anorexic woman in a pink sundress asked, "I have always wanted to write. Do you offer workshops?"

Rose tapped her false fingernails impatiently on the coffee table. She said, "Don't believe in 'em. You either have the talent or you don't. I'm tellin' ya, honey, you can't squeeze blood from a stone."

The anorexic woman looked crestfallen. "But didn't you?"

"I was hailed as a prodigy by the late Truman Capote," Rose said, continuing to tap her fingernails on the coffee table. "The MFA. from Alabama was irrelevant."

"Well." Mary Alice cleared her throat. "There is the parable of the talents, if you know your scripture. Would any of you like to see your children? They're in the art room now. They're doing collage today."

Mary Alice led the parents away. It was a parable I should have absorbed—it would have saved me years and years of channeling my energy in the wrong direction.

"Hold down the fort, Gary. You've been a great help," Mary Alice called from the open door. The wind blew the insurance agreement off the desk. "The phone's stopped ringing. That's a good sign." She gave me a thumbs-up.

The parents of Clover Flower were much worse than customers at Creamy Freeze or Domino's. I couldn't take much more—thought I might go postal. Good that they didn't have any pistols lying around.

Gudrun huffed, trying to get up. "*Aaach*, where is my *Liebchen*? My bon-bon. Where has he gone? Something is wrong."

Dagmar was lying in front of the bathroom door, looking glum, her head resting on her paws.

A few minutes later, Aengus came in, followed by Ashley. He wiped his muddy boots on the mat before coming into the office.

The preppy-looking father had not followed the other mothers, who had gone with Mary Alice. He and Bill, who both had sizeable paunches, were surveying the wide selection of doughnuts on the table. "Are you working on a new book?"

"Sure am," Bill said, taking a bite out of a doughnut. "Informers in the IRA. Fascinating underworld." A few traces of powdered sugar were smudged on his nose.

"Here she is," Aengus said. "Delivered, safe and sound, she is." His blonde hair had been tousled by the wind.

Rose picked up the straw basket. "We've come to rescue you from imminent danger and mayhem," she said. "Go pack your bag."

Ashley rolled her eyes. "What are *you* talking about, Aunt Rose? I am, like, just about to win the archery competition. I was told there was an emergency."

"I am talkin' about the murder next door," Rose said.

"That," Ashley said, "has nothing to do with us. As usual, you are overreacting. Blowing things way out of proportion, like *WAY* out of proportion."

"Don't give me any lip," Rose said. "Go on and get your things packed. It's for your own good."

Gudrun knocked on the bathroom door. "Kharalombos. Open up. Are you in there? You didn't drown in the toilet? *Nein. Nein.*"

Dagmar whined. "Dagmar, what is wrong with my *Liebchen?*" She bent down to pet Dagmar. "My back!" Gudrun had difficulty standing up straight again. She wandered to the doughnut table and picked up a cruller. "The crullers are the best. Gary, did you have your breakfast?"

Gudrun held up a doughnut, but I declined. If I didn't restrain myself, I would soon turn into a butterball.

Bill was saying, "Anyone who informed just disappeared. Or they were eventually murdered. Tribal punishment."

Gudrun said, "We have some Irish people working at our camp. I am not sure where they are from. Aengus, where are you from in Ireland? This man is writing a book about the Irish Republican Army."

Aengus blanched. He held out his hand. "My pleasure," he said. "They call it The Troubles. But we're from Dublin and remote from all that, like. Didn't affect us so much, aye. Everything's changed since the Good Friday Agreement."

Why was he lying? What had he said about his father? Had "raised him on hate."

"I'd love to interview you if you've got any free time," Bill said.

"Eh," Aengus said. "Maybe later. With the recent trouble here, we're a bit short-handed, if ya know what I mean. We've lost all our cooks, we have. Gary, yer wanted in the kitchen."

"I can't be in two places at the same time. I'm supposed to be answering the phone."

"Phones don't seem to be a-ringin'," Aengus said. He couldn't get away fast enough. "It's quiet enough here, it is."

Ashley begged, "Please, Uncle Bill. I'm in charge of the camp closing. Head of the Comanches. We have a special ceremony."

"Well," Bill said, "I don't see why not. We just came to see if you were all right. Your father wanted us to make sure."

Rose was furious. "She's not your niece. I'm the one in charge. Why are you pullin' the rug out from under me?"

Bill raised his hands. "What are you talking about? There's no imminent danger. You're as nervous as a long-tailed cat in a room full of rocking chairs!"

The bathroom door finally opened.

As soon as she saw Kharalombos, Ashley simpered. "I'm perfectly adult. Aren't I, Kharalombos?" A strap of her tank top fell off her shoulder.

"Ashley Leigh," Rose hissed. "That dog won't hunt. You don't think I know you're tryin' it on?" Had someone told her that Ashley was going around with Kharalombos?

Ashley said, "Bitch. You can't make me! I have my car. And my credit card."

Rose's lip quivered. She looked like she might cry. For all of her tough talk, she was vulnerable.

"Now," Bill said. "Ashley, that is no way to talk to your aunt. We drove all the way over here from Austin because we care about you. Apologize right now."

"Will not," Ashley said. "I meant every freckin' word." Ashley stood with her hands on her hips. She was wearing very short shorts.

Kharalombos stared at the group as if we were from another world. His eyes were red.

Gudrun went up to him and pinched his cheek. "My *Liebchen*, what is it? You look so sad."

"*Allah yerhamoh,*" he said, shaking his head. "Nunu. Nunu," he said, sobbing.

Gudrun shook her head. "Nunu? Nunu? Who is that?"

"You won't talk to me that way," Rose said, wiping a tear from her eye with the back of her hand. "Ashley Ann Rosemary Taylor Leigh, I took care of you since the time you were a tot. This is just unacceptable."

Ashley said, "Look, Aunt Rose, it's not my problem your biological clock has run out!"

I remembered one of my fights with Rachel—she was shouting at me, "Why didn't you tell me from the beginning that you didn't want kids?"

"Missy, do you want me to tan your hide?" Bill said. "That's Ee-nough."

Scarlett started yapping. Dagmar answered back. Soon the office was drowning in a cacophony of barking.

"I think it's best we be on our way. Scoot on down the road," Bill said. "Come on, now, hon."

Gudrun appealed to me. "What happened to my *Liebchen?* Did someone die? Do you know? Who is the Nunu? You keep talking about the Nunu."

"Kharalombos has just had some bad news. He will have to tell you himself," I said.

"*Aacch,*" Gudrun said to Rose and Bill. "If you'll excuse me, this is a situation."

Bill took Rose by the arm. "We were just leaving." Scarlett wouldn't stop barking.

Chapter 12

Summoned

DR KLAUS AND CAMERON WILEY WERE COMING TO Schulenburg to give their statements to Charlie. The four cooks from Mexico had quit and were on a Greyhound bus headed for the Rio Grande Valley. They had been promised work in the kitchen at the Brownsville country club.

At least they had escaped a humiliating roundup by the INS. The border area was more porous, and closer to home. Mexicans went back and forth between the two countries all the time.

"We're short-handed for good," Sinead said. "They cleared out after lunch. I wish them well, I do. We've only a few more weeks to the end, so we have. Our numbers are down."

Speedy was breathless. "There's a truck marked US Army at the bottom of the road. From Fort Hood. They're carrying boxes out of Azzurro's garage. That dude was in deep."

"The documents from the Baghdad Museum," I said. I wish I had investigated further. Objects Looted. Objects Recovered. If Azzurro, or Patrick, or whatever his name was, had absconded with any loot, just where was it? Was it still stashed in his garage? Or buried in his back yard? In the septic tank?

"*Amigo,*" Speedy said, "how do you know?"

Sinead put a lock of red hair behind her ear. "I'd say Chancer has plenty of secrets, he does. What else are ya keepin' from us?" She winked at me.

Why was she flirting with me now? Did she still want...?

"Mary Alice and I poked our noses in his garage when the septic tank went kaput. We saw the boxes. That's all. Clearly marked. We were looking for Azzurro. Thought he might help us fix the septic tank."

"The two of yous are here for the *craic* or you've come to work?" Sinead said, handing me a knife. Was she annoyed that I ignored her?

"What are you making?" I asked.

"Haven't a clue, Gary. Can't get excited. We've visitors tonight."

"What am I supposed to chop if you haven't made up yer mind?" I didn't want to play any more games.

"By the time ya put on yer hairnet, I'll know. Put on the bloody hairnet before Mary Alice turns up."

I rummaged around in the drawer. There were very few hairnets left, and the elastic was stretched out on the ones that were there. Why would anyone steal hairnets? One could understand someone pilfering bacon or a roast, but cheap, ugly hairnets? Were they reselling them somewhere?

Mary Alice marched in. "The situation is still tenable, if we don't have any more disasters. We've only had seventy campers withdraw."

Sinead nodded to the bowl full of zucchini. "We'll be having a frittata with courgettes. Get to it. Thin slices. Where's yer woman, Speedy?"

"I thought she was here," Speedy said.

"Can ya give a hand?" Sinead said. "Now we know ya can cook."

Speedy poured himself a cup of coffee and leaned against the counter. "I'm weeding in the front yard. Aengus's orders." He folded his arms.

"Yer always tryin' it on," Sinead said. "He's got a machine for that, he does. In America, they call it a Weed Eater."

Speedy grabbed a cupcake iced with chocolate frosting on his way out. "Later," he said, waving to me.

"He's a right sod," Sinead said. "Worthless. Dunno what Letty sees in 'im.'"

"He's not a bad guy." If he had not come up with the false driver's license, I would be history. I wondered if he had stolen more than one car. Surely he had not done something worse?

Mary Alice's voice boomed, "Just where is the second cook in command?"

Sinead shrugged. "Haven't a clue." Sinead was pouring cream into a big bowl and mixing it with eggs. "Haven't a clue," she muttered again, while she lugged a huge frying pan out of the cupboard.

Letty was huffing when she came into the kitchen, as if she had been running. "Sorry I'm late. I had to go back to the bus station because Maria forgot her purse."

"I told you at least ten times," Mary Alice said, "that Charlie wouldn't tip off the INS. Why did you find them other jobs?"

"You don't know the INS like we do. Those *pendejos* would never feel bad putting you on a plane," Letty said. "Anyway, they were spooked. One of them said she saw a ghost."

"Azzurro's ghost?" Mary Alice said. "I never heard such a foolish thing. That's ridiculous!"

"Aye," Sinead said. "Once I was workin' in a house in Monaghan County. A house for artists. And one of the rooms was haunted by a spirit. Her name was Miss Bunty Worby, it was. The companion of Lady Guthrie's grandmother. She wanted to be buried in England, but they never let her go home. Spirits have to be put to rest, they have. One of the writers said they felt weird energy in the room. Like a whoosh."

Mary Alice said, "You're pulling my leg."

"Dead serious," Sinead said. "That's the real reason the ladies left, I'd say. A ghost."

Mary Alice snorted. "I didn't expect that from you, Sinead," she said. "Dr Klaus and Cameron Wiley are coming for dinner. What are you making?"

Sinead really had the most natural, charming smile. But was she as straightforward as she pretended to be? Would I dump Boriana if I had a chance with Sinead? Of course, this was just an infatuation! She was sexy. What was happening with Boriana's divorce papers? I was too easily distracted.

"All fresh. Light food for summer. Frittatta with courgettes and parmesan, salad with rocket, fruit salad. Letty, can you get on with the mangos, like? Gary's chopping the courgettes, so he is. How ya doin' there, Gary? You've gone quiet."

"Are the US military trucks still out there?"

"There's a convoy," Mary Alice said. "Seems a bit excessive for four cardboard boxes. Overkill. But that's the US army. They could have sent a little jeep over."

"Does Charlie think it's related to the murder?" I asked.

Mary Alice cleared her throat. "Charlie is a professional. He never breaches the code of confidentiality. He hasn't discussed the case with me."

But he had involved her in the cooks' statements.

The kitchen door swung open wide. Gudrun called out, "Has anyone seen my *Liebchen?* Is he here?"

Dagmar followed her into the kitchen.

We all shook our heads.

"Out with the gouger. The health inspector will flatten us," Sinead called out.

Mary Alice clapped her hands. "Shoo, shoo," she said, nudging the dog toward the door.

Beads of sweat covered Gudrun's forehead. She wiped her brow with a pink and green tie-dyed handkerchief. "So, you always knew Nunu belonged to Kharalombos? All that time. Even in Egypt. I was just a toy?"

Mary Alice was surprised. "The Big Man's grandson. Does everyone know but us? Did you know, Sinead?"

"Of course you're not a toy," I said, wiping my hands on my apron. "It was love at first sight when he saw you at the airport in Cairo."

I had fallen for Boriana the day she had come to the Knights Templar Museum in Malta. I couldn't resist her mischievous brown eyes, or her hearty, inimitable laugh. So I had also been star-struck, like Kharalombos with Gudrun. But would I follow through this time?

"Seen a fair bit in my life," Sinead said. "Aye, nothing surprises me in this world."

"He's never even seen Nunu," I said. "Yasmine was taken away to Morocco. And now they've all been murdered."

What did Gudrun want? Yasmine and the baby were gone. Kharalombos had not seen her for more than two years.

"They're worse than the cartels," Letty said, shaking her head. She was peeling a mango very slowly. "Although that is real hard to imagine, anyone meaner than the cartels. Maybe those terrorists on 9/11."

Sinead shrugged. "At this rate, you might as well grow the mangoes."

Gudrun was distraught. "Men are no good. I am losing my language. My first husband was a devoted Dadda for seventeen years and then one day he just ran away with his young secretary."

"It's not the same story," I said. Why did women always seize on this kind of anecdote and then generalize? All men were not bastards. Although I hadn't tried very hard to resist my attraction for Sinead!

The air crackled. A voice said, "Over," Mary Alice said, "And out."

Aengus's voice boomed through the walkie-talkie. "Eh," Aengus said. "Think ya better know that Ashley's car's gone missing. And Kharalombos didn't show up to his dance class."

Mary Alice gave me a reproachful look, as if I were the enemy. Did she know about my little tryst with Sinead? She took Gudrun by the arm. "We've got to get back to headquarters."

When I rang the gong outside at dinner, I noticed that our numbers had gone down even more significantly. The picnic tables were half full. We had made way too much salad and fruit salad—which would probably get thrown out. At the last minute, Sinead had made homemade ice cream with nuggets of white chocolate and raspberries. "The wee ones always prefer ice cream if they can get it," she said.

I was tempted to promote my Dad's old company, Creamy Freeze, now Velvet Red Bucket, but then decided to let it go.

Mary Alice's brow was furrowed. "We've lost another fifty children," she said. "I really hope we don't have to declare Chapter 11."

Mary Alice was strolling around the picnic tables with her hands behind her back. "After the prayer, tell the children to line up, Gary. They're always hungry after swimming."

The children lined up. Mary Alice gestured to me, murmuring, "Does Kharalombos have a bad reputation? We might be looking at another lawsuit."

"They haven't returned?"

Mary Alice shook her head. She was in a dark mood. "I'm prepared for the worst," she said. "Keep this to yourself, Gary. I don't want Gudrun to worry. She has enough on her plate. Dr Klaus gave his statement today to Charlie."

"It's not what you think," I said. "Kharalombos is too sad and depressed to do anything like that. He probably asked Ashley to drive him somewhere. You forget, he doesn't know how to drive."

"Let's hope you're right," Mary Alice said. "Ashley is under seventeen. Still a minor. Could be considered statutory rape."

I shook my head. "He's thinking about Yasmine and Nunu."

"Then why did he go off with that young girl?" Mary Alice said. "You'll have to fib. Play for time."

Rose and Bill were making their way toward us. Bill waved.

"Who invited them?" I asked.

"It was my bright idea. They said they were staying in Fredericksburg last night. I wanted to reassure them about Ashley," Mary Alice said.

Rose was wearing a red halter top and white short shorts. She teetered in the same spiky Roman sandals.

"Lord," Mary Alice said. "That's some outfit. Did she go around Cairo like that? We had a strict dress code when I ran the school there. Nylons. Dresses."

But Bill was bearing down on us before I could answer. He shook my hand so firmly that it hurt. "Hello, buddy, how's the farm?" He was wearing a baseball cap, a tee-shirt that said "The Crimson Tide," and ragged Levi cutoffs.

"I've been helping out in the kitchen today," I said.

Rose stared past me at a huge oak tree.

"Hope you're in better spirits today?" Mary Alice said, addressing Rose.

Rose folded her arms. "You just don't know."

Bill frowned. "Rose," he said. "That's water under the bridge now. We agreed that it wouldn't spoil our trip."

Her mouth was turned down in a tight frown. "I don't think I'll ever recover."

What had happened? She acted as if her mother had died. I missed my mother's voice—how much longer could I put off calling her?

"Pssshaw," Bill said. "Come on, now, gimme some sugar." Bill turned his cheek toward her.

"Can it," she said, teetering off toward the oak tree. There was a wooden swing hanging from one of the high branches.

"She could make a preacher cuss," Bill said. "God love 'er."

"I'm needed in the kitchen," I said. Did I really care why Rose was in a sour mood? How did he live with all these tantrums?

Mary Alice gave me a significant look.

Bill was saying to Mary Alice, "Well, she's used to livin' in high cotton. There's always an off season."

Mary Alice nodded vigorously. "Don't we know."

I was tempted to say that I had been living in an off season for at least two years, but I doubted Bill would care. Anyway, he might start telling me about new ways that prisoners could be tortured in dungeons!

Rose was swinging higher and higher in the air.

"Huff & Huff cancelled the promotional tour of her new novel in Denmark. Budget cuts. Said it was too American-centered to export. Now we can all promote ourselves through social media. Is Clover Flower on Facebook?" Bill asked.

"Our good reputation. Word of mouth," Mary Alice said. "Don't believe in Facebook."

When I got back to the kitchen, Sinead was filling up the bowl of fruit salad. Letty was spooning out small helpings of the homemade ice cream with white chocolate and raspberries.

"Guests arrived?" Sinead asked. "The wee princess who is so particular? Any complaints about the food?"

I waved. "Rose's back."

"Two princesses in one place," Sinead said. "That will never do, it won't, Gary."

At just that moment, Gudrun burst in through the kitchen door. She was followed by Dr Kaiser, Cameron Wiley, and his wife, Miss Universe. Aengus brought up the rear.

Gudrun said, "This is our wonderful staff. Sinead, this is my cousin, Dr Kaiser. He is teaching at Baylor."

He had on the same wool flat cap as last time but instead of Bermuda shorts, he was wearing lederhosen, which were too tight through the crotch. Rather than shaking her hand, he lifted it to his lips and kissed it. Dr Kaiser said, "So you are the cook of this marvelous, exotic food?"

"We work as a team, we do," Sinead said. "Gotta give credit where it's due. That was Letty's recipe. And the cooks who've..." She waved her hand at the empty air near the griddle, where the Mexican ladies used to cluster.

Dr Kaiser lifted Letty's hand to his lips. Letty giggled. "Ordinary food in South Texas. We like it real spicy."

"Eh," Aengus said. "Mister Wiley, I'd like ya to meet my wife, Sinead."

Cameron Wiley held out his hand. "Pleased to meet you," he said. "I've heard so much about you."

Sinead laughed nervously. "So is Aengus lettin' out the family secrets?" she said. "He's a great one for the *craic*."

"It's all good, except if she's tied one on, if ya know what I mean," Aengus said.

I remembered rocking and petting Sinead on that night of the barbecue— her tongue in my ear. "*Be a man! I'm yer bitch*."

Sinead elbowed him. "Aye," she said. "Who doesn't go for the *craic*?"

"I visited Ireland when I was Miss Universe," Miss Universe said. "All it ever does is rain. I mean, it is so boring. Bor-ing. Rain. Rain. Rain. How do you stand the rain?"

"Aye," Aengus said. "Yer so right, ya are, Mrs Wiley. That's why we came to Texas. For the sunshine."

Was it? Or was there some other reason?

"Sorry," Cameron said, "I forgot to introduce my wife, Dixie."

No one had introduced me, either. But I didn't care.

Dixie rolled her eyes. "I am just the wife," she said, waving her monstrous diamond ring at me. She eyed me. "The Shawnee chief! I posted your picture on Facebook."

The intelligence services must troll Facebook for hours, looking for fugitives. That might be the clincher—a picture as a Shawnee chief at Clover Flower. At least she didn't know my full name.

"Captain Cook."

She giggled. "Last time you were Buffalo Bill Cody."

Gudrun said, "Everyone is hungry. What did you make today, Sinead? Something delicious?"

"It's all fresh, it is," Sinead said. "Straight from the fruit stand in town. A frittata. Fresh salads. We've plenty."

"My nutritionist says I can't have cream," Dixie said.

Sinead said, "So you don't. There's no cream in the frittata. It's all low-fat."

Dixie said, "There should be no fat."

"We'll be outside. I am sure Gary or Sinead can put some salmon or fish in the oven for you," Gudrun said. "Or something that will be satisfactory."

The retinue trooped outside to the picnic tables.

"She can eat shiiit and die," Sinead shouted, as soon as they were out of sight, slamming an empty pot on the counter. "Maybe we should do the Mongol Tuna again for her. Whadda ya say there, Gary?"

Letty giggled.

"I don't know if we have any Mongol Tuna left," I said.

Sinead looked up at the ceiling. "Check the freezer. We might have some leftover chicken," she said.

Dixie didn't look pleased with the chicken breast when I set the plate down in front of her. Cameron said, "For crying out loud, Dixie, nothing makes you happy!"

Admittedly, the chicken breast looked like a wrinkled prune. I'd put a few sprigs of fresh rosemary on it, after the microwave. But how long had it been in there? A month?

Later, when the children were loading their dishes onto the conveyor belt, I helped Letty scrape the dishes and load the dishwasher.

"Women like that are real expensive," Letty said, drying the huge frying pan, which we had used for the frittata. "Did you see that rock on her hand? I used to work for this anglo *puta* in the Valley. She was just as mean as her Doberman pinscher, Pancho Villa. One day, her neighbor shot her dog. I wasn't even sorry."

Sinead snorted. "If she says she wants something else, Gary, tell 'er the kitchen's closed. We're not waiting till that lot has finished to eat. I'm famished."

When I'd finished helping them, I fixed myself a plate and sat at a nearby picnic table. Kharalombos still had not shown up. Surely, he hadn't run off with Ashley? Did I know Kharalombos as well as I thought? Was anyone completely known?

Mary Alice sidled up to the table and said, "Has there been a sighting?"

"I haven't seen him," I said, taking a bite of the frittata. "I don't know where he is. I am sure there's a reasonable explanation. Did you try the frittata?"

"Not hungry," Mary Alice murmured. "Thinking that I might have to file a missing person's report. Don't think it's been twenty-four hours."

"Have they asked about her?"

"Not yet," Mary Alice said, her hands behind her back. "They're talking about their new books."

I shook my head. Maybe I was more modest than I thought?

"I'll be patrolling," Mary Alice said, strolling away.

A little further down the picnic table, Dr Kaiser had positioned himself next to Rose and was peering down her halter top in between bites of the frittata. "Could you tell me a little bit about your research pro-cess to find out about those fundamentalists? A most curious, peculiar practice in the modern world. Did they let you visit when they were praying with the snakes?"

"Why, it was a nest on the ground," Rose said, leaning down further.

Gudrun interjected, "There were birds flapping around the church with the snakes?"

"No, no, I meant it was easy," Rose said.

"What was easy?" Gudrun asked. "I am always missing the line punch. I mean, the punch line."

But Dr Kaiser was focused on Rose's cleavage. "In Abrahamic tradition, the serpent is a symbol of sexual desire."

"I told 'em I needed their healin'. After the layin' on of hands, the snakes come out of the box," Rose said.

Gudrun chortled as she speared a tomato. "Even if I bring you the dictionary, Klaus," she said, "you will not understand their English. Russian is a piece of strudel compared to this."

"These snakes are very dangerous," Dr Kaiser said. "You were not afraid of the bites? Sometimes, it can be fatal. The rattlesnake is a nasty creature."

Bill was deep in conversation with Cameron Wiley. "You know, Cameron," he said earnestly, as if he had known Cameron his entire life, "there has been a severe erosion of civil liberties in our country since 9/11."

Cameron adjusted the granny glasses on his nose. "I never thought of it that way," he said. "The Bushes are personal friends. But I think Bush Senior is disappointed in George W."

"Well, hell, if you'd like to read my book," Bill said, "I just happen to have a few extra copies from my publisher in the trunk of our car."

Dixie was pushing the shriveled chicken breast around on her plate. She set down her fork. "I read your book," she said, addressing Rose.

"Which one?" Rose asked brightly. "And?"

"Can I take your plate?" I asked Bill, piling up empties on a tray.

"Why, thanks, buddy," he said. "Don't know what we'd do without you."

I was ready to teach again. But that was over now; I had to accept invisibility. I no longer had any kind of public presence in life, except as a stage hand in the wings. Was this how people who lived under the social radar felt? People without papers. The Mexican ladies who worked in the kitchen, who had fled. I had never gotten to know them. On the other hand, had Sinead and Aengus sought out invisibility? Surely they weren't on the run from the police, too?

"We also have homemade ice cream," I said. "White chocolate and raspberry."

Dixie stabbed a tiny piece of chicken with her fork. "I don't eat any fat," she said. "*The Wobbly Ferris Wheel* or something like that?"

"*The Last Roller Coaster Ride*," Rose said. "I was shortlisted for the National Book Award."

"I didn't finish it. Too depressing. All of those carnival people." Dixie was gazing at her pink fingernails. "Have you read *Fifty Shades of Grey*? Now that's a good book. Couldn't put it down."

"There were snake cults in the Canaanite religion in the Bronze Age," Dr Kaiser said, ogling Rose's breasts. "And some of the African sects have a cult of the python."

Dixie, who was on the other side of Dr Kaiser, scooted closer. She was playing footsie with him under the table. Why?

Dr Kaiser squirmed. Then he coughed. "Sometimes, the poison was seen as the elixir of life. Immortality. Divine intoxication."

What was going on under the table?! It looked like Dixie was massaging Dr Kaiser's leg. Or had her hand moved up his thigh? Was this her way of getting back at Cameron?

Cameron was staring at Bill. "I had no idea it was that bad."

He must be detailing all the detainees tortured outside the jurisdiction of the United States. Or waterboarding, his favorite topic.

Rose squinted at Dixie. "Well, darlin', that trash looks like your kind of book. Right up your alley."

"Now," Bill said, "don't be going off like a pistol half-cocked, Rose. We've come here to…"

"Should I bring you dessert?" I asked. I was still standing there with the tray of dirty dishes.

"Do you make any money from your books?" Dixie asked. "Otherwise, I don't see the point."

Rose took a long swallow of water. "As a matter of fact," she said. Then she tapped her fingernails on the picnic table. "My question for you is…"

"I'm warnin' you," Bill said, "Rose."

But even if Bill threatened to divorce her, she wouldn't stop now. "Does anyone give a fat rat's ass that you were Miss Universe twenty years ago?" she said.

"We have goot, homemade ice cream," Gudrun said. "Gary, can you please?"

"Where's Ashley?" Bill said. "I'm sure she doesn't care if we're here or not. After her behavior yesterday."

Mary Alice, who had been circling the table like a hawk, said, "She's supervising the youngsters for the closing ceremony."

Cameron stared at Dixie from across the table. "No dessert."

I almost felt sorry for Cameron, except that he was the one who had chosen her. Maybe she had her sweet moments. Still, no one could be all bad.

"Can I take your plate, Dr Kaiser?" I asked. "Gudrun told us that you were an expert on Coptic manuscripts."

"He has such a wide breadth of knowledge," Cameron said. "Arabic, Greek, Aramaic. Hebrew. With his knowledge and my capital, we'll be building one of the best theological libraries in the region. Maybe in the United States. Or even the entire world!"

Dr Kaiser said, "You are too kind. If you are European, learning languages is the second nature. I am no better than…"

"He was always destined for a great academic future. Even in the *gymnasium*, he was brilliant," Gudrun said.

"Did you give Charlie your statement?" What was in the garage? Why had he gone there?

"Gary!" Mary Alice said. "That's confidential."

Dr Kaiser said, "I did nothing wrong. I was just asked by this gentleman Count Triksky to identify a manuscript."

Gudrun sighed. "We are plagued by this Triksky even in America. He is like a possum that will never die!" she said.

"Possums carry typhus," I said. "If you trap them, they are almost impossible to kill. You must have possums here."

"Charlie advised you not to discuss your statement with anyone," Mary Alice said ominously. "The investigation is ongoing. It has not been concluded."

"She's right," Cameron said. "We've been advised by our lawyers not to discuss the matter."

But Dr Kaiser pressed on. "I always thought there was something fishy about this Triksky from the beginning. I advised Cameron not to buy, but...."

"Dr Kaiser," Cameron said, "I'd rather you not discuss our affairs so casually."

"Gary," Dr Kaiser said, addressing me, "I have nothing to hide. That manuscript was found in a jar in a cave in Egypt. That story could change..."

Kharalombos and Ashley were standing in front of us.

Bill looked puzzled. "I thought you said Ashley was supervising the awards ceremony?"

Mary Alice looked embarrassed. "Well, sometimes the troops. She's safe and sound. The main thing."

Kharalombos was in a much better mood. He was carrying a huge paper which he held up triumphantly. "*Rumi* cheese! Egyptian cheese!"

"Ashley," Rose said, "have you been motorin' around the state of Texas without tellin' anybody? That is just plain irresponsible."

Ashley was breathless. "We kept driving around, looking for this gas station in the middle of nowhere. They sell *rumi* cheese. Tastes like parmesan to me! Kharalombos said that was the only thing that would make him feel better. And the guy is Egyptian and he wants to talk to Kharalombos in Arabic and tell him his whole life story. And then his wife insisted we stay for lunch and have this okra stew. I never had it that way with lamb. Amazing! It's much better than fried okra. They were so cool. And then they insisted we have tea and rice pudding. So we stayed for another two hours. When we were about a hundred miles away, I got this flat tire and we have to change it, like, wow. I want to go to Cairo. It sounds like such a cool, exciting place!"

"Next time, young lady, let people know where you're goin'," Bill said, his arms folded. "You can cause an awful lot of worry."

Rose said, "Come on now, gimme some sugar." She embraced Ashley.

Gudrun sniffed the air. "This cannot be our property."

Mary Alice's face was grim. "Fire!"

Chapter 13

Fire

MARY ALICE SHOUTED, "QUICK! THE STABLES! The animals!" All of us ran toward the green pasture. At least three fire engines chugged up the drive.

Gudrun wailed, "Can we take another disaster?" I was jogging alongside of her. "This is worse than the Russians taking Berlin."

I laughed out loud.

"This is not a joke, ha, ha," Gudrun said. "We could lose everything."

"But I thought you only had horses."

I prayed they would not assign me to the stable next. I could not keep bragging that I was Buffalo Bill Cody, or even Billy the Kid, since I had no gift with horses. The few times I had tried to ride at the Pyramids, the horses had bucked me off. My experiences riding trail horses as a kid had not been a success. One horse had gotten so spooked when I was putting on my poncho that it ran into a tree.

Dr Kaiser, who was huffing beside Gudrun, piped up, "The petting zoo was my idea. Good for the children. Understanding the natural world is important for their education!"

"I completely agree," I said. "As long as they're not raccoons! Or rattlesnakes!"

Behind me, Rose screamed, "Scarlett! You get back here. On the count of three." She was trying to run in those spiky Roman sandals. Bill was offering her a hand.

Scarlett O'Hara scampered up the road, straight toward the fire. Smoke billowed up into the blue sky.

"We will be eating pea-meal for the rest of our lives. Just like after the War. I will have to sell my house and go live with Klaus in Waco. Spend the rest of my days making strudel," Gudrun said, breathing heavily—all those doughnuts! I wondered vaguely if she had had her cholesterol checked. What about me? I had not had a medical checkup for two years.

When we reached the barn, flames were still blazing from the top. Half of the roof had caved in. The sides were burnt away and the horse stalls were smoking embers. Where were the horses?

A fireman was spraying water on the flames. It looked as if they had almost contained the fire.

Dr Kaiser said, "Where have all my precious animals gone?"

A fireman shouted at him, "Stay back! The smoke!"

Dr Kaiser pulled a monogrammed silk handkerchief from his lederhosen and covered his mouth. Gudrun had lapsed into German.

Rose wailed. "It's not enough that Scarlett O'Hara was left in Cairo to die during the Egyptian Revolution, but now she's going to be burned to a crisp, like a slab of salt pork!"

"Now there you go again, Rose, borrowing trouble," Bill said.

A few yards away, Mary Alice was talking to a cluster of firemen. She was shaking her head.

Out of nowhere, Scarlett O' Hara appeared and started barking. She wagged her tail, as if she were having a ball.

Rose scooped Scarlett up and hugged her. "I almost lost you again, darlin'." She glared at me. What a monster I was! It was fun being a bad boy!

"You don't know what we faced in Cairo after you left," I said. Why bother trying to help? If they disappeared during the Egyptian Revolution, they wouldn't hang around for cleanup or even moral support after a barn fire.

"We'd like to stay," Rose said, her voice suddenly hard. "Help you clean up this godawful mess, but we've got to get back to Austin. I've got a book signing for *Murder among the Serpents* tomorrow at Barnes and Noble, and then an interview on NPR on 'All Things Considered.'" She gave me a very slight smile and added, "Your day will come."

When? I was on the run from Interpol, a wanted cyber-terrorist, traveling on a forged Romanian passport. No university for miles would touch me. And I had completely lost interest in my academic work: contaminated water and the environment. Working in a real, natural environment had diminished my interest in the academic study of it. Besides that, I had also lost my opus, which I now admitted was not very good and maybe better safely buried in a trash dump at Moqattam Hills or used as scrap paper for expat grocery lists.

And—every writer's fear—I was not writing, except a few hurried, scribbled lines. Did I have the patience to write another novel?

"Go on and get packed up, Ashley. Come on home with us," Bill said, gently grabbing Ashley's arm. "Like a good girl. Easy does it."

Ashley stuck her lip out. "This place is cool. Like, why would I want to come home with you and sit around the house, waiting for my senior year to start? I mean, like, what's the point? Waiting to be shipped off to Birmingham, Alabama. *Boring!*"

"The point is that I'm telling you, young lady," Bill said. "Not asking you."

"I am not a lady," Ashley said. "Never was. Never will be. You can put that in your pipe and smoke it. And my mom can just stuff the idea of cotillion into her pantyhose!"

Rose said, her hands on her hips, "That's enough, missy. You're pushing it." Her knees were caked in mud. Scarlett barked nervously.

Ashley twirled a strand of hair with her finger. "What*ever*," she muttered.

Just then, Mary Alice joined the group.

"Mary Alice," Ashley pleaded, "please tell them that you need me for the rest of the session. I don't wanna go home. I don't wanna. Like, this is the coolest summer job, *ev*-er. We have the most awesome closing ceremony planned. The Comanches won all the prizes."

Mary Alice put her pencil behind her ear. "She's one of our finest counselors. We need her on deck. Don't we, Gary?" Mary Alice winked at me.

"Err," I said. "Yes, well, she's been a big help this summer. Don't know what we'd have done without her."

Ashley hugged me and gave me a big, sloppy kiss on the cheek. "Uncle Gary, I love you! You are the coolest! Even if you are an old coot, you are still cool!" The strap fell off of her tank top, exposing a creamy white shoulder.

She thought I was ugly? So what! Boriana had called me "Romeo." I remembered Sinead's bold hand, desperately searching for the zipper on my shorts.

Rose chimed in, "He's got *character*. A lot of *personality*! In *The Last Roller Coaster Ride*, my novel shortlisted for the National Book Award, the carnie fella who runs the dart booth has a wart on his nose and no girl would touch him with a ten-foot pole, but let me tell you, he's the kindest character in the novel! And kindness always counts for something! Dudn't it? Well, Ashley, darlin', if you do stay, you promise to be-have. No more gallivantin' around the state."

Bill was cleaning his ear with the tip of his pen. "Where's Kharalombos? We are concerned."

Mary Alice ignored him. "We have an important mission for Ashley. Only if she agrees to the assignment can she stay for the next two weeks."

Ashley was smiling; her white teeth were perfect. She bent over and tossed her long blonde hair back, jutted her left hip out.

"Anything," she said. "I'll do it cheerfully. No complaints, I promise! Shoveling manure in the barn? Cleaning up after archery? Baking chocolate chip cookies? Washing dishes?"

Mary Alice smiled. "It's a special job. Only you can do it. It's important for our operation."

"I can't wait! How can I help?"

Mary Alice said. "You will *not* let McKenzie out of your sight. You will be her bodyguard for the rest of the summer. On call *all night.*"

Ashley's smile disappeared. She spat, "That little turd! Pest. She's the biggest pill in the entire camp. Nobody can stand her. Why me? She's not in my cabin."

Rose said, "Well, if you're not up to the challenge, you can always come back with us to Austin. Come to my book signing!"

Ashley looked down at her manicured toes. They were luminous blue with white glitter. "It's definitely not a cool assignment. Bummer. I mean, I would rather clean toilets in the cabins than hang out with that brat."

Mary Alice folded her arms. "That's the deal. Are you up to it, young lady? You're to report to me daily."

Bill was now cleaning the other ear. He had discovered a wad of orange wax. "We do want to make sure. As Ashley's uncle and aunt, we are concerned. We don't want any untoward behavior that could result in…"

Ashley rolled her eyes. "Pleez, and I mean, *pleez.* I know about the birds and the bees…"

"For Pete's sake, Bill," Rose said. "Why don't you just call a spade a spade? Where is the gentleman in question? Or should we say, Don Juan?"

Mary Alice echoed, looking to me, "Where is Kharalombos?"

"Eating cheese?" In the confusion and panic, Kharalombos had disappeared. Maybe he was devouring the *rumi* cheese alone and singing Asmahan songs, nostalgic for Cairo. Couldn't say I blamed him.

The firemen were now rolling up their hoses. One of the fireman called out, "You're in the clear, Mary Alice. Fire's out."

Mary Alice said, "Thanks, Captain. I don't know how to thank you."

A white van marked Channel 5 San Antonio was driving up the road. I really couldn't be caught on camera. Or, was I positively thriving as a Wanted Man?! I ducked into the barn.

"Well, now," Mary Alice said, marching in behind me. "Let's see what's now happened to…"

She strolled through the barn, making notes on her clipboard. While she wandered over to the cages, I peeked out of the barn.

Next to the barn, Gudrun and Dr Kaiser were being interviewed by a reporter, whose hair looked like a stiff, brown helmet. The reporter was saying in a loud voice:

"The Clover Flower Girls' Camp has been plagued by a series of disasters this summer. The plot resembles an Agatha Christie who-done-it. First, a mysterious murder on the neighboring property. And now, a fire in their stables."

When I turned around, Cameron the oilman and his trophy wife, Dixie, had walked into the barn.

"Oooo! Gross!" Horse manure was oozing between Dixie's manicured toes.

Mary Alice was shaking her head. "I am sorry, Dixie. One of the hazards of walking in a barn."

Cameron adjusted the granny glasses on his nose. "Mary Alice, you don't suspect our daughter? I would hate to think."

"As you recall, she burned down a cabin last year," Mary Alice said. "Of course, I am grateful for your support."

"Cameron, you promised," Dixie cried. "She's not going to spoil our plans again."

Cameron smiled, as if we were trying to cajole Mary Alice. "As you can imagine, we've run through a lot of babysitters. You know, we've always believed in the values of this camp. And we are committed to your enterprise in more ways than one. The Christian atmosphere. Sharing. The Golden Rule."

How hard that was in reality!

Dixie was wiping her feet gingerly with a Kleenex. She gagged. "Be a doll and get me a hose."

"There probably is one," I said, searching around through the hay.

Dixie batted her false eyelashes at me. "Do you think you could?"

Mary Alice frowned. "I think that might be part of the problem. I think you need to spend more time with your daughter."

"Dixie," Cameron said. "Mary Alice is talking to us about our daughter. Why aren't you interested?"

She hissed, "I am trying to get this crap off my feet. Could you give me a minute?"

The green hose was twisted up and looked like an unruly python. When I turned on the tap, the hose bucked toward her, and the nozzle gushed open, spraying her in the face.

"Turn it off, you idiot! Can't you do anything right?"

Her heavy black eyeliner and mascara ran down her cheeks. She pulled a compact out of her giant purple Gucci purse. When she saw her face, she yelled, "Now look what you've done!"

"I'm sorry," I said, turning off the tap and twisting the nozzle off the hose.

"He was trying to help," Mary Alice said. "It looks like that hose also needs to be repaired. Should make a note of that." Mary Alice scribbled it down with a tiny nub of pencil. She murmured, "We never have anything decent to write with around here. Pretty soon, I'll be writing with a twig!"

Cameron handed Mary Alice a gold Cross pen.

"You're not sorry. You're the one who started the fire, aren't you? My baby would never have done such a thing," Dixie said. "You said you were Captain Cook."

"What are you talking about? I haven't even been out here," I said. "I work in the kitchen."

"That's a serious accusation," Cameron said. "What's wrong with you, Sugarpie?"

"I am not your sugarpie. Stop treating me like a baby!"

"Look, take off your sandals and I'll rinse off your feet," I said, directing the water toward her feet. The manure on them reeked.

"I won't let that man touch me," Dixie said. "You can't touch my toes. No one touches my toes except my manicurist! Or Cameron. Pervert! You have a foot fetish!"

I handed her the hose. "Go ahead." Had she become completely unhinged? And why?

Mary Alice rolled her eyes. "Dixie."

"Very decent of you. Dixie doesn't mean…." Cameron said, shaking his head.

I shrugged. "Anyone would do the same. I was just trying to help out."

Dixie sobbed. The mascara mixed with her tears to streak her cheeks black. She looked exactly like a raccoon, except there was no expression on her face because of the Botox.

"Nothing ever goes right for me. Ever…I'm diagnosed with breast cancer and will lose all of my hair. Pops has Alzheimer's. The tile on our swimming pool went moldy. Then our A.C. went out when the temperature was over a hundred degrees! We were burning up in our River Oaks mansion. The next day, I lost my favorite diamond ring in the disposal. Even my cheerleading friends from high school have deserted me. And now our Italian cruise is going to be cancelled! No one, and I mean no one, has worse luck than I do."

So Dixie had her own cross to bear. I had only seen her before as a bimbo, but it looked like she was a lonely woman without any friends. Was her beauty a curse?

Cameron was apologetic. "I really need to take her away. You know the camp has our full support."

Mary Alice was shaking her head. "I can see that. Well, you'll have to leave the discipline to me, then. Your pen." Mary Alice handed his gold Cross pen back to him.

Cameron took Dixie's arm. "Now, Sugarpie, let's get you cleaned up." He led the sobbing ex-beauty queen out of the barn.

Mary Alice sighed.

The birds' cages were lined up against the side of the barn, far from the horses' stalls. Most of the birds were lying belly up, completely still. How come I had never been out here? What a shame! They had a cage of green and yellow parakeets—it looked like a male and female. Another white rabbit bites the dust. Poor Blanca! What was this old girl's name? And a red-tailed Amazonian parrot with a blue throat!

"That's a red-tailed Amazonian parrot! Threatened by habitat loss. Considered vulnerable! How did that get in your collection?"

Mary Alice looked at me sternly. "How do you know that?"

"Spent a summer in Brazil, studying wildlife," I said, almost instinctively, forgetting that I was not supposed to reveal anything personal. Besides the blue frogs, I had seen many varieties of parrots.

Mary Alice cleared her throat, "Dr Kaiser donated all of the birds. I had no idea."

"There is a huge international illegal trade in parrots," I said. "Birds are taken out of their habitat."

For a moment, Mary Alice stood next to me, staring sadly at the corpses of the birds.

"Well, Gary," she said, "I want to believe that Dr Kaiser is not party to any of this. Maybe he didn't know. Where is Gudrun?"

The thieves who dealt in rare birds reminded me again of Weddo Silva's case. Why did this incident from the past seem so poignant to me now? Did Dad know his foreman, Weddo Silva, was tied to a Mexican gang? How long had Weddo been smuggling the cocaine in the Creamy Freeze trucks?

"What?" I asked, lost in thought.

"Where is Gudrun?"

"Oh, she's talking to a reporter from Channel 5."

Mary Alice looked up toward the blue sky, now visible through the caved-in roof. "Mercy. The only thing left to do is pray."

Even though the barn was now empty, her voice suddenly dropped to a whisper, "I do have an important mission for you, Gary." It reminded me of the voice in my novel, *Pure Water*. "I was on a mission."

"I love the animals, but I don't want to take care of them. One died on my watch in Cairo."

Mary Alice nodded, as if she already knew the story. "That's not what I have in mind. The assignment will require you to be clever. Cunning. Discreet. Secretive."

"Sounds like intelligence work."

Mary Alice cleared her throat. "You will guard that brat."

"I thought that was Ashley's assignment?"

"You're the daytime shift," Mary Alice said. "You can't let her out of your sight. One more disaster and we'll lose this whole kit and caboodle. We'll all end up as Walmart greeters for the rest of our lives!"

"Why didn't you tell Cameron and Dixie to take her home?"

"They made a donation for the new pool. Remember?" Mary Alice said, grimacing. "My hands are tied. We cashed the check to cover hay and fodder. And our vet bills have been outrageous!"

"Oh," I said. "Right. I forgot." Details regarding money had never interested me—which is why I would make a terrible businessman. I was fine, as long as a steady paycheck kept coming in. Of course, now we were just living hand to mouth at the camp. Unlike Dad, who had known where every penny went.

Mary Alice was looking down at her clipboard, studying a long list.

"Do you want me to bury them?" I didn't relish the task of digging the graves, but I couldn't stand looking at the corpses of the birds and animals. That beautiful red-tailed Amazonian parrot! Oh, no! There was also a tiny baby rabbit, belly up, next to the mother. I felt miserable about poor Blanca. Had the porter eaten her that day we had left her?

"Well," she said, clearing her throat. "We should do that. For reasons of hygiene. And of course, it will be upsetting for the children. But now, the priority is to catch the ones who are alive."

"You have more?!"

She took out her red half-glasses and put them on. "One zebra. Two ponies. Three nags. Five chickens. But let's forget about the chickens." She drew a line through them. "Chickens are not rare."

"A zebra?"

"Keeping it for the Waco zoo. One of Dr Kaiser's projects," Mary Alice said. "I was against the idea. Not practical. Gudrun overruled me on that one."

"Did I hear my name?" Gudrun said, huffing into the barn. Dr Kaiser followed her. He was wiping the sweat off his forehead with the monogrammed silk handkerchief.

He pointed to the cages, "Gudrun, look what's happened to the birds. Such a pity!"

At that moment, Charlie rolled up in his cruiser, just outside the barn. The siren was still whining. "Got here as soon as I could. I was on the other side of the county. Big burglary."

"We know who started the fire," Mary Alice said. "Open-and-shut case."

"Don't be so sure," Charlie said. "You do realize you're contaminating the scene. Everyone out."

"You think you could turn that thing off?" Mary Alice said.

The red siren on top of his car whined insistently, as if he were still in hot pursuit of a suspect. Reaching into his car, he clicked it off. At the same time, he grabbed a small reporter's notebook from behind the dash. A pencil jutted from his ear. Had he checked my driver's license? Work history? "Howdy," he said, nodding to me, but he didn't give anything away. One of his trouser legs was tucked into his cowboy boots; the other hung loose. He strode into the barn.

Charlie was inspecting the cages. Speedy's pickup squealed to a stop outside of the barn, and Speedy and Aengus ran in.

Mary Alice barked, "You three will track down the missing animals. They are the priority since they belong to the zoo."

"Why don't you just call the zoo?" I asked.

"That's not an option," Mary Alice said. "Aengus, you know the drill."

Aengus stood with his arms folded, as if he were a commando. "We'll need some rope, we will."

"Are we going to lasso them?" I asked. As an Eagle Scout, I had racked up the badges: Bird Study, Emergency Preparedness, Reptile and Amphibian Study, and Citizenship in the World. But I had pointedly ignored Knots for Land and Water and Other Emergencies. I was always voted "The Best Sport" at every session at camp, recognized for my good humor during disaster, scandals, and fiascos.

Aengus muttered, "We're going to try."

"Shit, Mary Alice," Speedy said, sucking on a cigarette he held between forefinger and thumb, as if he were Gary Cooper. "You have no luck. Remember when you were sued because the macaroni and cheese burned some brat's tongue? Hee! hee!" His baseball cap was turned backward on his head and he looked goofy.

Mary Alice roared, "We've just had a fire that nearly burned down the barn! Put out that cigarette now!"

Speedy turned to me. "You are now about to become a *vaquero* on the King Ranch! Ready for the ride?"

"Stop acting the maggot!" Aengus shouted.

Speedy laughed. "So now I'm a maggot? *Cabron.*"

"Eff off!" Aengus said. "Let's crack on before it gets dark."

The giraffe was the first one we spotted because of her height, not far from the barn. She was feeding on the leaves of a live oak tree a little way outside the fence. The tree, with its crooked limbs, was majestic and huge. Because of her long neck, the giraffe could reach the leaves on the top of the oak.

"Come on, Lady Bird Johnson," Speedy said, nudging her with a long stick. She loped back into the fenced-in area. She was gargantuan.

Meanwhile, Aengus was looping a rope around the neck of a shaggy bull not far away. The hair drooped over his eyes and reminded me of a sheep dog.

At first, I thought he might be a longhorn, or even a bison. He weighed over a ton. His horns curled outward and he looked fierce. Aengus acted as if he were putting a leash on a friendly Labrador retriever.

"That's a Tibetan yak!" I said.

"I had to look on the map to see where that country is. Anyway, that baby is the nicest of them all," Speedy said.

"Why do they need that for a petting zoo?"

Speedy guffawed. "Ay! You don't know by now that those ladies are *locas*? Completely crazy."

The zebra galloped past us, as if she were teasing us. She whinnied. "That mother is mean. Meaner than a mule. They bite," Speedy said, making a loop from the rope, effortlessly.

"How do you know how to do that?" I asked. I kept learning about the vast practical skills of the staff at this camp.

"Worked on a ranch. A little like the King Ranch. Called Rusty Nail," Speedy said, shrugging. "But then, I knocked up the owner's daughter." Speedy approached the zebra very carefully, as if he were approaching a poisonous snake. "*Que chula. Que bonita.* That's a good girl. Come with us, Frida Kahlo." She looked cartoonish and cute with the black and white stripes, but her ears flattened and she bared her teeth at us—they were monstrous.

"Gary," Speedy said, "stay back. She's not like a horse."

When she saw the rope, Frida made a strange barking noise and galloped away.

"How will we ever catch her?"

Speedy kept talking in a soothing voice, "*Que bonita!* You are the most beautiful girl in the world. You want to come to your Uncle Speedy, don't you?"

Speedy started to chase Frida. Because he was running, I started running, too.

"Don't get too close," he shouted. "Watch out! Get back. Get back!"

I got a vicious kick in the shin and fell back hard onto the ground, and the wind was knocked out of me.

My eyes were blurry and I saw something red. Was I crying? My cheeks felt wet. I felt as if I were in a long tunnel.

Speedy was kneeling beside me. "My friend, you never worked on a farm. For sure."

I couldn't speak. I was still stunned. "I am not…"

"Take it easy," Speedy said, patting my shoulder. "Just lie there for a minute."

Speedy plucked a red bandanna off of a sagebush. "There's only one *gato* who still wears these around here, besides Willie Nelson." He sniffed it. "Weed." Then, he sniffed again. "Unfiltered Camels." He sniffed a third time, "And…"

"Who?"

But he stared past me. "Thought I knew all the caves on this land."

Shrubs camouflaged the opening of the cave in the limestone.

"There are lots of these kinds of caves around here. There's a big one called Bracken Cave not too far from here. People go to watch the bats. Not my idea of fun, but…"

"What about the zebra?"

Speedy pulled me up, effortlessly. "Let's check it out."

"I'm claustrophobic," I said. "You go. Can't stand closed spaces."

"Have some *cojones*. Be a man!"

I stood up slowly. My leg hurt. I suddenly missed Cairo very much and wished I were going back there. I ducked my head and followed Speedy into the cave. He flicked his lighter again. The cave was much bigger than one would have guessed from the opening.

I sneezed. "What's that smell?"

"Bat shit," Speedy said.

I felt a desire to sneeze a second time. There was another strong smell— medicinal. Weird shadows flickered against the wall of the cave.

"That *cabron* is at it again."

"What?" I said. "Look, this place feels weird."

"You afraid of ghosts?" Speedy laughed. He held up a test tube. "You ever seen the movie *Frankenstein*?"

"Long time ago," I said. I felt very woozy.

He kept flicking the lighter. "Look's like I'm running out. My timing is always shitty. Story of my life."

The light dimmed and flickered against the wall of the cave. In the corner, he picked up packets, neatly stacked against the wall. He sniffed.

"What?" I said, sneezing again. My nose tickled.

"Josiah's stash. It's worth thousands. Could nab it, but meth is not my thing. And Josiah is one mean *gato*. Don't want to mess with his shit."

There was a whole layer of the world I was not aware of, except from the newspaper and television. How could I make up for years and years of academic life?

"Let's get out of here. That *cabron* is probably around. He's not the kind of guy you want to meet in a dark alley. Watch your head."

"Are you going to tell Charlie?" I asked, blinking as we went back into the light. The dusk sky was streaked orange and pink. It was beautiful, but I didn't care. My leg throbbed.

"Why don't you do it? Your record is cleaner than mine. I don't think Aengus is Mr Squeaky Clean, either," Speedy said. "*Chingauzos*, Frida gave you a kick."

I limped behind him.

Speedy talked on. "I mean, that *cabron* can do anything. Must have trained with the Irish Green Berets, or whatever you call them. Once, we were fooling around, he flipped me upside down, like a judo master. He's a perfect shot. And he can kill a rattlesnake with his bare hands."

"I saw him kill a snake once, but it was only a king snake." He had twisted the neck of that snake, as if he were twisting a lid off a jar of peanut butter. Was Speedy exaggerating?

Speedy was saying, "He acts like he's just a yardman, but don't be fooled. Once when we were trashed, he said he met that dictator, the Clown Man, when he was in Libya!"

"What?! He met the Clown Man!"

"Jeezus, Mary, and Joseph," Aengus bellowed. "Speedy! Speedy!"

Speedy ran toward a crashing in the brush. An odd-looking creature with a hump was spitting at Aengus.

Aengus shouted, "Where the feck have you been?" He motioned for me to stay back. "Give 'er a wide berth, Gary. Wide berth, I say!"

Let the boys handle it.

The creature with the hump charged Aengus. He was trying to lasso it from the front. The creature didn't see Speedy tiptoeing behind him. From a fair distance, Speedy threw the lasso and it landed around its neck. He pulled the rope tight. Suddenly, the creature turned its head and spat a green glob at Speedy. "Shit!" Speedy said, wiping the blob out of his eye with his sleeve. With the other hand, he held the rope tight. The creature bucked some, but finally Speedy led it back to the fenced-in yard.

"God, that's a Peruvian llama!" I said. "What the hell?"

"Eee, worth a fair bit, they are. It doesn't make any sense to have it at the camp, but Gudrun insisted. A few chickens and a pig would be enough for the wee ones."

The pain was so intense now that I was barely listening. "Sure." My leg was bruised and it hurt to put weight on it.

"Looks like you're hurt," Aengus said. "Better get some ice on it. Frida do that to you?"

I nodded. "It hurts like hell."

"She got away, eh?" Aengus sighed. "Not the first time. I'll report to the captain. You get some ice on yer leg, quick like."

Chapter 14

Bodyguard

A SERIOUS-LOOKING WOMAN BURST INTO THE OFFICE. Her face was swallowed by a pair of severe, black-rimmed glasses. "There's a zebra running through downtown Schulenburg! I almost had a wreck on my way over here."

I laughed.

Mary Alice glared at me. "Can you give us the exact location? I should let...."

She wasn't going to ask me to help catch Frida again!

The woman shrugged. "I don't know. Next to Jalisco's Mexican restaurant? Across from the post office?" The woman was staring at me. "What happened to you?"

"My wife kicked me."

If Aengus found out I was dallying with his wife, he would punch me in the face. Or worse. But Sinead kept studiously ignoring me, as if nothing had happened. Was I still hoping?

The woman didn't look like the other manicured mothers. She was wearing a plain navy blazer with a straight skirt. Her hair was pulled back in a round old-fashioned bun. "I raise money for battered women in San Antonio. Violence against women is not a joke."

I knew this from hard-won experience since I had confronted Boriana's bull of a husband, Dragomir. Admittedly, I had spun a tale, instead of fighting a duel, but it worked—and he had slunk away, without taking another slug at Boriana. (She was hiding in the wardrobe.)

"I'm sorry," I said. "That was in bad taste. I've been under a lot of pressure lately."

"Gary, just sit over there and answer the phone," Mary Alice said, pointing to the black swivel chair. "I will handle this."

"I'm pulling my daughter out of your camp. I don't believe it's safe. First a murder and now a fire! The next thing will be terrorists!"

Mary Alice smiled sweetly. "He's new."

The woman stared at me in disbelief. "He doesn't look like a terrorist."

And yet that's how the US government had classified me! People could still get away with murder if they didn't fit the stereotypes. Ted Bundy, who confessed to thirty gruesome murders, looked like the boy-next-door with his wavy brown hair and diffident smile. Had I slipped through the net because I didn't look dangerous? And even if I were a computer hack (which I was not), capable of creating that pernicious virus, what would I look like? Dr No in a James Bond movie? Wearing a Mao-like uniform, stroking a white Persian cat?

"Of course not. He's our handyman," Mary Alice said, convincingly. She put her arm around the woman, like a doting grandmother. "Come see your daughter, Bonnie. Let's stroll over to the art room together. They are making macramé bracelets today."

After dozens of frantic calls from parents, I unplugged the phone and surfed the internet on Mary Alice's old PC. First, I sent Boriana a short email: "Meet you soon, in Malta or Sofia. Love, Gary." I couldn't just disappear.

I was still dizzy from the fall, but I could still read Google with Mary Alice's reader glasses. "IRA and The Clown Man" resulted in three thousand hits. Just one headline after another about The Clown Man supplying weapons and arms to the IRA. "Attacks carried out with Libyan Semtex included Enniskillen bombing in 1987." Wasn't Enniskillen Aengus's hometown? The Clown Man resumed supplying the IRA after his adopted daughter, Zeinab, was killed in American air strikes in 1986. Was there a tie-in? I needed to bone up on modern Irish history.

When Mary Alice returned, I asked, "Is Aengus an IRA sympathizer?"

"Keep this hunch under your hat, Gary," Mary Alice whispered. "Mum's the word."

"So you know?" I asked, incredulous.

Mary Alice shrugged. "We had over a hundred complaints about Letty's cooking. The lard. Aengus and Sinead showed up at the right time. They're hard-working. Salt of the earth."

I pressed further. "So was he more than a sympathizer?"

And yet Sinead and Aengus thought no one knew. What kind of game were they playing? Were they pretending to be salt of the earth?

"So do they know that you know?"

Mary Alice glared at me.

"You made a deal?"

Mary Alice snorted, like the Peruvian llama. "We'll also ignore what we know about you, Gary, and your checkered past!"

Better cool it for now. I ventured over to the doughnut table, but it was bare except for a box of bran buds and skim milk. No crullers. No chocolate glazed doughnuts. No doughnuts filled with strawberry jam. No sugar, even.

"No doughnuts?" I asked. It was the one day I really craved a chocolate glazed doughnut. I felt lousy.

"New austerity program," Mary Alice barked. "Cutting luxury items."

I poured a few bran buds into a plastic bowl and choked down a bite. It tasted like cardboard. No good Italian coffee, either. Just bland, tasteless Lipton tea bags. I poured myself boiling water and swallowed a few aspirin.

"Where's Gudrun?"

"Went to the Hilltop Café with Klaus. For chicken-fried steak. Had to get away. She's very upset about what happened to the animals." Mary Alice was using a yellow high lighter to underline numbers in the spreadsheet. Her voice softened. "Why don't you get the nurse to look at your leg? I believe she's in the clinic. Your assignment starts tomorrow."

I was dying to throw a tantrum like Dixie had in the barn. "What about Frida Kahlo?"

"Back to the zoo," Mary Alice said. "If they can catch her. I called Waco zoo this morning and told them to come get the animals. Too much liability. One of the children could get hurt. Gudrun's not talking to me."

"Oh," I said. "I'm sorry."

Mary Alice grimaced. "It's not the first time." She resumed looking at the spreadsheet. "She'll get over it."

Even though I had excruciating pain in my leg, I didn't go to the clinic. Instead, I wandered over to the kitchen. It was deserted, except for Sinead and Letty. I remembered my first day when Sinead had been making pizzas—the bustling, happy atmosphere. But there were no delicious aromas wafting in the air this time.

Sinead was singing, "I wish I was a fisherman tumbling on the seas far from dry land and its bitter memories, casting out my sweet line with abandonment and love, no ceiling bearing down on me save the starry sky above." She was chopping celery expertly, crossways, with a huge kitchen knife.

Letty was sitting on the stool. She was eating an enormous flour-tortilla taco while she studied *The San Antonio Star*. "Listen to this. The fate of the 44 students who disappeared from a training college in San Luis Potosí state is now known."

What had happened to the guy who had murdered Weddo, Dad's foreman? The fantasy of summer camp had been pierced by nearby violence, and violence from afar.

Sinead said, "The world's a right mess, it is. A number of boys disappeared during the Troubles. Many of 'em were found later in the bog. The IRA couldn't abide informers. Cooperating with the Brits."

"But I thought you…?" Had I said that out loud? I better keep my trap shut. I had the bad habit of frankness.

Letty asked, "What's a bog?"

"A swamp," I said.

"Ah, it's Gary, so it is." Sinead had dark circles under her eyes and red blotches on her forehead.

"Back to the zoo, if they can catch her," I said. "The last sighting was in downtown Schulenburg across from Jalisco's."

But Sinead didn't laugh. And she didn't ask what happened. Was she more preoccupied with the past?

Letty took another bite of her taco and kept reading. She muttered again, "*Muy feo.*"

"Letty, can ya get off yer arse and do a little work around here?" Sinead said, putting an unruly red curl behind her ear.

Masses of tacos wrapped in foil were piled on the sideboard. Letty nodded her head toward me. Jalisco's. "Real cheap. There's bean and egg, bean and potato, chorizo and egg, eggs with hot sauce. I can't eat them all. Take one. I haven't felt like making gorditas since my cousins left."

Sinead snorted. It sounded like the ungraceful snort of a pig. The crudeness turned me off.

"Jalisco's. That's where the zebra was last seen," I said.

Sinead shook her head. "They even killed a mother of ten. Didn't even find her body until 2003."

The Disappeared refers to those abducted and murdered by the Provisional IRA for being informers to the British authorities. Would she get suspicious if I started asking questions?

Letty looked up from *The San Antonio Star.* "Those *pinche cabrons* would even kill their own mothers. The gangs are *muy feo.* And so are the police! The police in Mejico took the boys and handed them over to that cartel."

"I am not talking about bloody Mexico," Sinead said.

"You're not listening!" Letty said.

"Neither are you! Don't you lot know anything about the world out there across the ocean?" Sinead said, dumping the chopped celery into a small bowl.

"The IRA," I answered.

"Who?" Letty asked.

"Don't bother yerself," Sinead said. "The Irish Republican Army. Do we have to educate yous about the world? Wanted the Brits out of Northern Ireland and wanted to reunite with the South. The South is independent and it's called the Republic."

If Aengus was hiding because he was IRA, why would Sinead talk about it so openly? Or was she banking on the fact that no one in Schulenburg would suspect them?

Letty looked puzzled. "Are you talking about all that fighting over there? We heard about it on CBS News. The bombs in garbage cans. But I never could understand what they were fighting about."

Letty had a point—even the people fighting probably forgot why they were fighting. But the Provisional IRA calculated specific targets—and they were ruthless. From my research: *The Provisional IRA was a paramilitary group which used violence to achieve its goals: against the Royal Ulster Constabulary, British army, and British institutions.* Did Aengus belong to the Provisional IRA?

Sinead sighed. "Jahsas. Gary, can you lend a hand? Eggs from the back."

There were almost no supplies in the freezer. No meat. No chicken. Only one crate of yellowing broccoli. Two dozen eggs. Frozen peas and French fries and fish sticks. Only a few pink crumbs from a cupcake were left in the dessert leftover container. My stomach growled.

A rank odor stank up the kitchen. Sinead was dumping cans of Mongol Tuna into a bowl.

"You're feeding them the tuna for stray cats?"

"Can't always be inspired, creative, can ya, Gary? Besides that, we've got very little in the larder, as ya saw fer yerself."

"They've also cut out doughnuts and coffee in the office."

"The trick is homemade mayonnaise. That will bury the taste, it will," Sinead said. "And we'll serve it with fries. They won't complain, they won't. Wee ones like taters."

The refried beans reminded me of *ful*, fava beans, in Cairo. In the morning, security guards at the embassies often ate their *ful* sandwiches off of newspapers on the hoods of cars. Part of me really ached to go back. But what about Boriana? I would have to make a choice.

Letty turned the page of the newspaper and said, "The bean tacos are the best. Jalisco's makes better beans than I do. They don't have to worry about lard. Not like here."

The bean taco was delicious but seemed a little greasy.

Letty read out loud, "The gang then burned the bodies at a garbage dump. After that, they dumped the bags in the river. One bag was found, the human remains intact."

The memory surged to the surface: Weddo Silva's decomposed body had been wrapped in a tarp and dumped in a stagnant pond on an isolated farm outside of Oklahoma City. Gagging, I ran over to the garbage and spat out the beans.

Sinead said, "Jahsus, Letty, we're not interested in this bloody article. Could ya just read to yerself, like, silently?"

Letty's eyes filled with tears. "Oh, my God. My cousin Maria's son is listed! Carlos! And you're such a *puta*, you don't even care!"

I had known Weddo Silva since I was small child. Whenever I showed up with Dad to check the ice cream vats, he would shake my hand and leave a piece of butterscotch candy inside. He would pinch me on the cheek, saying, "*Mi hijo.*" My son.

"Maria's son?" I asked.

Sinead said, "Ah, there, Letty. I didn't know that. Why didn't you say so from the beginning? I just thought...."

"You just thought? What? It didn't matter. *No le hace.* It's someone far away. In a country you don't care about? It's someone else's son?" Letty threw the newspaper down on the counter. Then she untied her apron and threw it in the hamper. "You're always talkin'. Ireland, this. Ireland, that. Why can't I even breathe a word about Mexico?"

"Aw, come on, now, Letty, we all have our worries."

Letty said, "I quit! I wouldn't even come back if you begged me!" She pushed her way through the swinging doors, as if she were a sheriff.

Sinead repeated, "We all have our worries, providing for our wee men."

Weddo Silva had a wife and four children. Did Weddo have a pension? Retirement? What about all those years of loyalty to Creamy Freeze and our family? Had Dad abandoned them? Was that the American way? "Every man for himself?"

As the door swung back and forth, one of the hinges squeaked defiantly.

Sinead glanced at me. "Why the long face?"

I didn't feel like explaining Weddo Silva's tragedy to her. Maybe she was keeping things to herself, as well.

Her eyes were bloodshot, as if she had not gotten any sleep. "We only have a few days left until the end."

During Weddo Silva's trial, Mom had knocked on the door to my room. Her eyes were bloodshot. She said, "This trial has been hard on your Dad. You could be a little kinder to him." That was when I was in high school and he had insisted I play football. "You mean, I'm not supposed to quit football now."

"Why the long face?" Sinead asked again.

"You might say a ghost from the past," I said. "Tell you another time."

Now, other memories that I had not thought of for years appeared. The day after the trial, I had shouted at my Dad, "You wanted me to play football because you could never even make the team!" I had expected an explosion, but instead, his eyes were pensive. "You are right, my boy. It is not life or death. Do what makes you happy."

Sinead lowered her voice, "Can you keep a secret?" She handed me a spoon of homemade mayonnaise.

"No, thanks," I said.

She whispered, "We're leaving."

"Why?"

Sinead put her fingers to her lips and nodded to the swinging doors, as if she thought Letty might still be nearby.

"You might say, the well has run dry."

I could barely focus on what Sinead was saying. Weddo Silva had started dipping his hand into the well—taking too much of the profits. He was double-crossing the gang. How much?

"What does that have to do with Letty?"

"Nothing," Sinead said. "Were ya born yesterday, like? Sometimes it's better not to blab everything. Show your hand. Cameron Wiley has offered him a job in West Texas. He's fed up catching zebras. Can't say I blame him."

Weddo Silva supposedly had made thousands of dollars, but they never found the money. One day, I overheard the drivers in Dad's warehouse saying that it was buried near Tahlequah, Oklahoma, capital of the Cherokee Nation. I never learned if this was true or not.

Were they leaving town in a hurry because Aengus was implicated in the murder? I didn't want to believe that. But wasn't it a convenient time to leave?

Weddo Silva's killer was stabbed in the throat during a prison brawl. No one was charged.

—⚉—

I finally started my new job as McKenzie's baby sitter. Ashley delivered her to me. She was sucking her thumb.

"Aren't you a little old for that?" I asked.

"Mom says you're a pervert," she said matter-of-factly. She took her thumb out of her mouth so she could stick her tongue out at me. Then she added, "And a dumbo. You don't even know how to turn on the faucet."

Ashley said, "Girl, you want a whuppin'. That's no way to speak to Uncle Gary."

"How did the night shift go?" I asked.

Ashley yawned. "Up half the night, playing Go Fish."

"Well, now," I said. My voice sounded artificial, even to me. "What should we do for fun?"

I prayed McKenzie didn't suggest horseback riding.

McKenzie glared at me. "Mister, you remind me of my math teacher at St. Mary's, Mr Goober. He's an old dork. We put gum on his chair."

Ashley adjusted the spaghetti strap on her shoulder. She flashed me a pristine smile. "Should I stick around?"

"Up to you," I said. "I thought you had other duties as the chief of the Comanches."

Had Ashley given up on Kharalombos? Why was she flirting with me now?

Ashley winked at me. "Pepe has invited me to play Monopoly at his cabin. Why don't we all go?"

McKenzie stuck her lip out. "I saw that! That's what my daddy does when he wants my mother to take her clothes off."

"That's a wonderful idea, Ashley," I said. I had no ideas at all how to entertain this brat. I longed to be back in the kitchen, washing dishes.

"I don't want to," McKenzie said. "Hey, Mister, I wanna ride my horse, Star."

"The stable is closed now."

"If you beat me at Monopoly," Ashley said, "I'll take you into Schulenburg for a chocolate dipped cone at Dairy Queen in my MG convertible."

Ashley was fantastic! What a brilliant bribe.

McKenzie scrutinized me. "Have you seen my mother naked?"

"No. Of course not! I barely know your mother."

Ashley said, "Pleeez. McKenzie, you are impossible!"

McKenzie said, confidently, "Ashley, you took off your clothes for Mr Kharalombos! I'm gonna tell."

Had she? Surely not.

Ashley's face turned purple.

"I'm gonna tell," McKenzie said. "Gonna tell."

Ashley twisted the little girl's arm. "Now listen here, kid. We're going to play Monopoly whether you like it or not. And if you complain, you're going straight to Time Out for the entire afternoon. You can read *The Lion, The Witch, and the Wardrobe* over and over again by yourself."

"Awwww," McKenzie started wailing. "That hurts. Please, Mister. Help! She's hurting my arm."

"I agree with Ashley," I said. "We're going to play Monopoly at Pepe's cabin. And if you don't behave, straight to Time Out."

"This is not fair," McKenzie said. "Not fair."

The three of us trooped down to Letty's cabin. When we knocked, Pepe opened the door. He looked disappointed when he saw the three of us. I had not seen him since the goat barbecue.

"Yo, dude," he said, shaking my hand vigorously. "We meet again." He was wearing Rap jeans, which were hitched so low on his hips that you could see his red, white, and blue underwear—a Hispanic rap style?

McKenzie pointed at him. "Your hair looks funny. Are you an Indian?"

Ashley giggled.

Pepe ran his hand through his purple mohawk. "Who's the little kid? Are you baby sitting?"

McKenzie stuck her tongue out at him. "I'm not a baby."

"Yeah, right," Ashley said. She let the spaghetti strap fall off her shoulder. "So, Pepe," she said, glancing at me out of the corner of her eye. "We'll play Spin the Bottle another time."

So he didn't think girls were gross any more? Within the span of a month, he had changed into a horny devil.

I cleared my throat. "Is your mom home?"

"Dude, the owner of La Concha Bakery called her. New job. She's gonna make pan dulces. She said, 'This camp sucks big mammoth...'" Then he stopped suddenly. "Is Sinead your friend?"

Ashley became prim and nodded her head toward McKenzie. "Hey, Pepe, watch your language."

"Kind of," I said. "Don't know her very well, but you could say she's a friend."

Weren't they all new friends? Until...until what?

But Pepe was staring at Ashley's chest.

I waved my hand in front of his eyes, "Hello. Anybody home?"

McKenzie piped up, "My mom has big boobs. I saw her once when she was getting out of the shower."

"McKenzie, that's not nice," Ashley said.

She squealed. "But it's true!"

"That's enough, McKenzie," Ashley said.

McKenzie asked, "Are your boobs real?"

Pepe guffawed. "Dude, where did you get this kid? She's like, like something from reality TV. Did you ever see Anna Nicole Smith's show?"

"I thought we came to play Monopoly," I said.

McKenzie continued, "Lots of my mom's friends have those operations to make their boobs bigger. Their husbands won't like them unless they have big boobs."

"Pepe," I said. "Let's set up the board."

Pepe was laughing so hard he was bent over so you could see the crack in his butt. "Dude." He could barely talk. "Dude."

"My name is Gary," I said. "Remember?"

When he caught his breath, he said, "So, dude, Gary, whatever your name is, we can't play."

"Why not?"

"Juan José put the dice up his nose," Pepe said. "And he ate the card for Park Place."

McKenzie giggled. "Ooooh, gross. Does Juan José eat his boogers? Babies do that."

"Okay," I said. "Why don't we play cards?"

Ashley said brightly, "That's a great idea. Why don't we play Go Fish?"

McKenzie whined. "I don't wanna. I don't wanna. I don't wanna."

Pepe was rummaging through a cabinet, looking for the cards. "Maybe Dad took them. Put them in another place. He plays poker on Friday nights."

Ashley gritted her teeth. "If you don't behave, we're gonna drown you in the river."

"My dad says…" Pepe waved his hand.

McKenzie said, "You'll go to jail for that."

Pepe continued, "My dad says you fell flat on your ass trying to catch that zebra." He chuckled.

"Dude," Pepe said. "Did you break anything?"

I sighed. "Could you stop calling me dude?"

Pepe hitched his jeans up a little, since they kept sliding down his hips.

McKenzie pointed at him and started giggling. "Your pants are falling down. Falling down. Falling down. Soon, you'll be *naked!*"

Ashley pinched her arm. "Cut it out! You're annoying."

"So, Du... I mean, Gary," Pepe said. "My dad says there's no way you could be undercover. You're not *muy*." Pepe's pants kept sliding further and further down his pelvis.

"*Muy* what?"

"You're just not *muy*. Kind of. Like."

"Like what?" Did I really care what Speedy said about me to his kids?

"Well," Pepe said, then hesitated. "My ma says you don't have any common sense. Like dude, you don't even know how to do the basic things. I mean, even a fourteen year-old kid like me knows how to..."

McKenzie was wailing. "She hurt me. Uncle Gary, please. Do something. Ashley's attacking me."

Pepe's pants had slid down, close to the crucial areas. He had on huge boxer shorts with a Batman and Robin motif.

"Maybe we should change the activity," Ashley said. "You haven't even found a deck of cards. This is seriously un-funny."

"I'm not *muy* what?" Why didn't I just let it go? My feelings would just get hurt. Why did I want Pepe's approval anyway?

Ashley said, "Batman and Robin are so retro. How can you wear that hideous underwear?"

"Pepe's wearing Batman and Robin underwear!" McKenzie squealed, delighted. She started singing the Batman song "Batman! Nananananana, Batman! Let's watch cartoons. I don't wanna play cards. I don't wanna."

Pepe shrugged. "I don't know where my dad put his cards. We only have one deck because we're poor. He might have stuck them in his underwear drawer. Hee, hee! That's where he puts his *Playboy* magazine or anything he wants to hide."

"I think we should do something else. Let's go to the art room," I said. "We could make bread boards."

McKenzie shouted, "*Boring!*"

Ashley said, "Good idea! I'm officially off duty as of right now."

"You're not coming?"

Ashley tossed her hair back. "Nope. She's all yours."

McKenzie whined. "But I want you to come. Uncle Gary is *boring*!"

"But I thought you didn't like Ashley?"

McKenzie stuck her lip out. "She's more fun than you."

"Let's go," I said, taking her by the hand. "Pepe, when's your mom coming back?"

I didn't know if it was a good idea to leave Ashley with Pepe, but she was seventeen, a big girl. I wasn't her bodyguard. Not my problem.

Pepe said, "Any minute. She has to make homemade tortillas for my Dad, every day, rain or shine. He's traditional. Has to have beans and tortillas every day. I don't get it! I'd rather have a Whataburger!"

"Why don't we all go to the art room?"

Ashley smirked at me. "And do what? Play with Play-Doh?"

"Don't you have to organize the closing ceremony for the Comanches?" I asked.

Ashley folded her arms. "Like, whatever."

"I thought you were excited about it before?"

Ashley rolled her eyes. "Mary Alice cancelled it."

"Really?"

McKenzie whined. "I wanna play with Play-Doh." I dragged McKenzie behind me, as she wailed, "I wanna stay. I wanna stay. I wanna stay."

The door slammed shut.

The next day, Mary Alice summoned me to the office. She was swiveling around in her black chair, her chin cupped in her hands, when I arrived.

"You do know that you left Ashley unchaperoned with Pepe yesterday? She is a well-developed young lady."

"Did they elope?"

"This is not a joking matter! We are not running a brothel around here!"

"Ashley refused to leave," I said. "What was I supposed to do? Drag her by the ear?"

"*Yes!*" Mary Alice said. "You're a teacher. Don't you know that you have to use *fear*?"

"What happened?"

"Letty found them in their birthday suits, playing strip poker! She is so upset she has refused to go to work."

Did she know that Letty had another job at La Concha? That Sinead was planning to quit? Did I need to be the messenger of bad news?

"Well, at least they weren't doing the deed."

I still longed to do the deed with Sinead. I had to stop thinking about her.

Mary Alice waved her hand. She suddenly lowered her voice. "That's not the real reason I summoned you."

So Mary Alice was not as prudish as she pretended to be?

"Oh," I said. "What's happened now?"

"McKenzie didn't burn down the barn," Mary Alice whispered, although there was no one in the office.

"Who did, then?"

"Someone was operating a meth lab. Do you think Speedy?"

"No," I said. "Not Speedy. He likes booze. Maybe he smokes a little pot every once in a while."

"But he's had a few brushes with the law."

"Remember Josiah?" I said. "We met him in Azzurro's garage. The creep with the wandering eye."

Mary Alice nodded. "Of course, that unpleasant cedar chopper."

"Maybe he's operating the meth lab," I said.

Mary Alice looked up at the ceiling. "Could be."

"Listen, this is off the subject of brothels, meth labs, drug deals, and arson. But do you think I might relinquish my job as bodyguard?"

Mary Alice slammed her fist down on the desk. "No!" she said. "You'll guard her until the bitter end. Until she is safely back in the hands of her parents."

I moaned. "Aye, aye."

Mary Alice lowered her voice. "There is something else. And," she sighed heavily, "I wish you would stop making jokes."

How else could I deal with this crazy situation?

"I can't imagine what it could be."

"I went back to Azzurro's garage. Do you know what I found?"

"More lists of looted objects from the Baghdad Museum?"

"You have to swear on the Bible you won't tell a soul," Mary Alice said.

She nodded at me grimly to put my hand on the Bible and swear. I had never noticed the Bible before. In danger of Chapter 11, had she decided she should consult it more often?

"I swear," I said, solemn. Not really! "So what's the big deal?"

"Documents in Arabic from the Libyan Secret Service. That tell of torture in underground prisons." Her face was grim.

"Libya?!"

"And the IRA's involvement in Libya. Munitions deals." She pursed her lips.

"And?"

"Lists of the names of IRA members involved. Special training." Mary Alice put her finger to her lips. "Don't say another word!"

"I was right."

"Aengus mustn't know you suspect him," Mary Alice said. "It could be dangerous for you."

I really didn't want to believe Aengus was implicated. He seemed like such a nice guy. Could a murderer also be a nice guy? What an absurd question! But just because he was listed didn't mean he had done Azzurro, or Patrick, in. Or was he just a talented actor? Were we all being played? Had Dad been playing Mom and me? Had he been more involved with Weddo Silva's operation than he admitted? Was that why he became so sad?

"So the documents are now in the hands of the army, who came with their six trucks to pick them up?" I asked.

"No!" Mary Alice said. "I have them."

"What?" I said. "But that's tampering with…"

Mary Alice said, "I have my reasons."

Chapter 15

The Last Waltz

MOSQUITOES BUZZED AROUND MY EARS. I could not stop wondering why Mary Alice had taken those documents. And what did they say, exactly? After another two hours of swatting mosquitoes in my cabin, I grabbed the flashlight and shined it on my watch: 3 a.m. The large skeleton key to the office was hanging on a nail, next to the cabin door. A label said: SPARE KEY.

I had never opened the office at night. Still, these ladies didn't seem the type to go in for high-tech alarms.

Of course, when I stuck the key into the keyhole, it didn't open immediately. There must be a trick. I pushed this way and that. Still nothing. Just pretend you are a real detective, Gary! Finally, I pulled the door back, with the key in the lock, and it suddenly opened. Open Sesame!

Now, if I were Mary Alice, where would I hide important documents? I sat down in the swivel chair and opened drawers. Maybe the desk was too obvious a hiding place? And all of the drawers were unlocked. Nothing but insurance agreements and old bills.

Where else could they be? I opened the closet to the right of the desk. A first-aid kit: gauze bandages, Band-Aids, peroxide, Pepto-Bismol, antibiotic ointment, suppositories. I rifled through the bottom of the closet: Indian costumes and headdresses. This was hokier than my novel, *Pure Water*. Why would she hide these documents in a box of Kotex? But men would never look there! There was a shelf on the top of the closet: enough cowboy hats for a rodeo. As I felt along the ledge, my hand hit something—a bulky envelope.

A voice boomed, "Just what do you think you are doing?"

When I turned around, the flashlight was so strong it almost blinded me.

Mary Alice was wearing a white cotton nightgown, tied at the neck with a red bow, and a pair of clunky hiking boots without any socks.

"Ointment for chiggers," I said, without missing a beat.

She waved the huge yellow flashlight as if it were a gun. "You won't find anything. I've destroyed them."

"The ointment?"

"Sit down," she said, waving me over to the couch. "On the double."

"Why?"

"Because I'm the captain of this ship," she said.

"I don't dispute that," I said. "But why did you destroy the documents?"

Mary Alice cleared her throat. "You don't need to know. Just like no one needs to know you are wanted by Interpol."

Like one of the campers who was being disciplined, I protested, "But I didn't do anything wrong."

Mary Alice snorted. She held out the palm of her hand. "The key."

I handed over the skeleton key.

As if I were a kid, she said. "Go back to your cabin. Forget we ever had this conversation. Unless you want to be arrested!"

On my way back to the cabin, I passed Gudrun's house. I tapped on her bedroom window.

Kharalombos's massive figure appeared at the window. He was singing, "*Maalel amar maaloh. Maginash 'ala baloh.*" "What's wrong with the moon? Why didn't she remember us?" From one of Mohamed Fauzy's most touching songs, "What's Wrong with the Moon?"

"*Meen?*" Kharalombos asked, first in Arabic. Who is it?

A large figure in the bed wheezed and snored. Dagmar yapped.

"It's me, Gary," I whispered.

"Ssssh. You'll wake her up," Kharalombos said.

I chuckled.

"It's not funny!"

Kharalombos and I walked into the back yard. "You usually sleep early. Why are you walking in the woods in the middle of the night?"

Dagmar had followed us out. We sat in the plastic chairs for children, since there was no other place to sit. But Kharalombos split the tiny chair in two. He tossed it to the side and sat on the damp ground in a pile of leaves.

"Mary Alice knows I'm wanted by Interpol," I said.

Kharalombos laughed heartily. "*Tab'an!* Of course. Why else would she know that she doesn't have to pay you?"

"But we did get paid."

"*Aiwa,*" Kharalombos said. "A few piastres here and there. Enough for a *ful* sandwich! Some free bacon from their gourmet cafeteria! A few cans of sardines. I should have stayed in Cairo. A producer wants me to work on the new Ramadan serial. The life of King Farouk. I could be making thousands of pounds."

"You're going to teach the king how to waltz?"

Kharalombos shook his head. "They start filming in a week. That is a lost chance. Another lost chance. *Khosaara!*"

"Mary Alice found some documents in Azzuro's garage. *Mukhabarat.* Libyan intelligence," I said.

"Why does she care? If she is just a little old lady who runs a girls' camp? Don't you see? It's another American conspiracy." Dagmar yapped in agreement. "Shhh, Dagmar," he said, scooping her up and petting her with his huge hand. "You have to be quiet. That's a good girl. *Mashmousha*. My little apricot!"

"So anyone who speaks Arabic well is linked to a conspiracy?"

In Cairo, that's what everyone believed—and that's what Kharalombos believed, although he was now in the United States. And it was true—after 9/11, the demand for Arabic speakers in the US intelligence services had skyrocketed and Middle Eastern programs had flourished. Few seemed to see the value in knowing another language, unless it had direct utility. Yet who could ever determine the utility of knowledge? And how might that knowledge might be connected, internationally? Did an Irishman named Aengus have a nefarious connection with Libya? And was it a coincidence that Azzurro had worked in Libya?

Dagmar yapped, as if she understood what we were saying.

Kharalombos snorted. "You believe everything people tell you. That's your problem. You are *saazeg*. Too naïve. Maybe she was using the church as a cover. She does not seem very religious to me."

Well, that much was true. However, it did not mean she had been recruited. Maybe she had just lost her piety. Grandmother Grace had believed, but she didn't make sanctimonious references to God all the time.

"Do you know what the documents say?" Kharalombos asked.

"The IRA was being supplied by the Libyans," I said.

"That's no big secret." Kharalombos snorted. "That was reported in the Egyptian newspapers since 1985, when the Americans bombed Libya."

"Maybe she was trying to protect Aengus," I said, theorizing.

"Did you read the documents?" Kharalombos asked.

I shook my head but pressed on. I could not resist spinning a tale: "Maybe Aengus was an informer. He's hiding out in a small town in central Texas because he's a marked man."

Why had they left Ireland? Was the job at Clover Flower such a plum?

"We are being castrated by all these women," Kharalombos said. "Did she threaten you?"

I nodded.

Kharalombos whispered, "We must make our escape. Before…"

Before we had no balls left?

But something else occurred to me. "Maybe the murder has something to do with the past. Azzurro, or Patrick, knew something about Aengus? And Aengus didn't want anyone to find out."

Kharalombos shrugged. "Maybe, if it were like a *taar*, a blood feud in Upper Egypt. That happens with these gangs. But I don't think Aengus…? You have no proof for anything you are saying. But such a wild imagination! You can write the detective novels for children, like Mahmoud Salem, my hero. Your next book!"

"So you don't believe me? You just said you thought it was a conspiracy!"

Kharalombos didn't put much stock in any of my theories. He was much shrewder than I was politically. He sighed. "Look, America is not to my taste, as I have told you many times. I am Mediterranean. I have wanted to leave this crooked circus for weeks. Did you get your leg x-rayed? Did they take you to a doctor?"

"What does that have to do with what I am saying?!"

"You see, they are so *bukhala…gelda*. Stingy. They won't even pay for a doctor. So everything I say about them is true!"

Gudrun was shouting, "My bonbon! Where are you? Are you hiding from me?"

"One more thing," I said. "Can you give McKenzie a dancing lesson? I have to entertain her, and I can't think up anything more to do."

"*Baiza awi. Metdalla'a.* Such a spoiled little girl," Kharalombos said.

Gudrun shouted, "Please, my darling, can you make me some hot tea? I am having a sore throat."

Kharalombos cradled Dagmar in the crook of his arm. "I have to go. We will plan the escape later."

I had never been to the dance studio. The place was covered with long mirrors. You could not escape looking at yourself, even if you tried. Every wall of the room was covered with a mirror. A drained, pale, middle-aged man stared back from the looking-glass—the image was less flattering than Dixie's photograph. I had never noticed the wrinkles on my neck or the furrows in my forehead. And if I looked at myself from the side, a little paunch bulged out. I was getting fat from the gourmet food at the camp. Was that me? Could we ever see ourselves as others saw us? Was that what happened to Dad, after he sold the company? He wasn't the busy mogul any more, full of plans—just a morose man with few hobbies or friends. He felt he was no longer needed. I lounged on a stack of yoga mats. I had been up all night and was dying for a nap.

Kharalombos stood in front of his pupils: Ashley, Pepe, and McKenzie. "Now," he said, gesturing with his huge hand, "the first rule of the waltz is to count: One, two, three. One, two, three…"

His pupils did not look excited. "We will demonstrate," Kharalombos said, standing straight. He was wearing his formal black leather dancing shoes. "Gary."

"I can't dance," I said. "As you know."

Kharalombos glared at me. "*Ya raagel!* I am doing the favor. Make my burden lighter. *Teezak hamra.* Your ass is red like a monkey's."

Pepe laughed. "That's a good one."

I struggled up from the yoga mats. Kharalombos put one of his hands on my waist, the other on my shoulder. He was so much taller than me, he had to bend way over. We started to waltz. "And one, two, three, one, two, three…"

I followed, but just barely. And then, I missed a step. Kharalombos's huge foot came crashing down on mine.

"Awwwww!!!!" I yelled.

Pepe was bent over laughing. "Dudes," he said. "What goofballs!"

McKenzie whooped. "Is Mister Kharalump a homo?"

She was only seven!

What a wonderful evening we had with Rose and Bill, waltzing!

Ashley tossed her blonde hair back. "The waltz is for old fogies. It's, like, so uncool. My mother wants me to learn it for cotillion. Why don't you teach us how to belly dance?"

Pepe bowed and said, "May I have the next waltz?"

But Ashley ignored him and tied a wide purple sash around her hips. She went to the other side of the room and stood in front of the mirror, where she practiced moving her hips provocatively. She didn't have the right technique and looked as if she were doing a sixties rock-and-roll dance with a hula hoop.

McKenzie followed her. She stood next to her, copying every move she made.

Kharalombos stopped. "You said they wanted to learn how to waltz!" My foot was on fire. I limped back to the stack of yoga mats.

"I meant any kind of dancing lesson," I said.

"Dude," Pepe said, breathless. "Can you teach me how to breakdance?"

Kharalombos sniffed. "My name is Mr Kharalombos. In Egypt, we don't address teachers and elders as 'Dude.' I teach salsa, rumba, the tango, the waltz. The more refined dances."

Pepe had slipped a Michael Jackson tape into the recorder and turned up the volume at full blast: "You better run, Better do what you can, Don't wanna see no blood, don't be a macho man. So beat it."

And of course, Michael Jackson had not wanted to be a macho man, after all—and had plastic surgery to make his face look more feminine.

Pepe made ungainly leaps across the floor that did not resemble Michael Jackson's moves. McKenzie giggled and clapped her hands. He came dangerously close to my mat.

"Hey, Pepe, you could hurt yourself. Watch out!" I said.

"Just beat it. Beat it . . . "

Ashley was still gazing at herself in the mirror. She put her fingers in her ears, mouthing, "Michael Jackson is gross!"

Gudrun stood at the door, in an orange muumuu. "Ah, my *Liebchen*, have you seen Dagmar?"

But all we could hear was: "They're out to get you, better leave while you can. Don't wanna be a boy, you wanna be a man."

Pepe was singing at the top of his lungs, "Just beat it. Beat it."

Gudrun marched across the wooden floor. "Just be . . . " Suddenly, the place went silent.

"That is the American garbage that is exported to Europe," Gudrun said, shaking her mop of carrot-red hair. "Not like the classics. Frank Sinatra. Andy Williams."

Pepe moaned. "Oh, man!"

As soon as Ashley saw Gudrun in the mirror, she sashayed over to Kharalombos and stood in front of him, jutting one of her hips to the side. She was wearing very short blue jean cutoffs. "Kharalombos and I were just going to waltz, weren't we?"

Kharalombos gingerly picked Ashley's hand off his shoulder, as if it were a horsefly that had landed on his long-sleeved white oxford-cloth shirt.

Pepe started howling as if he were a wolf. "Busted!"

McKenzie imitated him. "Busted!"

At this rate, Kharalombos couldn't be counted on to entertain them for the morning. I would have to come up with some other plan. But what?

Ashley stuck her lip out and her eyes filled with tears. She picked up her duffel bag, whispering under her breath, "I'm outta here! I am so over him. Like, what was I thinking?"

I didn't know what to say to her. He's too old for you? It's a summer infatuation? I nodded sympathetically. Hopefully, Kharalombos had not led her on or . . .

As Ashley fled, Gudrun stood in front of Kharalombos in her orange muu-muu. With her flaming hair and dress, she looked like a giant navel orange. But who was I to throw stones? It wasn't as if I really looked like Gary Cooper, either. But I could make Boriana swoon. And Sinead.

"My *Liebchen*, may I have this dance?" Gudrun asked.

Kharalombos nodded solemnly and they waltzed around the studio. But I could see Kharalombos's face in the mirror on the adjacent wall, and his brown eyes looked melancholy. Gudrun's eyes looked dreamy, as he artfully glided her around the room. Andy Williams crooned, "Moon River, wider than a mile… Two drifters, off to see the world, there's such a lot of world to see."

Pepe put his finger in his mouth, as if he were about to gag. "Dude, can you stomach this stuff? It's like cough syrup!"

"We're after the same rainbow's end."

Mary Alice poked her head into the studio, summoning me with her forefinger. I got up from my comfy perch. Oh, God! Maybe she needed me for some other odd job. Please, God, no . . . "

She cleared her throat. "Charlie would like a word with you. He's outside."

Charlie was sitting in his black Lexus patrol car.

After a tense, silent ride into town, I was taken into a room, bare except for a table and two wooden chairs. The beefy-looking cop I had seen at the crime scene was standing near the door, sending text messages on his cell phone. I glanced down—even a cop in the countryside could afford a smartphone!

A simple search had shown that I was not from Missouri. That the driver's license was a fake. The game was up.

"You have to tell me the truth," Charlie said. "This is a murder investigation. All sorts of ugly things come out."

That I'm a wanted man? A cyber-terrorist on the run?

"One of your hairs was found in Captain Quinn's garage," Charlie said, pursing his lips. "We have a good forensics team. Very professional."

"But I don't have any hair," I said, running my hand over my bald head.

"Can the jokes," Charlie said, sighing. "I know you're a wanted man."

"Of course you do," I said. "You must. So when are you turning me over?"

"It's not my jurisdiction," he said. "I am concerned about the murder in *my* county. Kerr County."

"You're not arresting me?" I was flabbergasted.

Charlie bounced his Number 2 pencil up and down on the desk. "Not if you answer my questions truthfully." He looked me straight in the eye. "Son."

"I'm fifty."

Charlie snorted. "I'm old enough for you to be my son. What were you doing in the garage?"

"Mary Alice and I were looking for Azzurro or Captain Quinn. She thought he might help us with the septic tank. It was the Fourth of July weekend and the septic tank had overflowed. All the companies were closed. We found the boxes labeled Baghdad Museum. Mary Alice gave me some rubber gloves and asked me to look through the boxes."

Charlie looked up at the ceiling thoughtfully. "Did you read the documents?"

"There was an army unit assigned to recover looted objects from the Baghdad Museum. It looked like the report of the unit. A list of looted objects. The ones recovered."

"Umm-hum," Charlie said. "I see. How long were you there?"

"About five minutes. Maybe ten."

"What happened after that?"

"Josiah came in. He told us Azzurro had gone on a trip."

"A long one," Charlie said, "at that."

I curbed a chuckle.

"That was not said in a spirit of levity," Charlie said. "You do realize this is a murder investigation?"

"Do you think Josiah . . ?"

"Everyone is a suspect."

I squirmed in my chair. "Do you suspect me?"

Charlie said, "I haven't ruled anyone out. But what I want to know is this…"

Why Mary Alice had made me put on the rubber gloves? About the missing document in Arabic that Mary Alice had destroyed? Why wasn't he interviewing Mary Alice? Or was Kharalombos's suspicion about her correct? She was not in his jurisdiction—working for the federal government. Should I mention the meth in the cave? A voice shouted in my ear, "Just answer the question. Nothing more."

"In your statement, you mentioned hearing three voices going up to Captain Quinn's place. You knew the second voice, but you lied about it. Strictly speaking, you perjured yourself in your statement."

I groaned. "A fraud named Count Triksky."

"Did you know him in Cairo?"

"He was a friend of Gudrun's. He was acting as her escort. They were going on a Nile cruise but then the revolution…" I waved my hand.

Charlie raised his eyebrows. "Go on."

"We think he's an antiquities smuggler," I said.

Charlie nodded. "I see. Is there anything else you want to tell me?"

"I am not a cyber-terrorist!" I shouted. I felt I really was starting to lose it this time. "You have to believe me! I can't even run a scan on my computer! I hate technology! How could I create a virus that would destroy all of the new books at Zadorf Publishers?"

How could I have lost self-control? Harry Houdini would never have shown his cards like that!

"Could be," Charlie said. But he kept a straight face, and I couldn't tell what he was thinking or feeling. What genius.

"Are you letting me go?"

"For now," Charlie said. "Don't go far. I'd prefer if you didn't repeat our conversation to anyone. The murderer could be in your midst. Understood? And it could be dangerous for you."

I nodded. Charlie was much more terrifying than Mary Alice.

"Jeremy."

"Chief?" the other cop said, looking up from his cell phone.

"Can you run Gary back to Clover Flower?"

"Sure thing, Chief."

Part IV

Twists in the Tale

Chapter 16

The Signing

I DIDN'T DISCUSS CHARLIE'S CONVERSATIONS WITH ANYONE, even Mary Alice. Who knows, maybe Mary Alice was The One? But why? What was her possible motive?

When I returned, Mary Alice barked, "You've got a new assignment."

"Who's baby sitting McKenzie?"

"Ashley will take care of her the last two days. She's on duty, day and night. Round the clock. You're needed in the office."

I groaned. I hated office work—it was like having a phone chained to your foot.

"On the double," Mary Alice said.

But instead of anorexic mothers arriving in their Mercedes, giant brown UPS trucks were driving up our steep gravel driveway. The UPS drivers usually just dumped the box onto the gravel and stuck a clipboard in my face: "Sign here." If I happened to be out of the office, I received an automated message which said: "A UPS driver will deliver a package to you at 6 p.m. If you do not sign, the package will be returned to UPS. You must pick up the package yourself between 10 and 11:05 a.m. on Mondays only. Thank you for using UPS." When I called UPS, I *always* received an automated message: "Thank you for calling UPS. All lines are busy at this time. If you are calling about a package, please press 1. If you are calling about a complaint, please press . . . " I never spoke to a live human being.

There were so many boxes they filled the entire office. We didn't even have enough room to wriggle past them to go to the bathroom.

The return address: Huff & Huff Publishers, New York, New York. Rose's novel? Was she doing this to torture me? But, why? "Could you tell me what's in the boxes?"

Mary Alice said, "You don't know? Gudrun didn't tell you?"

Gudrun was biting into a doughnut. She held up the sack: Dunkin' Donuts. "This is from my own pocket money. I didn't take the money from the kitty."

"Tell me what?"

Mary Alice pulled out the metal box marked "Petty Cash" from the drawer. There was a huge lock on it. She patted it and put it back in the drawer.

"Would you prefer the chocolate glazed, the coconut dipped, or the crullers?" Gudrun dipped her large bejeweled hand into the bag, smiling at me. "My *Liebchen*."

She had never called me that before! I hoped she wasn't getting any ideas.

"Go on," Mary Alice said. "Tell him."

"I'll take coconut," I said. At breakfast, they had served packets of instant oatmeal and prunes. They were really scraping the bottom of the barrel.

"You see, my *Liebchen*," Gudrun said, "I don't know why I didn't see how adorable you were before. Like a little munchkin."

I growled. "I'm Billy the Kid."

Mary Alice's voice boomed. "Ramses el-Kibir has sent us his latest book on mummies. It's a coffee-table book. Animal mummies."

"Why?" I asked.

Gudrun pinched my cheek. Her fingers were dusty with powdered sugar. "Ramses will sign his books for the children at the closing ceremony."

"But we don't have any kids left," I said. "It doesn't sound like a book for kids. And we've got at least five hundred books here!"

"Gudrun has not been paying attention! She has been preoccupied with other things. As you know," Mary Alice said.

"You didn't tell Ramses el-Kibir that we don't have any kids left at the camp?" I turned toward Gudrun.

Gudrun laughed. "Don't worry," she said. "You worry too much. Ramses el-Kibir is so famous. Everyone from Schulenburg and San Antonio will come for his mummy book. You will see."

Mary Alice frowned. "You can't keep promising things that you don't deliver. Gary, I want you to put ads on Facebook. In all the local newspapers. Do whatever it takes."

This was a worse job than signing for boxes.

Speedy and I were in charge of lugging all the boxes of books from the office to Gudrun's house on the day of the book signing. Then we were assigned the task of hanging a huge banner from the porch: "We Love You, Captain Mummy," in red, white, and blue.

Gudrun was inside, making an elaborate German dessert. When I opened the door, an aroma of vanilla permeated the air. She was wearing a large apron with a colorful flowery print—red geraniums. She was also wearing a chef's hat, made from the same geranium print. *Hausfrau* was written across her massive chest.

Kharalombos was lounging on the sofa, petting Dagmar. A series of Shiner Bock beer bottles were lined up in front of him. Next to them was a cutting board with a variety of different kinds of sausages, neatly sliced.

"Mind if I taste?" I asked, picking up a slice and popping it into my mouth.

Dagmar yapped.

"Delicious. Is she serving this at the book signing?"

Kharalombos chuckled and shook his head emphatically. "*La*. That's *Blutwurst*. Consanguine pig's blood."

I had already swallowed it. "I think you mean congealed."

"You see how America has destroyed my English. I was a graduate of Manor House secondary school," Kharalombos gestured with his huge hands. "We only had the very best teachers who spoke proper British English. Americans have ruined the language!"

I felt like punching him in the nose. He was becoming insufferable. Needed to be shipped back to Cairo.

Speedy took a swig out of a Shiner Bock bottle. "Hey, *amigo*, are any of those sausages venison?"

"My *Liebchen*," Gudrun called out, "would you like to sample the *Bienenstich*?"

She was just pulling out the pastry from the oven. As she was bending over, we could see her enormous rump.

Speedy giggled.

Kharalombos shook his head. "I don't have the taste for sweets. And I ate too much sausage." He rubbed his protruding belly.

Gudrun started talking baby talk. "My *Liebchen*," she said, sticking out her lip, "my bonbon, you won't even try one teeny weeny bite from your *Hausfrau*?"

"Hey," I put in, "don't you think you might give us a hand? The book signing is going to start any minute."

Kharalombos stared at the television. "I will not lift my pinkie finger for that *homaar. Ibn kalb waati.* I will never forget the way he cuckolded me."

Speedy was downing the rest of Kharalombos's Shiner Bock in one swig. "What's he's saying?"

"Expletives."

"Gary, I didn't even go to junior college," Speedy said. "You know that by now."

"Son of a donkey."

Gudrun pinched my cheek. "My little munchkin. Won't you try my *Bienenstich*?" She shoved a plate with the pastry in my face.

Speedy had wandered over to the refrigerator and was peering inside. Shiner Bock bottles had taken over an entire shelf. He snatched one and popped off the metal cap with his teeth.

I took a bite of Gudrun's pastry. The top was caramelized almonds, filled with vanilla cream—heavenly. She stood in front of me, waiting for the verdict. Kharalombos switched channels with the remote. He looked bored.

"It's wonderful," I said. "What's it called?"

"*Ja-aa*," Gudrun said, smiling. "It's the *Bienenstich*. This means in German, 'the bee's sting.' Won't you try it?"

Kharalombos sighed. "In America, you can never find out what's happening in the rest of the world. It's as if America is the center of the universe. I hate American football. It is so uncivilized! What beasts! They crash their heads together!"

Gudrun laughed. "Ah, don't be a sour pussy...I mean, puss."

Speedy spewed beer all over the kitchen floor.

Mary Alice marched in with her clipboard. "Just what do you think you are doing?"

Speedy set the beer down on the counter. "We came in to get more chairs."

I handed the pastry to Mary Alice. "I never tasted anything like it. It's called *Bienenstich*. Bee sting."

Mary Alice's eyes narrowed. "We agreed that the money for this reception is not coming from the camp budget."

Gudrun shook her mop of orange hair. "This is from my very own purse. I didn't touch the kitty. I swear on the Bible of Martin Luther. I am German and I never break my contracts. I mean promises."

Mary Alice couldn't resist taking a bite of the *Bienenstich*. "Ummm," she said. "Delicious."

Gudrun had served up a generous portion for Speedy. "No thanks, Mrs Grunewald."

"*Aacch*," she said, handing the china plate, decorated with blue swans, to Kharalombos. "You have to taste my honey."

Speedy looked as if he might burst.

Gudrun looked astonished. "What is this funny business?"

Mary Alice cleared her throat. "Let's get to the business at hand. Huff & Huff publishers have also sent us a box of Indiana Jones hats. They want us to sell those at the signing. Thirty dollars a pop."

"That's a lot," I said.

Speedy looked doubtful. "Thirty bucks? Too much."

Gudrun was saying, "Open, my *Liebchen*." She was trying to feed Kharalombos a bite of her pastry.

Dagmar barked in Kharalombos's defense.

Kharalombos refused to open his mouth. He had folded his arms and was staring at a Viagra commercial on television. A man and a woman were walking hand in hand on a beach, looking out at a wide expanse of blue sea. "Always consult your doctor. Side effects can be, but are not limited to, heart attacks, strokes, and paralysis…"

"Gudrun," Mary Alice said, "where are your folding chairs?"

She gestured toward the spare bedroom. Mary Alice nodded and we trooped in to get them.

"How do we even know if anyone will come?" Speedy asked.

"You have a point," Mary Alice replied. "But Ramses is hugely successful."

"One hundred and fifty people on Facebook said they were coming," I said. "Why don't we just stack the books on the tables for now?"

Gudrun had speared the pastry with a fork and left it in front of Kharalombos.

Mary Alice's voice boomed. "Why aren't you more involved? Ramses is your friend. You are the one who promised him."

Gudrun looked puzzled. "*Nein*, I never promised him. That was never my idea. I thought you were the one who invited him."

Dagmar had leaped up on the table and wolfed down the pastry in one bite. She was licking the cream off the plate.

"Are you getting dementia?" Mary Alice asked. "We talked about it yesterday. Why would I invite him? I think he's a pill."

Gudrun shrugged. "A pill? After all these years in America, my English is still . . . The right hand and left hand are not going at the same time. In the same direction. Are confused!"

Mary Alice asked, "Who told Huff & Huff Publishers to send us five hundred copies of his book, then?"

Gudrun shook her mop of orange hair. "Maybe he was saying something last time he was here. But he never confirmed the appointment."

Mary Alice snorted. "We could use some good publicity around here. Gary, you and Speedy just stack the books."

Speedy followed me out onto the front porch. "Man, oh, man, can you believe all those pussy jokes...."

"Forget about pus . . . " I said, opening up one of the cardboard boxes. Mary Alice had followed us outside.

I handed Speedy an Indiana Jones hat. "Might bring you luck next time you have to lasso a zebra."

"Thanks," Speedy said, "I always wanted one of these. Is it free?"

"Who's counting?" I started arranging some of the books on the table. Next to the books, I set a sign reading, "Please wait in line."

Speedy flipped through one of the books. "I hate to read," Speedy said. "And I am no expert. But would kids be interested in crocodile mummies? It seems like a book for professors." Then he whistled. "Forty-five bucks. Lotta *dinero*. When you think of how many six-packs of Corona you could buy at Walmart!"

Pepe was carrying a blue raft onto the front porch. "Hey, Dad, yo, want to come swimming with us?"

Ashley and McKenzie were close behind him. McKenzie had yellow floaties on her arms. She was wearing a bikini and looked like one of those children from the "baby-doll" beauty contests. When she saw me, she stuck out her tongue and pointed. "It's the pervert!"

Ashley was wearing a thong. You could see the cheeks of her ass. Her breasts were barely covered by tiny triangles of red cloth.

Mary Alice shook her head. "That's not an acceptable bathing suit!"

Ashley batted her eyelashes. "So fire me!"

"Young lady," Mary Alice said, "you are treading a thin line."

"Captain Mummy is coming. Don't you want to meet him?" I asked.

McKenzie shouted, "It's our last day to swim in the river."

"Hans, the neighbor across the way, is going to let us ride in his speedboat," Ashley said. "That's very cool. He's cooler than Captain Mummy. Way awesome."

Pepe chimed in, "Yo, dude, he puts the pedal to the metal."

Mary Alice's eyes narrowed. "Speedy, do you think you could keep an eye on them? A little adult supervision might be in order."

"Sure," Speedy said. "I'll just change into my bathing suit."

Pepe whooped. "I told you guys he would come!"

Mary Alice scrutinized me. "You'll be the bartender for the book signing. Do you know how to make drinks? I'd like for you to wear the camp uniform."

"I thought we were just serving beer?"

Mary Alice pulled out the Indian headdress with the long feathers from behind her back and handed it to me. "Put it on."

"What about your austerity program?"

"It's on Gudrun's nickel," Mary Alice said. "Not from the camp budget."

A light blue Volkswagen bug sputtered up the circular driveway. It lurched to a stop and Dr Kaiser crawled out, unfolding his gangly legs from the seat with difficulty. He was wearing the same Baylor tee-shirt embossed with a giant bear, the brown knee socks with leather sandals, and red, white, and blue plaid Bermuda shorts.

"I jumped in my car right after my lecture on Paul's conversion on the road to Damascus, as soon as I heard." Dr Kaiser said. "It's a rare thing."

"Crocodile mummies?" I asked.

Dr Kaiser looked puzzled. "No, no. I have the wish for the *Bienenstich*. It's something my nana used to make for me when I was a child. Even in the German bakeries in Fredericksburg, they do not know how to make it properly. They are only doing the common apple strudel."

"Hello, Dr Kaiser," Mary Alice said. "So glad you could make it today."

Dr Kaiser took her hand and kissed it. "You are most welcome, my lady."

Mary Alice blushed. "You are not proposing. A simple handshake will do."

He bowed. "A man my age still has vim and vigor, if you know what I mean! Ha! Ha! Of course, after I lost my Gertrude, may God rest her soul in heaven, I am spending all of the weekends on bird-watching expeditions and bluebonnet walks in the hill country. The natural beauty of the place is majestic. You wouldn't . . ?"

"I might be interested in going," I said. "I would like to add more birds to my list."

But Dr Kaiser had his eye on Mary Alice.

Mary Alice frowned. "I don't have time to look at bluebonnets! I'm running Clover Flower!"

Then he whispered, "Is there any more news on that heinous crime?"

"That is completely confidential," Mary Alice said.

Did she know something more, or was she just being officious? She avoided looking at me.

"Of course. Of course," Dr Kaiser said, putting his hands behind his back. "I would never transgress upon…"

"Would you like a beer?" I asked. "We have Doppelbock, Eisbock, Waitrose, German Pils, Shiner Bock."

Dr Kaiser glanced down at his watch and then waved his hand. He had a small, expensive-looking black onyx ring on his pinkie finger. "Well, my rule is never to have a drink before one. Two minutes until the hour. To be exact!" He waved his forefinger at me. "We must adhere to rules to keep the discipline! But thank you for your kind offer, anyway."

The door slammed. Gudrun rushed out with a plate, piled high with her homemade pastries.

"Klaus!" Gudrun said. "I made the *Bienenstich*. I found Mama's old recipe in a drawer yesterday. She would have been ninety-nine if she were alive today. I hope you will find it to your liking." Then she lapsed into German.

Dr Kaiser closed his eyes as he chewed the pastry slowly. He looked as if he were having an orgasm.

Mary Alice looked concerned. "What time is the book signing?"

"One o'clock," I said.

Dr Kaiser and Gudrun were chatting in German.

Mary Alice lowered her voice. "Why isn't anyone here?"

"They all drowned in the river?" I ventured.

"Very funny," Mary Alice said.

I couldn't care less about Ramses el-Kibir. No skin off my nose. I didn't care if he sold a single book. But maybe Mary Alice was hoping the book signing would redeem Clover Flower camp: good publicity, rather than bad. For a change.

"Would you like coffee to go with your pastry?" I asked.

Dr Kaiser nodded. "I take it black. Thank you. I am sorry but I don't know your name."

"Gary," I said.

"Ah, yes," Dr Kaiser said. "You are the one who served us those delicious enchiladas the last time. So exotic!"

"I've been promoted," I said.

Dr Kaiser looked surprised, but then he smiled. He was missing a side tooth and looked like a jack o'lantern. "In America, I can never tell when people are hurling a joke. I laugh at the serious things, but do not laugh when everyone else is laughing. Sometimes it causes embarrassment in committee meetings."

Mary Alice glared at me. "Just make the coffee."

Kharalombos had decided to move to the front porch. He was carrying a wooden cutting board, full of cut-up sausage. Under the crook of his arm was a bottle of Shiner Bock. Dagmar followed him, wagging her tail.

When I returned with the coffee, Dr Kaiser was sampling the sausages on the cutting board.

"Now, my dear boy," Dr Kaiser was saying to Kharalombos, "this is *Leber-wurst*. Made from veal and pork liver." He was spreading it on a cracker. "A real delicacy."

I set his black coffee on the table beside him. He rocked back and forth in the rocking chair.

"Thank you for your kindness, Gary," Dr Kaiser said. "Kharalombos here is from Cairo. He was telling me about how the government killed all the pigs during the swine flu epidemic. Apparently, they threw them in pits and then covered them with lime. Most unfortunate."

I nodded. "The World Heath Organization told them the pigs were not a threat." I was not supposed to talk about Cairo—my other life. I had to censor almost every idea or thought I had because invariably it related to Cairo. My conversation in Schulenburg was limited to the weather, food, septic tanks, snakes, and raccoons—comparatively inoffensive topics.

Kharalombos had started to feed Dagmar little pieces of sausage. She would jump up on her hind legs and grab a piece of sausage from the palm of his huge hand.

Dr Kaiser was horrified. "You are spoiling her! This is most distressing. Such a waste! You are feeding her the *Bragenwurst*. The sausage made from the pork belly. Gudrun brought it back in her suitcase the last time she came back from Germany. As you know, it's strictly forbidden to bring food into the United States. And she could have been fined a thousand dollars! Gone to prison!"

Mary Alice stacked more books on the table. "Gary, are you sure you put ads in all the local papers? It's now one-thirty."

"Advertised everywhere," I said.

Why wasn't anyone here? I had hundreds of "likes" on Facebook for the event.

Dr Kaiser said, "I must insist that you do not feed the little dog any more sausage. This is too decadent! When I was a child after the War, we raised rabbits so we could have meat. Everything was rationed."

I thought of poor Blanca. Surely, the porter in Cairo had not....

Kharalombos stared pensively at the river down below. "Gary and I met in a mental hospital. I was hiding from the Big Man. And now…"

I shot Kharalombos a look. What was he doing? I wanted to keep my identity a secret.

"*Aaach*, Klaus," Gudrun said. "You've forgotten that I already told you Gary and Kharalombos saved me from that wicked cobra at the Pyramids when we were filming *The Marvelous Adventures of Ramses el-Kibir*. My darling, won't you tell us what happened at the mental hospital? You are not keeping any more secrets from me?"

So Gudrun had blabbed. Probably everyone in the little town knew.

"*Ja-aa*," Dr Kaiser said. "We got on the CBS news today that the Big Man and his family are now back in Egypt. In the Sharm el-Sheikh."

"*Ya Salaam!* They're alive! They're alive!" Kharalombos said, jumping up from his chair. He embraced me and kissed me on the cheek. "Nunu is alive! *Al-hamdu lellah! Al-hamdu lellaah!*" He twirled me around the front porch in a waltz. "La! La! La! La!"

"*Aaach*," Dr Kaiser said. "I am not against the gays, but you are not . . ?"

"I thought they were dead!" I said.

"Who is Nunu?" Dr Kaiser asked.

Gudrun's eyes suddenly filled with tears. She rushed back inside the house with the empty plate—nothing left, except for a few caramelized almonds.

Rose and Bill rolled up the circular driveway in a shiny red Jeep Cherokee with Alabama plates and parked behind Dr Kaiser's battered light-blue Volkswagen. The doors slammed. Rose had a papoose strapped to the front of her sun dress, festooned with the colors of the old Confederate flag. She was wearing Roman sandals, the leather crisscrossed up to her knees.

"I thought the Confederate flag was considered offensive in some quarters," Dr Kaiser said, popping a piece of pork sausage into his mouth. He chewed it thoughtfully.

"You're right. Many consider it," I said, preparing to explain.

But they had reached the front porch. "Howdy, all!" Bill called out. He was wearing a maroon tee-shirt that said, "Hail the Mighty Tide!" His shorts matched. And he was wearing maroon high-top sneakers without any socks.

Rose plopped down into one of the chairs. "How y'all doing?" Before anyone could answer, she started singing, "You've got to know when to hold 'em, when to fold 'em, know when to walk away, you never count your money when you're sittin' at the table...."

Something yapped from the papoose, which, added to her substantial size, made it look as if she had one enormous breast. The snout of Scarlett O'Hara, her Chihuahua, peeked out from the papoose.

Bill gestured to the road. "We've just come from the Kenny Rogers concert at the LBJ Ranch." He looked at the books on the table, "Expecting company?"

Mary Alice nodded. "We thought you might be here for the book signing."

Bill looked surprised. "What? There's been some misunderstanding."

Rose whispered in baby talk, "Now, Scarlett, darlin', baby, boo-boo, you gotta behave. My sweet wittle Scarlett Warlett, are you gonna behave for your Mommy Wommy?"

"Ramses El-Kibir's new book," I said. "Would you like a beer?"

"Aaaah," Bill said, chuckling. "Rose has so many book signings I just can't keep up. Ya know, Gary, a beer sounds mighty good. I'll take a Coors Light."

"We only have German beer," I said. "Doppelbock, Eisbock, Waitrose, German Pils, Shiner Bock."

"What did you say? My hearing's not so good." Bill cocked his ear toward me.

"Doppelbock, Eisbock, Waitrose, German Pils, Shiner Bock..."

Rose said, "Well, I know what I want. Bourbon and Coke for me. A twist of lime." She fiddled with the diamond stud on her nose. It glinted in the sunlight.

Dr Kaiser pointed to the Jeep Cherokee. "You didn't have that a few weeks ago. Did you purchase a new car?"

"What's wrong with American beer?" Bill asked.

"Shiner Bock is local," I said. "Made in Schulenburg."

"Is it a dark beer?" Bill asked.

Dr Kaiser repeated, "Did you purchase a new car?"

Bill chuckled, "Pardon me, Dr Kaiser. Just drove it off the lot yesterday. The proceeds from Rose's new novel, *Murder among the Serpents*, have already..."

"Aaah, yes," Dr Kaiser said. "She was explaining to me last time we met about her research pro-cess for the book. About the rattlesnakes and faith. You know, my royalties on Coptic theology are never so much. But what I can say, they are carrying my book at Harvard University library!"

Mary Alice was shaking her head. "Something is not right. Ramses el-Kibir is one hour late for his signing. Not a single customer in sight!"

"Shiner Bock is dark beer," I said. "A lager."

Bill shook his head. "You know, buddy, it just doesn't do it for me. Could you bring me some tap water?"

When I returned with the water, Bill said, "Changed my mind, bud. Think I will try the Shiner, after all."

I felt like strangling him.

Rose tapped her long fingernails on the table. "Where's Khara-whatsamajiggy?"

Kharalombos had disappeared. "He might be making a phone call."

Bill had folded his arms and was talking to Mary Alice. "I am sure there's a logical explanation for it. I believe the other camps in the area might have their closing ceremonies today."

Mary Alice's eyes pierced me. "You didn't check?"

"How was I supposed to know?" I asked.

Maybe Ashley had never mailed the checks to pay for the advertising in the newspapers! Mary Alice didn't believe in online banking. She was paranoid about identity theft and she was right!

"Well, I'd say your competition is Kenny Rogers," Bill said. "He's more famous around these parts than Ramses What's-His-Name."

Rose was sipping from a small silver flask, embossed with pink elephants. "Dr Kaiser, darlin', I'd like to show you something. It's spanking brand new."

Dr Kaiser scooted his rocking chair closer to Rose. Rose unlaced the leather straps that ran up to her knees. She hitched up her sun dress so we could see the side of her thigh. She sang, "Every gambler knows the secret to survivin' is knowin' what to keep . . . 'cause every hand is a winner . . . "

A blue scorpion was tattooed on the back of her calf. Just like Azzurro's tattoo. Was there a connection? But what? How would Rose know Patrick Quinn? This was a real stretch. Was she somehow implicated? Was this the symbol of a secret group?

She had very smooth, tanned legs. She looked up at Dr Kaiser expectantly.

Dr Kaiser said, "That's an abomination! You have ruined your flesh. Tattoos are for sailors! Truck drivers! Harlots!"

Mary Alice nodded. "Yes, in my day, piercing your ears was something radical. My father thought piercing your ears made you look cheap. He said, 'If you get your ears pierced, you'll have to pierce your nose!'"

"Awww," Rose said. "What planet are you livin' on? I have that and more," she said, pointing to the diamond stud in her nose.

Dr Kaiser huffed. "This is a barbaric practice!"

She winked at me. "Your next novel can be called *Pure Flesh*!" Then, she pointed at my Indian headdress. She put her hand to her mouth and made an Indian war cry.

Bill was suddenly alert. "Now, Rose, I think you've had enough."

"Am I putting too much pepper in your gumbo? Should I...?"

"Rose," Bill said, in a menacing voice. "That's enough."

"Call me old-fashioned, but the young generation has taken the tattoos too far," Dr Kaiser said. "I do not approve of such."

Rose stuck her tongue out and wiggled it at us. Two brass balls pierced the middle of her tongue.

A few people drove up looking for Ramses el-Kibir, but when they learned he was not around, they left. So my advertising campaign wasn't a total flop. We sold two hats, but no books. Maybe I could go into advertising, if it didn't work out to stay at Clover Flower.

Mary Alice strolled up and down the porch, with her hands behind her back. "Gary, are you sure you told Ramses the right time?"

Yikes. Had I? I thought Gudrun was supposed to communicate with him. Gudrun was the only one who had his email. Ramses had refused to give anyone else his email since he said he had no time to deal with the deluge of fan mail.

"Sure did," I said, trying my hand at another bluff.

Mary Alice snorted. "Not like him to miss his own book signing."

At that moment, two black Land Rovers with shaded windows drove slowly up behind the drive and parked behind Rose's shiny red Jeep. Wasn't this the car of choice for Egyptian bigwigs? Did they bother with the Secret Service for Ramses? A huge entourage descended upon the porch, led by a man in dark Ray-Ban sunglasses. A cameraman ran behind him, filming his walk up to the front porch. Other members of the entourage were taking pictures of him with their smart phones. They were all wearing Ray-Bans with their cheap oversized suits, a signature of Egyptian security. Except they were also all wearing oversized cowboy hats.

As soon as he took off his sunglasses, you could see the surprise on his face. "Ramses el-Kibir that means 'The Great' in Arabic has arrived! Where are…?"

Mary Alice said, "You're two hours late!"

Ramses looked perturbed. "I was asked to identify stolen objects from the Egyptian Museum as part of a murder investigation. I was delayed!"

"Charlie never mentioned it," Mary Alice said. "But he doesn't tell me everything."

Wasn't everything supposed to be confidential? What did she know about us?

"Would you like something to drink?" I asked.

"You might be unaware that I saved the Museum, during the first revolution, with a soup ladle," Ramses said. "Without me, the entire cultural heritage of Egypt would have gone awry! The protestors followed me in protecting the museum."

"We know!" Mary Alice said, her voice booming. "The story was widely covered by CNN."

Ramses bowed. "Ramses did not mean to offend. Will Gudrun be present at my signing?"

Mary Alice gestured to the group. "Your audience."

Ramses scanned the tiny group. Dr Kaiser stood and held out his hand. "Dr Kaiser, Professor of Coptic Studies and Theology at Baylor. We met a few weeks ago. It is my pleasure."

Bill waved. "Name's Bill. Professor of Human Rights, Visiting, the University of Texas."

"Howdy! Remember me?" Rose said. "I write about sin, lust, and murder, if you do recall!" Her legs were splayed open.

Ramses's eyes looked her up and down for a minute, from the pink hair to the open legs. Then he saw me. "You look familiar!"

"Don't think we would have met," I said. "I own Hansel and Gretel Brewery in Schulenburg. We do craft beers. Been here for years. I rarely travel outside the United States."

Rose hooted. "Craft beers! Boyfriend, you lyin' like a legless dog! A tad more Jim Beam?"

Bill made the "T" sign with his hands. Time out. No more.

But Ramses was mesmerized by the river—his entourage of Egyptian security had run across the road and jumped into the river with their clothes on. Some of them were swinging on the rope, tied to the huge oak tree, that swung out over the water. The river was irresistible.

I prayed he'd forgotten about the cobra scene at the Pyramids. Where was Kharalombos? He would kill Ramses if he showed up.

Ramses sighed and took off his Indiana Jones hat. "Ramses will have a whiskey."

"What kind?" I asked.

Ramses frowned again. "Ramses the Great only drinks Glenfiddich." His eye spotted the cut-up sausages on the bread board. Did he eat pork?

Did he ever use the word "I"?

"Coming right up," I said. I didn't remember seeing any Glenfiddich in Gudrun's liquor cabinet. What would we do if we didn't have it?

Gudrun was piling cookies on a plate when I came into the house. I started rifling through her liquor cabinet: Ouzo 12, Old Crow Kentucky Bourbon, peppermint schnapps, local Mexican tequila with a striped worm, Bailey's, Kahlua. No Glenfiddich. Here was Teacher's Scotch. I took a sip. It was disgusting!

"Ramses is outside," I said.

Gudrun's eyes were red. "Tell me that Kharalombos will not be leaving me."

I shook my head. "I'm sorry, Gudrun. Nothing lasts forever."

"You are saying the truth. After all these years, I wish I could live without the expectations of grand romance. From the moment we met, it felt like one of those romance novels...Harlequin Romance? *Aacch*, but life is more complicated. After my husband ran off with my sister, I took all of the money from the divorce and decided to start new. In a place where no one will know. Klaus told me about Clover Flower. Mary Alice was looking for another investor."

So it had not been the secretary? This was much worse! We never knew what other sadness and misery other people were carrying.

I set down the ice trays on the counter. "Come here. Humphrey Bogart thinks you need a hug." I gave her a warm embrace.

Gudrun giggled and then squealed like a young girl. "Shame on you! You are flirting with me. You are not suggesting that we...?"

"No," I said. "Of course not. Your bee-sting pastries were wonderful." I was trying to cheer her up. "Did you make something else?"

She smiled briefly. "These are the gingerbread cookies with chocolate chunks. I made them in the shape of mummies. Some are in the shape of scarabs."

I followed her out the door with Ramses's drink. She sounded cheerful. "*Aaaach*, Ramses, so you have arrived at last! We were waiting for you for so long! How is the movie star? You are more handsome than Omar Sharif!"

She set the cookies down on the table and made a great show of kissing him on both cheeks.

Ramses couldn't resist giving her a little pat on her behind. Gudrun giggled. "Ramses, you mustn't be a naughty boy! I have made some mummy cookies for you to celebrate your latest new book on the animal mummies."

I handed Ramses the cheap Scotch.

He shook his head. "Ambrosia of the gods! I never drink anything but Glenfiddich!"

"*Aaach*," Gudrun said. "You have to try my mummy cookies. These were prepared especially for you and for the event."

Ramses put his hand on his chest. "Ramses can never thank you enough for this handsome, generous hospitality, but I have to confess that I have the sugar disease."

Gudrun looked concerned. "*Aacch*, so you are diabetic. *Zuckerkrankheit.* The sugar disease in German. That is a pity you can't sample."

Dr Kaiser reached toward the plate with his slender fingers. "I will try the gingerbread mummies."

Mary Alice asked, "Dr Ramses, can you tell us the Egyptian objects that you identified at the Ingrum police station?"

Ramses had forgotten about Gudrun, and his eyes had wandered back toward Rose's sleek legs.

"They are the *shabti* figurines buried with mummies," Ramses said, as Rose opened her legs wider. "Wooden models who do the tasks for the dead in the afterlife: bakers, brewers, laborers. New Kingdom. Made from terra cotta."

Ramses held out his glass as if I were a servant. "More Glenfiddich?"

When I returned, Dr Kaiser was saying, "If I understand you correctly, Dr Ramses, there were not so many pharaonic objects found on the property."

Ramses nodded, but he seemed distracted. "That is correct, Dr Kaiser. Most of the objects were stolen from Iraq and Libya. Mr Charlie will have to get an archaeologist who is an expert on those."

Rose was unstrapping her papoose. "Scarlett, darlin', you are just obstructin' my movements. I have to breathe."

"Dr Ramses, maybe you might be interested in my book on torture," Bill said. "I happen to have a few extra copies…"

Ramses's face was flushed. "The Americans have ruined our tourist industry! They are telling everyone it's not safe in Egypt. I have never seen such a conspiracy!"

"I couldn't agree more," Bill said, taking off his baseball cap, which said "Alabama Football National Champs." "We have ruined the political map of the Middle East. Our leadership has been very poor since George W."

Ramses looked bewildered. "I am talking about how our tourism has been destroyed by the American State Department! They keep renewing the travel warning."

Rose said, "Well, darlin', I wouldn't trade my experience in Egypt for anything in this world. Even the revolution. It was just a ball!"

Once Rose had finished taking off the papoose, it was clear that she had no straps at all on her dress—she really was wearing a Confederate flag! She was not wearing a bra, either.

All of the men on the porch were staring at Rose.

Mary Alice murmured, "Lord."

Bill was saying to Ramses, "We really have to close Guantánamo Bay. That is a clear violation of civil liberties."

Rose winked at me but gestured to Dr Kaiser. "Would you like to come here and hold Scarlett?"

Gudrun said, "Anyone for more cookies?" But gingerbread cookies were not as big a draw as Rose's tight-fitting dress.

Dr Kaiser was rocking back and forth in his rocking chair, faster and faster. "Ever since I was a child, I have been loving the dogs."

"Chihuahuas are feisty dogs," I said. "I would be careful if I were you, Dr Kaiser. She bites." She had taken a chunk out of Kharalombos's hand in Cairo.

Dr Kaiser winked at Rose. "Goot. Very goot. Maybe you would all like to know something about the object which I saw at the property."

"We have been told not discuss the case," Mary Alice said sternly. "It's an ongoing murder investigation."

"But you were the one asking Dr Ramses about what he identified," Dr Kaiser said, crossing his spindly legs to hide the bulge in his shorts. "Why shouldn't I?"

"Well, I, for one, want to know. Even though you told me an hour ago," Rose said, licking her lips, "that tattoos were barbaric. That I had besmirched my own flesh."

"The manuscript that Azzurro owned," Dr Kaiser said, "was found in a cave in Minya. It would change the way we see Jesus. Jesus was a man."

Rose laughed. "Of course, darlin'. How profound!"

"Would you cut it out, Rose?" Bill said. "Let Dr Kaiser finish."

"He was a man with instincts. Natural impulses. The manuscript tells us about Jesus's relationship with a woman named Irene. She was an important disciple, but she was left out of the four synoptic gospels."

"Oh, please," Rose said. "This is a bunch of hogwash. You are just trying…"

"I read it myself in Coptic. Verified the authenticity for…" Dr Kaiser said, pausing. "Dr Ramses, why didn't Lieutenant Charles ask you about the manuscript?"

Gudrun had forgotten the second plate from the first batch of pastries on the table. A yellow jacket landed near the sticky caramel.

"Ramses always says that the Coptic artifacts are just as important to the Egyptian heritage as the pharaonic and the Islamic." Ramses was waving his hands wildly.

Disturbed by the sudden, erratic movement, the yellow jacket started buzzing around Ramses's head. It landed on his ear.

"That's a wasp," I said. "Don't provoke it."

He swatted it, as if it were a fly. "Ramses does not deny." The yellow jacket circled and nosedived for a second assault. "The importance of such a manuscript for…" The wasp then went straight for Ramses's throat.

"Oh, my God!" Rose shouted, jumping up out of her chair. "Oh, my God! I'm allergic!"

"Now," Bill said. "Let's just stay calm, Rose."

A huge red welt appeared almost immediately on Ramses's throat. "Ra … " but he couldn't speak. Within minutes, it looked as if he was breathing with difficulty.

Mary Alice drew me to the side, murmuring, "Very discreetly, go to the office. Look for the first-aid kit. Epinephrine. It's clearly labeled. Fourth drawer on the right. Go!"

I sprinted to the office. Switched on the light. One, two, three, four. Fourth drawer on the right. I yanked it out so quickly that he entire drawer fell onto the floor. I pawed through the drawer, searching for the first-aid kit. I heard the siren in the distance. A skull and crossbones was embossed on the front: Dangerous Emergencies. A leaflet: what to do if you are bitten by a rattlesnake. Calamine lotion. Big help for a rattlesnake bite! A splint. Another leaflet: allergies to bees, hornets, and wasps. Okay, great. Anti-snake serum. What to do if you are bitten by a rabid dog. What to do in cases of diabetic coma. Where was it? Empty injections. Tiny capsules labeled "epinephrine." Got it!

At the bottom of the small box was a folded letter in Arabic. Whose was that? I grabbed the letter and started reading: *Azizati Zeinab, my dearest daughter: I believe I am in the last hours of my life.* Why did Mary Alice have the letter? Gudrun couldn't read Arabic. Had Mary Alice found this in Patrick Quinn's garage? That certainly didn't look like a document from the Libyan intelligence. I shoved the letter in my pocket and ran back to the front porch of Gudrun's house.

"You're a little late," Rose said. "Fifteen minutes to be exact." She was stirring the Coke with her manicured finger. A bottle of Jim Beam sat on the table. She stuck her finger in her mouth and sucked it.

"He didn't die?"

Bill shook his head. "Naw. He's all right. When he was able to speak, he was speaking in Arabic. Shock. Forgot his English. Kharalombos went with them to the emergency room to translate."

I could imagine how happy that would make Kharalombos. To be translating for the man he believed had cuckolded him, the son of a donkey.

"I'm allergic. I've had anaphylactic attacks before," Rose said. "I also have asthma." She waved her inhaler at me. She was now wearing a hugely oversized red tee-shirt over her Confederate flag dress. It said: "Slip, Slide, and Away Water Resorts. EASY SLIDING AT SLICK PRICES. South Padre Island, Texas."

Scarlett barked at me when she saw the injection. Scruffy little rat with beady brown eyes. Who would ever want such a mean-spirited dog?

Rose laughed. "She remembers when you gave her the insulin. Life was just a ball in Cairo! When I think about how dull my life is now in Austin, except of course unless I'm doin' a book signing for *Murder among the Serpents*. I've got an idea for a novel about Cairo."

"What?" I couldn't believe my ears. What did she know about Cairo? She had been there a year.

"You know, buddy," Bill said. "We were thinking of going back to Egypt. Do you think it's safe now? Rose has just gotten an offer."

"You have to be flexible," I said, setting the thimble of epinephrine on the patio table, next to a green fern.

"Well," Bill said, folding his arms matter-of-factly. "We are that. As you must recall."

They had fled to Cyprus and left me in their apartment with a rabbit and a diabetic dog. The capacity for self-delusion was endless! On the other hand, how was I deluding myself? That I was a writer? That Boriana loved me? That I would ever get out of my scrape with the law?

Rose sang, "Every gambler knows the secret to survivin' is knowin' what to keep...."

Had I made the wrong gambles? I started to pick up glasses and plates from the front porch. "Did everyone go to the emergency room?"

"Yep," Bill said. "Need a hand?"

"You could put Ramses's books back in the boxes," I said. "Don't think anyone's coming to the book signing now."

"Always happy to help, buddy," Bill said. "Like a good neighbor."

Were they good neighbors? I wasn't so sure.

Rose didn't budge. She sang to herself, "'Cause every hand is a winner... Every hand is a loser . . . "

Chapter 17

The Found Letter

I GAVE UP WAITING FOR THE GROUP TO COME BACK from the emergency room. They had been gone for hours. I went to bed.

Pulling the letter out of my shorts, I flipped on the light overhead, but the bulb flickered. I picked up the flashlight and clicked it on. I had never been particularly good at reading Arabic handwriting, which is not as clear as reading a printed text. I put on my glasses and read the scrawled, hurried script.

Bismillah el-Rahman el-Rahim

Azizati, Zeinab, my dearest, lost daughter, flower in the desert:

I believe I am in my last hours of life on this earth. *"Wa alallahi fal yatawakalel motawakeloun."* (Whoever believeth in God should rely upon Him.) I have sent the letter with my trusted advisor, who has left me to tell his wife about the death of their son in a village very far from here.

My soldiers are devout believers and will fight to the last breath the Western imperialists who are raining bombs upon us from the sky. Our chef is wounded and we eat plain pasta with no salt, which we are boiling in the water we find in the drainage ditches because the water towers and tanks have been pierced by the imperialists' bullets and where is the water?! Where is the water?! Who can live without good water? Our throats are parched from savage thirst! I always provided for my people! Tasty chickens nourished naturally have all but disappeared in this village, and the nutrition has gone. But who can blame the hungry? We have a saying, "One must eat well." My chef, Ashour, lost his arm in a bombing raid and he keeps losing blood and cries in his sleep. I sit next to him and pray for him because there is no sleeping now. Only prayers. At the leader's palace, Ashour used to make delicious tagines with couscous for our foreign visitors and he used only the best herbs and tasty lamb and he even made his own couscous and now that is over, and we cannot deny that fact! I was always afraid someone would poison me and Ashour was the cook and the taster at once and now we are eating pasta if we eat, drained in sewage water, and anyone who is hungry will cook in our entourage, but as for me, I do not touch it. Idrees, my bodyguard, bound Ashour's arm with a sheet, but Ashour has lost too much blood and I fear for him, that he will not last another night. He calls me "master" and I tell him that, before God, we are as equal as the teeth of a comb. We have no medicine and the doctors have also fled. I am moving from house to house every few days. The people have left their doors open and we walk in, as if they are our neighbors. The milk has curdled. Everything has spoiled in the refrigerators and the smell makes you want to vomit. Where have they gone? Are these rats heading to Tripoli?

This is not my house and I am writing with a copy pencil, which I found in a child's room. I picked up a teddy bear from the floor, when I was looking for a blanket. This is what made me think of you, Zeinab, dear daughter, and I feel the sadness and the regret that I sent you far away when you were such a tiny girl, but I had my reasons when the Americans bombed my palace in 1986. But I know you were well provided for and a father must provide for his daughters, which is my duty as a father. You are like Lucy Manet to me, whose father mastered carpentry in *A Tale of Two Cities*. Girls are emotional and have the softness for the motherhood. Hens lay eggs, so do women, and that's why they should both stay in the shed.

I always thought I was better than my cousins in the tribe because I had so many more sons, but my sons are fighting among themselves and hate each other and do not treat each other in a brotherly way. The boys are directing the battle. I am not sure who is alive and who has been killed by the imperialists' bombs, may God rest their souls in peace. And the West is chasing us now! My heart is as heavy as a lion's and I am a tired one. We have no electricity and are cold at night. We found a few stubs of candles in a kitchen cupboard, but the wax burns too quickly and we must only burn the candles to see our way around when we are boiling tea, and believe me, that is our only pleasure apart from scouring our minds for jokes. At night, we sit in the dark except for the candle shadows which flicker on the walls. We drink heavy tea without sugar. Where is the sweetness left in our lives?

The years passed quickly, like the sand of our great desert, and the shadows on the walls are like the friends who have vanished, but where is the power? Where are the Italianos?!! They just came for the bloody oil. Beware of greed, my dear! My big friends who greeted me in Europe could not find a shelter for me and I will not be sorry to die in my hometown—I was never a coward and I never threw in the towel, and that's what counts. If they want to come and get me, I'm game. We call our cousins of our tribe to see if they can tell us where the forces against us are—those rats who want to kill us. The Open Door Policy Man told me I was a Clown. I heard the Big Man has fled to Morocco because his people want him out. I offered him shelter, but he, like the Open Door Policy Man, calls me the Clown and chose to go to Morocco. There is a funny story about the Big Man when he was a pilot and landed in the desert in Morocco. The Berber tribes thought his helicopter was a hornet and tied it to a palm tree! That was long before the 1967 Setback of Egypt by the Zionists.

Dear daughter, politics has nothing to do with you and it is a wicked, nefarious business, indeed. Medicine is a noble profession and I am glad you have devoted your life to curing the sick, and if you were with us now, you would know how to save Ashour, the cook. The Communists always took me to the best casinos in Paris.

So many loved the common sense and philosophy of the Green Book! I advise you to read it, if you have not. The important thing is one's flesh and blood and the tribe, and you were a flower blooming on one of the steps of a mosque. I hear gunfire. People are screaming... I must... Farewell, my dear daughter who must by now have blossomed into maturity. May you live a long . . .

A letter from the Clown Man? But I didn't understand what it was doing in Mary Alice's office drawer underneath the first-aid kit labeled Dangerous Emergencies. I thought the baby daughter was killed in an American bombing? Why was Mary Alice keeping this letter? And, if she had found it in Azzurro's garage, why did he have it? Should I put it back? I shone the flashlight on my watch: midnight. Not too late for Kharalombos.

I put my clothes back on and laced up my tennis shoes. I didn't bother with socks. The light bobbed and widened as I walked down the short path to Gudrun's house. The familiar melody of Arabic music—the voice of Abdel Wahab—floated from the porch.

The candles in the lanterns flickered.

"Kharalombos?"

I shone the light on the front porch. Kharalombos was spreading paté on a cracker. Probably *Leberwurst*. I had no appetite.

"Gary! *Eshta! Cool!* You're just in time for a snack. I am recovering from eight hours in the emergency room with Ramses el-Kibir! It was like an Egyptian soap opera. His bodyguards insisted on going into the room with the doctor. They were all wearing wet clothes! The doctor refused and he called the police. I also had to translate between the old man, Mr Charlie, and Abdel Hafez, the security guy."

"Will he be okay?"

He took a bite out of the cracker and paused. "As you must imagine, it was not the most enviable job, for me as the cuckold, to translate. But he will live. He was so tired he forgot his English."

"I don't think Gudrun really cares about him," I said. "She is heartbroken that you are leaving."

"My feeling about America," Kharalombos said, "has not really changed. I am a fish out of the water here. I am tired of adventure. I just want to go home."

"When are you going back?"

"As soon as possible," Kharalombos said. "I have made contact with Yasmine. And she has agreed for me to see Nunu, my son. Will you return to Cairo?"

"I don't know," I said. "I'm still wanted by Interpol."

It was unbelievable that I had not been arrested. Everyone in this town seemed to know my story—it was as if it had been broadcast from the rooftops.

Kharalombos sighed. "*La'. La'*. I cannot take the blandness any more. The schedules. The organization. It is suffocating!"

"What are you talking about? This camp has been crazy. Like a circus," I said.

Kharalombos pointed his finger to Gudrun's room. He whispered, "She won't stop crying."

"She really loves you," I said. Did Boriana love me like that? The tiny hope mixed with real doubt.

Kharalombos sighed again. "Love could be bad for your health, my friend, like Abdul Wahab said, "*Wa menal hubbi ma qatal*."

I handed Kharalombos the Clown Man's letter. "I found this underneath the first-aid kit in Mary Alice's desk. Read it!"

Kharalombos was surprised. "*Ya salaam! Bil arabi*."

"She reads Arabic. She spent ten years at Ramses College," I said.

Kharalombos grabbed the flashlight from me and read. He moved his lips as he read.

When he finished, I asked, "Well?"

"I always knew she was connected," Kharalombos said.

"Connected to who?"

"The CIA!"

I laughed. "She's a little old lady who worked for the Presbyterian Church. What on earth could she do for the CIA?"

"Why else would she have this letter? It's a letter from the Clown Man," Kharalombos said. "His last moments before he perished. As we would say, *Kalb wi rah*. He was a dog no one should mourn."

"There are plenty of other reasons why she might have this letter."

"Like what?" Kharalombos asked. "This is your American naiveté! Innocence."

I couldn't think of a single reason why Mary Alice might have the letter. "I don't know. It's his last letter to his daughter."

Kharalombos said, "One blood daughter. There was also an adopted daughter, a baby. Zeinab. The Clown Man said she was killed in a bombing in 1986. Maybe she is alive."

"Okay," I said. "Mary Alice said she had destroyed some documents from the Libyan intelligence from Azzurro's garage. Maybe she found the letter there. But why did Azzurro have the letter?"

I had sworn on the Bible not to tell a soul about the destruction of these documents. But Kharalombos was my best friend. And yes, why was Mary Alice destroying documents from the Libyan intelligence? Who gave her the right to?

Kharalombos folded his arms. "You see."

"But why would she keep the letter?"

Kharalombos shrugged. "It proves my point."

"Does it?" I asked. "What should I do with the letter?"

"Look, my friend," Kharalombos said. "*Wana mali.* This has nothing to do with me. I am escaping before I become involved in a new swamp of problems. You will have to decide. We will celebrate my return to Cairo with a shot of Scotch. Just wait there, while I get the bottle."

Chapter 18

The Last Supper

ARY ALICE SENT ME TO HELP OUT IN THE KITCHEN. I was dying to ask her about the Clown Man's letter. Why did she have this strange missive? I had hidden the letter underneath the mattress in my cabin. I highly doubted anyone would look for it there. My spiral notebook, with my notes about the camp, was also under the mattress.

Letty was sitting on a stool, reading a newspaper, as if she had never left.

"I thought you had a job at a bakery?"

Letty yawned. "I had to be there at 4:30 every morning. Too early for this girl!"

Sinead waved. "Ah, there ya are, Gary. Are ya grand on this here our last day? We are preparing for the fi-nal-ly!" She was slicing tomatoes with a huge knife. "The last show in this circus."

Speedy was flipping hamburger patties. "Did you hear what happened to the Big Gato? Hee! Hee!" His hair was tied up in a ponytail. He was wearing a red tennis headband.

"Anaphylactic attack," I said. "I heard he's okay now."

"Just deserts, I'd say," Sinead said, waving her knife. "Sometimes people get what they deserve. We could use a hand, like."

Speedy laughed. "Man, it will take you years to pack up all the Gato's books!"

"What do you want me to do?" I asked. I grabbed a white apron and looped the tie around my waist.

Sinead waved her knife. "Cut some onions." She waved her knife at the onions next to the tomatoes. "I'll fetch the frozen taters from the back."

Onions were a killer! I had to keep up the macho front.

"How many people today?"

Speedy flipped another burger. "Only thirty. Twenty kids and a few guests."

"Why are you cooking?"

Speedy winked at me. "Because I'm a Nice Guy! *Comprendes*? And because I worked at Whataburger for years and this is real easy for me."

I took the knife and started to slice the onions. "You're talented."

Sinead was carrying in huge packages of frozen French fries. "Everything frozen today, except for the strawberries, tomatoes, and onions," Sinead said. "On a tight budget, we are. Mary Alice's orders."

Almost as soon as I started cutting the onions, my eyes began to water. Soon it looked as if I were weeping because my mother had died. Or maybe I was crying because I now had no future? I imagined Boriana motoring up to the penitentiary for conjugal visits. Was I crying because I had not been kinder to my father? And now it was too late.

Letty turned the page of the *The San Antonio Star*. "Eeeeeeh," she said. "Listen to this: 'Josiah Stoner was arrested yesterday, the leader of a huge ring of thieves in Kerr County. Other charges include: possession of meth-amphetamine, possession of explosive and noxious materials, possession of paraphernalia, intent to sell, and jeopardizing the safety of someone else's property.'"

Speedy was patting the grease off of a hamburger patty. "Shit! He's going back to the slammer, for sure. Screwed up his parole, big time."

Tears were streaming down my face. I had to stop cutting the onions. What kind of fantasy was I spinning? Could I really work in a circus? Marry a Bulgarian girl whom I barely knew?

Letty's voice became sharp. "Speedy, you don't know anything about Josiah's meth lab, do you?"

God, had Speedy lied to me?

Sinead dropped the French fries into a vat of sizzling hot grease. "Gary, you should've told me you couldn't manage the onions."

Speedy gave me a significant look. "I had no idea that Josiah was dealing again."

So he had not told Letty about finding Josiah's stash in the cave. Did Speedy know something more?

"Aaah," Sinead said, putting a red curl behind her ear. "Gary, you're suffering, like. Just put the tomatoes on the dish and I'll finish up the onions."

The French fries were sizzling and spitting in the hot grease.

Letty said, "You better be tellin' the truth."

Charlie was on the ball. He had cracked a theft and drug ring. Why hadn't he arrested me?

"Awww, Letty. You gotta believe me. I'm clean. How about a burger? I make the best burgers in South Texas," Speedy said, handing Letty a dish with a fat hamburger patty. The juice oozed off the sides.

Letty put the folded newspaper on the counter. "Not hungry," she said.

—∽—

We decided to serve the food family style, since we only had thirty people. Compared to the opening, it was a very small group—very few parents and campers. I wondered if Mary Alice and Gudrun would go broke. Would I still be on the run next summer? I felt the vise tightening. Maybe I needed to make another plan. But what? Kharalombos was leaving for Cairo. Just where was I going to go? I had no money. Charlie knew about the false passport.

The guests we had could be counted on one hand: Rose, Bill, Dr Kaiser, Cameron Wiley, and his wife, Dixie. A few other parents were seated at a nearby picnic table.

Mary Alice surveyed the area, with her hands behind her back. Gudrun stood beside her. Gudrun had decided to wear the camp uniform with the Indian headdress. Mary Alice was wearing khaki shorts, which were very high-waisted. The two of them looked like Laurel and Hardy.

I set the plate of hamburger patties down on Rose and Bill's table. Dr Kaiser was saying, "One of my colleagues gave me an intriguing article today about the stolen antiquities. Baldo Durante was the hero of the Baghdad Museum story. He was a classics scholar in the army who organized a team to find the Treasures of Nineveh."

"That's like the Monument Men who saved great art in Europe," Bill said. "Hitler had planned to have his own Super Museum."

Dr Kaiser shook his head. "Of course, that is a great shame for us. So many terrible things happened in the War."

Dixie chimed in, "I just love Matt Damon! He is my favorite actor."

Dr Kaiser shook his head. "Indeed, this movie trivialized the issues about art and the heroism of that unit in the American army, which saved some very valuable pieces of art."

Bill gestured with his head toward Azzurro's house. "Well, sure as shootin' Azzurro must've had other loot, besides the story of I-rene."

"We were asked not to discuss the case, Dr Kaiser," Cameron said. "That's what our lawyers have advised us."

"But the Treasures of Nineveh have nothing to do with...Unless...," Dr Kaiser said, frowning.

Dixie pointed at the meat and made a face.

"Coming right up," I said. "At your service." Had no idea what I'd find in the cupboard this time.

Bill called out, "Buddy, while you're at it, could you bring me a Shiner Bock?"

Kharalombos sat at an empty picnic table with Dagmar, who was sitting defiantly on top of it. Karalombos stroked her back while he swayed. He had earphones on—probably listening to Arabic music.

Michael Jackson's voice blasted, "You better run. Better do what you can. Don't wanna see no blood, don't be a macho man."

Pepe and Ashley were doing a break dance. McKenzie had joined them. Their dancing was terrible, but the three of them looked cute together. Did it matter if they were any good? Sometimes enjoyment was more important than achievement. What a hard lesson.

Mary Alice gestured for Kharalombos to take his earphones out. Kharalombos shrugged and put his earphones back in.

Mary Alice shouted in my ear, "Were you in on the planning of this?" She pointed to Pepe, Ashley, and McKenzie. Since Cameron had donated the money for the pool, maybe she hesitated about stopping the dance.

I shook my head. "Didn't know anything about it."

Why was Charlie here?! And he had brought his beefy number two. They were in uniform. And if he was taking me in, why now?

Michael Jackson screamed, "Don't wanna be a boy. You wanna be a man."

Charlie and whatever his name was, Jeremy, were walking toward me. Should I make a run for it? But where would I go now? I felt miserable. I should say goodbye to Kharalombos. Once I went to jail, I would probably never see him again. It was unlikely he would return to the US for a visit.

I walked up to him. "I just want you to know that I'll never forget you. You have been a wonderful friend."

We had only been here a few months, but Kharalombos had not integrated into American life in the way I had imagined he would. But how hard it was—this integration that encouraged you to leave your language and culture behind, and demanded you flatten yourself into a slice of bland Wonder Bread. Even though he was fluent in English, he sang melancholic Egyptian songs because he pined for that other noisy, emotional world, so far from the strict Protestant regimen of Clover Flower. How he would hate corporate America! Or even the bureaucracy of the intelligence services! Kharalombos was now singing Mohamed Qandeel's song, "*Talaat salamaat ya waheshni. Talaat teyyam.*" Three greetings of farewells to you...whom I will miss for three days.

Kharalombos looked bewildered. "Eh?"

Michael Jackson's voice drowned me out, "So beat it, just beat it!"

"You've been a great pal!" I shouted.

He took his earplugs out. "*Habibi,* what are you saying? I cannot hear a word."

At that moment, Mary Alice switched off the music. Instead of Michael Jackson, there was a cacophony of barking. Dagmar leapt off the table and started yapping, which made Scarlett join in.

Charlie had stopped at Cameron Wiley's table and was talking to him. A courtesy greeting before I was taken away. The remaining parents rushed over to the table, curious about what was happening.

Kharalombos nodded his head toward Charlie, as if he finally understood. He got up and embraced me in a big bear hug. "*Salaam ya sahibi.*" Farewell, my friend.

"This is the end of the road," I said. There was nowhere to run. I was cornered, at last. As the narrator in *Pure Water* said on the last page, "This is the end for yours truly."

But Cameron was shaking his head. He didn't look happy. From afar, it looked like a serious discussion, not a polite greeting.

McKenzie ran toward her father. "Daddy! Daddy!"

Dagmar and Scarlett were barking at Cameron. Kharalombos chased after Dagmar. McKenzie had buried her head in the crook of her father's arm.

I had a few minutes left to myself. Dixie was taking her smartphone out of her purse. Kharalombos motioned to me, then gave me a thumbs-up. After all we had been through together? How could he?

But Kharalombos was smiling. He didn't look upset. Wouldn't he be upset if I were being arrested?

Charlie was saying, "Anything you say or do can be used against you in a court of law. You have the right to remain silent."

The dogs were still barking. Rose had scooped up Scarlett and put her in her wicker basket.

In between the insistent yapping, I heard the phrase "…accessory to murder."

Cameron was adjusting the granny glasses on his nose.

Bill came over to me. "Buddy, did you have any idea? Were you in on the sting operation?"

Dixie said coolly, "Sugar, just tell me what you want me to do." So she was not as helpless as she pretended to be?

Mary Alice said, "Surely, there's been some kind of mistake?" She was standing in her usual pose with her hands behind her back.

Bill looked at me, puzzled. He mouthed, "Buddy?"

"Jeremy, could you clear the area?" Charlie asked.

But none of the parents would budge. Someone said, "That's Cameron Wiley, the famous oilman."

Bill elbowed me. I was mute. I shook my head.

Dr Kaiser said, "Cameron is a very respectable man. Are you sure you have the right man?"

"We have significant DNA evidence," Charlie said. "Now, Cameron, you can come quietly with us down to the station or…"

Jeremy touched the metal cuffs looped in his belt.

Dixie was waving her phone. "Which firm do you want me to call?"

Dr Kaiser and Gudrun had lapsed into German.

Cameron stood up. "Hilderburton, Blackberry, Huckleberry, and Huckleberry."

McKenzie whined. "Daddy! Daddy! I want some French fries!"

Rose, who was standing next to Bill, said, "Why, I'll be. I always thought it was you, Gary."

I was speechless.

Bill said, "Rose, could you put a lid on it?"

I managed to say, "What would be my motive?"

Rose laughed. "Let me see." She put her forefinger coyly to her head. "Buried treasure?"

"This is not the Hardy Boys!" I said. I stifled a murderous impulse. I really wanted to wring her neck!

Dr Kaiser was mopping his brow with a monogrammed handkerchief. He had to sit down. Was he having a heart attack?

"Are you all right?" I asked, bending over Dr Kaiser. "Should I get you some water?"

Dr Kaiser had his hand on his chest, as if it were caving in. "Some water would be goot. He must have gone back later after I identified the manuscript."

Gudrun was patting his hand. "Do not speak. You will have to testify. We will have to hire lawyers. I have just finished paying them off for the macaroni and cheese case. I can…"

Cameron was being led away by Charlie and Jeremy.

Mary Alice was shaking her head, "Hard to believe. But innocent until proven guilty in a democracy."

But so often the innocent could not pay for the best legal counsel. And then they were found guilty.

Rose said, "I think we all need a drink."

Bill was shaking his head. "Who would have thought?"

Dr Kaiser whispered, "He would do anything to have the most famous theological library in the world."

—⁓—

Sinead was scooping ice cream into small bowls.

"We won't be serving dessert," I said.

"Awww, Gary," Sinead said, putting a wisp of a curl behind her ear. "Are ya tryin' it on?"

"I'm dead serious." I put the tray, stacked with dirty dishes, on the counter. "The party's over."

She eyed the plates—most of the food was untouched. "They didn't like Speedy's burgers?"

"Cameron Wiley was just arrested for murder," I said.

"What?! Jahsus, Mary, and Joseph! Yer jokin'." She left the metal scoop dug into the middle of the frozen ice cream—it was Velvet Red Bucket.

"Am not," I said. I took a deep breath. "I thought Charlie had come to arrest me."

"Anyone in their right mind can see yer a harmless rogue, ya are," Sinead said, slapping the kitchen towel against the counter. "That cyber-terrorism is some kind of trumped-up charge. Who thought that one up?"

"Cameron Wiley looks harmless, too," I said. "I need a beer. Or something stronger."

Sinead opened the door underneath the sink and brought up a bottle of whiskey. It was right next to the Palmolive dish soap. I had never noticed it.

"This here's very special Irish whiskey for emergencies." She poured me a glass. "Tealing."

It was very smooth. "I never would have thought Cameron…"

Sinead groaned. "That is very bad luck for us, it is. Cameron just offered Aengus a permanent job in West Texas."

So she had given up on the idea of running away with me? Or maybe we both had?

"Oh," I said. "I'm sorry. I think I might have to sit down." I still could not believe what had happened. I sat down on Letty's stool.

"Do you think he did it?"

"Charlie said he had DNA evidence," I said. "Who can argue with DNA?"

"Was yer man after the buried treasure?" Sinead said. She started scraping the food into the trash, ever practical.

"An early manuscript," I said, "that tells the story of Jesus's relationship with a woman, Irene."

Sinead hooted. "My ma always made me go to confession. As soon as I was old enough, I said, 'I'm not going back there and yous can whip me if you like.' I never had any use for the church."

"Did you know that Captain Quinn had connections with the IRA?"

Sinead swatted the towel against the counter. "Aengus knew 'im."

"What?!"

"They were in Libya together on some mission. Years ago. When Quinn moved into the house next door, we were none too happy, I can say now. Of all the places to choose in America!"

"Why didn't Aengus ever say anything?"

"We came to America to get away from all that. Live peacefully," Sinead said. "And Charlie told Aengus to keep mum about Libya and the training missions with the Clown Man."

I couldn't believe it. And yet, I had always suspected that Aengus was affiliated with the IRA.

Sinead shook her head. "Gary, that's all over since the Good Friday agreement. Sometimes, the past is really over and ya just have to move on, like. We just want to provide for our two wee men."

Chapter 19

A Final Surprise

"HAVE A SEAT." MARY ALICE GESTURED TO THE CHAIR in front of her desk. I felt as if I had been called in to the principal's office.

She held out the palm of her hand. "The letter, please."

"Why should I?"

"Don't be a smart aleck. It's part of a fair trade," Mary Alice said. "I have something for you if you relinquish the letter."

Why should I keep the Clown Man's letter? What would I do with it, anyway?

Mary Alice had a folded copy of the *New York Times* on her desk. She thrust it at me and pointed to the headline: "Wrong Man Accused of Masterminding Computer Virus."

"Dr Gary Watson, the biology professor accused of bringing down the entire computer system of Zadorf Publishers, was cleared of any wrongdoing yesterday. All charges against him have been dropped. Watson, who has been on the run for two years, lived a colorful life, working various jobs until he was recently located in a small town in central Texas: a clown in a Bulgarian circus; a maker of wax knights at the Knights Templar Museum in Valletta, Malta; a plumber at the LBJ Ranch; a dishwasher at Jalisco's Mexican restaurant; an attendant for gorillas at the Houston Zoo; and most recently, horse trainer at the Clover Flower Girls' Camp in Schulenburg, Texas. The real perpetrator of the crime was a radical offshoot of the ACFT, or Anti-Capitalism Front Today, protesting the takeover of publishing companies and the hegemony of huge conglomerates, as well as the homogenization of American cultural life."

I was stunned. "Why didn't the reporters find me?"

Mary Alice smiled. "I steered them in another direction."

My eye scanned the date at the top: three weeks before.

"Why didn't you tell me?"

"Charlie asked me not to," Mary Alice said. "He needed your help."

"Did they find Triksky?"

"Tony the Tuna. His real name is Tony Attatunabunabuna. Arrested in New Jersey for fraud, antiquities trafficking, and murder."

"So he was connected to the Mob?"

Mary Alice nodded. She loved bad news. "You bet."

"He was an incredible mimic. Sounded like an upper-class Brit."

"What are you going to do now?"

"I don't know. I want to call my girlfriend, Boriana. She's in Bulgaria now with her folks."

"You're not going back to Cairo with Kharalombos?" Mary Alice asked.

"I don't know," I said. "But I don't understand why you told me about the Libyan documents. The IRA connection."

"I didn't know myself if Aengus was innocent or not. Didn't want you to ask any more questions."

"But wasn't Captain Quinn linked to the IRA?"

"At one time," Mary Alice said. "He took a false name because he went AWOL from the Monuments Team in Iraq. Called himself Azzurro Agua. 'Blue water' in Spanish. Started dealing in stolen antiquities."

"You're not working for the army, are you? Kharalombos was convinced you were."

Mary Alice chortled. "No, no, no. But I did read the documents for the army at Fort Hood. All of their Arabic translators were too busy, listening to tapes. Since the Patriot Act...." She waved her hand. "They hired me freelance to tell them what the documents said since I read Arabic."

"Oh," I said. So Kharalombos wasn't completely off base. "Where did you find the Clown Man's letter?"

Mary Alice shook her head. "At the bottom of the box. Mixed in with the other documents. They don't know I have it."

"Why do you want it?"

Mary Alice clasped her hands, as if she were offering a prayer. "You see, Gary, I knew that little girl, Zeinab. She was one of my pupils at Ramses College many years ago. The headmistress told me her story. The girl doesn't know that the Clown Man was her first adoptive father. The Libyan ambassador in Cairo gave her a good home. One wonders . . . "

"Are you going to give her the letter?"

Mary Alice cleared her throat. "You know, I have lost a lot of sleep over that question the last few weeks. I have prayed about it, but the way forward is unclear. Do you think I should?"

"I really don't know," I said. "I would be horrified to learn that the Clown Man was my adoptive father."

My father had loved me, but he was so reserved and such a perfectionist that he rarely praised me. But I had also been determined to reject the mantle of the family business, Creamy Freeze—and had been mean to him at a time when he was vulnerable. I didn't want to believe he knew about or was involved in Weddo Silva's cocaine-smuggling operation. Had that tragedy wrecked his health and, later, his retirement? But the Clown Man had never been Zeinab's biological father or had any hand in raising her—she had been raised as an ambassador's daughter. Could you have two sets of adoptive parents? That might be even more confusing in terms of identity than a real set of parents, plus adoptive parents. And what could be gained for Zeinab? Would this revelation wreck her life? But didn't she have a right to know that the Clown Man had found her on the steps of a mosque and, for a brief moment, was touched? Often, the way forward is full of moral tangles.

Mary Alice said, "Well, I'll have to sleep on it a little more, I think. Let's keep this conversation between ourselves. In the meantime, would you like to make that phone call?"

She pushed the old-fashioned black rotary phone toward me.

Epilogue:

Final Destinies and
Resolutions

M
Y ADVENTURES WITH KHARALOMBOS HAD FINALLY come to an end. The producer still wanted him to come and work on the Ramadan soap opera, but his series would focus on his favorite singer, Asmahan. He finally saw his son, Nunu, in Sharm el-Sheikh. Yasmine had married Eek, the son of a mineral-water mogul. She was pregnant with a second child.

Azzurro was Captain Quinn, part of the Monument Team in Iraq. But the real unsung hero was Lieutenant Colonel Baldo Durante, a classics scholar and judo expert who had been in charge of the Monument Men's team in Iraq. The team had recovered almost all the Treasures of Nineveh for the Baghdad Museum: cylinder seals, gold coins, rosettes, bracelets, and the Mask of Warka. Many of these objects had been hidden in the Louis XV sofas in the garage. After a great deal of bureaucratic red tape with the US Customs Office, they were returned to the Baghdad Museum, the rightful owners.

A half-bust of Artemis from Libya was found in Azzurro's garage. The bust was hidden under the hood of one of Azzurro's antique cars, a blue 1967 Mustang, in place of the engine.

The Coptic manuscript from Minya was returned to the Coptic Museum in Cairo, where it was placed in a remote glass case on the third floor. The story of Irene did not change the history of the church, as Dr Kaiser had predicted.

Josiah Stoner was convicted on all counts and returned to Huntsville for a significant amount of time.

Aengus and Sinead moved to San Angelo in West Texas. Aengus was hired by another fracking company.

Tony the Tuna was being tried in a federal court for many other crimes besides antiquities theft and murder.

Ramses signed a new contract with *National Geographic* for a show on his latest mummy discovery.

Mary Alice bought out Gudrun's share of the camp. Gudrun went to live with her cousin, Dr Kaiser, in Waco and started a small German bakery.

After dealing with so much paperwork for the federal government and customs, Charlie retired. It was his last case.

Mary Alice and Charlie got married in a quiet ceremony at the Schulenburg courthouse. They bought a small Winnebago and planned to take long camping trips, when Mary Alice was not running Clover Flower in the summers.

Rose and Bill returned to Tuscaloosa, Alabama. Rose declined the teaching offer at the university in Cairo.

Ashley pledged Chi Omega sorority at the University of Alabama, Tuscaloosa.

Dixie and McKenzie moved out of the mansion in River Oaks, into a two-bedroom condo.

Cameron Wiley was tried as an accessory to murder, but because he had one of the most expensive lawyers in the state, his sentence was commuted.

Speedy and Letty moved back to the Rio Grande Valley near the Mexican border. Letty was offered a job at El Pato as the manager and she never again had to worry about how much lard she added to her tortillas. Speedy was hired as the handyman, repairing cotton pickers for a local farmer. Next fall, he will be competing in the World Tournament of Poker in Las Vegas.

And finally, the fate of your humble narrator:

First, I visited my mother, as any dutiful son should, in Taos, New Mexico. We laughed a lot, and in the end she said, "Oh, Gary, you should have been on the stage!"

A very smart techie from Zadorf Publishers retrieved a copy of my lost novel, *Pure Water*, from their hard drive and they offered me a two-book deal—what I had dreamed of for years. But you have to be careful what you wish for, that old truism. Of course, by now, I realized *Pure Water* was greatly flawed and should be radically revised, even scrapped altogether as a book project; however, the editors completely disagreed with me and had already picked a cover—thousands of dead tilapia, floating in the Nile. The second book must be a memoir.

The university offered me my old job back. But would I promise to be in charge of The Creative Portfolio Committee and the The Mean Green Center? Of course, I was always tempted by Cairo—the Mother of Stories! One hears them in taxis, at home, in the street, in the shops—no one is shy about chewing off your ear! Still, after you have been sedated and hauled away in front of your colleagues, could you ever return home? I had my doubts.

Instead, I decided to move to Bulgaria to be with Boriana, who had given up her job as a traveling acrobat and was coaching young girls in gymnastics for the Olympic team. I am now studying Bulgarian. It is almost as difficult as Arabic.

Alas, when I received the contract from Zadorf, the legalese cramped my style and made me squirm. I must strictly promise to write my memoirs, not fiction. Frankly, I didn't know if I could pull it off. Stretching the truth is part of the fun. There is a fine line between memoir and fiction, and a writer or two (no names mentioned) have fallen down the rabbit hole while promising to deliver "a true story."

Dear reader, in this lengthy tome, I must confess to the sins of exaggeration and hyperbole in my adventures with the other knight errant, Kharalombos— all for the sake of a good old-fashioned yarn, as my dear old friend Mark Twain was fond of saying.

A final postscript:

I hope you will forgive me for taking A FEW LIBERTIES with the FACTS.

The End

Acknowledgments

WRITING FICTION IS RISKY, LONELY BUSINESS. Writing novels is even riskier. Learning to write novels does not happen quickly. So many people encouraged me along the way and they should be acknowledged.

My parents, Graham and Anne McCullough, encouraged me to read at an early age, and emphasized the importance of education and a curiosity about the world beyond our little town.

Sam and Martha Peterson, who have been like an uncle and aunt to me, shared my love for Egypt and the Egyptian people. I am grateful for this rich friendship, ever since we met in Cairo in 1985.

Many writers encouraged me to write and were important in my development as a writer: Jaimy Gordon, R.V. Cassill, Robert Coover, Tamas Aczel, Allen Wier, John Keeble, and George Garrett.

Part I was adapted from a novella, *Pure Water*, first published in *Shahrazad's Tooth* (Cairo: Afaq Publishing House and Bookshop, 2013). Thanks to Sawsan Bashier and Mostafa El-Sheikh for that publication.

I would like to thank the American University in Cairo for generously funding:

A Research Grant for a writer's residency at the Tyrone Guthrie Centre, Ireland, July 2013. At this wonderful house on the lake, all dreams are possible—homemade scones in a basket, jack rabbits in the front yard, an impromptu concert at sunset. Thanks to Jacinta O'Reilly for her creative energy and sense of joy.

A Professional Development Leave, Spring 2016. The stretch of the spring and the summer gave me the uninterrupted time to finish the book. Special thanks to Rob Switzer, Ghada El-Shimi, and Michelle Henry.

Besides residencies at the Tyrone Guthrie Center, sections of the novel were written at the Skopelos Foundation for the Arts, Skopelos Island, Greece. Thanks to Jill Somer for giving up her office so I could have the view!

Thanks as well to the Green Olive Arts Foundation in Tetouan, Morocco. My time in Tetouan was fruitful and enjoyable. Jeff McRobbie and Rachel Pearsey, thank you for your enthusiasm and commitment to art and artists.

Thanks to the Community of Writers at Squaw Valley, who understand what writers need: Brett Hall Jones, Sands Hall, Lisa Alvarez, and the staff. Thank you to Tom Lutz for that encouraging meeting.

Many writers and friends gave me constructive feedback and comments on early drafts of this novel:

Allen Wier, who first started me on this winding journey of novel writing in the 1990s in Tuscaloosa, Alabama. Little did I know how long it would take to shepherd a novel into print!

Jennifer Horne, who has been a steadfast, loyal friend since graduate school. She has always cheered me on whatever the literary weather.

William Melaney, for his passionate, encyclopedic knowledge of literature and talent with the scissors.

Melanie Carter, who always sees possibilities in any manuscript, for her optimism.

Sonallah Ibrahim, for his wry humor, honesty, and political vision.

Mohamed Metwalli, who gave me marvelous suggestions and practical support. Thank you for your precision in English and Arabic.

Thanks also to Lana Abdel Rahman, who kept urging me to send the novel out.

I am also grateful to Raphael Cohen and Rob Latham for editing suggestions on the novel. Jody Baboukis, for her careful copy editing and gentle suggestions.

Thanks to Musa Al-Halool for his friendship in Syria—and for an auspicious introduction. Thanks to Scott C. Davis for his support and enthusiasm. Finally, thank you to the dedicated team at Cune Press.

Cune Press

Cune Press was founded in 1994 to publish thoughtful writing of public importance. Our name is derived from "cuneiform." (In Latin *cuni* means "wedge.")

In the ancient Near East the development of cuneiform script—simpler and more adaptable than hieroglyphics—enabled a large class of merchants and landowners to become literate. Clay tablets inscribed with wedge-shaped stylus marks made possible a broad inter-meshing of individual efforts in trade and commerce.

Cuneiform enabled scholarship to exist and art to flower, and created what historians define as the world's first civilization. When the Phoenicians developed their sound-based alphabet, they expressed it in cuneiform.

The idea of Cune Press is the democratization of learning, the faith that rarefied ideas, pulled from dusty pedestals and displayed in the streets, can transform the lives of ordinary people. And it is the conviction that ordinary people, trusted with the most precious gifts of civilization, will give our culture elasticity and depth—a necessity if we are to survive in a time of rapid change.

Books from Cune Press

 Aswat: Voices from a Small Planet (a series from Cune Press)
Looking Both Ways   Pauline Kaldas
Stage Warriors   Sarah Imes Borden
Stories My Father Told Me   Helen Zughaib & Elia Zughaib
Girl Fighters   Carolyn Han

 Syria Crossroads (a series from Cune Press)
Leaving Syria   Bill Dienst & Madi Williamson
Visit the Old City of Aleppo   Khaldoun Fansa
Stories My Father Told Me   Helen Zughaib, Elia Zughai
Steel & Silk   Sami Moubayed
The Road from Damascus   Scott C. Davis
A Pen of Damascus Steel   Ali Ferzat
White Carnations   Musa Rahum Abbas
The Dusk Visitor   Musa al-Halool
Jinwar and Other Stories   Alex Poppe
Jews in Damascus   Azza Ali Akbik

 Bridge Between the Cultures (a series from Cune Press)
Empower a Refugee   Patricia Martin Holt
Muslims, Arabs & Arab Americans Nawar Shora
Afghanistan and Beyond   Linda Sartor
Music Has No Boundaries   Rafique Gangat
Apartheid Is a Crime   Mats Svensson
Curse of the Achille Lauro   Reem al-Nimer
Arab Boy Delivered   Paul A. Zarou

WCW West Coast Writers
Fluid   Lisa Teasley
Definitely Maybe   Stephen Fife
The Other Side of the Wall   Richard Hardigan
Kivu   Frederic Hunter
Finding Melody Sullivan   Alice Rothchild, MD
Afghanistan & Beyond   Linda Sartor

Cune Press: www.cunepress.com | www.cunepress.net

Gretchen McCullough was raised in Harlingen, Texas close to the Mexican border. After graduating from Brown University in 1984, she taught in Egypt, Turkey, and Japan. She earned her MFA in Creative Writing from the University of Alabama and was awarded a teaching Fulbright to Syria from 1997 to 1999. Her stories, essays, and reviews have appeared in *The Barcelona Review*, *Archipelago*, *National Public Radio*, *Story South*, *Guernica*, *The Common*, *The Millions*, and the *LA Review of Books*. Gretchen's translations in English and Arabic have been published in Oman-based *Nizwa*, UK-published *Banipal*, *Exchanges*, *Brooklyn Rail in Translation*, *World Literature Today*, and *Washington Square Review* with Mohamed Metwalli. Her bilingual book of short stories in English and Arabic, *Three Stories from Cairo*, translated with Mohamed Metwalli, was published in July 2011 by AFAQ Publishing, Cairo. A collection of short stories about expatriate life in Cairo, *Shahrazad's Tooth*, was also published by AFAQ in 2013. Currently, she teaches writing at the American University in Cairo. She lives with her husband, the Egyptian poet, Mohamed Metwalli, in Cairo.

Coming soon from Cune Press:
   Sharazad's Gift: Short Stories
   by Gretchen McCullough

CPSIA information can be obtained
at www.ICGtesting.com
Printed in the USA
JSHW011458030922
29975JS00002B/2